IN THE WHISPERS OF THE TREES

Amanda Maynard-Schubert
Willow and Owl Publishing

In the Whispers of the Trees
Book 1 in The Lorekeepers Trilogy
Amanda Maynard-Schubert
Previously published as 'The Bards of Birchtree Hall'
Daisy Lane Publishing 2019

ISBN: 978-0-6459258-0-7 (paperback)
ISBN: 978-0-6459258-1-4 (ebook)

In the Whispers of the Trees

AMANDA MAYNARD-SCHUBERT

Willow and Owl Publishing

For Daniel, Alannah, and Ethan.
To whom my heart belongs.

Of memories lost and time erased,
Of Kings on thrones of gold.
Of Lords and Ladies dancing wild,
Of ancient tales told

Of magic and myth and creatures dark,
Of truth and lies and secrets.
Of Fae and Men and all between,
Of promises and regrets.

Harken now and heed the call
Lorekeepers, thou hold the keys.
For an ancient power is stirring
In the whispers of the trees.

~ 1 ~

"That's the last one, ma'am. I'll just get Mick to take it inside, then we'll leave you to it." The furniture salesman gestured for the large man beside him to carry the final box into the house.

Neala had been standing off to the side, admiring the cottage she would share with her mother. It was just as lovely as the pictures; built with white-washed stone and nestled amongst the rolling green hills and towering trees, it could have materialised out of a fairytale.

There were brightly-coloured fuchsia flowers and hydrangea bushes everywhere, and the sound of the Atlantic Ocean was audible even over the wind whistling through the trees. Though she had yet to inspect the inside, the tension in Neala's shoulders lifted at the sight their new house.

But it won't be the same without Dad.

The thought came unbidden into her mind, and she frowned, willing it out. "Fresh start!" she muttered under her breath, clenching her fists until her fingernails dug into her palm.

"Are you okay, sweetie?" asked Neala's mother, Dana, as she waved to the truck winding its way down the quiet road, returning to the nearby city.

"Oh, yes, Mum. I'm fine. Just excited to get inside and have a look." Neala released her fists and stretched her fingers, her knuckles popping lightly. "Race you to the best bedroom!"

She and Dana laughed as they hurried up the paving stone steps, playfully poking each other with their elbows as they jostled their way to the front door. Neala was first to squeeze her way into the cottage, and she paused in the entrance, gazing around her.

The cottage was small but airy, with a brightly-lit kitchen on the left and a combined dining and lounge area on her right, featuring a lovely old fireplace with massive windows either side to allow the sunshine in. A sliding glass door in the far-right corner led out into a little walled courtyard, though Neala couldn't see much of it from her angle.

Walking into the main room a little further, she saw a door on the left, just beyond the kitchen area, which she guessed led to the bathroom, toilet and laundry. The bedrooms waited at the end of the passageway, one door on the left, the other on the right. *That one would overlook the courtyard*, Neala realised. Turning back around, Neala saw her mother watching her from the doorway, a nervous expression on her face.

"You can choose one of the bedrooms first honey; whichever you want. They're both about the same size. I know it's a bit small, but I hope it will be okay?"

Neala gave Dana a reassuring grin and walked down the narrow passageway. Opening the door to the right, she entered the bedroom and looked around. There was a large window seat opposite the doorway, which provided a view of the overgrown garden sprawling along the back wall of the courtyard.

Beyond the crumbling wall, a dense woodland wound its way up the hill, a far cry from the stretches of golden grain paddocks she'd had back home. The sheer size of the trees and the lush greenery was mind-boggling to the girl from the Australian outback. One tree in particular made her pause; it seemed to almost be glowing, its leaves rustling hypnotizingly. Blinking, Neala shook her head. *I need sleep - my brain's going cuckoo.*

Though they had not wanted to bring too much of their large furniture with them, Neala's decorative redwood bed was one of the items she had insisted be shipped across. Her father had built it for her when she was a young girl, and she couldn't bear the thought of leaving it behind. Her lip wobbled as she imagined her father standing beside her, explaining how the sunshine would illuminate the rich redwood just perfectly through that window.

Returning to the main room, Neala's trembling mouth shifted into a soft smile as she heard a meow from the corner. Having picked up the family cat, Sox, from quarantine after arriving at the airport, she was pleased to see that he had been released from his carry cage and was sniffing the air curiously.

"Hey Soxy!" Neala called, bending over and patting her knees with her hands. Sox looked up and padded over to her, mewing happily. She scooped the cat up into her arms and buried her face in his soft ginger fur, the vibrations of his happy purr rumbling against her cheek. Giving a quick nod to her mother, Neala smiled. "I'm happy with that room, Mum. Is it okay if I start putting some of my things away?"

Dana let out a long breath and smiled in relief. "Oh, that's great to hear, honey. Yes, I think most of your boxes are...ah..." She glanced around the lounge room, looking at the large stacks of moving boxes. "I think that's them there, by that window."

With a roll of her shoulders, Neala turned toward the living room windows and spotted a box with her name on it. "Well, here goes..." she muttered, wrapping her arms around the box and lifting it off the pile with a grunt. Placing it on the ground, she stood behind it and pushed it along the polished floorboards, sliding it toward her new room.

She repeated the steps with all the boxes of her possessions, while Dana started gathering her own things. Once she had moved all her belongings into her room, Neala began rifling through the boxes, searching for her speakers. Locating them in the third box she tried, she placed them on her desk and plugged her phone into the audio jack. Sighing happily as her favourite song started playing, she got stuck into the task, singing loudly as she worked.

Several hours later, Neala looked around her newly-furnished room with a sigh. The evening sun had just dropped below the horizon and a cold breeze was wafting through her window, carrying the scent of the ocean and the sweet perfume of flowers closing for the night.

Stretching her arms above her head, she turned off her music and yawned. Shuffling out of her room, she realised Dana was still busy arranging her things; she could hear her humming to herself. Not wanting to disturb her, Neala padded out to the courtyard, desperate for some fresh air. Turning her face to the darkening sky, she closed her eyes and breathed deeply.

Neala...

"Yeah, Mum?" she muttered, tilting her head to the side.

Neala...

Opening her eyes, Neala turned around. But Dana was nowhere to be seen. A shiver ran up her spine. "Hello?" she choked out. A rustling sound from the garden made her jump.

Peering over the crumbling wall of the courtyard, Neala stared into the shadowy woods, her eyes locking onto the tree she'd seen from her bedroom. There was something familiar about it, though she couldn't place it.

"A closer look won't hurt..." she mumbled, climbing carefully over the wall and making her way up the narrow path through the stinging nettles and hawthorn bushes rambling over the woodland floor.

Drawing nearer to the mysterious tree, she felt a strange tingling, like pins and needles, creep over her skin. The wind was swirling wildly now, tugging at her clothes and hair. It seemed to be whispering, almost singing, as though speaking a language Neala almost understood, but couldn't quite make out.

As the leaves fluttered above her, Neala realised why it looked familiar; she had a mark on her shoulder that looked just like these leaves. An odd patch of white pigment. She'd had it since birth. Her mother had told her not to worry about it, that it was probably just a rare birthmark, and she'd never given it another thought. Until now.

"What in the world..." Curious, she reached toward the tree, placing her trembling hand against its bark –

"Neala? Honey, are you out here?"

The whistling of the wind nearly drowned out Neala's shriek as she clutched at her shoulder blade. It was burning intensely, as though someone had pressed a hot poker right into her birthmark; the fire raced through her body, like she'd been electrocuted. Then, as suddenly as it had appeared, the painful sensation was gone.

Gasping, she rubbed her aching shoulder and stumbled away from the tree, back to the courtyard. Dana's face appeared over the wall, paling visibly.

"Get away from there, Neala!"

"Why? Mum, what's wrong?"

Dana's eyes were wide, her body tense. "That ash tree - did you touch it?"

Neala clambered over the wall, brow cocked in confusion. "Huh? Well, yeah, but it's just a tree. What -"

Hands shaking, Dana pressed trembling fingers to Neala's aching shoulder. Closing her eyes, she muttered something inaudible. Once she'd composed herself, she gave a light cough and shifted her hand to smooth over Neala's hair. "It's nothing, I'm sorry if I scared you. It's - just stay out of the woods for now, okay. At least until we've settled in more. I'd hate for something to happen to you."

"But—"

"No buts. Now," Dana gently guided Neala back into the courtyard, turning her away from the woods. "Did you get all your things put away?"

Neala opened her mouth, then closed it sharply. *Maybe she's right - it'd be just my luck to get lost in the woods the day we arrive. Eaten by the big, bad wolf or something.* Squashing down her questions, she grinned crookedly.

"Yep, everything's put away. I swear, I never want to see another screwdriver ever again, though."

Dana chuckled. "Assembling beds is not your true calling, then?"

Neala rolled her eyes. "Eurgh, I sure hope not."

Giving her daughter an affectionate nudge, Dana turned her face up to the now-dark sky, the first rays of the emerging moon starting to creep across the land.

"Well, here we are; our first night in Ireland together. It means so much having you here with me, honey."

Neala closed her eyes and breathed deep, letting the cold, salty breeze fill her lungs. A yawn followed shortly after, causing Dana to reach over and place her hand tenderly on Neala's head.

"Go to bed, my baby. Tomorrow's going to be a big day. We'll go and see Nanna first thing in the morning; I know how much she's looking forward to seeing you again. I think you were only nine or ten the last time she came to see us." Patting Neala gently, she murmured, "I love you, sweetheart. Thank you for all your help today."

Neala grinned sleepily. "I love you too, Mum. G'night!" With legs that suddenly seemed to be made of stone, she turned and headed back into the house, desperate for her bed. Barely able to keep her eyes open, she stripped off her clothes and reached for her pyjamas, vowing to shower in the morning when she wasn't as likely to fall over.

Climbing carefully under her soft, down-filled doona, she wriggled around a little, trying to find a comfortable position on the new mattress. Her shoulder was still aching slightly, which made her frown. *Too much heavy lifting, that's all. It'll be fine by morning.* Breathing deep, she smiled at the familiar, comforting smell of home emanating from her doona. Before she'd even had time to worry about what was coming the next day, Neala had slipped into sleepy darkness.

*****

The dream she had that night was more vivid than any she could remember having before. Standing at a crossroads in the woods behind her cottage, Neala watched as an icy fog swirled around her ankles, shifting eerily in the slight breeze. In the distance, an owl hooted mournfully.

Neala was surprised to find she did not feel nervous or afraid at all. On the contrary, she felt quite at home here. In the shadows, a flicker of movement sent a puff of fog whirling into the air. Brow furrowing with curiosity, she peered through the trees, trying to spot the furry creature she was sure she'd glimpsed.

"Hello, little one. Don't be shy - let me see you," she called, the words echoing in the murky darkness.

A soft voice whispered in response, *"Not yet."*

It took a moment for Neala to realise she had heard the voice in her mind, rather than with her ears. Momentarily disoriented, she mumbled, "What? But - why not?"

"You have not proven it yet."

There was a pause as Neala tried to make sense of what was happening. Where was the strange whispery voice coming from? "Proven it? Proven *what*?"

"That you are ready."

*****

"Meowwww!"

Neala woke with a start, gasping as she lurched upwards. Panicked, she ran her hands over her goosebump-covered skin, the bitter cold of the fog still lingering in her memory. With a scowl, she glared down at Sox, who was nonchalantly licking his paws and cleaning his ears, the picture of innocence.

"Sox! What was that for?" she growled. With a snooty sniff, Sox turned and padded to the door. It was then that Neala caught the first wafts of freshly-brewed coffee coming from the kitchen. Rubbing her eyes, she glanced at the window, surprised to see how bright it was outside.

Yawning, she swung her legs over the side of the bed and hoisted herself to her feet with a grunt. She groaned as her muscles protested, working out the stiffness of spending almost twenty-four hours crammed in an economy plane seat. She kneaded her shoulders rhythmically as she made her way out into the kitchen.

Dana was leaning against the bench, already dressed, clutching a mug of steaming coffee in her hands. She had opened the windows, and a cool breeze was swirling around the room, carrying the promise of a lovely summer's day ahead.

Neala plonked herself on a chair at the new dining table they'd bought yesterday, rubbing the sleep from her eyes. "Would you like a cuppa, sleepyhead?" Dana teased, pulling a mug from the cupboard.

"Mmph," Neala mumbled, resting her head in her hands and closing her eyes. Try as she might, she couldn't bring back the memories of the creature she'd spoken with in her dream. She only emerged from her thoughts when she heard her mother placing the mug down on the table.

Dana kissed her on the head and sat in the chair opposite her, placing her own coffee mug on the table. As the first mouthful of hot English tea made its way down her throat, Neala sighed happily. Opening her eyes, she grinned at her mother.

"Good morning, Mummy-dearest!" she trilled brightly. "I'm awake now."

"Yes, good *morning*. Well...just." Slowly and carefully, Dana picked up her coffee and sipped it, raising an eyebrow knowingly. Neala eyed her suspiciously, taking another gulp of tea.

"...What?"

Dana lowered her mug, then smiled sweetly at her daughter. "Oh, nothing really..." She sighed, staring ponderously out the sliding door toward the courtyard. "I was only wondering if you'd noticed how bright and sunny it is already? Or how plentiful our bounty is?" She gestured to the overflowing fruit bowl on the bench, then to the mugs they were drinking from.

Now that her mother mentioned it, Neala frowned. When had they gone shopping for food? With a confused frown at her tea, she eyed her mother over the top of her mug.

"Did you go to the shops yesterday? I don't remember stopping anywhere, did I fall asleep?"

"No, I went this morning, actually. There's a lovely little general store not far down the road, I noticed it when we drove in. There's not much else in the village, but it was a pleasant walk."

"But how...What time is it?"

"Oh...almost noon." Dana smiled into her mug.

Neala nearly spilled her tea as she threw herself back from the table.

"Aaargh, Mother!" she growled. "I still need to shower and everything! What about Nanna?"

Dana gave a soft laugh. "You needed the sleep, my dear. Nanna is expecting us for lunch now, instead."

Throwing down the last of her tea, milk dribbling from the corners of her mouth, Neala raced from the table into her room. Grabbing the first clothes she came across, she bolted into the bathroom. As she waited for the water to warm up, she rifled through her toiletries drawer, where she had unceremoniously dumped all of her products the evening before, until she found her shampoo. Stepping into the steamy shower, she tried to breathe steadily, letting the hot water flow over her face and calm her nerves.

"It's just a visit with Nanna...not tea with the Queen...she'll forgive me..." she murmured to herself as she worked the shampoo through her hair, enjoying its fruity smell.

Once she felt clean and refreshed, Neala turned off the water and reached for her towel, wrapping it around her body. Looking in the mirror, she studied her reflection. Her dark brown hair was plastered to her skin, though usually it hung in light waves to her shoulders. Neala had inherited her mother's thick, wavy locks, but her eyes were all her father's, sharing his light blue-grey, as opposed to her mother's deep chocolate brown.

Shivering as a cold drop of water ran down her back, she quickly wrapped a second towel around her head. *Focus, Neala - Nanna's waiting*, she reminded herself sternly.

Once dry and dressed, she tied her damp hair up in a messy ponytail and made her way back to the lounge area. Dana was in the kitchen again, tapping her fingers rhythmically on the bench, staring out the window, deep in thought.

Neala gave a light cough and Dana jumped slightly, turning to face her daughter. "How do I look?" Neala asked, twirling for her mother like she used to do when she was a young girl.

Dana smiled warmly. "You look lovely, darling. Shall we go see Nanna?"

Neala nodded cheerfully, then stopped, her brow creasing with puzzlement. "Wait - what car are we taking?" The rental they'd borrowed to travel from the airport had been collected the day before.

Dana chuckled and placed an arm around Neala's shoulders, giving her a squeeze. "The bus-shaped one. The towns are a lot closer over here, it's much easier to get around. There's a bus stop just down the road that runs into the city."

Neala cocked a brow. She'd never been on a proper bus before; they were a city-person thing. The closest she'd come to riding one was the time her neighbour, Sam, had bought an old, broken-down school bus to gut and convert into a kind of sleepout for one of his on-site farm hands. It was hardly the same thing.

I'm sure it'll be fine, she reassured herself. *What could go wrong?* Reaching for her backpack, she smiled at Dana. "Well, better not keep Nanna waiting any longer than I already have." Dana gave her a gentle nudge with her shoulder then grabbed the keys, following Neala to the door and shooing Sox back into the house as he tried to squeeze past them.

~ 2 ~

For much of the bus ride, Neala had her nose pressed to the glass, gawking open-mouthed at the scenery that flashed by. Seeing the beauty of the Irish countryside in the flesh was so much more than she'd imagined when poring through books.

Beside her, Neala heard a sigh escape her mother's lips and she tore her gaze away from the window, studying her curiously. Dana was fiddling absently with the golden wedding band on her finger, her eyes distant.

"Everything okay, Mum?"

As if breaking out of a trance, Dana blinked and gave her head a slight shake. "Oh, honey. Yes. More than okay." Patting Neala's knee gently, Dana frowned at the bus route in her hand and narrowed her eyes, studying it carefully. "We need to get off soon, Nanna's house is only a few streets away. We'd better make sure to ring the bell before it's too late."

Neala gathered her backpack onto her lap, feeling anxious. Looking around at the other passengers, she met the eyes of a boy around her age. He was seated across the aisle and several seats in front and was watching her and Dana curiously. Blushing shyly, Neala looked down and clutched her pack to her now-tight stomach.

Stealing another peek at the boy, she realised he was still watching them, smiling openly now. A blonde-haired girl beside him was also glancing at her, trying to see what had captured her friend's attention. Feeling more annoyed than embarrassed now, Neala raised her eyebrows at him in a silent challenge, mouth twisted in frustration.

To her horror, the boy laughed and got out of his seat. Her shoulders tensed as he made his way towards them, flopping onto the seat in front and casually slinging an arm over the headrests so he was face-to-face with her.

"Sorry for staring," he said cheerfully in the lilting Irish accent Neala loved. "I couldn't help but overhear that you're wanting to get off here soon. There's a stop coming up in a wee while, d'ya need help ringing the bell?"

Neala felt her pride prickle. She hated feeling helpless. Or worse, like she was stupid. More icily than she'd intended, she shot back, "I think we can handle something as simple as ringing a *bell*, thanks."

Ignoring the admonishing look from Dana, Neala watched as the boy shrugged his shoulders and stood, the friendly grin never leaving his face. He ran a casual hand over his red-brown hair and winked.

"Okay then. You ladies enjoy your day."

Once he'd returned to his seat, Dana glared at Neala. "What was that about? He was being nice."

Already regretting her sharpness, Neala slumped back in her chair and closed her eyes with a wince. "Sorry, I don't know why I was rude. Just tired and grumpy, I guess."

Dana pressed her lips together tightly and glanced out the window. Letting out a sudden gasp, she clutched Neala's arm. "Oh, that's our stop! Neala, the bell!"

Flustered, Neala reached up, fingers searching for the button to alert the driver. Before she could press anything, a ringing sound echoed through the bus and they began to slow, pulling over to the side of the road. Ears burning, she lifted her eyes to peer at the boy and the blonde-haired girl.

He was grinning sheepishly at her, shrugging as he lowered his hand away from the bell. Taking a deep breath, Neala tried to compose herself. She purposely ignored Dana, who was chuckling with amusement as she gathered her handbag.

Following her mother down the aisle, she almost ran into Dana's back as she halted beside the boy.

"Thanks for that - we would have missed our stop if it weren't for you. We *both* appreciate it." She looked pointedly at Neala, who scuffed her feet.

Forcing herself to meet the boy's gaze, Neala mumbled her thanks. His blue eyes glittered with mirth, and he pretended to tip an invisible hat to them.

"Pleasure to help you, ladies. Have a grand day."

Dana beamed and nodded back, shuffling her way to the front of the bus. Unable to resist, Neala glanced once more at the boy and his companion. Unlike her cheerful friend, the girl was staring down at her hands, flushing as badly as Neala was.

As Neala turned to leave, the boy called out, "Name's Torin Greenwood, by the way. I hope we'll see you again."

Neala gave a half-hearted wave back, lips pulled into a tight, unconvincing smile as she exited the bus. As it pulled away, she let out a huff and turned to face her mother.

"Sorry, Mum. I guess we'll eventually figure out how to use a bus properly."

Dana laughed heartily. "Plenty of time to practice, my darling. Now, Nanna's place is just around the corner there. I would have loved to make an arrangement for her, but I guess I can put something together once we get to the shop."

This time Neala's smile was genuine. Flower arranging was her mother's great hobby. She'd always said that if she wasn't a farmer's wife, she would be a florist. They'd had a large garden at home and Dana always kept fresh flowers in vases all around the house. Before they'd moved here, Nanna had suggested Dana finally pursue her dreams and sell floral arrangements in her shop. Dana had almost wept with joy.

As her mother chatted about how excited she was to be working in Nanna's shop, Neala breathed deeply and looked around, taking in the surrounding sights and smells.

Her memories of her grandmother were vague, having not seen her for several years now. They'd spoken on the phone many times, but Neala still struggled to picture her. She remembered the smells of lavender and mint, and that her Nanna always wore skirts or dresses, never pants. Glancing down at her own black jeans, Neala wondered whether she'd picked the wrong outfit.

As they rounded the corner onto Nanna's street, Neala gawked at the sheer number of houses, as pretty as she had expected them to be. Tidy little homes were spread out in rows, surrounded by well-tended gardens and window boxes. Large trees were scattered around the area, giving shade on this warm summer's afternoon. Turning to her mother as they walked down one of the avenues, Neala asked, "Which one is Nanna's? They all look the same."

"Nanna's is number twenty-two, sweetheart." She gestured to the homes they were passing. "A lot of people in this area are elderly, and most are retired, so they're quite a close community. Nanna said there's a friendly rivalry between the residents here; they regularly hold baking competitions, bowls or croquet nights, craft afternoons, and so on. She said it gets quite competitive." Neala grinned to herself and gave a shy wave to a gentleman who was walking his dog down the lane opposite them.

As they approached Nanna's house, Neala's hands began to sweat, and her blood seemed to hum with nerves. Dana must have sensed it, because she reached out and squeezed her daughter's hand. "Here we go, darling." Lifting her free hand to her face, she cupped it around her lips and let out a loud "Oo-roo!"

Neala blushed, looking around to see if anyone had heard them. A man around her mother's age who was pulling weeds in the garden next door glanced up. He gave Neala a tiny, knowing smile, then went back to his work, pulling his floppy hat down over his face. Dana called out again, and Neala was startled to hear an answering call come from the doorway of number twenty-two.

A large, vibrant woman stood holding the door open, her face lit with joy. Dana dropped Neala's hand and hurried up the path, whooping with laughter as she embraced her mother. Neala followed a little slower, not wanting to interrupt their reunion.

Nanna Kennedy gave Dana one last squeeze, then peered around her, looking for Neala. When she spotted the girl hovering back on the path beside the rose bushes, she called jovially, "Come here, dear one, and let me look at you."

Neala took a tentative step toward her. "Hi Nanna. It's good to see you."

Nanna stepped forward and opened her arms wide. "Oh, you've grown into such a beautiful young lassie, just like your Ma." In seconds, Neala was enveloped in a soft hug. Her nose tickled as wafts of lavender and mint washed over her. She giggled at the smell; it was exactly how she remembered from when she was younger. Once released, she grinned with greater confidence.

Nanna's bright brown eyes lit up and she patted Neala's cheek. "Ah now, that's better. Not so shy with your old nan, now, aye?" Turning back to the door, Nanna held it open and gestured for Dana and Neala to go in. "Come, I have some tea brewed and ready. We've got a lot of catching up to do."

*****

Several hours and too many shortbreads later, Neala was feeling very sleepy. The jet lag was kicking in big-time, and she was resisting the urge to lay down on the plush couch cushions and take a nap. Dana and Nanna had pulled out an old photo album and were seated at the dining table, poring over the images, cooing and reminiscing about earlier years.

A knock on the door jolted Neala out of her daze, and she lifted her head curiously. Nanna's expression was puzzled, but she closed the photo album anyway, groaning as she stood up. "That could be Marjorie from next door, she was meant to pop around later today to pick up an old fiddle with her friend. He's, uh, a music teacher."

All traces of tiredness disappeared, and Neala sat up eagerly. Back in Australia, she'd been home-schooled. Her family had lived too remotely to attend any mainstream school. As part of her learning, her mother had insisted that she learn to play at least one musical instrument. Neala's father had been a talented pianist, and Dana herself was adept at several instruments. "It runs in the family," she had claimed proudly.

Neala had chosen the flute, and she had taken to music with ease. So much so that she had eventually taught herself to play the piano, saxophone, and trumpet, as well as the guitar. Her fingers itched to try out Nanna's fiddle, and she shuffled restlessly on the couch while Nanna greeted Marjorie.

"Ah, come in, my dear. I'd love you to meet my daughter and granddaughter - they flew in from Australia yesterday," Nanna chatted amiably as she held the door open. Peering out further, she called, "You may as well join us, scallywag. Plenty of tea to go around."

Neala frowned with curiosity. Who else was Nanna inviting in? Realising she should be polite, Neala rose from the couch and made her way over to greet Marjorie and the mystery guest.

Marjorie was a short, slight woman, barely reaching Neala's shoulder, but her handshake was firm and commanding. "Pleasure to meet you, girlie. Bridge has not stopped raving about having you and Dana coming to live here - anyone would think she was a wee bit excited."

Nanna laughed as she shuffled back to the table, giving Marjorie a pat on the arm as she passed. Peering further out the doorway, Neala finally spotted their extra guest; the man who'd been pulling weeds in the garden earlier was taking off his hat and brushing his boots on the mat carefully, making sure he wouldn't track any mud into the house. With a friendly smile, the man caught her eye and came over.

"Hey there. Neala, is it? I'm Finley Talbot. Marjorie is an old friend of mine."

"Not *that* old, you pup," Marjorie snapped, though a hint of mirth tinged the glare she gave Finley.

"You teach music," Neala blurted out, clumsily offering a hand. Finley looked confused, forehead furrowing thoughtfully, then his face split into a beaming smile and he shook Neala's hand warmly.

"Ah, my reputation precedes me. I suppose I do teach a bit of music sometimes. I don't suppose you play?"

"Actually, Neala is a wonderful musician," Dana chimed in, standing to introduce herself to Finley while Nanna and Marjorie chatted in the kitchen, preparing a fresh pot of tea. "Hi, I'm Dana Moran, Neala's mother. Come, take a seat. It's a pleasure to meet you, Finley."

"Ah, call me Finn, everyone else does," he laughed. Pulling a chair out, Finn folded his wiry body down and propped his chin on his hand. Neala sat down opposite him and her mother, feeling nervous. "So, what do you play?" he asked her curiously.

"I-uh, a bit of everything, really," Neala stammered, twisting her fingers together. "Mum taught me the flute, but I can also play piano, trumpet, saxophone, and guitar. Um, I play mainly classical music, but have tried some pop songs and stuff..." Neala knew her face was glowing pink now, and she stuttered to a halt. Dana gave her a warm smile and winked.

Finn was studying her attentively, listening to every word. "You said your mother here taught you the flute, but who taught you the others?" He looked at Dana with a raised brow. "Was that you, as well?"

Dana shook her head, smiling proudly.

"No, she taught herself the other instruments. Her father, Gary, was a pianist, and he showed her the basics, such as which keys were which, but as far as technique and so forth, she just picked it up by herself. Same with the saxophone and trumpet – they were handed down to me from my own grandfather. Her guitar was a gift from our friend, Angie, and after playing around with it a few times, Neala had it mastered. She seems to have a...talent for it."

Neala tucked her arms under the side of the table and lowered her head shyly; her mother made it sound so much more impressive than it really was. She'd just enjoyed playing, that was all.

Stealing a glance at Finn, Neala saw that he was staring into the distance thoughtfully, tapping his fingers periodically on the table. Neala frowned, watching the pattern his fingers were making. There was something about the rhythm, the way they moved. It wasn't random...

Her thoughts were interrupted by Marjorie and Nanna returning with the tea and some extra cups. Once everyone was served, Nanna and Dana began rifling through the photos again, relaying the stories to Marjorie. Neala listened for a while, but soon found her attention being drawn back to Finn's hand, which was still tapping out a rhythm.

As she stared, the air above his hand began to shimmer, like concrete on a hot day. Hypnotised, she watched as the ripples began to form shapes and colours, morphing before her eyes. Within moments, she could see the notes playing above his fingers, as though they were being written in the air.

Almost against her will, she began to hum softly, reading the notes in the air as they wavered in front of her gaze. Finn grinned, and said loudly enough to startle Neala, "Ah, 'Requiem' - one of my favourites."

Neala jumped, the notes disappearing as Finn's fingers stopped playing. Looking up, she realised the adults were all staring at her. Confused and embarrassed, she stammered, "Sorry, what? I-I wasn't listening."

Finn chuckled. "'Requiem', the song you were humming. Mozart is one of my favourites."

"I-I'm sorry, I didn't realise I was humming, I just...the music..." Neala's voice trailed off. Had she really seen the notes floating in the air? Maybe she was more tired than she realised.

Shaking her head, she tried to brush it off. "I guess the jet lag is kicking in stronger than I thought." The ladies laughed, but Finn met her eyes and raised an eyebrow knowingly.

Before she could feel any more rattled, Finn cleared his throat and mumbled to Nanna, "Sorry to interrupt, Brigit.

I was just wondering if I may have a look at that fiddle you're wanting to sell?" Keeping his tone casual, Finn asked, "Neala, have you played a violin before?"

Still unsettled by the vision of music notes in the air, she shook her head absently.

Beaming, Finn tapped his hands on the table and stood with a stretch. "Wonderful. Well, would you like me to teach you a wee bit while we're here? Long as you don't mind, Bridge?"

Nanna rose from the table, flapping her hands dismissively. "Ah, lad, you can do what you like with it, it's yours now. Neala, would you like to have a try?"

Finally registering what they were saying, Neala sat straighter in her chair, eyes widening with excitement, all confusion vanished. She nodded eagerly, hands already itching to hold the violin.

The others laughed. "Seems like a yes, then." Nanna huffed with pleasure. "All right, I'll just grab it for you, Finn. Hold on a tick."

Gesturing for Neala to stand, Finn flicked his head toward the living area, just off from the kitchen. "Come, I'll give you a quick lesson, then."

"Um, thank you, sir," Neala said awkwardly, rising from her chair.

Finn snorted. "No need for this 'sir' business; 'Finn' will do just fine. I'm just a common man, after all." He laughed, his eyes crinkling at the corners. Neala had already grown fond of him; he reminded her a little of Sam, Angie's husband and their only neighbour back home. They had the same easy-going, friendly nature. Relaxing her shoulders, Neala let out a long breath.

Finn held out a hand to Nanna as she returned with the violin in a dusty, battered case. He eyed it with a frown, the corner of his mouth drooping sadly. Nanna must have noticed as she muttered, "No one's played it since John died, rest his soul."

Nodding in understanding, Finn held the case up and blew the dust off sharply. It whooshed into the air, straight toward Neala. She closed her eyes tightly, coughing as she tried to catch her breath; there was a lot more dust in the air than she expected.

Ignoring the stinging of her eyes, Neala squinted at Finn through the cloud of dust. For the briefest second, she thought she saw a coppery glow around his hands, illuminating the particles as they suddenly dispersed, as though whisked away on an imperceptible wind.

Catching her narrowed stare, Finn opened his mouth to say something, then closed it. Instead, he shrugged nonchalantly and crouched to open the violin case. After a moment of hesitation, he mumbled "Sorry about the dust - bit more there than I thought." Clearing his throat, he said in a cheerier tone, "Well, then - let's have some fun with this beautiful lady, shall we?"

He sighed as he drew the violin from the case and eyed it lovingly. "Ah, such a pretty thing. Your grandfather obviously looked after it wonderfully well. I'll just give her a quick tune..."

Finn took the bow in his long fingers and carefully ran it over the strings, making them hum. Neala felt the notes echo through her whole body, and she smiled broadly, even as she rubbed the last of the dust from her eyes.

Shifting her weight restlessly from one foot to the other, she waited impatiently as Finn turned the pegs of the violin strings carefully, making sure each note sounded perfect before moving on to the next.

Once he was done, he faced Neala and propped the violin on his shoulder, wiggling it until it sat comfortably. "Playing a violin is similar to the guitar, but instead of plucking the strings, you stroke them, gentle-like, running the bow along them just like this..." He drew the bow across one of the strings, the high A-note echoing around the small living room. In the kitchen, Neala was dimly aware that the others had stopped talking.

With a smile, Finn launched into a heartfelt rendition of 'Dance of the Sugar Plum Fairy', swaying his body as he drew the bow effortlessly across the strings. Neala forgot where she was, losing herself completely in the music. As the notes rang out, she swore the room flickered with lights, like sparkling stars hovering around Finn as he played. The coppery glow was back, but it was not contained to his hands this time – instead, it seemed to shimmer around his entire body.

The edges of her vision grew blurry, and she closed her eyes, feeling a little dizzy. Once her eyes were closed, she could see the picture the song was painting clearly in her mind. A large oak tree stood alone in a snow-covered field, and she could see tiny lights dancing beneath it. Neala approached quietly, her feet leaving no trace on the snow.

Once she was close enough, she crouched down and watched the balls of light dance, her heart lifting with joy. There were seven balls altogether, flashing with every colour of the rainbow. The blue one, pale as a summer sky, drifted closer to Neala, bobbing almost within reach of her fingers. Before she could touch it, the ball flickered and spun its way back to its companions, seamlessly re-joining their whirling dance. In the distant corner of her mind, Neala felt a tug on her awareness; the song was coming to an end.

As Finn played the final notes, Neala was drawn away completely, coming back into her body and opening her eyes. She blinked rapidly, trying to refocus her vision; she could see the flowered wallpaper of her Nanna's living room, could smell the lavender and mint.

As though emerging from a dream, Neala stretched her arms above her head and sighed. For a second, she was sure a drop of melted snow was running down her neck. But when she placed her hand on her skin, it was warm and dry. Curious, Neala looked at Finn.

"Sorry, I must've been, like, sleep-standing or something; I had this really vivid dream." She shook her head, feeling silly. *Dancing balls of rainbow light. Seriously?* "Anyway, that was amazing; you're very good."

Finn, looking a little dazed himself, placed the violin and bow down by his side. She couldn't read the expression on his face as he murmured, "Thank you. I've had a lot of practice." Cocking his head, he asked, "I'm curious - what did you dream about, if you don't mind me being nosy?"

Neala blushed. "Oh, there were some...lights. Under an oak tree in the snow. Nothing really." She ran a hand over her hair. There had been something about that pale blue light, something wildly familiar. Giving her head a sharp shake, she scoffed, "I really have been knocked for a six by this jetlag; my dreams have been so strange and clear since I got here. Anyone would think I'm losing my mind."

Cheeks flushing with awkwardness, Neala tried to steer the conversation away from her dreams.

"Um, is it still okay if I have a turn? With the violin, I mean. I don't know how much longer we're staying here..." Neala was startled to see her mother standing in the doorway. "Oh, Mum, how long have you been there?"

"I came in to listen. Now, it's getting close to dinner time, Neala, so we won't stay too late. The bus leaves at a quarter past five, so we'll go just before then, okay?"

Neala nodded happily. Looking back at Finn, she stared hopefully at the violin in his hands.

Finn chuckled at her expression. "All right, I've got time to go through the basics at least. Come on up here, give her a hold."

Finn passed the violin over as Neala held out her hands eagerly. Taking the instrument with gentle fingers, she could feel warmth emanating from it. She didn't think much of it; surely it was just warm from being in Finn's hands? Propping the base under her chin, Neala shifted the violin around until it was comfortable in her grasp. Finn watched her with a raised brow. Noticing, Neala felt a little self-conscious.

"Am I doing it wrong?" she asked worriedly.

Finn shook his head, amused.

"No, quite the opposite. Holding a violin looks easy, but it's actually pretty tricky to get it in the right spot straight away. You've got it perfectly, though."

"Oh, um, thank you," she stammered, not sure how to respond. Feeling her hands sweating slightly, she wiped her free palm on her jeans as Finn passed her the bow.

"Now, the bow dips down a little in the middle, which is where we want it. That's the whole idea of the 'bow' name; if it's too tight, and the hairs are too straight, it will damage it. Now, just for this lesson, put your thumb under the bit here at the end of the bow there, pinkie there, and pointer finger just there. It's not perfect, but this will do for now."

Neala set her fingers, getting used to their placement. It reminded her a little of the grip on the end of her flute, and she found it quickly felt comfortable. Once set, she looked to Finn for the next instruction. Smiling, he pointed to the strings on the violin, starting with the one closest to her body.

"There are less strings on here than a guitar, and they increase by fifths; you know about those?" Neala nodded in response, and Finn beamed. "Oh, thank goodness. Then you're already my favourite student. Anyway, they start with G, then D, A and E. To get the note, just draw the bow over them one at a time, starting with G. Don't worry about using the fingerboard yet."

Neala did as she was told, cringing at the scraping sound the strings made as she drew the bow over them. She knew intuitively that her pressure was all wrong and that she was being way too heavy-handed. Readjusting, she tried again and again, until the notes finally came out cleanly.

Feeling proud, she looked at Finn, who nodded, impressed. "Very good, nice adjustment. Just have a play around with it – get used to the instrument, and let it get used to you. Use the finger board, try pressing on the different parts, and see if you can tell what notes are where."

Excited, Neala settled the violin comfortably again and started running the bow over the strings, using her left hand to press and release different parts of the strings along the finger board, hearing how the notes changed as she moved her fingers. This was more familiar to her, as it was similar to playing the guitar.

Before she knew it, Neala was lost in the music, sensing the violin reacting to her movements more willingly the more she played. The sound became cleaner and crisper, becoming less like nails on a chalkboard. The bow felt like part of her arm, and she drew it across the strings with more confidence, closing her eyes to hear the notes more keenly.

Buoyed by her success, Neala started playing one of the easiest songs she knew: 'Twinkle, Twinkle, Little Star'.

As the last note faded out, she opened her eyes, fighting the desire to yawn. As her vision refocused, she realised she had an audience. Finn was leaning against the wall by the door, arms folded, with his head cocked to the side, a strange look on his face. Dana, Marjorie, and Nanna had all taken seats around the room, and they were clapping enthusiastically.

Blushing Neala lowered the violin and scuffed her feet awkwardly; she wasn't accustomed to having so many people watching her when she played.

Pushing off from the wall, Finn came over and held his hands out for the violin. Neala passed it over with an internal sigh; she had enjoyed the beautiful instrument very much. As he packed it away, Finn asked curiously, "You've definitely never played a violin before, Neala?"

Unsure of his tone, Neala cleared her throat and answered, "Um, no, I haven't. Only guitar and the other ones I said before."

Finn nodded firmly, as if confirming something within himself. Standing, he faced her and tapped his chin thoughtfully. The ladies had started chatting to one another again, and Finn leaned closer so only Neala could hear him.

"Just so you know, I have never seen anyone take to an instrument as quickly as you just did. Did you realise how well you were playing? You have a great talent for this. Perhaps you can find a way to use it, hmm?"

Neala's skin prickled, goosebumps racing over her arms and making her hair stand on end.

With a quick pat on her shoulder, Finn turned to Marjorie and said kindly, "Well, Marjorie, my old friend, shall we get you back home and ready for dinner?"

Marjorie cuffed him lightly on the arm. "Call me old one more time, lad, and it'll be the end of you."

Finn chuckled, his affection for the stern woman obvious to everyone. Allowing her to link her hand through his arm, he patted it warmly then bowed his head to Neala and her mother. "It was lovely to meet you both. I hope we will meet again soon."

As he led Marjorie to the door, Finn and Dana exchanged a knowing look. Neala noticed it but was too busy pondering what he had meant by 'using her talent' to give it much thought. Shrugging it off, she went to stand by her mother as they waved farewell.

Closing the door behind them, Nanna sighed wistfully. "I suppose this is today over for you, too. You and Neala won't want to miss the bus; it gets dark much quicker here than you're used to, even in summer."

Dana gave her a warm hug. "You won't have to wait so long for visits anymore, Mother, I promise. We'll spend a bit of time settling in over the next week or so, but we'll be back for a cuppa again soon. Besides, we'll be joining you in the shop sooner rather than later. I'll be surprised if you don't get sick of us before long!"

"Yeah, I reckon you'll be retiring a week after we start, just to get away from us," Neala joked. The family laughed and said their final goodbyes before Neala and Dana made their way down the path, waving to Nanna as she disappeared from view.

Once they were out of sight of the house, Dana casually reached out and took Neala's hand, swinging it lightly as they walked.

"So, I have a musical prodigy on my hands, do I?"

Neala rolled her eyes. "Hardly. Nanna said he was a music teacher - I'm sure he was just looking to get a new student on-board."

Dana cocked her head to the side thoughtfully. "You know, it's not a bad idea. Joining a music school. There's a lot of opportunities here for you, darling - lots of ways to use your talents."

"Yeah, that's what Finn said. But, well..." She screwed her nose up crookedly. "I've been here for *one* day. Can't we just start working in the shop and see how that goes before planning my violin world-tour?"

Dana gave Neala's hand a squeeze then let go, moving aside to avoid running into a tree growing through the sidewalk.

"That's true. And I agree wholeheartedly; I'm not ready for you to fly the nest just yet, anyway." Dana chewed her lip, shoulders slumping. "Though, obviously, if you did decide that's what you wanted, I wouldn't stop you. I'd never want to hold you back, that's not what I meant..."

Neala shook her head quickly. "Nah, that's okay, Mum. Honestly, I never thought I'd become a famous musician or anything. I even told Finn I only play for fun. Besides, I want to work with you and Nanna - I can make coffee better than anyone, right?"

Dana smiled, but her eyes still looked miserable. Angry with herself for upsetting her mother, Neala changed the subject.

"So, do you reckon we'll have a helpful Irish lad to assist us with ringing the bus bell on the way home?"

Neala could tell Dana's mind was still elsewhere, but she made the effort to plant a smile on her face then elbowed Neala lightly. "That would be nice. As long as you don't go biting the head off this one."

Neala placed her hand on her chest in mock indignation.

"Gasp! Mother, how you jest! I'm an absolute delight, I would never."

The pair laughed, and Dana linked her arm through Neala's, all talk of music abandoned for the moment.

~ 3 ~

Neala yawned as she slapped her alarm clock off, thoughts already turning to the day ahead. Several weeks had passed since she and Dana had arrived in Ireland and had begun working in Nanna's shop, 'Heartful Soul'. It had been her passion for almost twenty years; a combination of gift shop and café.

Now, though, she was looking forward to taking a step back and handing the bulk of the work over to Dana. This suited Dana perfectly, as it gave her an opportunity to put her floristry skills to use and expand the business, while Neala worked the café. It was joyful work, and Neala was beginning to feel genuinely happy for the first time since her father's accident.

But every now and then, when she least expected it, a memory of him would pop into her mind and her joy would be smothered by waves of grief. It was a tiring battle.

Enough moping, she admonished herself. *I've got some running to do.* Trying to rein her mind back to the present, Neala pulled on her sneakers and yanked her hair into a ponytail. "A run a day keeps the insanity away," she mumbled to herself, wandering into the kitchen to fill her water bottle.

Though she enjoyed working for Nanna, there was a constant niggle in the back of her mind – a thought she couldn't shake. Finn's words had become lodged in her mind - what he'd said about her musical talent - and she often wondered whether she really could be good enough to pursue it. Or was she just dreaming?

Neala frowned, suddenly reminded of something else. After that first night, she'd had several more vivid dreams about the crossroad in the woods. But no matter how many times she'd called, the mysterious voice hadn't appeared again.

Last night, though, there had been a change. The owl that always hooted mournfully was still present, but this time, a fox had been sitting by the roadside on the path leading to her left.

She had been confused; this fox, unlike its red-coated cousins, had been covered in jet-black fur, with flecks of white scattered around its muzzle and tail. Its eyes, too, had been unusual – they were a bright, almost-glowing blue. Neala had tried to reach out to it, but the moment she did, it had disappeared into the underbrush.

Shaking her head to clear the memory, Neala grabbed her phone and strapped it to her arm, securing the headphones in her ears. As the music blared, she scribbled a note for her mother and gave her legs a quick stretch. Once she felt limbered up, she opened the door, cautiously eyeing the area around her feet in case Sox was waiting to make a sneaky break for the outdoors. She locked it behind her, checking routinely that the spare key was still hidden inside the pot plant by the door.

She was beaming as she leapt down the short steps and started jogging towards the beach, the moonlight casting a soft glow over her surroundings. Neala loved running just before dawn; there was something magical about watching the landscape slowly come to life before her eyes.

As she rounded the bluff, Neala stumbled and almost tripped as she spotted something swimming out in the ocean. Slowing to a stop, she placed her hands on her knees and breathed deeply, scanning the waves, trying to decipher the shadowy patterns.

What in the world was that? she thought, her mind scrambling to make sense of what she'd seen.

For a moment, she could have sworn she'd seen a large, black horse floundering in the water. She stared out over the dark ocean for a long moment, hands on her hips. When nothing appeared except a few seagulls, she shook her head and snorted.

"Good lord, I'm losing my mind. Must've been a seal or something." Neala looked around, making sure no one had seen her. Giving her shoulders a quick stretch, she continued running, forcing herself to move a little faster this time.

By the time Neala returned home, the sun had risen fully, and Dana was awake, cooking some scrambled eggs on the stove-top. Neala's stomach growled as she opened the door, greeting her mother breathlessly.

Dana smiled at her. "Morning baby, did you have a good run?"

Grabbing her water bottle off the bench, Neala sat on the cool floor and started stretching her legs out.

"Wasn't bad, I didn't quite get the five k's today, but that's all right; I did some hill running so that makes up for it. It's warming up out there, though. I thought you promised me cold weather here," Neala teased, brushing her dark hair off her sweaty face. Dana chuckled.

"Hey now - compared to an Aussie summer, this is nothing. Which do you prefer?"

"Yeah, fair point." Neala laughed. Getting to her feet, she glanced down at her worn shoes. "Hey, Mum is there a chance I could buy some new shoes today? These ones have just about had it. I was thinking I might be able to leave the shop an hour early, perhaps?"

Dana nodded thoughtfully. "That should be okay. I have a delivery to make just before closing, so as long as you're back by four, I can give you a ride home."

Neala bobbed her head in agreement, reaching for a bowl as Dana turned and dished up the eggs. Feeling in a silly mood, Neala drew a smiley face on her eggs with the tomato sauce, making Dana grin. "They look like some happy eggs."

Neala shrugged, scooping the eggs up with her fork. "I'm feeling really good about this week, Mum. There's just something in the air, I'm excited," Neala beamed as she shovelled her breakfast into her mouth.

Once she'd finished eating Neala grabbed some fresh clothes and showered, feeling the endorphin rush fading. Emerging from the bathroom, she sat down at the computer desk to check her bank account, making sure there was enough in there for some new shoes.

Dana was pottering around in the kitchen, humming softly. Despite herself, Neala picked up the tune her mother was humming, and she started to sing along, harmonising the lyrics. She was startled to feel her mother's hand on her shoulder. Glancing up, she saw sadness echoing in Dana's eyes.

"Baby, you know it's not too late to look into music lessons. You don't have to stay at the shop if there's something you'd rather be pursuing."

Neala frowned and turned to face her mother more squarely. "Mum, we've talked about this. I love the shop, and I love working with you and Nanna. One day I might look at doing something else, but, right now, I'm happy where I am. Please don't worry about it anymore, okay?"

Dana pursed her lips, but nodded, smiling faintly. "How did I get blessed with such an amazing daughter?"

Neala shook her head, the corner of her mouth twitching upwards. Dana squeezed her shoulder gently, then said, "Well, shall we load up the van? I have a couple of deliveries to make on the way to work. Just let me grab the invoices and we'll get going."

Dana left the room and Neala let out a sigh. From the moment she could walk, she had worked with her family on the farm back home. Now, once again, here she was - working in a family business. She wondered if she'd ever find her own path – her own adventure.

Wandering aimlessly out into the courtyard, Neala glanced up at the mysterious ash tree at the edge the woods, partially concealed by the newly-repaired wall. True to her word, she had not gone near it again; she wouldn't risk upsetting her mother, not when she was finally happy.

That's me - always putting others first. Always the good girl, making everyone else happy. She rubbed her face dejectedly and turned her back on the tree, retreating back to the safety of the cottage. *Pursue my own dreams? I wouldn't even know where to start...*

Planting a smile on her face as her mother emerged from her room, Neala threw the pack on her shoulders and they headed out the door.

*****

Neala let out a long sigh and dropped her pack down beside her chair. Slumping into the seat, she leaned back and folded her hands behind her head, closing her eyes. She'd just returned from shopping for new running shoes, and she was exhausted.

The café had been busier than usual that morning - she'd hardly been able to catch her breath. Now she finally had a chance to sit and enjoy her own lunch; a blue-berry turnover she had been eyeing off hungrily since she arrived. Just as she was bringing the turnover to her lips, Neala heard a male voice call, "Hey, bus girl!"

Turning, she stared confusedly at the boy sitting a few tables behind her. Her mouth dropped open as she recognised him - he'd rung the bell for her and her mother on the bus, their first day here. *What was his name? Todd? No, something unusual...Tarkin? Oh, Torin. That was it.*

She gave what she hoped was a friendly 'I-see-you-but-please-don't-come-over-here' wave and turned back to her pastry. Wincing as she heard the scrape of chair legs on pavement, Neala grit her teeth. She smiled tensely as he dropped into a chair opposite her, a broad grin splashed across his face.

Sighing internally, she tried to be more friendly. *Gotta keep up that customer service*, she thought to herself wryly. As politely as she could, she said, "Hey. It's Torin, right?"

The boy beamed. "Great memory. How have your bus trips been lately? You got that pesky bell all figured out?"

"Yep, mastered it. You're out of a job, sorry buddy."

"Ha! That's grand - the boss was a real jerk anyway," he winked. Despite herself, Neala snorted. Sensing the change in her attitude, Torin slung his arm over the back of his chair and cocked his head at her. "So, I never caught your name. As charming as 'bus girl' is, I'm sure your real name is much nicer."

She grinned crookedly. "Neala Moran."

Torin held out a broad hand. "Nice to meet you, officially. You're Australian?"

Neala shook his hand, noticing how calloused his knuckles were. Looking at him properly, she could see bruises around his blue eyes, just beginning to fade from purple to pinky-brown. A frown twitched at her brows as she nodded.

"Yeah, my mum and I moved here a little while ago, at the start of June. It was actually our first proper day here, when we saw you on the bus." She was itching to ask about the bruising, but, just at that moment, Dana walked past with an armful of flower arrangements.

Spotting Neala, she called out, "All right honey, I'll be back in about half an hour. Nanna is finishing up, then we'll head home." Realising she had company, Dana gave her a not-so-subtle wink and continued walking to the van.

Blushing, Neala hurriedly picked up her abandoned turnover and plucked off a tiny chunk, popping it carefully into her mouth. She felt terribly self-conscious about taking a decent bite, hoping she wouldn't do something embarrassing like spill jam all down her front.

As though he sensed she was feeling awkward, Torin stood and patted his pockets, pulling out a worn leather wallet.

"Sounds like you'll be closing soon. You mind if I go order one last coffee then come back?"

With a rush of gratitude, Neala nodded. "Nah, that'd be great. I'll wait here."

With a casual flick of his fingers, Torin loped off, leaving Neala to eat her pastry in peace.

She'd just brushed the last crumbs off her lap when he returned, flopping into the chair with a sigh. Propping his chin in his hand, he leaned forward and gazed at her.

"So, where were we? You said you moved here with your ma?"

Neala nodded. "Yeah, she was born here, but she moved to Australia years ago, before I was born. After my dad die—" She cut herself off, not wanting to share any more with this stranger.

Torin eyed her curiously, his forehead furrowing at her sudden silence. For a brief moment, she pondered the idea of opening up to him. There was something warm and inviting in the prospect. Still...

No. That's my business, not his. Instead, Neala cleared her throat. "Anyway, that's not important. All that matters is we're living here now, working in my Nanna's shop." She gestured around her.

Wanting to avoid any more personal questions, she turned the conversation back on him. "But what about you? Apart from riding around pressing bus bells, what else do you do?"

Sensing the topic was closed, Torin leaned back and folded his hands over his stomach. "Well, I was born in Wicklow, on the east coast. I'm a Taurus, I enjoy long walks on the beach and candlelit dinners..."

Neala rolled her eyes, though she couldn't stop the corners of her mouth from pulling into an amused smile.

He gave her a quick wink and tilted his head to the side as he continued, "As you can tell, I am incredibly serious by nature and have no tolerance for foolishness or any sort of craic."

Grinning as Neala outright giggled this time, he rubbed his nose absentmindedly, then winced. "Ah, yeah, so, about this," he gestured to his face. "Before you get the wrong idea, I'm a boxer in my spare time. A good one, usually, but I had a bit of a tough gig on the weekend."

Neala sighed with relief. "Oh, that's good." Stammering, she hurried to correct herself. "I mean, good that it was from, like, sport, and not that you were getting beaten up for no reason or anything."

"Not lately." Despite the light tone, she didn't miss the pained look that crossed his face. He must've noticed, as he quickly covered it with a cough. Before he could continue, Nanna appeared with his coffee, giving Neala a warm smile as she placed it down.

"Ah, did you find your shoes, sweetheart? Just letting you know, lad, we're closing in a few minutes, so I'll need to steal her away from you shortly, okay?"

Neala covered her eyes with her hands as Torin chuckled.

"You have my word, ma'am - I'll have her home by curfew, I promise."

Nanna laughed heartily and patted Neala on the shoulder. "Ah, he seems a good enough sort. I'll leave you to your chin-wagging."

Torin smiled softly to himself and turned his attention to his coffee, stirring it absentmindedly. Neala blinked, not quite believing what she was seeing – he wasn't using a spoon.

Staring open-mouthed, she watched as the liquid swirled around in the mug, seemingly moving by itself. His finger was moving in slow, steady circles several centimetres above the coffee, not touching it at all. About to ask him how he was doing it, Neala was distracted by a dog barking as its owner passed them.

By the time she looked back, the coffee was still – no trace of a ripple. *No...no, I must have imagined it. Surely...*

Realising her own drink was getting cold, Neala hurriedly took a sip.

Clearing his throat, Torin picked up his mug, his eyes darting to the side sheepishly. "So, what are your plans for the rest of the afternoon? I could show you around the city, if you'd like?"

Neala lowered her eyes shyly. The idea of spending more time with Torin sounded like fun. She'd never really had any friends back home; they'd lived over an hour away from the nearest town, and she hadn't had many opportunities to meet people, other than Sam and Angie.

She was about to accept his invitation when she grimaced; her mother would be back to pick her up in a few minutes. Relaying this information to him, Neala gave an apologetic shrug and fiddled with her cup.

"Ah, that's okay. Maybe some other time, though? Here, why don't you give me your number?"

Neala hesitated, then drew her phone out of her pocket. Stuttering a little, she explained, "Ah, yeah, just let me – I had to get a new SIM over here, I haven't memorised my new number or anything yet, I'll just, um, look it up...somewhere..."

Torin laughed. "How about I just give you mine, then? That makes it nice and easy."

Neala smiled, and opened a new contact tab. She was a little embarrassed to realise she only had two other contacts in her new phone: her mother and Nanna. Handing the phone over, she sat awkwardly while Torin added his number, unsure what to do with herself.

Once he was done, he handed the phone back with a cheeky grin. Neala glanced down and snorted; he'd entered his phone number under the name 'Obnoxious Bus Guy.'

"Thanks for that, O.B.G," Neala chuckled, slipping her phone back into her pocket.

Torin tapped his chin thoughtfully. "You know, I like that. O.B.G. It makes me sound like some kind of rapper or something." He lowered his voice as deep as it could go and shaped his fingers into what Neala guessed was meant to be some kind of gang sign. "Yo, yo, let's give it up for the big dawg himself, the Disreputable O.B.G!"

"Oh my god," Neala scoffed, fighting back giggles. "Please, for the love of everything you hold dear...never, *ever* do that again."

Torin chortled with laughter as Neala reached for her pack and stood, her own face lit with humour.

"Well, as nice as it's been meeting you, Disreputable O.B.G., I do need to get back to work. Not all of us can be millionaire rap celebrities."

Torin bolted down the last of his coffee and stood, too, stretching his arms above his head. "Hey, I'm always happy to make time for my adoring fans."

Grinning cheerily, he shoved his hands in his pockets. "But, if it's not too much to ask..." He narrowed his eyes furtively and lowered his head, gesturing for Neala to lean closer.

Not quite sure what was happening, Neala flicked her head from side to side, then bowed so she could hear his whispers.

"You see," Torin murmured, "this is a right proper dangerous neighbourhood, and I'm just a poor, weak scrap of a lad. Would you mind walking me to the bus stop? I'd never make it on my own."

Neala stifled her laugh, fixing a look of concern on her face.

"Oh, absolutely. I can totally understand why a six-foot tall, professional boxer like yourself would feel intimidated around here. I mean, all these old ladies packing heat in their floral handbags, brazenly walking their fluffy little attack terriers out in the open like this. Why, it's positively abhorrent. Of course I'll protect you, you poor thing."

Falling into step beside each other, the pair made their way down the street and around the corner towards the bus stop. Realising how short the walk really was, Neala screwed up her nose; it hardly seemed worth the effort. Nevertheless, Torin came to a halt and gave her a beaming smile.

"Well, that was a thrilling two seconds," he mumbled as Neala giggled. Running a hand over his red-brown hair, he smiled crookedly. "Anyway, this part is always somewhat awkward and stuff, so how about we just count to three, say goodbye and wave, then you can toddle off back that way all casual and not remotely self-consciously. Then you'll glance back wistfully - just once - while I stare longingly after you."

Neala guffawed, covering her mouth in embarrassment at the garbled squawking sound she'd made.

Once she was composed, she said, "You know what, that sounds great. I hate awkward goodbye moments."

"Excellent, so on the count of three, yeah? You remember what you need to do?"

Neala nodded firmly, "Yep, all set."

Torin took his hands from his pockets and readied one to wave. "Okay then, here goes. One..."

Neala joined him and they counted simultaneously, "Two...three...goodbye!"

Neala giggled as Torin waved vigorously, then she turned on her heel and walked away, trying to keep her expression solemn. When she was almost around the corner, she whipped her head back and stared at him with puppy-dog eyes, as promised.

Unable to control her laughter, she almost tripped over her own feet. Torin was clinging to the bus pole as though his life depended on it, reaching one hand toward her and pretending to sob desperately.

A man passing by stared worriedly before giving him a wide berth. Clutching his chest, Torin cried, "Do you miss me yet, Bus Girl?"

"Oh, I'm pining something awful, O.B.G!" she called back, hand pressed to her forehead dramatically. Taking one last look at Torin's beaming face, Neala turned the corner and he disappeared from view.

Pausing, she smiled to herself and scuffed her feet, clutching the strap of her pack tightly. She'd never met anyone like Torin before. Was it always this easy, making friends? Or was he just special?

She pulled out her phone and opened her contacts list, thrilled to see the new entry. Distracted by an older couple walking past, she shoved her phone back in her pocket, blushing slightly. Nevertheless, there was an extra spring in her step when she returned to her family's shop.

~ 4 ~

Neala had taken the beach path again on her run today, testing out her new sneakers. As she rounded the bend, she suddenly remembered: last time she'd come this way, she'd been sure a horse had been floundering out in the ocean. But that had been a mistake, right?

Slowing, she stopped and looked out over the waves, searching for the slightest movement, any trace of something unusual. After several moments, she rolled her eyes and started running again, mentally berating herself for being so foolish.

But before she'd gone more than a few metres, something drew her eyes back to the water; her senses were on-edge, and she could feel goosebumps rising on her arms. There, that flicker of black...

No way - that's impossible...

She stumbled to a halt, gasping in disbelief. Out in the shallows, she saw a horse's head break through the surface of the ocean, steam huffing from its nostrils in the cold air.

As she watched, dumbfounded, the horse dragged itself from the surf, black fur streaked with salt and foam. Its mane was tangled with seaweed, and it pawed at the sand restlessly, tossing its head from side to side.

Neala's mouth dropped open in shock; it was huge, far larger than any horse she'd ever seen before. *It's the size of a freaking car! What the hell?*

Spotting Neala up on ridge, the horse reared defiantly, issuing a challenge. Her heart skipped a beat – it's eyes were glowing with golden fire, unnaturally bright in the dim light of dawn. It let out a screaming whinny, and lowered its head, preparing to charge.

Terrified, Neala bolted, praying that she wouldn't hear the dreaded sound of hoofbeats behind her. Not daring to look back, she sprinted faster than she ever had, feet pounding on the dirt. Only when her legs were burning too much to continue did she stop, breathless and trembling.

"What the heck is happening? I'm losing my mind." Hugging herself tightly, Neala waited until her nerves had settled then turned for home, giving the beach a wide berth.

*****

"Do you have that latte, dear?" Nanna's voice broke into Neala's thoughts, and she hurriedly shook her head to refocus.

"Um, yes, sorry Nanna." Turning away from the coffee grinder, she handed the mug to the gentleman waiting at the counter. "Sorry sir, here's your latte. Have a lovely day."

Dana smiled at her over the top of the roses she was wiring. "Neala's had a busy morning, Mother. The business just keeps growing by the day."

Nanna beamed. "Well, with my two new stars working here, I'm not surprised. It will be a shame to see you go, Neala."

Neala froze, dropping the cloth she'd been wiping down the benches with. Shocked, she turned to her grandmother, eyes wide with panic. "Why? I mean, w-where am I going? Are you firing me?"

Nanna looked horrified. "Oh, no honey, that's not it at all. I just thought...Hasn't Finley spoken to you? About Birchtree Hall, the academy? Dana, you said it would be arranged?"

Mouth open, Neala stared at her mother, an uncomfortable weight settling in her stomach. Dana pursed her lips, her face white. "Mother, we spoke about this last time."

Nanna huffed through her nose. "Dana, this girl has a gift, she deserves the chance to use her talents. I know Finley would have seen it; that's why I invited him over that day. It's a wonder he hasn't been to visit her again yet."

"This isn't the time. I will speak with Neala about it at home. Later." Dana's face was livid, her hands shaking.

"Hmm, will you though?"

Dana bristled. "Mother, stop. We have discussed it over and over—"

"Oh, poppycock. You can't hold her back just because you chose not to walk that path."

"It has nothing to do with that!"

Nanna raised her brows and planted her hands on her hips. "Don't play me for a fool. I know you, my girl. It is just such a *waste*. Neala could be doing great things—"

With a growl, Neala threw down her cloth. "Would you both please stop talking about what I should be doing with my life? It's like I'm not even here. Don't I get to decide things for myself? I don't know what this *Birchtree* is all about, and I don't want to. Just leave me alone!"

With ripples of anger bubbling under her skin, she stalked out of the shop, ignoring the stares from the customers. Not knowing where else to go, Neala ran to the bus stop and threw herself onto the bench, tucking her knees to her chest and clutching her face in her hands.

*****

Back in the shop, Dana dropped her stalks of roses and made to follow Neala, but Nanna placed a firm hand around her wrist and shook her head. "Give her space, Dana. Besides, we need to talk."

With a sigh, Dana lowered herself onto her stool and rubbed her temples, eyes closed tightly. Nanna watched her with pursed lips. "You haven't told her anything, have you? You promised you would."

Dana clenched her fist and shook her head. "No, I haven't," she whispered, meeting her mother's eyes sadly. "I don't want that life for her. That responsibility..."

Nanna's face softened, and she took Dana's hand gently. "I know, sweetheart. But you know what she is to them, why you had to bring her back. You can't run from it any longer, my love; she needs to know what's coming."

"I know that, I do," Dana murmured sadly. "But she's only sixteen. It seems so young now, looking back..."

Nanna sat down beside her and folded her hands over her stomach, nodding slowly.

"It is indeed. I remember when you were that age, quite vividly," she replied. "But keeping her from it all will do no one any good. You need to send her to Birchtree; Finn has already confirmed it, you know he never misses the signs."

Nanna tapped her chin thoughtfully. "What if...what if I get him to meet us here, after close? He's used to explaining this to the new ones. It may be better for her to hear it from someone with his knowledge and experience, rather than us just dumping the whole story on her."

Dana sighed and closed her eyes. "I suppose...I know I should have told her as soon as we got here, but I didn't know where to start. I told myself I'd give her a week to settle in - just a few days to get used to being here, that's all. Then one week turned into two, and two became four...now it's almost too late."

She winced. "Maybe a Tracker like Finn *would* be able to explain it better. He's the best, after all. But I just don't know how she's going to react." Dana's voice became little more than a whisper. "What will I do if she never forgives me?"

Nanna clucked her tongue. "True, true. She will be angry and hurt, to be sure. There's no avoiding that, darling. But you know her better than anyone - you will find a way to get through this. Together." She groaned and pushed back from the table, getting to her feet with a grimace.

"But, love, you'll need to tell her everything eventually. The truth about us."

Dana nodded absently, fiddling with one of her roses. Nanna watched her for a moment, then turned to the doorway, making her way back to the counter to serve the line of customers that had formed in their absence.

*****

Once she'd calmed down, Neala had hung her head and huffed out a sigh, ashamed of how she had spoken to her mother and Nanna. She'd debated whether to return to the shop now and apologise, or just take the bus home and deal with it later.

Gritting her teeth, she stood and walked away from the bench; she couldn't shake her curiosity about the academy Nanna had mentioned - Birchtree Hall.

"I don't need distractions, I need answers," she muttered, turning back toward the shop. Her resolve trembled as she opened the door, hearing the little bell chime, but she steeled herself and walked in.

Nanna spotted her immediately and gestured for her to go back outside. Feeling a little miffed, Neala retreated out the door and sat down at one of the empty tables to wait.

Once Nanna took a seat beside her, Neala glanced at her sidelong; she didn't seem angry, so Neala tentatively said, "Sorry for being so rude, Nanna."

Nanna leaned back and smiled at Neala softly. "It's okay, sweetheart. I shouldn't have pushed so hard." Studying her carefully, Nanna seemed to be weighing her words. After a moment, she cleared her throat and said, "You know your mother loves you and only wants the best for you, as do I. I want to know, and answer honestly, please - is this what you want, darling? If you could do anything with your life, would this be it?"

Neala paused, considering her answer. Choosing her words thoughtfully, she explained, "I've never really known any different, Nanna. You know I've always just helped Mum and Dad on the farm. I guess I just assumed I'd eventually take over running things one day, after they retired. Then, when that all fell apart, we came here."

Cocking her head to the side, she said wistfully, "I've honestly never imagined being anything else. A lawyer, a doctor, nothing like that. I like being outdoors and working on the land, not being shut-up in an office all day. Studying was never my forte, either. I guess the only thing I've ever really enjoyed doing, like, apart from the farm work, is playing music. But I never thought of making a career out of it or anything."

Until now, she thought to herself, hardly daring to breathe.

Meeting Nanna's eyes, she murmured, "Nanna, if there's a chance I could go to a music school, like where Finley works or whatever, that would be wonderful, truly. But-but am I good enough? Honestly?"

Her face drooped. "Then I'd have to leave Mum all alone, and we've only just moved here, and I wouldn't be able to help you in the shop right when you're getting so busy, and—"

"Neala, honey, slow down," Nanna said gently, placing a hand on Neala's arm. "I'll have Finley come by, hopefully this afternoon, and he can explain it all a wee bit better. But believe me - you are more capable and amazing than you know. One day I hope you realise that. You were born to go to Birchtree Hall, darling - they've been waiting for you."

She didn't take her eyes off Neala's face, even as tears welled in the corners. "You've always put others before yourself, sweetheart; now it's time for you to discover your own path."

Neala let out a long breath, her stomach churning wildly. She had squashed the idea of doing anything but helping her family down so far that it had almost disappeared. But in just a few words, Nanna had sparked the flickering ember into a raging fire. Neala would not be able to let go of the idea now, not now that she could imagine it coming true.

Her hands were trembling as she turned to Nanna and asked breathlessly, "Will they really take me? Birchtree?"

Nanna smiled and placed a hand on her cheek.

"I think we'd best call Finley."

~ 5 ~

"Okay, Neala, come on in." Finley's voice cut through Neala's daydream, sending the butterflies in her stomach scattering. Two weeks had passed since Nanna had made the phone call, asking him to help prepare Neala to join Birchtree Hall.

As predicted, Finn had been thrilled. What followed was a whirlwind of planning; an audition with the Birchtree staff panel had been arranged, and Neala had been told to prepare a musical piece to present. Despite Nanna's prompting, he had not been willing to provide any more information about the school until after her audition.

Curious, Neala had scoured the internet for information on Birchtree Hall, but it had proved fruitless - there was nothing about the music academy anywhere. She had asked Dana why, but her mother had been extremely quiet since the argument at the café and had merely waved off her questions. Nanna had been just as dismissive.

"It's very exclusive, Neala. That's all. Finley has already said you'll find out more after your audition."

The time had passed so swiftly that Neala could hardly believe she was already here, waiting in front of the community theatre, trembling nervously and wondering if she was about to make a fool of herself. Glancing down at her phone, Neala read Torin's message for the tenth time:

Good luck! Let me know how it goes. Don't break anything, unless it's a leg, haha! (I'm hilarious)

She smiled to herself, grateful for her friend's support. Wanting to avoid any humiliation if she failed, Neala had told him only that she was auditioning for a position in a local band; she promised herself she'd tell him the truth if she got accepted, though.

Taking a deep, shuddering breath, she picked up her guitar and walked over to the doorway where Finn was waiting. When she reached him, he stopped her and smiled warmly. "Don't worry, Neala, this is just a formality. So, relax - you'll be fine."

Neala was puzzled; what did he mean about it just being a formality? Had she already been accepted? Then why did she still need to audition? Worried, she followed him up into the wings, trembling when she saw the spotlight shining on the stage before her.

Dana, who seemed more like her usual self today than she had for weeks, hurried over to give Neala a final hug. "Do your best, honey. You are amazing, no matter what, okay?"

Neala gave her a shaky smile and hugged her back hard.

"Thanks, Mum," she whispered, afraid that if she said anything more, she would throw up.

Placing a gentle but firm hand on her back, Finn gave Neala a slight push, directing her out into the spotlight. Blinking in the brightness, Neala spotted some shadowy people sitting midway up the theatre, though she couldn't make out their faces.

With a wink, Finn shuffled off to the side of the stage, hurrying down the stairs and out into the audience. Neala's hands were shaking uncontrollably, and a sheen of sweat had already started beading on her forehead.

"You are Neala Moran, correct?" A woman's stern voice spoke from the darkness.

Fighting the urge to place a hand over her eyes so she could see them better, Neala nodded and stuttered hoarsely, "Ye-yes, that's me."

The voice spoke again, without a hint of emotion. "It is understood you wish to attend Birchtree Hall. Finley Talbot has recommended you based on your musical prowess. What is your experience?"

Neala licked her lips, throat as dry as sandpaper. "Um, well, I...I, uh, I've played the flute, guitar, and piano since I was little...at home...Oh, and saxophone and-and the trumpet..." A blush crept over her cheeks; it hardly seemed impressive.

"Mm-hm, I see. And your mother taught you, Dana Moran - previously known as Dana Kennedy?"

"Yes, and my father, Gary Moran."

Neala could hear someone coughing. She tried to subtly wipe her hands on her shorts, feeling the guitar slip in her grip.

With a bang, it fell from her hands and crashed onto the stage floor. Horrified, Neala hurriedly picked it up, face crimson. "S-sorry, I'm sorry," she mumbled, wishing she'd kept her hair down so she could hide behind it.

"What will you be playing for us today?" A man's voice spoke this time, gentler than the woman.

Taking a breath, Neala tried to compose herself. "It's a song I-I wrote myself. An original."

This was met with murmured whispers by the shadowy figures. The man spoke again. "Very well. In your own time, then."

Hoisting the guitar strap over her head, Neala settled the instrument comfortably in front of her, placing her fingers carefully. As soon as she struck the first chord, her whole body relaxed. Smiling, she closed her eyes and lost herself in the music. Her hands moved along the strings deftly, filling the theatre with sound...

*****

With her eyes closed, Neala couldn't see that she was beginning to glow - pale, teal-coloured light was spreading out from her body and sweeping into the darkness, illuminating the people in the audience. With a raised brow, the stern woman looked over at Finley, who gave her a knowing smile.

Lips pursed, the woman glanced at her companions. The man who had spoken to Neala leaned over and whispered, "She makes seven, Imelda, if she truly has the mark. She is the last one – the last Lorekeeper."

The woman, Imelda, raised a long finger to her lips. "I know, Brian. Finley found her, so it was to be expected. Still, it is good to have it confirmed."

Turning to her other companion, seated on her right, Imelda whispered, "Clodagh, I believe she is the one you Saw in your vision?"

The woman, Clodagh, nodded silently, watching Neala with a soft smile.

Imelda hissed lightly under her breath. "Well, then. I suppose we shall see what the Fates have in store for us all soon enough."

Turning back to the girl on the stage, Imelda and the others watched as the light faded and Neala's song drew to a close, all of them lost in their own thoughts.

*****

By the time Neala opened her eyes, the last note fading into silence, there was no trace of the mysterious coloured light. Swaying slightly, she shook her head, trying to clear her mind.

As she'd played, she'd imagined herself at the cross-road from her dreams. This time, the fog that had always clouded the paths ahead had cleared slightly, revealing the one to her left, where the black fox sat, watching her. The path wound away into the trees, disappearing around a sharp bend in the distance. Curious, Neala had taken a step forward, looking to walk further along it.

But the fox had trotted across and sat in front of her, blocking her. When she had tried to move past it, it had moved with her, not allowing her to pass. Frustrated, Neala had drawn back into awareness in the theatre, just as she played the final chord on her guitar.

Blinking, she glanced out into the dark, trying vainly to see the teachers once more. Out the corner of her eye, she swore she saw the flick of a furry black tail disappear under one of the seats. Dismissing it as nonsense, Neala planted a smile on her face and tried to look confident; she had been so distracted by the daydream, she hoped she had still played well.

Imelda's voice rang out. "Thank you, Miss Moran. We will be in touch soon."

Neala waited to see if there would be more, but the only noise she heard was Finley clapping as he climbed the stairs to join her on stage.

Confused, she looked at him and whispered, "Is-is that it?"

"For now, yes. You did very well, Neala, don't worry. I'm sure they saw the same thing I did – that you belong with us. And, if I may," Finn glanced around then whispered to Neala, "I'd be thinking about packing my bags sooner rather than later."

He gave her a wink, then guided her off the stage and back to the room where Dana was waiting. The adrenaline was still coursing through her veins, making her feel giddy.

Giving her mother a big smile, Neala took her guitar and packed it carefully into the case, hands trembling. She ran Finn's words over in her mind; he meant she had been accepted, right? If he was telling her to start packing? Glancing up at him, she spotted Dana gesturing him over and the adults moved away from Neala to talk, where she couldn't overhear them.

Unsure what to do next, Neala clicked her guitar case closed and sat on it, wringing her hands absentmindedly.

*****

Watching her daughter out the corner of her eye, Dana leaned close to Finn and whispered fervently, "How did she go? Is-is she...one of them?" Finn met Dana's eyes firmly, all trace of his usual humour gone.

"Aye, without a doubt. I was sure when you introduced her to me, but now there is no denying it. She is the final one. Another girl was found in the spring, she will be joining Neala at Birchtree this year. Now that they are all gathered, things will begin to move more quickly. With the number of creature sightings growing by the day, there can be no doubt; the Veil is weakening."

Dana gasped, covering her mouth quickly and turning so Neala wouldn't see her expression.

Tersely, she whispered, "But-but how?"

"We aren't sure. My scouts are gathering as much information as we can. But whatever the reason, Neala and the others will need to be trained as soon as possible. As it is," he glanced at the girl, "she'll need to be told, Dana. You simply cannot keep it from her any longer. I have avoided mentioning it up to this point, as you requested, but it is highly unusual to have someone come to the academy with so little knowledge of what they are. It will be a big shock."

Dana hung her head sadly.

"I know. I should have done it sooner, as my mother has reminded me ceaselessly." With a firm nod, she steeled her shoulders and met Finn's firm gaze squarely. "Leave it with me. She will know everything she needs to; I promise."

Finn's expression softened, and he placed a gentle hand on Dana's shoulder.

"Thank you, Dana. For bringing her back to us. I'll keep her safe; you have my word."

Dana took a shaky breath and planted a smile on her face. Turning, she slowly walked over to Neala, composing herself.

*****

Neala watched her mother approach, confused by the tension in her features. But by the time Dana reached her, she was beaming brightly. "Finn says you did well, honey. I'm so proud of you."

Shoulders relaxing, Neala peered up at her mother, meeting her smile with her own excited one. "Thanks, Mum. I think they were happy with my song. Finn seems to think I'll get in..." Neala trailed off, worry creasing her brow.

Standing, she wrapped her arms around her mother's waist. "Will you really be okay without me?"

There was a slight quiver in Dana's voice as she replied, "My sweet baby, you always put others before yourself. I'll be fine. Of course, I'll miss you terribly, but you are going to do so many amazing things, and I could not be prouder of you."

Neala almost believed her. But she didn't miss the single tear that slid down her mother's cheek as she turned away.

~ 6 ~

A loud beep roused Neala from her thoughts, and she glanced down at her phone.

Meet me in town today at Monnighan's Bakery on Donoghue. I have a surprise for you!

Neala read Torin's message absently, wiping sweat off her forehead. She had just returned from her morning run and was feeling out of sorts. The day after her audition, she had received a phone call from Finley; she had been accepted into Birchtree Hall. Though she had been expecting more information, he had kept the conversation quite vague, reassuring her only that "everything would be taken care of."

True to her word, she had texted Torin immediately, and he had been extremely enthusiastic about the news – more than she had expected him to be, truth be told. Though she'd been excited, too, she couldn't ignore the trickle of fear that had run down her spine. Things had moved so quickly it was making her head spin. What was the big rush about?

Dana had also been acting strangely since the phone call. A week later, she was still wandering around the house absently and seemed to be lost in her thoughts more often than not. The only time she ever came alive was when she was working with her flowers in the shop.

Neala had tried to talk to her, but whenever she asked about it, Dana just smiled and waved her concerns off, insisting she was fine.

Placing her phone on the bench, Neala spotted a note from Dana explaining that she'd left early to visit the markets, off to purchase more fresh flowers. With Nanna busy in the shop training the new girl, Tilly, it seemed Neala would have the whole day all to herself. The sense of freedom was exhilarating.

A distant voice in her head reminded her she should be packing for Birchtree, but she ignored it. Instead, she picked her phone up and read the text message again. Blowing a stray hair off her face, she typed a reply.

Sounds good. What time?

Leaving her phone in the kitchen, Neala strode into her room and gathered her clothes together. Once she had showered and changed, she returned to see if Torin had answered. She couldn't stop the smile from spreading over her face when she saw the little message icon flashing. Opening Torin's text, she read:

How does 10ish sound? My shout!

Neala glanced at the clock. She had about an hour until she'd be meeting up with him, so she headed to her room and stared at her suitcase in the corner. It seemed like she had barely finished unpacking, and now she needed to go through it all over again.

Her heart twinged painfully when she eyed her bedframe. She'd gone to such lengths to bring it over with her. And for what, in the end? Birchtree was a boarding school, she'd been told that much. All the effort she'd put into making this new place feel like home seemed wasted.

How many times do I need to start over? Will I ever find somewhere I can call home?

Thinking of how simple things were before her dad died, Neala let out a long sigh. Walking over to the calendar on her wall, she flipped the page up and traced her finger over the date circled in red: the new school year would begin on Monday, the second of September.

Her heart squeezed in her chest; that was barely two weeks away. "Where has that time gone?" she whispered. With mixed emotions, she plugged in her headphones and began sorting through her wardrobe.

*****

A short while later, Neala leapt off the bus, backpack bumping her spine painfully. Grimacing, she adjusted it until her water bottle was sitting more comfortably, then set off for Monnighan's Bakery. She felt a little awkward; she hadn't really been to any other cafés apart from her Nanna's. Wondering if this counted as a minor or major betrayal to her grandmother, Neala glanced up and realised she was close to the bakery now.

With a grin, she spotted Torin waving happily. Her smile dimmed a little as she noticed he had a female companion with him.

As she drew closer, she saw that the girl was around her age, with long honey-blonde hair tied in a braid under a floppy sunhat. She was very pretty, with creamy skin and bright green eyes, emphasised by her flowing white sundress dotted with mint-green flowers.

Neala felt positively grubby next to this immaculate creature, and she glanced down at her own denim cut-offs and sky-blue blouse with disdain. Squashing her envy deep down inside, she planted a smile on her face and strolled over to the table.

The moment the girl met Neala's eye, she dropped her gaze to her lap and hid her face beneath her sunhat. Torin, however, stood and held his arms out wide, greeting Neala with a warm hug. Tensing slightly, she patted his back awkwardly, unused to such shows of affection.

Gesturing to the empty seat, Torin said cheerfully, "Thanks for coming, Neals. I'm going to order some drinks, what would you like?"

Neala dropped her backpack on the ground and pulled out her chair, wincing as it scraped on the pavement. "Ah, I'll just grab a milkshake, thanks. Chocolate, please?"

"Aye, that's grand. Coming right up. Bet they won't be as good as yours, though." He gave her a wink, then tilted his head at his companion. "Neala, this is Áine Holloway. Áine, Neala Moran. Just chat amongst yourselves, I'll be back in a tick."

Torin gave them a quick wave then entered the bakery, pulling out his battered wallet. Feeling slightly abandoned, Neala folded her hands in her lap and looked over at Áine. The girl lifted her chin tentatively, then ducked her head down once more, a blush creeping over her pale cheeks. Stifling a sigh, Neala realised it would be up to her to initiate conversation.

Leaning her arms onto the table, she tapped her fingers restlessly. "So, Áine, was it? It's nice to meet you. Are you a friend of Torin's?"

Neala winced as she thought to herself, *Sure, because he invited her out because they're complete strangers, dunderhead.*

Áine placed her delicate hands on the table and said in a voice little more than a whisper, "Oh, yes, we've known each other since we were children."

Feeling buoyed that Áine was speaking to her, Neala tried to keep the conversation flowing. "That's great, it's nice to have friends."

Neala closed her eyes in dismay; making small talk had never come easily to her. Ploughing on, she continued, "I haven't lived here all that long, my mother and I moved here only a couple of months ago. Torin is one of the first people we met, and he's been really nice."

Áine looked up. "Yes, I was sitting with Torin on the bus that day. You were with your mother, weren't you?"

Neala frowned. Her memories of that first day here had all but faded. "Yeah, that was my mum. She was born here in Ireland but moved to Australia in her teens."

The other girl nodded, but this time she didn't add anything to the conversation. She briefly licked her lips, as though she wanted to say more, but then she hid her face behind her hat once again.

Sitting back, Neala glanced around at the other diners, trying not to look awkward. The silence dragged on uncomfortably.

Just when she thought she would burst, Torin returned, flopping casually into his chair. His eyes flicked from Neala to Áine, picking up on the odd energy, and he raised an eyebrow curiously.

Leaning back, he tucked his arms behind his head and cocked his chin at Neala. "So, I can finally say congratulations in person. I'm so glad you're coming to Birchtree, that's awesome. Even if you did lie about it to start with –

'local band', my arse." He wagged his finger at her in mock indignation.

Neala relaxed, returning his smile with her own. "Thanks again. I know, I'm sorry I didn't tell you earlier. It was so crazy how it all came about. I had no idea it even existed until now."

Torin nodded knowingly, stealing a glance at Áine out the corner of his eye. Neala noticed the look, and her brows furrowed.

He'd just opened his mouth to say something more when he was interrupted by the waitress delivering their drinks. Once everyone was served, he took a sip of his cappuccino and tried again.

"Anyway, what I was *about* to say was, are you ready for my surprise?"

Neala, who had just placed a spoonful of milkshake froth in her mouth, nodded quickly, trying to swallow as fast as she could. "Yep, sure am."

Torin grinned at Áine, then leaned closer to Neala, propping himself on his elbows. "Aye, well...Áine and I will be with you at Birchtree - we're Bards, too!" He watched Neala's face excitedly, waiting for her reaction.

Neala frowned in confusion. What was a Bard? And what did he mean 'with you at Birchtree'? That revelation, at least, finally clicked into place and she raised her eyebrows in surprise. "Wait, you go to Birchtree Hall? Both of you?"

Torin beamed. "I'm in my second year. Áine will be starting with you as an initiate - a first year. Sorry I couldn't say anything earlier, but you know how secretive everyone is about the magic and all. Finley would have strung me up by my ankles."

Finally registering the blank expression on Neala's face, his smile faded slightly, and was replaced with a worried frown. "Wait...you have no idea what I'm talking about, do you?"

Neala shook her head slowly, and Áine finally raised her head, staring at Torin with wide, panicked eyes.

Sitting straighter, Torin's tone turned serious. "Neals, hasn't anyone told you? About being a Bard? Surely Finn would have told you when he found you – it's his job as a Tracker..."

Neala was beginning to feel frustrated. "Look, either get to the point or forget about it. All I know is that Birchtree is a boarding school, an academy where they teach music, and Finn is a teacher there."

Áine spoke up softly. "Neala, while that's all true, there's more to it than that. Birchtree Hall is an academy, yes, but for Bards, like us. We learn more than music there; we also learn how to use our power - our magic."

Torin continued, "If you're coming to Birchtree, you must have Faerie blood somewhere in your family. It's where the magic comes from."

Neala flicked her glazed eyes from Torin to Áine, the thudding of her heart almost painful. Pushing back from the table, she picked up her backpack. "Okay, this is insane.

Magic isn't real, it only exists in books and movies. Do you think I'm an idiot? Was this some kind of joke?"

Torin reached out and gently grabbed Neala by the wrist, a pleading expression in his eyes.

"Neala, please, I'm so sorry. I just assumed you knew all of this – you told me about going to Birchtree over a week ago. But if no one's explained anything, well...then, yeah, it must sound crazy, I know."

Neala watched him steadily, one hand on her pack, the other clasped in his grip.

Áine added gently, "Please, will you stay and let us explain?"

Shifting her gaze to Áine, Neala hesitated, then lowered herself back into her chair slowly, body still tensed to run. Only when she was sitting did Torin release her hand. He looked at Áine, who nodded.

As she cleared her throat, her body straightened, all traces of shyness dropping away. "You may already be familiar with the term 'bard' as someone who sings songs and recites stories, yes? Like in the old courts of royalty?"

Neala gave a short nod.

"Well, that's the very basics of what we can do, what is most easily accepted by humans. Music, art, dance; they are all part of a Bard's power and usually one of the first indicators of Bardic magic, which Trackers like Finn look for when identifying new Bards – like you.

"Bards are very in-tune with nature and the rhythms of the universe, and this is the core of our power. It comes from the Faerie side of us, which is a whole other history. Our Bard magic typically begins to emerge at the age of sixteen, when we reach maturity."

Neala's head was spinning wildly, trying to take in everything Áine was saying. "So, Bards are just...really good musicians and dancers?"

Áine sighed sadly, pinching the bridge of her delicate nose. "I'm really not explaining this well at all, am I? I'm sorry. Finn is much better at this."

She tilted her head from side to side, weighing her words. "To answer your question, yes, we are, but that barely scrapes the surface of what it means to be a Bard. To be a Bard means to be sensitive to all aspects of nature, and to be able to manipulate the energy around us. All life, all matter, is made up of vibrations, yes?"

Neala bobbed her head dimly, eyes squinted in concentration. Her shoulders were aching, tucked up around her ears, and her teeth were practically squeaking, she was clenching her jaw so tightly.

"Well, we are like super-conductors of those vibrations. A Bard can tune into this and use it to create magic, to manipulate matter. The measure of our power is based on how sensitive our magic is."

Frustration was beginning to bubble under Neala's skin. Áine was making no sense to her, and the more she spoke, the more confused Neala felt. She was about to snap when Torin placed a hand on her arm gently.

"At a guess, I'd say your Faerie blood comes from your mother's side. Maybe she can help?"

Neala snorted, crossing her arms and shaking her head vehemently. "No, there's no way Mum knows any of this; she would have told me. We've always been honest with each...other..." Her voice trailed off.

Her mother's odd behaviour over the past couple of weeks was beginning to make sense. Neala had believed she had just been sad about her going away. But now...

Torin and Áine exchanged glances, watching the colour drain from Neala's face. Her legs were like jelly as she jerked upwards and shoved herself backwards, her abandoned milkshake sloshing over the side of the glass and running over the edge of the table, dripping onto the ground with a splatter.

In a voice that shook, she stammered, "I, uh, I have to go. I'll have a t-talk to Mum tonight. Thanks for the milkshake, Torin, and I, uh, I guess I'll catch up with you guys again soon."

She slung her bag onto her back and gave a little wave. "Nice to meet you, Áine." Stumbling slightly, she turned her back on them and walked swiftly towards the bus stop, almost bumping into the waitress carrying a mug of hot chocolate.

Mumbling an apology, Neala frowned and kept walking, her mind a tornado of images and words. So many odd things had happened since she'd arrived here – the tree, the dreams, the horse with the glowing yellow eyes...

"It can't be...*magic*, though...can it?" she whispered to herself.

Unexpectedly, a laugh bubbled up from her stomach, exploding out of her mouth. Neala stopped, feeling oddly hysterical. A woman walking her dog diverted around her, giving her a worried look, but Neala couldn't stop. Breathlessly, she grabbed her side, waiting for the giggles to subside.

Once she could breathe again, she inhaled deeply, shaking her head. "What on *earth* are you thinking, doofus? That you're a frickin' Faerie? That you can do magic and talk to unicorns and sprinkle pixie dust all over the place? You've lost it, officially."

Muttering to herself about the ridiculousness of it all, Neala flopped onto the bench at the bus stop and settled in to wait.

They were messing with you, you know that, right? the voice in her mind said tauntingly. *You're nothing special.*

Scuffing her foot, Neala scowled. *So much for making friends.*

When the bus pulled up several minutes later, Neala boarded silently, swiping the bitter tears off her cheeks.

~ 7 ~

By the time Dana got home from work, Neala had already started cooking dinner. Walking through the door, Dana sniffed appreciatively, hanging her bag on the rack. Neala, startled by the noise, glanced over and eyed her mother warily.

"Hey Mum. Did it all go well today?"

Sighing, Dana took a seat at the table and slipped her shoes off with a groan. "Hey baby. Yes, it was another busy day, but a good one. It's strange not having you there, but Nanna is hopeful that Tilly will be a nice fit."

Neala pursed her lips in a tight smile, raising her brows, then went back to stirring the pasta sauce.

"That's great, I'm so glad you guys will be okay without me. Must be a huge relief."

Dana obviously didn't catch the twinge of sarcasm in Neala's tone, because she merely leaned back in her chair, folding her hands over her stomach. "It sure is. It's nice to have all the details out of the way. By the time you're off to Birchtree, it should all be running smoothly again."

At the mention of Birchtree, Neala stiffened. Clenching her jaw, she reached for the spaghetti noodles and snapped them sharply, dumping them into the boiling water more violently than she'd intended.

This time Dana noticed the tension in the air and looked at her in concern. "Sweetheart, are you okay?"

Turning the sauce down to simmer, Neala slowly rotated to face her mother, leaning against the bench and folding her arms. "I met up with Torin today, and he introduced me to a friend of his, a girl called Áine."

Dana frowned in puzzlement at Neala's tone. "Well now, that all sounds...nice. What happened?"

Neala chewed the inside of her cheek. *May as well go all in.* "Well, we got talking, and Torin said that both he and Áine go to Birchtree, too. What are the odds?"

Dana's face froze, her brown eyes flashing with something Neala couldn't place. Fear? Anxiety? Guilt? Pushing it aside, she barrelled on, "And, you know, the funny thing is, *they* seem to think that Birchtree Hall is some kind of – get this – some sort of *magic* school. For Bards. Apparently, they said, only Bards are allowed to go there, so the fact that I'm going must, logically, mean that I'm some sort of Faerie-human hybrid with magical powers, like them. Would you believe that?"

Dana let out a long breath, sitting taller in her chair. "Neala, I...I meant to tell you, a long time ago..."

It was as though someone had dumped ice-water over Neala's head. She'd expected her mother to deny it. To laugh and say it was ridiculous; of course Birchtree Hall wasn't magical. It was just a normal academy of music, nothing to worry about. The lack of protest from Dana set Neala's pulse racing.

Breathlessly, she whispered, "So, it's true? What they said? I'm a Faerie?"

Dana clasped her hands tightly in her lap. "A *Bard*, yes. Your Nanna Kennedy and I are also Bards, as was your grandfather, and your uncle Jimmy - James, my brother - who lives in Wales."

Neala felt like the world was crumbling beneath her feet. If she hadn't been leaning on the bench, she was sure she would have collapsed. In a trembling voice, she asked, "Did-did Dad know? Was he magic, too?"

Dana shook her head sadly. "No, he wasn't. Neala, the reason I left Ireland is because I...I didn't want to be a Bard; I didn't want that life. When my powers emerged, just before my sixteenth birthday, I was angry and afraid. I had no interest in magic, in using my powers. Not like James, who was already attending Birchtree by then.

"So, I left for Australia, trying to get as far away from here as possible. But it doesn't work like that. The magic is a part of me; I couldn't just run from it. So, instead, I tried to hide it, to ignore it and hope it would just go away. When I met your father, I found an outlet in the farm; I could use my abilities to tend to the land and the animals. Then, when you were born, I wondered if you were like me - if you had the gift."

Biting hard on her lip, Neala forced herself to keep listening. She ached to run, to cover her ears and not hear anymore, to pretend that this was all a dream.

Dana continued, head drooping lower with every word. "I decided to keep it from you. Even knowing you could be like me, I couldn't bear to reveal the secret I'd hidden from your father for so many years. I thought that, perhaps, if I taught you to play music, that would be enough. That you could express your power through music, as a talent. But..."

Dana closed her eyes, a tear trickling out and falling into her lap. "That odd, white pattern, the one on your shoulder that looks like a leaf? I've always told you it was just a rare pigment quirk. But it's more than that. It's a special mark, one that was foretold centuries ago by our ancestor; it marks you as one of the Lorekeepers. One trusted with protecting the Veil."

Her breath hitched in her throat. Without warning, she curled her hand into a fist and thumped it on her knee, startling Neala out of her shocked stupor. "I had been a *fool*, keeping you in the dark. A selfish fool. Word reached me that the Veil was under threat, and I knew the time had come. It was vital that you learned to use your power properly.

"I had no choice but to tell your father the truth. I should have known he wouldn't have batted an eye; your dad was the most amazing man I've ever met." Her lower lip quivered.

"When he learned what I was, what *you* were, he immediately said we needed to move here, so you could be educated. He began saving every spare dollar, planning for us all to move as soon as possible. But then...the accident..."

Dana's voice hitched and Neala hugged herself tightly, trying to ignore the ache of grief.

After a long pause, Dana looked up, eyes burning with regret. "I have made so many mistakes, Neala. I am so, *so* sorry."

Neala swallowed past the lump in her throat, hands shaking. Breathing heavily, she realised the fog of sadness triggered by memories of her father was fading, dissolved by the rush of anger roaring through her. She could feel the rage building in her chest, burning her like acid.

Eyes blazing, she spat, "My whole life...my *whole* life, you have been lying to me. You say you moved here for me? So, I could 'start over' or whatever? But even then, you tried to keep me from Birchtree, didn't you? That's what Nanna meant. Five seconds ago, you were saying I was some prophesised 'chosen one'. But apparently going to the school where I might actually learn what I am supposed to do about it would be too much for me?"

"I was trying to protect you-"

"That wasn't your decision to make!" Neala shouted, fists bunching at her sides. "What matters is that you *knew*! All my life, you knew what I was and never said a word, not even the slightest hint – not even when we moved here. A 'fresh start', right? That was your reason for dragging me to the other side of the world – not 'you're going to magic school because you're a Bard'."

A lightbulb flicked in her mind. "Nanna and Finley – they wanted to tell me, didn't they? But you wouldn't let them. If Torin hadn't spilled the beans, were you even going to tell me any of this before I left? Or were you going to just let me rock up to Birchtree and be all like, 'Ta-da! You're a goddamn Faerie!'?"

Dana was aghast. "Neala! Mind your temper – this isn't like you. I know you're upset, you have every right to be-"

"No. No more." Neala was sure her chest was about to explode. Fighting the urge to punch the wall, she stormed around the bench and headed to the door.

Dana stood and reached for her, worry etched across her face. "Neala, please wait…"

Neala turned and glared at Dana so fiercely that she took a step back. Heat radiated from Neala's body in waves, causing her to shimmer slightly. "Don't touch me," she hissed. For the briefest second, Neala was sure sparks of lightning had flashed from her eyes.

Falling back into her seat, Dana tucked her chin to her chest, hiding her face in her hands.

Squashing down the part of her that wanted desperately to comfort her mother, Neala reached for the door handle and disappeared into the inky darkness, slamming the door behind her.

Not knowing what else to do, she started to run.

*****

Back inside, Dana, sobbing hard, slowly made her way over to the stove, turning off the smoking pasta sauce. Hands trembling, she reached for her phone and called Finley Talbot's number.

"Finn...She knows. She knows..." She tried to ease her gasps, the terror at what she'd seen lurking in Neala's eyes wrapping icy hands around her throat. "I – I think it's happening. She was so angry, more than she's ever been. I could see...I could see the storm in her. Oh, Finn – please, I think she's in danger."

Dana dropped her phone on the bench without hanging up. Wrapping her arms tightly around her chest, she pressed her back against the cupboard and slid to the floor. "Great Goddess, please help her. Keep her safe."

But no response came. Dana tucked her head in her arms and bawled.

*****

By the time her anger had started to ebb, Neala was approaching the beach. Breathing hard, she slowed, eyes puffy with tears. Peering down onto the sand, glistening in the pale light of the waning moon, Neala stopped and began climbing down the rocks towards the water's edge.

Once she was on the shore, she stepped lightly over the piles of seaweed until she reached a large, flat rock, where she could sit comfortably. Settling herself, she hugged her knees to her chest and closed her eyes, letting the salty breeze caress her face.

A Lorekeeper from some ancient prophecy? What does that even mean? That kind of stuff isn't real, is it? she mused, throat tight. *It's all so crazy. My whole life has been a lie. Who even am I anymore? What am I?*

Unable to fight it anymore, Neala rested her forehead on her knees and wept, the hot tears streaming down her cheeks.

After a while, her cries faded, and she hiccupped softly. Raising her head, she let her legs fall until she was sitting upright on her rock, face turned up to the moon. Empty of emotion, she breathed deeply, tasting the briny tang of the ocean.

Opening her eyes, she gazed out over the silvery waves, letting her eyes drift over the rippling water...then froze.

She hadn't been thinking when she took off. Driven purely by instinct, she hadn't paid any attention to where her legs had been carrying her. Staring out at the ocean now, a trickle of fear ran down her spine – this was where she'd seen the horse.

The giant, black horse with the bright yellow eyes.

Hardly daring to breathe, Neala slowly slid off the rock, eyes wide as she scanned the dark water anxiously. *It wasn't real...it wasn't real...*

Her lungs were tight with suppressed panic. Swallowing past the lump in her throat, she backed carefully toward the low cliff, never turning her face from the waves. Only when her hands pressed against the rough stone did she let out a trembling sigh. She did a final sweep of the shoreline, then bit her lip. *Please don't appear. Please, please, please...*

Gathering her courage, she turned and started scrambling up the rocks as quickly as she could. But she was shaking so badly that she kept losing her grip. Her nails scraped painfully down the limestone before she sprawled on the sand, spitting loudly as she tried to clear the grit from her mouth.

About to try again, Neala heard the sound she'd been dreading; there was a loud splash, followed closely by a sharp, huffing snort. Trembling uncontrollably, she glanced over her shoulder.

She was sure her blood had turned to ice in her veins. Terror had her gripped tightly in its claws, and she clapped her hands over her mouth to stop herself from screaming.

There, on the opposite side of the little cove, the black horse with its bright, golden eyes was emerging from the surf, like some demonic beast rising from the depths of hell. Its nose was raised, and puffs of steam glowed eerily in the moonlight as it sniffed, turning its massive head from side to side, searching for something.

With a thrill of terror, Neala realised it was looking for her.

It had sensed her fear. She was sure it had. Because the horse's head whipped around, its terrible eyes locking on her, and it let out a piercing whinny that split the silence like a knife.

Slowly and deliberately, it began trotting through the waves, eyes burning into her. Whimpering, she lurched back towards the rocky cliff face and scrambled against the unyielding surface, breath coming in short gasps.

But no matter how hard she tried, how desperately she clawed at the rock, she couldn't get a good grip. A moan of despair burst from her lips. Her fingertips were in ribbons, the blood dripping slowly over her knuckles, her hand, her wrists.

The horse was mere metres from her now. Neala could hear it huffing, its nostrils flaring as it breathed in her scent. With a thudding stomp that set the sand rippling, it let out another piercing cry.

"Please, don't hurt me. Please!" she begged, her words little more than whispers on the still, icy air. Exhausted, she slid back down the rocks once more, muscles weak with fatigue. Curling into a ball, she lay down on the sand and wailed.

A hot, sour burst of air flowed over her hair, tickling the nape of her neck and sending goosebumps racing over her flesh. Any minute now. Any minute now, it would crush her beneath those terrible hooves...any second—

A crack of thunder boomed around the cove, the rocks shaking with the force of it. Sand rained down on Neala's cheeks as she clamped her hands over her ringing ears.

The horse reared, screaming wildly, adding to the still-rumbling sound of the thunder crack.

Heart pounding with adrenaline, Neala sat up; the sky had been clear a moment ago. Where had the thunder come from? She cowered as she became aware of the monstrous horse looming her, and she gripped herself tightly, screeching, "No! Leave me alone! Please, please don't hurt me!"

But its demonic gaze was no longer fixed on her. Its ears were pinned flat against its skull, and it was baring its huge, vicious teeth in the opposite direction to the girl it had been stalking.

Hardly daring to move, Neala peered past it and saw a man standing on the shore, the pale moonlight bouncing off the sand surrounding him, as though he was standing in shards of broken mirror.

Transfixed, she lurched back as the horse reared again, but it seemed to have forgotten about her completely. Instead, it began charging at the man, head lowered and tail flicking furiously, sand churning beneath its powerful hooves.

Neala scrambled to her knees, reaching a hand towards the strange man reflexively, yelling for him to run.

But the man stood squarely, hands hanging loosely by his side, head bowed. His blonde hair, sheened with silver in the moonlight, fluttered softly in the wind. It was the only sign of movement coming from him. Neala's screams died in her throat, and she watched in horror, unable to tear her eyes away from the impending slaughter.

The horse seemed to sense its victory, as it tossed its head wildly and gave a sinister whinny, reminding Neala eerily of a human cackle. But in the split second before the horse would have barrelled through him, the man disappeared. Vanished without a trace.

Neala's mouth popped opened in shock. The horse skidded to a halt, sand and shards of the sparkly mirror-like substance spraying from its hooves. It hopped angrily on the spot, head whirling as it tried to make sense of what had happened. It spotted the man in the same moment Neala did; he was in the same pose, head bowed and hands hanging loose. But he now stood twenty metres away, the foamy surf almost lapping his sneakers.

Gathering itself, the horse gave one last jerk of its head then charged again. Like before, the second the horse would have crushed him beneath its deadly hooves, the man disappeared once more.

Inexplicably, the horse dropped to the sand, writhing and kicking, eyes rolling with terror as it let out an awful, rage-filled squeal. Clambering to its feet, it bucked and kicked at an invisible enemy, lashing out again and again. Despite its frenzy, though, Neala noticed that it was barely moving from its spot; it almost seemed trapped by an invisible barrier.

The thought had hardly entered her mind when, right before her eyes, Neala watched as a large, metal cage materialised from the air, surrounding the creature. Sure enough, it was trapped within the thick, black metal bars. At one point, its rump nudged up against the cage and Neala could have sworn tendrils of greenish-grey smoke rose from its sweaty fur.

A hand suddenly gripped her shoulder, fingers digging painfully into her collarbone. She let out a sharp cry and lashed out with her fist, connecting squarely with something hard. The thing she'd punched growled and released her, snarling, "Hit me again and I'll throw you in there with it."

Glancing up, Neala found herself face-to-face with a young man, his sharp green eyes glaring at her as he rubbed his jaw. "What are you doing here?" She spluttered, recognising him as the stranger from the beach.

She wasn't sure when he'd appeared, or how. A faint buzzing sound was humming deep in her mind, threatening to overwhelm her. "How did you...how...the horse...what..."

Neala stared at the man in horror, not understanding what was happening. Noticing her expression, the man sighed and pinched the bridge of his nose tightly. His eyes flicked back to hers, but she found no trace of warmth in them.

"It's simple, all right?" He pointed at the horse, still fighting frantically against its prison. "I used an illusion. A basic one at that. I laid that trap hours ago – that cage is made of pure iron, of course. Then I merely covered it with a glamour to hide it until night fell. That's when púca are most active. Everyone knows that. Well. *Almost* everyone, apparently."

He gave her a withering look. "Why anyone in their right mind would come to a púca's lair after sundown..." Shaking his head, he jerked his chin back toward the cage. "Anyway, despite the...added complication of rescuing you, it was a simple matter of getting the ugly thing to run itself straight into it. This púca was exceptionally stupid, lucky for me. Of course," he smirked, "my illusions are always perfect, so I'm not surprised it fell for it so easily."

The man paused, cocking a brow at her. "Hey, now. You don't look so good."

Neala had barely registered what the man had said. Her skin had turned cold and clammy, and the buzzing in her ears had grown to a deafening roar. Closing her eyes, Neala was sure the world was tilting around her; she was swaying wildly, unable to keep her balance.

The man's voice was fading away, as though she were sinking under water. Somewhere inside her, she knew her brain was imploding. Reality had stopped existing, and she was floating in some sort of limbo. Not wanting to fight anymore, she let go, slipping into unconsciousness.

~ 8 ~

"Neala, wake up. It's me, Finley. Are you okay? Neala?"

Somewhere in her bleary mind, Neala sensed a hand gently patting her face. Frowning, she swatted absently at it, trying to shoo it away. After a moment, she realised she was lying on wet sand and she began to struggle, a scream bubbling up in her throat.

Opening her eyes with a snap, she searched for the demon-horse, scrambling to get to her feet. Strong hands gripped her shoulders and a soothing voice murmured gently, "It's okay, Neala, it's okay. Hush now. You're safe now. I promise."

Stretching her hands out desperately, Neala's fingers closed around a wiry forearm, and she gripped onto it for dear life, her heart pounding in her chest.

Her eyes rolled wildly in her skull until she landed on a familiar sight; the hazel eyes of Finley Talbot, watching her with concern. Clutching his arm to her like a life-preserver, Neala sobbed, wondering dimly how she still had any tears left in her body.

Once she had calmed a little, Finn eased his arm away from her and placed a gentle hand under her chin instead, turning her face from side to side. "There now, that's better. Are you okay? Are you hurt?"

Neala shook her head, tucking her legs beneath her until she was sitting cross-legged. Staring out over the water, she shivered violently. Noticing, Finn stood and slipped his jacket off, wrapping it around Neala's shoulders carefully. Though it helped keep the cold wind off her, she continued to tremble. Meeting Finn's gaze, she whispered, "Where is it? Where did the horse go?"

Finn rubbed a calloused palm against his cheek, wrapping his long fingers around his face, as though weighing up his answer. Finally, he sighed, placing his hands on his hips. "It has been dealt with. As has the boy who recklessly disobeyed orders and went hunting for the darn thing."

Neala remembered the cold, emerald eyes of the boy who'd saved her. "You know him? Who is he?"

"No one you need to concern yourself with," Finn murmured. "Not yet, anyway."

Before she could ask any more about the strange boy, Finn cleared his throat and gestured to the water.

"The horse that attacked you - it was a creature from the Otherworld, a shape-shifter known as a púca. It is not inherently evil; yes, they can be dangerous, but some are benevolent or even protective. Unfortunately, you happened upon one of the more violent kind."

When Neala frowned at him, Finn crouched down beside her. "What was it doing here? Are there more?" Neala felt like a young child, asking so many questions. But she was still trying to wrap her head around everything that had happened. Everything that she had believed impossible that was now becoming reality.

Finn, to his credit, didn't baulk at her interrogation. "As I said, púca are usually confined to the Otherworld, home of the Fae and dwelling place of other long-forgotten creatures. A world of myth and magic. Separated from ours for hundreds of years by the protective barrier known as the Veil. But things have...changed, lately."

As though wondering if he'd said too much, Finn came to a sudden halt. His brows knitted into a frown, and he placed a hand gently on Neala's back. "I know your mother has spoken to you. About what we are."

Neala bristled, but then her shoulders slumped, and she hung her head, ashamed.

"I yelled at her," she whispered, placing her hands over her face. "What if that thing, that púca, had hurt me? Had *killed* me? That would have been our last moment together. I never got to say goodbye to Dad, now it's nearly happened again."

Finn's expression softened, and his voiced was laced with sympathy as he murmured, "All that matters is that you're safe. Your mum is waiting for you at home. She will be very relieved to have you back."

"I never thanked him." Neala lifted her head suddenly, her eyes wide. "The man who saved me – I never got to thank him. I mean, I *punched* him, but that's hardly a show of gratitude..." She trailed off, staring across the sand at the place where the stranger had appeared.

Crawling forwards, she pushed herself to stand. Her legs trembled beneath her, but she forced them to work. Pointing to the patch of sand, where flashes of moonlight still glinted oddly, she explained, "There was a thunder-clap, then the guy was just standing there, on the sand, surrounded by all that shiny-looking...stuff. What is it? That stuff?"

Neala hardly bothered to check if Finn was following her as she trudged over to the spot, her heart quickening as she passed the deep hoofprints in the sand, evidence of the púca's attack.

As she drew closer to the strange markings, her mouth opened in awe. Extending several metres out from where the man had stood, curious glass-like formations were scattered, each one twisted and warped, amongst the sand.

Stopping to pick up a small, rough-edged spiral about the length of her pinkie, Neala marvelled at its warmth. She had expected it to be cold; it was the middle of the night, and she was almost blue herself. But the moment she'd touched it, it seemed to heat instantly. If she didn't know better, she would have almost said it was purring.

"May I see it?"

Neala started, unaware that Finn had come up beside her. Her fingers tingled as she held it out to him. As he took it, she was struck by a sudden urge to snatch it back. Instead, she tucked her hands under her armpits, hugging herself against the chilly ocean breeze.

Flicking his eyes over it, Finn pursed his lips. He let out a heavy sigh, then handed it back to her. She took it swiftly, clutching it tightly in her fist, its warmth humming through her body.

"Have you ever seen lightning strike sand, Neala?"

Neala shook her head, cocking her head at Finn curiously.

"When sand is heated to extreme temperatures, it can be used to make glass. When hit with lightning, the heat it generates is enough to make creations like that one, called fulgurite, or petrified lightning – glass-like tubes coated in sand. Of course, natural creations like that are imbued with the energy of the lightning, which gives them greater power than those made by glassworkers."

Finn scowled. "Working with lightning is extremely dangerous. Only the most reckless and foolhardy Bards would ever attempt it - it's notoriously volatile. There's only one Bard in existence who has ever come close to taming it, and...and he suffered greatly because of it." Sorrow etched Finn's face as he stared over the ocean, his eyes lost in some distant memory that Neala couldn't comprehend.

Stirring himself, Finn looked at Neala with concern. "You must be freezing. Come, let me get you home. Your mother is worried about you."

Pushing her curiosity about the lightning aside, Neala lowered her gaze, not wanting Finn to see the mix of guilt and anger that was coursing through her; she wasn't quite ready to forgive Dana for lying to her, despite feeling sorry for the way she had behaved.

Sighing, she cast one final glance at the moonlit ocean and the shimmering sand, then fell into step beside Finn as she let him lead her back to her house. When they were almost at the door, Neala stopped suddenly.

Frowning at him, she asked, "Wait – you never told me the man's name. Who was he? Is he a friend of yours? He was a Bard, right?"

Finn held up a hand to stop her, but he was chuckling with amusement. "Patience, young one. Soon you will get answers to your questions, I promise, but not tonight." He stifled a yawn, then gave her a kind smile. "I'm very much looking forward to having you at Birchtree, Neala."

With a nod, he turned and climbed the steps to the front door, knocking lightly. Before Neala could press him further, she was interrupted by Dana yanking the door open, her face mottled from crying and hair hanging in tangles.

Neala's heart ached to see her mother like this; it was exactly how she had looked when she'd found out Gary had been killed.

With a leap, Neala jumped up the steps and threw her arms around Dana's neck, pressing her face into her shoulder, all her rage evaporating for the moment. Dana gasped, but soon returned the hug ferociously.

"Oh, Neala, I'm so, so sorry, baby. If anything had happened to you –"

"She was attacked by a púca, Dana," Finn said sombrely.

Dana stiffened, her hands digging into Neala's back so painfully that she winced. Loosening her grip slightly, Dana pulled away, but kept one hand around Neala's waist protectively.

"A púca? Where?"

"In the cove. It wasn't one that we were tracking, but it seems one of our students must have known about it, as he came to Neala's rescue. I'll be having a long chat with him, and we'll do a full check of the area to see if there are any more Otherworld beings around. I'm sorry we didn't detect it sooner; my scouts are usually more reliable."

"I saw it a couple of months ago," Neala muttered sheepishly. Finn gaped at her in surprise. "It was the first time I went jogging along the beach road; I thought I saw a horse in the water, but when I looked again it was gone. I assumed it was just jet-lag playing tricks with my mind. Then I saw it again a few days later, but I...I didn't think it was possible. So, I just, kind of, pretended that – that it never happened."

Dana looked at Neala worriedly. "Honey, have you seen anything else since we've been here? Anything odd? Or even any visions, or dreams?"

Neala opened her mouth to tell her about the crossroad dreams, but she stopped herself. Bitterness was rising in her like a serpent, and it hissed, *Why should she be the one with all the secrets? No need to tell her everything; she has no problem keeping things from you, does she?*

Planting a smile on her face, Neala shook her head. "Nope, nothing else." Feigning a yawn, she glanced from Dana to Finn then shrugged weakly. "I'm sorry, it's been a very long and overwhelming day. Thank you, Finn, for coming to find me. I'll see you at Birchtree, if not before. And if you see him, please thank that man for me – the one who saved me."

Slipping out of her mother's hold, she walked backwards into the house, waving politely as she bid the adults good night. She kept her face neutral as she pretended not to notice the two of them exchange a worried look.

"C'mon, Soxy," she muttered as she passed the ginger cat, who watched her steadily. "Can you keep me company tonight?"

Obligingly, Sox followed the girl into her room as she shut the door.

*****

As Neala's door clicked shut, Dana dropped her head and sighed. Finn glanced at her sympathetically, before his gaze drifted to the closed door. "You had to tell her. I'm sure she'll forgive you, once she's had a chance to take it all in."

Dana pursed her lips and wrapped her arms around herself. "That's just it, though; I wasn't the one who told her. It was her friend, Torin, who broke the news. Unintentionally, I mean. He, quite fairly, assumed she knew about the existence of Bards, since she'd told him she was going to Birchtree." She peered up at Finn miserably. "I'll be lucky if she ever trusts me again."

Not knowing what to say, Finn scuffed his feet lightly on the mat. Glancing out at the night sky, he placed his hands on his hips, letting his mind wander. He gave a low whistle and murmured, "I should really get going, Dana. Are you sure you'll be okay?"

She smiled at him and nodded absently, still lost in her own thoughts.

"Oh, yes. I'll see my mother tomorrow and fill her in on what's happened. Thank you again for coming - I didn't know who else to call."

Finn shrugged, his lanky arms bouncing swiftly before he shoved his hands in his pockets. "Well, good night."

With that, he turned and strode down the path, realising too late that Neala still had his coat. Waving a hand dismissively, he disappeared into the darkness.

Dana waved at his back as he walked away, before closing the door behind him and locking it securely. About to turn out the light and go to bed, she paused, then placed her hands on the door, sealing it with some of her magic. Smiling faintly to herself, she turned and headed into her bedroom.

*****

In the room next door, Neala lay on her covers, turning the piece of lightning glass around in her fingers. It was hypnotising, watching the moonlight play over its surface, and she soon drifted off to sleep.

It was not a surprise when, in her dream, she found herself at the crossroad again, the familiar fog swirling around her ankles. Glancing to her left, she saw the path leading off in that direction was still much clearer than the other three, but that meant little to her.

Placing her hands on her hips, Neala called sharply, "I am getting pretty damn sick of this. Am I supposed to be getting some sort of wisdom or guidance or whatever from all of these dreams? It's always the same thing - I'm tired of games, and tricks, and riddles. If you have something to say to me, just come out and say it." But she got no response; even the black fox who had been showing up recently was not there tonight.

Frustrated, Neala kicked at the fog, letting out a feral scream. Falling to her knees, she burst into tears, hugging herself tightly. "Please...please, just make it stop. It's all too much, I can't take any more," she sobbed, curling into a ball on the ground and wrapping her arms around her head. As the fog enveloped her, Neala felt chilled to the bone. The last thing she heard was a distant, cackling laugh, like the cawing of a hundred crows.

~ 9 ~

If Neala hadn't known better, she would have thought she'd been run over by a truck in her sleep. Her whole body ached. Rolling onto her side, she heard a clatter as something fell off her chest onto the floor.

Blearily, she picked up the small spiral of crystallised sand, frowning at it. Memories crashed into her consciousness, and her stomach roiled with fear. Lurching upwards, she sucked in breath after breath, hands gripping her knees as her head spun.

Glancing down at herself, she realised she was still wearing the same clothes from yesterday, including Finley's coat. A dim corner of her brain wondered why her hands weren't bloody and scratched; she was certain her fingertips had been shredded in her desperate attempts to climb the rocky wall to safety. Yet, looking at them now, they had nothing to show for it other than some shiny, reddened patches of skin. Almost as if they'd healed overnight.

Closing her eyes, she lay back down on her bed, folding her arms across her face. An angry yowl made her force one eye open, and she spotted Sox by her door, tail flicking back and forth as he demanded she let him out. Groaning, she dragged herself out of bed and opened the door, muttering an apology to the cat.

Peeking out of her room, Neala didn't see Dana anywhere. She huffed out a breath; she couldn't pretend that she wasn't relieved. A frown creased her brow as she walked over to her wardrobe and pulled out some fresh clothes, glaring disdainfully at the trails of beach sand scattered all through her room. Realising her bed would be full of grit, too, she stripped her sheets and piled them in the corner, making a mental note to put a load of washing on later.

As she stared at the empty bed, her eyes welled with tears. Once upon a time, she never could have imagined leaving her family. Would never have dreamed that her mother could have kept such life-altering secrets from her. How could things have changed so much, so quickly?

Clenching her jaw, Neala scooped up her clothes and headed to the bathroom, shooting a pained look at her mother's bedroom door as she passed.

It was only once Neala had showered and was sitting at the dining table eating her breakfast that Dana emerged, looking worse for wear. Neala gave her a tiny, tight-lipped smile, then hastily shoved the last bite of her toast in her mouth.

She was just about to get up when Dana sat beside her, placing a tentative hand on her arm. Neala sighed internally and turned herself to face her mother. It was obvious Dana hadn't slept at all; her eyes were bloodshot and puffy.

She raised her hand to touch Neala's face but lowered it almost immediately.

"Honey, I'm not expecting you to forgive me today, or tomorrow, or anytime soon. What I've done, keeping this secret from you...It must be such a shock, and I'm sure you have questions. But please know that I never meant to hurt you; I only wanted to protect you."

Neala's jaw twitched and she stared at her hands, unsure how to react. Deep inside, she knew her mother had meant well. But the nerve was still too raw.

Shrugging her shoulders, she pulled away from Dana and stood. "I know, Mum. Honestly, I do. But it's all been too overwhelming. I'm angry, and sad, and all sorts of mixed-up right now. I-I'm going to send Torin a message and see if he wants to hang out today. Just for now, I want to pretend like everything is back to normal and forget about all of this. Please?"

Dana listened to Neala sadly, then nodded. "Of course, sweetheart. I'll be out late with deliveries tonight, so if you want to head out, that's fine. I - I will have to see Nanna, though, and tell her about...what's happened."

Neala sucked in a breath and let it out slowly. "Sure. Well, I'm going to, ah, send that message and then I'll head off. If Torin's busy, I might go to the library or something. There's plenty to do in the city."

With that, Neala grabbed her empty coffee mug and plate, placed them in the sink, and retreated to her room, closing the door behind her. Once inside, she leaned her back against the wall and sighed. She had never felt so awkward talking to her mother; they'd always been able to share everything. *Well, not everything, apparently,* she added bitterly.

*****

Give me an hour, okay? I'll call Áine and we'll meet you at the art gallery, the one on Cullain Street. Chin up – it'll all be okay x

Neala glanced out the bus window, her mood significantly lighter than earlier. *It was a good idea to catch up with Torin today. He's just what I need.* Almost as soon as she'd texted him that morning, explaining what had happened, he had been nothing but supportive and had vowed not to mention anything about magic, or Bards, or crazy demon horses. Neala was curious to see what he had in mind for the day.

Leaping off the bus once she reached her stop, she strolled down the road, spotting the gallery sign in the distance. After scanning the faces of everyone nearby, she realised Torin and Áine weren't there yet. Unsure what else to do, she leaned against the wall and pulled out her phone, pretending to be busy.

To her relief, she didn't have to wait long before she heard a shrill whistle. Glancing up with a smile, she spotted Torin and Áine walking toward her and she let out a sigh of envy when she saw the other girl. Once again, Áine looked effortlessly glamourous, dressed in her pretty floral skirt and white singlet.

Next to her, I'm a potato, Neala thought, playing with the end of her ponytail wistfully.

"Sorry we're late, were you waiting long?" Torin asked, holding his arms out to greet Neala with a hug.

Slightly less awkwardly than yesterday, Neala returned the embrace and replied, "Nah, only a few minutes." She flicked her eyes to Áine. "Um, hi. Good morning," she murmured, unsure if she was supposed to hug her, too.

When Áine made no move to do so, opting only for a quick return smile, Neala clasped her hands in front of herself instead. *That answers that, then,* she thought self-consciously.

Pushing aside her awkwardness, Neala shrugged and hitched her backpack further up her shoulders. "So, what's the plan for today?"

Torin grinned crookedly, folding his arms lightly across his chest. "Well, since you've had a, uh, rather stressful twenty-four hours, to put it lightly, I thought we'd do something relaxing today."

He chuckled and nudged Áine with his elbow. "Or, rather, Áine came up with the idea; my plan was to go out surfing. But given the incident on the beach last night—" Torin cut himself off, looking sheepish.

Áine gave him a horrified look as Neala cringed. Running a hand over his head, he laughed awkwardly, then continued, "So, yeah, anyway, we obviously scrapped that.

Áine seems to think a day of pampering and such would be more suitable, what do you think?"

Áine looked at Neala hopefully, scuffing her feet. "I-I wasn't sure if it would be something you'd enjoy? If it's not to your taste, we could do something else?"

Neala cocked her head thoughtfully. "Honestly, I've never actually had a, uh, 'pamper day'. Living on the farm, it just never really happened - you know, nails and massages and things. So, yeah, I'd be keen to see what it's like."

She frowned. Directing her question to Torin, she asked, "But what are you going to do?"

Feigning a look of outrage, Torin placed a hand on his chest and huffed, "Well, excuse you! Do I not also deserve to be treated like a queen? Boxing is absolute murder on my cuticles, they are in desperate need of a full buff, and polish, and...and whatever other things make sense right now, in the context of this event."

Neala burst out laughing, and even Áine's shoulders bounced with suppressed giggles. Meeting her eyes, Neala asked jokingly, "Is he always like this?"

"Oh, only on special occasions, I swear."

The girls shared their first genuine smile, and Neala's heart trilled with happiness. Turning back to Torin, she placed a hand on her hip and exclaimed, "Well, by all means, let us be going, then. I'd hate for your poor cuticles to suffer for even one more moment."

*****

A short while later, Torin leaned back in his chair, stretching his arms above his head luxuriously. Glancing over at the girls, he winked and adjusted the white fedora perched on his wavy chestnut hair. Áine and Neala exchanged a look, then giggled.

The first stop on the pamper day had been a quick trip to Áine's favourite boutique, where they had each picked out a fabulous hat to wear for the occasion.

Neala had chosen a traditional brown flat cap with a large blue flower pinned to it, while Áine's pale straw hat was embellished with small feathers and a jewelled pin, and it set off her golden locks beautifully.

Much to the chagrin of the shop assistant, Torin had insisted on parading his choices for the girls, before finally being shooed from the store with the fedora.

Once they were decked out in their fancy hats, Áine had taken them to a salon, where they were all currently reclining in large, cosy chairs, soaking their feet in bowls of warm, sweet-scented water while the beauticians showed them a selection of nail colours.

As Áine deliberated over two almost-identical shades of lavender, Neala glanced over at Torin and gave him a crooked smile. Torin beamed back, flicking his head lavishly.

"I honestly don't understand why more guys don't do pamper days," he muttered. "I've never felt so fabulous in my entire life."

Neala rolled her eyes with a chuckle, then turned her attention back to the colour chart in front of her.

"Um, okay, so I'm definitely going with the, ah, 'Pearlescence'," she told the woman waiting on her, who smiled and nodded, reaching behind her for the bottle of creamy-pink polish.

Curling her toes in the warm water, Neala lifted her feet as the beautician removed the basin and settled herself on a stool. Trying not to giggle as she started massaging her feet, Neala met Áine's eyes and grinned. Áine smiled back, face glowing with happiness.

It was mid-afternoon by the time they finished at the salon, and the trio were now walking toward Monnighan's Bakery, all sporting shiny, colourful nails. Torin was unashamedly flashing his coral-orange fingernails at anyone they passed, ignoring Áine's cringes of embarrassment.

Only when it seemed like Áine would combust from blushing so hard did Torin fall back into step with her, throwing an arm around her shoulders affectionately. "Thanks for today, Áine – it was a great idea, way better than mine."

"Definitely," Neala agreed, nodding happily. "Just what I needed."

Áine grinned with pleasure, adjusting her new hat to hide her flushed cheeks.

Once they reached Monnighan's, Torin went inside to order their lunch. Neala watched the staff laugh as he modelled his fancy hat and sparkling nails, a fond smile on her face.

"We can't take him anywhere, can we?" Áine muttered, but there was a trace of humour in her tone. "How I wish I had even a wee bit of his confidence."

"I don't think the world could handle that. One Torin is more than enough!" Neala joked. The girls giggled, then she continued warmly. "Seriously, though, Áine, thanks for this. It was good to chill out after such a crazy day yesterday."

Áine's cheeks flushed with pleasure. "You're welcome, Neala. It must have been such a shock, I'm glad we could help you relax today."

Her mouth popped into a delicate 'o' shape. "Oh, I almost forgot!" She reached into her bag and pulled out a small, hand-painted wooden box.

Eyes locked on her lap, she fiddled with the box as she explained, "I-I wanted to get you a little gift, since we're both going to be starting at Birchtree together soon. I know it hasn't been a great start for you, but I wanted to give you something to make it not seem so bad, or scary. It's not much, but I hope you like it."

Áine thrust the box at her, still avoiding her gaze. Neala, touched by the gesture, took the little box gently. Tracing her finger over the delicately painted rose on the lid, she flicked the latch carefully.

Inside the box lay a small, intricate silver brooch in the shape of a treble clef. A swell of gratitude filled Neala from head to toe. Without hesitating, she drew the brooch out and placed it on her shirt.

"Áine, I...this is beautiful, thank you so much. But I don't have anything for you..." Neala's face drooped, but Áine only shook her head.

"That's okay - I have a matching one of my own, see?" She rummaged in her bag and drew out her own pin; a treble clef like the one she'd given Neala, but in gold. With a small smile, she pinned it to her top, too. "So, now we have something in common." Áine beamed.

"I'm working on something for Torin, too; I wasn't sure he'd be too grateful for a fancy brooch." She chuckled, "Though, after today, I'm actually not sure he'd mind in the slightest."

*****

After what seemed like too short a time, Neala brushed the last crumbs off her lap and sighed. Noticing, Torin asked, "What's up, Neals? Are you okay?"

Neala fiddled with her napkin distractedly. "Yeah, I'm good. I just don't feel much like going home." Her jaw tightened. "I hate feeling like this; Mum and I have never fought or anything, it feels so weird. But I'm still just so mad."

Placing her empty mug back on the table, Áine cleared her throat. "Well, if you wanted, you could come back to my place for a while. You'd be welcome to stay the night, too, if you wish?"

Lifting her head, Neala gazed at Áine with raised eyebrows. "Really? Your parents won't mind?"

Áine shrugged her shoulders lightly. "They aren't home, and Colleen won't be bothered; she's our housekeeper. My sister is probably home, but that wouldn't be a problem."

Despite the thrill of excitement in her veins, Neala flushed slightly. "I, um, I've actually never had a sleepover before."

"You really were sheltered out on the farm, weren't you?" Torin teased good-naturedly. Neala stuck her tongue out at him, and he laughed. Áine looked at him and cocked her head to the side.

"Did you want to stay, too, Tor? Eilìs hasn't been to see Poppy in a while, I'm sure she'd love to hear how she's doing?"

Torin gave Áine a sad, knowing smile, then nodded. "Yeah, I'll come along. Can't let you girls have all the fun," he said, returning to his usual cheery self.

Neala listened to the exchange, feeling a bit left out; she'd forgotten how little she knew about her friends. About their lives, their families. About what it meant to be a Bard...

Curiosity stirred within her, and she asked quietly, "At your place, could you guys maybe...maybe tell me more about Bards, and your - our magic?"

Exchanging a look, Áine and Torin nodded. "Yeah, of course," Torin said, wrapping an arm around Neala's shoulders with a grin. "You're one of us now, aye?"

~ 10 ~

Neala couldn't help but stare; Áine's house was the biggest she'd ever seen. Nestled in the hills east of the city, the mansion stood at the end of a long, tree-lined driveway which wound its way to the top of the rise, overlooking the ocean.

Rather than take the bus, Áine had called her family's chauffeur, Charles, to pick them up in a car so flashy that Neala had been terrified to touch anything. As they drove towards the two-storey monolith, Neala tried not to press her nose against the spotless window. Torin gave her a sidelong wink.

"Yeah, I know, right? I mean, it's no medieval castle, but it tries."

Neala smiled back at him, shooting a glance at Áine to make sure she hadn't embarrassed her. But Áine was busy rifling through her bag, oblivious to the other two. Itching to ask a million questions, Neala shuffled in her seat, twisting her fingers together restlessly as the car pulled to a stop beside a huge decorative fountain.

As she started to open her door, Torin placed a gentle hand over hers and whispered, "Let Charles - he'll be offended if you do it." Neala raised her eyebrows but sat back and waited for the driver to unlatch her door.

Inclining his head to her as she exited, Charles murmured, "Welcome, Miss."

Flustered by the formality, Neala blurted out, "Thanks, you too."

Ducking her head as her face burned, she hurried away, feeling mortified. Seeking any kind of distraction, Neala let her gaze wander around the grounds, taking in the manicured lawn and perfectly-tended gardens. In the distance, she could see the ocean sparkling in the late afternoon sun.

More relaxed now that she had taken some deep breaths, she waited for Torin and Áine to join her. Once Charles had driven off, Áine turned and gave Neala a nervous smile, her eyes guarded.

"So, this is 'Château de Holloway'," she said dryly as she gestured behind her. "Please make yourself as comfortable as you can here."

Climbing the creamy marble steps, Áine pushed open the ornate door with a barely-audible sigh. Following her inside, Neala bit the inside of her cheek so she wouldn't gasp. It was like she'd just walked into the pages of a magazine; the entrance room oozed luxury and class, and Neala suddenly felt like a stray puppy who'd been rescued by a princess.

Torin, obviously used to the place, tugged off his sand-shoes and threw them towards a doorway leading off the right, not bothering to put them away neatly. Áine grimaced, then led Neala to the little side room, grabbing Torin's shoes as she went.

"This is the, ah, slush room. It's where we put our shoes, coats, and the like, so we don't track mud or anything into the house. Um, usually we would give guests complimentary house slippers, and you're welcome to have some, if you think you'd like them? With Mother and Father away, it's not such a big deal, though."

Neala stuttered nervously, "Oh, no, I don't think I need any. Unless you'd feel better if I wore them? Do most people wear them?"

Áine's expression drooped a little, and she lowered her eyes to the ground, letting her hair fall in front of her face. Neala felt awful.

With a sigh, she said "I'm sorry, Áine. I don't mean to make you feel ashamed or embarrassed or anything. You have a beautiful house, but I'm guessing it doesn't feel much like a home sometimes? Especially when gawkers like me come in, drooling and gasping like a dying fish."

This sparked a giggle out of Áine, and Neala grinned.

Reaching out, she touched Áine's arm softly. "Really, though, I'm sorry. I promise I'll be a little less star-struck, and more...Torin-ish."

The girls shared a smile, then Neala slipped off her shoes, placing them on the rack and flexing her toes.

"There, this will do fine. Besides, it shows off my pretty nail polish now."

Returning to the entrance hall, Neala realised Torin was missing. Before she could ask where he'd gone, Áine rolled her eyes and gestured with her head. "The kitchen," she said resignedly, then walked off. Neala raised an eyebrow.

"Seriously? We just had lunch."

"He can't help himself. You'll see why."

As she followed Áine towards the kitchen, Neala fiddled with her phone. Feeling torn, she considered ringing her mother, but settled for sending a quick text instead.

Hi Mum. Am at Áine Holloway's house, will be staying the night here. See you in the morning.

Hesitating, she sighed and added one last bit.

Love you xo

Slipping her phone back into her pocket, Neala's stomach gave a painful twist. *Time. I just need time. Once I talk to Torin and Áine, and learn more about all this Bard stuff, I'll be a bit better. Then things with Mum will go back to normal.*

Squashing down her doubts, she trotted to catch up to Áine, who was looking back for her.

"Here, this is the kitchen. Please help yourself to any snacks that you'd like. Colleen usually serves dinner at six, but I'll have a talk with her about maybe just doing some pizzas or something for us, what do you think? We can have them in the lounge instead."

Neala nodded happily. "Pizza sounds great. Will Colleen mind, though? You know, having extra people to feed?"

Áine shook her head with a tiny smile. "No, she actually quite enjoys it. Eilìs is the one who usually has heaps of friends over, Colleen will be pleased it's me for a change."

Áine shuffled awkwardly, then pushed the door open. "Anyway, we better check on Tor before he eats himself silly."

Walking into the vast kitchen, Neala clamped her jaw closed, remembering her promise to Áine about not being so overwhelmed.

But it was hard not to gape. The kitchen could easily accommodate three whole buses with room to spare. Modern appliances were scattered all around the place, and pots and pans hung from the roof in droves. Through the window, Neala caught glimpses of a sprawling veggie patch, and bunches of fresh and dried herbs filled the kitchen with their fragrance.

Peering at her sidelong, Áine watched Neala's expression nervously. Sensing eyes on her, Neala smiled, and called casually, as though she walked into kitchens the size of a small house every day, "Oi, Torin! Save some for the rest of us!"

Áine smiled gratefully and her whole body relaxed. Wandering further into the kitchen, Neala spotted Torin rifling through the massive, double-width fridge. "Hey gutso!" she said jokingly, startling him.

As he emerged with arms full of fruit and yoghurt, Torin ducked his head guiltily and shrugged.

"What can I say? I'm a growing boy."

As he spread the fruit out on the bench, Áine pulled a stool over and gestured for Neala to do the same. Taking a seat, Neala leaned forward and propped her head in her hands.

Torin, through a mouthful of strawberry, asked the girls, "Can I get you ladies a tea, or juice, or something?"

Neala cocked an eyebrow at him. "Juice sounds great, thanks. The way you're offering, anyone would think you lived here."

Áine and Torin exchanged a look, then he shrugged. "Well, that's probably because I did. Until a year ago, anyway."

Neala's mouth dropped opened in surprise.

"You did? Really?"

"Yeah, from when I was about thirteen until I turned seventeen. I mean, I live at Birchtree most of the time during the year now, but I got my own place last summer. The Holloways fostered me 'n' my sister. I'm happy to tell you about it, if you want to know?" Torin queried. "I'm not ashamed or anything."

"Here, I'll get the juice while Torin tells you the story," Áine said softly as she made her way around to the opposite side of the bench.

Taking her place, Torin spooned the last bit of yogurt into his mouth, then turned to Neala.

"Where to start? Hmm...So, back in the day, my father was a local boxing legend in Wicklow, where I'm from. He was the middleweight champion for close to a decade. Anyway, once my sister, Poppy, was born, he retired from competing and turned to coaching. I reckon this is when the trouble started for him, but that's another story. Sort of."

He shook his head, frowning.

"I won't go into too much detail, but let's just say Dad...well, he had a bit of a temper sometimes. When I was nine, he started coaching me, wanting me to basically become the next him. I did pretty well, but I always knew there was something a bit...different about me.

"None of my family had ever been Bards before, though - never even knew they existed. My mother, she knew how much I wanted to dance; that was my real passion, not boxing. But there was no way Dad would ever see his son 'prancing about like some sort of fairy'."

Torin's mouth twisted crookedly. "You see the irony there, of course? My sister, Poppy, was learning piano at this studio in town, but they also taught dance there. So, Mum used to pay for me to get private lessons after school, telling my dad I was getting tutoring for math and stuff. She paid for it out of her own money, putting little bits aside every payday so Dad never knew. My mother was...she was the best person ever."

Neala didn't miss the past tense. Her own grief gripped her keenly. Ignoring the ache spreading through her chest, she watched as Torin took a sip of juice, then continued. "She died when I was eleven, a stroke. I gave up dancing after that and channelled my energy into beating the snot out of opponents in the ring, much to my father's delight.

"His drinking was pretty bad by then, too, and things at home were kind of awful. Just when things couldn't get much worse, Poppy's magic emerged, and our family had its first ever Bard. Not knowing what that was, or what her new powers were, Dad freaked, calling her a witch and kicking her out of the house. For a drunk, he's pretty religious, my old man. He thought she'd been cursed by the Devil.

"She lived on the street for a bit, and I'd smuggle her food and blankets and what-not when I could. But things at home were worse than ever. Eventually I just joined her, running away from home one night and never going back."

He paused again, running a hand through his hair, eyes distant. "I think we lived on the streets for about a year or so? That's when Finley Talbot found us. He explained to Poppy what she was, then introduced us to the Holloways, who offered to take us in."

Letting out a long breath, he lifted his chin and gestured to the kitchen. "So, short story probably made longer than necessary, I lived here until my own Bard powers emerged. Since then, I board at Birchtree then rent my own apartment in the city over the summer break."

Neala stared at the bench, feeling hollow. "What about Poppy? Does she live with you, too?"

Torin's face clouded over. "No. Poppy...she's in the hospital now. She was trying to...well, she had an accident a few years ago and her brain was badly damaged. We tried looking after her here, but she took a turn a while back and she's been in a coma since then. The Holloways pay for her treatment, and she's being cared for in one of the best facilities in the country. I go visit her when I can."

He gave a sad laugh. "Magic's grand and all, but it can't fix everything."

"Torin, I—"

"Hey now, what's with all the doom and gloom? This is a party, isn't it?" Torin forced a smile onto his face, and nudged Neala with his elbow. "Seriously, Neals, don't overthink it, okay? I'm grand. Happy and all that."

Neala took a deep breath and smiled at him reassuringly. "Fair enough. I just have one last question, if I may?"

Torin raised an eyebrow at her cautiously.

"Yes?"

"You-you still box. Why? Didn't your dad *force* you to do that?"

Torin chuckled. "Yes and no. He wanted me to be like him, so it was boxing or nothing in the way of sports. But, honestly, I don't mind it. Dancing and boxing actually have more in common than my old man would ever admit. I mean, if you ignore the whole punching each other part, it's basically a two-step."

He winked and picked up his juice, taking a big mouthful.

Áine, who had stayed quiet while Torin talked, chimed in, "You'll have to come to one of his fights someday, Neala. He's really very good."

"Of course he is; just ask him," a strange voice called dryly. Startled, Neala swallowed her juice too quickly, and started to cough. Torin pounded her on the back, rolling his eyes in mock disgust.

"So nice of you to kill our guest, Eilìs."

Turning, Neala did her best to compose herself. Áine's sister was leaning in the doorway, grinning crookedly. Taken aback, Neala tried not to stare; Eilìs was nothing like the elegant Áine. Tall and broad-shouldered, with bright blue hair styled into a spiky pixie-cut, she was Neala's definition of a rock-goddess.

Twirling one of her ear piercings absently, Eilìs studied Neala just as intently. With a grin, she sauntered over and wrapped an arm around Neala's shoulders.

"Nah, this one's tougher than she looks; it'd take more than a bit of juice and spit to get rid of her."

Focusing her attention back on Torin, she chuckled and moved toward him, arms spread welcomingly. "C'mere, stranger. I love your new look." She grinned, gesturing to his orange fingernails.

With a laugh, Torin stood, admiring his manicure. "You know me, never one to miss a fashion trend." They laughed and wrapped each other in a warm hug.

Neala was amused to see that even Torin's large frame seemed dwarfed by the sheer presence of Eilìs. She squinted her eyes, unsure if she was imagining it; she was sure that Áine's sister had an aura around her, oozing power.

As though sensing Neala's scrutiny, Eilìs pulled out of the embrace and slowly turned, ice-blue eyes boring into her. After a little while, she gave a low whistle.

"Wow, you are something special, aren't you? What's your name, little one?"

Neala had been hypnotised by Eilìs' stare, and she blinked confusedly, trying to gather her thoughts. She opened her mouth to answer, but Áine got there first.

"Eilìs, stop scanning my friends, it's so embarrassing! This is Neala Moran, from Australia. Neala, please excuse my sister - she's an aura-reader, a Tracker. For some reason she thinks this means she can Read everybody she meets," Áine huffed, hands on her hips.

Eilìs rolled her eyes. "Ah, I didn't even look that hard. Don't have to with this one." She jerked her chin at Neala with a grin.

Neala's face flushed, and she looked down at her hands, twisting her fingers together. She had never liked being the centre of attention and was getting a little fed up with everyone fussing over her.

Noticing her friend's discomfort, Áine turned to Eilìs with a frown. "What do you want, anyway?"

Eilìs raised her left eyebrow, the piercing glinting as it shifted in the light. "I came to say hi when I sensed guests in the house, that's all."

Shrugging her shoulders, she scanned the trio and nodded, a knowing smile on her face. "But I can see now isn't the time; you were obviously in the middle of something."

Eilìs leaned past Neala and grabbed an apple off the bench. "Let Colleen know I'll be out late, okay?"

Áine's expression had softened considerably and she smiled at her sister. "I will. Have fun tonight."

With a salute to Neala and Torin, Eilìs bit into her apple and sauntered out of the room. Once she had left, Neala felt the pressure in the room physically drop. Eyes wide, she gaped at Áine. "Does your sister usually leave such an impression?"

Torin chuckled. "You felt it, then? Eilìs is one of the greatest Bards at Birchtree and a gifted Tracker. She's not quite as good as Finn, but she's not far off, either."

Neala shook her head. "Speaking of Birchtree..." she trailed off, feeling nervous.

Áine lifted her eyebrows at Torin, who shrugged.

"Whenever you're ready, Áine and I will try and answer your questions as best we can," he said, keeping his tone neutral.

"I don't even know where to start, though."

Torin nudged her with his foot. "I find the beginning works pretty well, from experience."

Neala rolled her eyes at him as Áine giggled.

"All right, well - if you've quite finished raiding the fridge, Tor, would you show Neala to the lounge? I just want to find Colleen and ask about the pizzas, then I'll be there. Would you like anything else while we're here? Like a tea, or coffee?"

"Um, maybe just some water?" Neala asked, butterflies beginning to stir in her stomach. Áine nodded, and Torin eased off his stool with a groan.

"If you'd care to adjourn to the parlour with me, ma'am," he said gallantly, offering Neala his arm.

Feeling the nerves ease a little, she grinned, linking her arm through his. "Why, thank you, good sir. It would be my pleasure."

As he led her down the hall to the lounge, Torin gave her a sidelong glance. "Out of curiosity, how much do you already know? About Bards and the like?"

Neala let out a sigh. "Only what you told me yesterday, really. My mum told me a little bit, but that was more along the personal side, like why she kept it secret. And something about some Lorekeepers and a prophecy of sorts? Then there was the run-in with the, um, I forgot the name - the demon horse thingy?"

"Púca."

"Yeah, that. Finn said it came from the Otherworld, but he didn't go into any more detail. All I know is that it's been dealt with."

Neala suddenly remembered the stranger with the iron cage. "Oh, and a guy was there, another Bard. He's the one who trapped it. I guess he would've been about our age, probably a little older. He appeared in a flash of lightning and turned the sand to glass. Here, I have a piece."

She paused to rummage in her jeans pocket, drawing out the little spiral to show Torin. For some reason, she hadn't been able to part with it, even for a moment. Instead, she'd shoved it in her pocket, wondering why it still seemed warm to her touch.

Torin took it curiously, turning it in his rough fingers.

"The guy was distracting the púca, creating illusions and stuff. That's how he tricked it into going into this cage he'd set up. I don't really know what happened after that, I blacked out. By the time I came around, he was gone, and Finn was there instead."

Torin tapped his chin, rubbing the faint stubble absently as he handed the glass spiral back to Neala. "Hmm, that is a bit odd. I mean, all Bards have elemental power, that's in our Faerie blood, but being able to manipulate lightning like that? That's something entirely different."

After a moment, he added, "I mean, the only ones I know of who might be capable would be the Fitzpatrick twins – Lorcan and Eamon - but I'm not sure if they can *actually* do it or not. They're an interesting couple of lads, to be sure, and a lot more advanced than this wee fellow." He tapped his broad chest lightly. "But you said something earlier, something about a prophecy?"

"Oh, yeah, so Mum said that I could be part of a prophecy about some Lorekeepers or something. It sounds so silly saying it aloud. But it supposedly has something to do with a birthmark I have, this pigment thing on my shoulder that looks like a leaf. I never gave it much thought, but Mum seems to think it's, like, some sign, or something?" Her ears were burning - the words sounded crazy, even to her. She regretted even mentioning it.

*Unless...I mean, there was that weird moment with the tree in the yard, I guess. It made my birthmark ache...*She cringed. *Eurgh, listen to me! This is ridiculous - magic birthmarks? Seriously?*

Torin frowned and ran his hand over his hair sheepishly. "Well, this 'Q&A' session isn't off to a great start. I'm sorry, Neals - if there *is* some legend about Lorekeepers and leaf-marks, it's not one I know. Sorry I can't help much with that."

Neala snorted, waving her hand dismissively. She was ready to forget about it completely.

"But, anyway, let's see if there is something I can help you with, or if I'm going to be completely useless. Here, come in and take a seat."

He gestured through the doorway and Neala entered the lounge. She still felt a little awed by the lavish rooms in the mansion, but she made herself sit casually on the plush sofa as if she lived like this all the time...

Out the corner of her eye, she saw Torin stifle his laughter as he watched her sink into the couch, trying desperately to straighten herself. It was just so *soft!* The more she struggled, the more she flopped sideways. She was certain a walrus would have shown more grace than her.

Once she was composed, Neala brushed a stray hair off her cheek and watched Torin through narrowed eyes as he lowered himself onto the sofa with the ease of practice. Once settled, he folded his arms behind his head and grinned at her. "Okay then - fire them at me."

Neala took a deep breath, trying to get the flurry of questions popping into her head under control. *Start at the beginning*, she thought with a smile.

Meeting Torin's eyes, she asked, "Okay - Faeries. You said Bards are part-Faerie, part-mortal, right? So, where are the Faeries now? And, I have to be honest - I hear 'Faerie' and think of little creatures with glittery wings. I'm guessing that's not quite right?"

Torin lowered his arms and twisted his neck from side to side. "Whew, this is going to be a long night, isn't it?"

Neala rolled her eyes at him, and he snorted. "Nah, I can give you the basic history. See, once upon a time, long ago, the Immortal and Mortal worlds intermingled much more frequently. The Otherworld, the home of the Immortals, exists parallel to our world, but in a different dimension of time and space.

"Ages ago - like, medieval times - a mortal might accidentally cross into the Otherworld and spend what they think is just one day there, only to find when they cross back that a whole week has passed in our world. Much more often, the Good Folk, the Faeries, would come here.

"The Fae are quite a mixed bag, like humans, I guess. You have the good ones, who would bless mortals or do other nice things, but there are also those who seek to cause harm. Many times, mortals would be seduced by the Fae, whether for genuine love, or through enchantment.

"As you'd expect, um..." Torin smirked, scratching his head and squirming slightly, "physical unions would happen on occasion, leading to the cross-breed known as Bards - mortals with magical powers, who gain longer life and the ability to connect more easily with nature and the Song of Life, the vibration that connects all living things."

His mouth tightened. "Not everyone was happy about Bards existing, though. Many so-called purists believed we were some sort of mockery of true Fae, being part-human and all. But, mostly, life carried on as it always had.

"Until, one day a few centuries ago, the magical portals between the worlds closed, out of nowhere. Something happened that effectively slammed the door in our faces. A Veil was created - an impenetrable wall of mist and magic."

Neala was listening intently. She'd heard the Veil mentioned before.

"That left us all in limbo a bit, really. I mean, we're technically part-immortal, from the Otherworld, but we can never go there, so we are stuck in the human world with these amazing powers we can't reveal to anyone." Torin shrugged, a sour twist to his features.

Neala frowned, mulling it all over. She was intensely curious as to why they had to hide the magic away, but she decided to follow a more intriguing line of thought for now.

"How common are Bards, then? If the Fae magic is passed on through blood, then there should be thousands. Millions, even. Like, that's simple math; one Bard has three kids carrying their bloodline, then they all have three kids, and so on? Over centuries, that's a lot of Bards running about the place."

Torin huffed out a long breath. "It's just one of those things, really. Like genetic luck. Sometimes the Fae part is triggered, and Bard powers emerge. Other times, for whatever reason, it stays dormant. I mean, look at my family - none of my immediate family had magic, until Poppy and me. There must have been some back down the line, but no one had the magic come out in recent times. Or, at least, none that anyone cared to mention. We just got lucky, and it popped up in us.

"Others have the reverse happen," he added. "Like Áine's family, who are fifth generation Bards. She has at least three cousins who never got powers when the rest did. It seems the Fae blood is as fickle as the ones it came from."

"The magic, that's probably the next thing I really want to know about," Neala muttered, wracking her brain for the right questions. "What sort of things can we do? Musical talent is obvious, but what else? And how do we do it? I've never performed any spells or done anything magical. You'd think I'd notice if I had."

This time, Torin took a longer pause before replying. "Ah, now, you see...this is another one I can't really answer. Everyone is different, and their abilities vary. You felt Eilìs' power, aye? Not all of us are that strong. I mean, you never picked up anything from Áine and me like that, even though you've been hanging out with us all day."

Neala cocked her head to the side, weighing that up.

Torin rubbed a hand over his face and went on, "I felt it a bit when I was with you, but it wasn't until you mentioned Birchtree that I knew what the vibe I was getting was." He gave her a flirty wink. "I thought it was just your radiance and beauty affecting me like that."

A blush crept over Neala's cheeks, even as she groaned at his corny line.

"Having said that," he went on, licking his lips and tilting his head back against the couch, "the general basis of our power is the same. A greater sensitivity to nature lets us manipulate and influence the elements."

Lowering his chin, he gave her a stern frown. "I won't say control, because that's misleading; natural forces *cannot* be controlled, that's a very important thing to remember, and one of the first things you'll be taught. Bards who have tried...well, it doesn't end well."

Neala gulped at the look on his face. His blue eyes were shadowed, and she wondered if he'd had personal experience in the matter. With a blink, his face relaxed and he sat back once more.

"I've heard that some Bards can even affect the time and space continuum, but that would take a lot of power – *massive* power - and is way more advanced than what I know. Healing, illusions, other tricks - they can be learned, too. I guess the simple answer is what we can do is as widely varied as normal human talents; you get ones who are good at math, others who make great builders, and so on. Bards are the same. It all comes down to where your talents lie."

"But I haven't done *anything* like control- I mean, manipulating elements." Neala tried to keep the anxiety out of her voice. "All I've done is play a few instruments. I turned sixteen in February - surely I should have done something by now, if that's when my powers supposedly emerged?"

Against her will, tears of frustration and shame welled in her eyes. "What if I'm not really a Bard at all, and I'm just good at music?"

Torin cocked his head and gave a light chuckle, glancing up as Áine entered the room and took a seat beside him, handing Neala a glass of water as she did so.

Looking from one to the other, Áine asked, "So, where are you up to?"

"Neala doesn't think she's a Bard, just a very good musician," Torin said, giving Neala a quick grin before he turned back to Áine. "She turned sixteen at the start of the year but says she hasn't done anything magical, ever."

"Oh, the whole 'sixteen' thing is a bit misleading," Áine muttered, taking over from Torin. "I mean, it's used as a baseline, but it varies from Bard to Bard. Think of it like, um, like..." She flapped her hands awkwardly, searching for the word.

"Like puberty!" Torin exclaimed, giving an exaggerated double thumbs-up and grinning broadly.

Áine gave him a withering glare, but she nodded.

"Thank you, Tor. Yes, that's pretty much what it's like. After all, it's like you're maturing into your true Bard-self, so that's accurate. You may have been showing subtle signs for a few years, Neala, without knowing what it was. The age of sixteen is used as a guideline, as most Bards' powers have awoken by then, but there are a few cases of Bards being a little younger, or a little older."

She smoothed the front of her shirt absently. "I mean, take the Fitzpatrick twins; they were only children, not even in their teens yet, when they started at Birchtree. That was completely unheard of. Eilìs says they're wildly powerful – no one else comes close to them."

Neala's ears pricked up. "Fitzpatrick? Like the lightning guy?"

Áine gave her a puzzled look, so Torin repeated what Neala had told him, about the boy who saved her from the púca.

As she studied the glass spiral Neala handed her, Áine rubbed her chin curiously. "Well, I'll have to ask Eilìs about that one. They're quite well-known around Birchtree. As anyone that powerful is bound to be, obviously. If one of them did do it, that would be a huge development; no one's ever mastered lightning before - it's way too unpredictable."

Her eyes had turned glassy as she studied the spiral, turning it over and over in her fingers. "It would be fascinating, really. The mechanics alone are mind-boggling; lightning as a force doesn't adhere to the usual elemental conventions. It is unique in essence and behaviour, quite apart from the fundamental–"

She cut herself off with a shake of her head, pressing her fingers against her temples. Without another word, she handed the glass back to Neala, who tucked it into her pocket protectively; she had grown immensely attached to it.

I'll have to get it made into a necklace or something, she thought absently. Realising Torin was saying something, she looked up and asked, "Sorry, I missed that."

Torin waved his hand nonchalantly. "I was just saying, did you want to try an experiment? As in, try some actual magic?"

Neala's brows shot up. "I could do that? But...but I haven't learned anything yet. Are you sure we're allowed to use our powers outside of school?"

Áine giggled and Torin tried, unsuccessfully, to hide his snicker as a cough.

"Um, I think you've read too many books about other kinds of magic," Torin said kindly. "Bards don't work like that, exactly. See, we're connected to nature - our power can be drawn from us without intention sometimes. What we learn at school is based around controlling our magic and shielding ourselves, so it doesn't break away from us."

He leaned forward. "Of course, we also learn history and about the Otherworld, all the myths and things, too. More scholarly pursuits and all that. But the magic's the fun part."

Neala's heart was pounding so loudly, she was sure it was visible under her shirt. "So...so I could do it? I could try actual magic...right now?"

"Sure. Why not?" Torin said, eyes shining. "Let's do it."

Flicking her eyes between Torin and Áine, Neala swallowed down the panic rising in her throat. *It's fine. It'll be fine. What's the worst that can happen, right?...*

"Now, I can shield us enough that nothing too bad can happen, but we're not exactly going to be summoning a typhoon or anything. I was just thinking you could try lifting the water out of that glass there, nice and simple."

Torin was giving Neala an encouraging smile as he pushed the glass of water closer to her, but it did little to reassure her.

Ignoring the faint buzzing in her ears, Neala stared at her glass of water. "Um, yeah, okay. I can-I can give it a go."

Áine raised an eyebrow at Torin. "Are you sure you can shield her enough?"

He glared at her, insulted. "I've shielded you enough times during your experiments, why wouldn't I be able to do the same for Neala?"

Áine flushed and sat back, tucking her hands into her lap without another word.

"Now, the first thing you're going to be doing is finding your power source, okay? It exists inside you, in the subconscious. Then all you have to do is just direct it to the element you're working with, sending your intention in your magic – what you want to make happen. Easy, right?"

Huffing dejectedly at the blank look on Neala's face, Torin settled himself on the edge of the couch, reaching for the glass of water. "It'll be easier if I show you. Here, hand me that."

Neala passed the glass over, watching him curiously. Dragging the coffee table a little closer to his knees, Torin placed the glass down and let his hand hover just above it. "Watch closely now, okay?"

A prickling sensation drew Neala's attention to her palms, which had begun sweating slightly. She wiped them on her jeans absentmindedly, determined to focus entirely on what Torin was doing.

Torin took a deep breath, eyes closed as he centred himself. His face went slack, and his hand wavered ever so slightly. Another breath, and Neala noticed a faint shimmer in the air around him, like the waves that come off asphalt when it's hot.

It was a shock when Neala saw Torin's eyes snap open, and she was embarrassed to admit that she'd jumped. The shimmer was growing larger and reaching toward the water, a tinge of rich purple colouring the air between Torin's fingers.

Enraptured, Neala stared wide-eyed as the shimmer, which had now taken on the faintest hint of that same purplish hue, touched the surface of the water and melted into it.

Mouth agape, Neala watched as Torin began to swirl his finger in small circles, as though he was stirring the water. Though he wasn't physically touching it, the water in the glass was responding to his movements, beginning to slosh and wobble.

A memory sprang into her mind and her eyes widened – she'd seen him do this once before, with a mug of coffee. Intrigued, she watched as the water began to spin faster, matching the speed of his finger.

Deliberately, Torin lifted his hand higher, and Neala gasped with joy as she watched the water funnel rise from the glass, like a mini whirlpool.

Once the waterspout had risen several centimetres above the table, Torin closed his fingers sharply, and the water fell back into the glass, droplets sprinkling to the sides, and the purple-ish glow of magic faded from his skin.

"So, what'd you think?" Torin beamed, gazing at Neala excitedly.

Sinking back into the couch cushions, she shook her head slowly.

"That was...wow. I'm still...still trying to wrap my head around what I just saw. It's – magic is...it's real."

Áine shifted her weight, shuffling slightly closer to Neala, and tilted her head to see her properly.

"Did you want to have a turn? Or would you rather wait until school starts?"

Neala sat up straighter. "Oh, no, I *definitely* want to try it now. I just...I still don't quite understand how he did that."

Torin nodded thoughtfully. "I can try to explain it better. I, um...I guess the first thing to understand is that the magic we use isn't some external force, okay? It all comes from inside you; it's your spirit, your aura, essence, whatever you want to call it. Every Bard has it – we're born with it.

"To create magic, what you need to do is take that energy and convert it into a tangible form, which you then send out. Think of it like you're sending electricity to a lamp or something, to make it power up. Your energy connects to your target – in this case, the water here," he gestured to the glass of water, "and this allows you to join with it, to connect to its vibration. Like tuning into a radio frequency. Does that make sense so far?"

Neala bobbed her head slowly, frowning in concentration. This explanation made it a little clearer, and she felt her palms itching, wanting to try it out.

Noticing her fidgeting, Torin chuckled. "All right, let's see what you can do then!"

Neala took a deep breath, trying to settle the nerves in her stomach, and looked at the glass of water. It was such an innocent looking thing; it shouldn't be making her feel so trembly.

Torin pushed it closer to her and continued, "You need to try and see it with your mind. How it comes through for you will be unique; it's different for everyone. Once you can feel its energy, you need to send a link to it, to connect your essence to it. Just see how you go, okay?"

Neala nodded, and closed her eyes, keeping her breath as steady as she could.

See the water, but don't use my eyes. Breathe, relax, focus. Send my energy to it. But where do I find my magic? Will I glow, too? What colour will it be? Neala grit her teeth and forced the thoughts to the back of her mind.

Vowing to focus only on her breathing, Neala drew a breath in slowly, then let it out, thinking about nothing but making the air flow steadily. *In...out...in...* she thought, not letting her brain interrupt with anything else.

After a little while, she sensed her body relaxing. When she finally felt ready, she tried to picture the glass of water in her mind. She thought of how water feels, how cool it is against her skin, how it flows, the way that it feels when swimming, totally weightless.

Out of nowhere, she saw a flash of blue light with her mind's eye, a flicker in the darkness. Fighting the urge to open her physical eyes, Neala tried to concentrate on that blue ball. But it seemed that every time she tried to focus on it, it slipped out of her vision, hovering on the very edges of her sight. Realising she was getting nowhere by chasing it, she stopped and waited.

After what seemed like an age, she saw the blue glow beginning to creep toward the centre of her vision. With an internal sigh, Neala thought, *I see what Torin meant about the elements not being controlled.* The voice in her head sounded simultaneously loud and distant.

As though it had heard her, the blue glow suddenly flared with an almost-painful brightness, then settled in front of her. Neala smiled to herself as she watched the glow form itself into a tear-drop shape.

Outside of her awareness, she murmured to Torin, "I can see it."

"Okay, now work on sending your energy to meet it." Torin's voice sounded as though he was speaking through a long tunnel.

Neala obeyed, wondering how she was supposed to reach the glow that was the water element. Squinting her eyes, she tried to throw her mind-self toward it, but that just resulted in her brain hurting.

I can't force it, she reminded herself. *How do I connect with water? What will make it accept me?* Letting a memory drift into her internal vision, she concentrated on how it felt to sink into a pool, feeling the water envelop her, welcoming her like a friend.

Pushing the memory aside, Neala took another deep breath and tried to bring her spirit into her mind's eye. The glowing tear drop seemed to tremble, and it leaned toward her slightly.

Feeling encouraged, Neala sent her vision deeper inside herself, looking for her core. A sudden flash caught her eye, and she froze. Deep in her centre, she found herself staring into a shimmering pool of blue-green light.

Tentatively, she poked it with her mind-self's hand. As she drew back from it, she saw a thin strand follow her. An idea began to form, and spirit-Neala smiled.

Returning to the plane of her mind where the water element sat waiting for her, spirit-Neala held up the long strand of what she knew was her essence. Keeping her movements steady, she held her magic thread out to the water, and it reached out a long tendril of its own, taking her essence gently.

Neala gasped as she felt the water's touch, and it began to draw her power in, allowing her to sink into the flow of its energy. With a sigh, Neala felt her spirit shift, merging with the water's, and, suddenly, she *was* water.

Reaching further, she sensed the water on the table and joined with it: she could feel the glass surrounding her, could see the wavering shapes of her own body and those of her friends sitting on the couch.

Neala could feel the tendrils of anxiety building in her mind, overwhelming her, but then she heard the water in her mind.

"Don't lose it now, you're so close." The water spoke to her in their joined minds, spreading a feeling of calm though Neala.

Composed, she spoke with her mind back to the water, *"Do you mind? If I make a funnel with you?"*

"That will be fun. I will do that for you."

Spirit-Neala chuckled to herself. There was a child-like energy to the water element, a playful spirit that made her smile.

Far in the distance, Neala knew her body was beginning to move, making circles with her finger, like Torin had. Even without seeing herself, Neala knew she looked awkward, and it made her spirit-self blush.

Picking up on her embarrassment, the water said patiently, *"I am here. Focus only on me."*

Returning her awareness to the water, Neala continued swirling. In her mind's eye, she could feel the water beginning to rise, and it filled her with excitement.

Curious, Neala drew more of her power forth, wondering how high she could lift the water...

In the distance, she felt a new tug on her magic. Something far more powerful and wild than the water in the glass. Whatever this spirit was, its presence sent a thrill of adrenaline through her veins. Her very bones seem to hum with the energy of it.

The water element hesitated.

"Storm-father calls."

"Who is storm-father?"

When Neala got no answer, she tugged on her power, adding more of her own soul to her water form. Her awareness grew, and she sensed more water elements calling to her, curious about this visitor joined with their sister. Water from the garden, in the pool, even the faintest echoes of the salty ocean.

But one called to her far more than the others - the one in the sky above her. *This* is who had awoken something within her. The storm clouds, rolling and roiling overhead. Her essence yearned to join with it, to *become* it. She wasn't Neala anymore – she belonged to the storm.

"*Storm-daughter. I can hear you. Why are you trapped?*"

Neala blanched, clinging to her soul. She wasn't the storm – she was human. She had to stay focused. She had to stay in control. "*I-I'm Neala, Storm-father. I'm just a girl, a human. A-a Bard.*"

"*You are water, Storm-daughter. Come, join us.*"

The part of her that was human screamed to leave, to retreat back into her physical body. But the call of the water bond, the drive that all water has to join with one another, tugged at her. It seemed to be chanting through every fibre of her being: *The storm is safety. The storm is family. The storm is...home.*

Unable to resist that call any longer, spirit-Neala and the water element she was bonded with flew out of the open window, rising to join the mass of clouds above them.

Neala whooped excitedly, a wild kind of freedom overcoming her. Reaching out, she and the water touched the other droplets, the ones that formed the clouds, merging with them as easy as blinking.

With a gasp, Neala could suddenly 'see' through the storm; it was as though she had become a cloud and was looking over the city from high up in the sky.

The other clouds gathered around her, bumping and jostling her in their excitement. Neala could feel a strange pressure building and it made her cloud-self itch. When the itchiness became unbearable, she let out a shriek.

To her shocked delight, a bolt of lightning shot from her cloud-body and struck a building below her, the rumble of thunder following it. With glee, Neala realised she had contributed to the power of the storm. All around her, the other clouds hummed, proud of their newest member's efforts.

Overjoyed, Neala started bumping into her companions excitedly, building that electricity up again. As she let off another bolt, cloud-Neala whooped, and the thunderous boom echoed around them, the air vibrating with the power of it.

Glancing down, Neala suddenly realised that she had strayed a long way from her body. Far below, the buildings of the city had filtered into acres of farmland and forest. Panicking, Neala tried to get back to her physical self, but she didn't know how.

To her horror, she finally became aware of another problem; she had started to rain. The water vapour that formed her body was cooling and falling to the earth as she and her brothers and sisters moved further and further away from the ocean.

Neala baulked, trying vainly to separate herself from the seething mass of clouds and electricity. She was utterly terrified; if she lost her cloud form, would she ever get back to her human body? Would she *die*?

A tug on her magic made her pause, the pulsing echo of concern and love vibrating through every fibre of her being. With a jolt, she realised that the other clouds were worried and trying to comfort her, drawing her back into the protection of their cluster. *The storm is safety. The storm is family. The storm is home.*

Somewhere, in a vague part of her awareness, she could just make out a strange sensation; someone was shaking her physical body wildly. Her humanity tugged at her, begging her to release herself from the storm's hold. In desperation, she called out to the heart of the storm, hoping it could help her.

"Storm-father, please - I need to go back!"

"Storm-daughter, you are one of us."

"No! No, I'm a human. I'm a human!" she shrieked. But her cries were swallowed up in the sheer power of the storm. It was unstoppable, unrelenting. A force unlike any other. Who was she, to fight against it? She, a mere human child—

Suddenly, a wind gust broke ranks and yanked at Neala, breaking her out of the spiralling mass that was the storm. In an instant, she was a lonely puff of cloud, separate from her brothers and sisters. Isolated and alone, Neala fought to return to them, even though she knew she would become trapped again. Water longed to be connected. The impulse was too strong to resist...

But the wind was forceful, deliberate. Through her haze, Neala thought there was something familiar about it. Something in its energy that she had felt in her human form...

With a jolt, she recognised the power that drove it: Eilìs.

Wrapping her in a cocoon of air, Eilìs raced back to the house, and cloud-Neala could sense her body getting closer. As she and Eilìs slipped through the window, back into the Holloways' lounge room, Neala could see her body slumped against the couch.

Her hair was whipping wildly in the wind that was Eilìs, and cloud-Neala reached out with her power, longing to connect with her source again. Deep inside her mind, she could see the blue-green pool that was her magic, and she dived for it...

Her whole body jerked, her soul finally connecting once more to her physical self. Neala gasped and opened her eyes, her real eyes. Overcome with exhaustion, she leaned forward, placing her elbows on her knees. Her head was swirling, and the voices around her were disoriented and warbled.

In her ear, she heard Torin's voice more clearly than the others', asking, "Neala, are you okay? I'm so sorry, please say something."

Still quite disoriented, Neala closed her eyes, feeling the world spin beneath her. The pressure of Torin's hand on her back helped keep her anchored, and she took a deep breath before opening her eyes again.

Tilting her head slightly to the right, she saw Torin's familiar blue eyes studying hers worriedly. She smiled as best she could and tried to reassure him that she was okay, but the moment she opened her mouth, she felt a wave of nausea sweep over her. Leaning forward, she felt herself dry-heave, and someone shoved a bowl under her mouth reactively.

Only once she felt a little more composed did Neala raise her head, her cheeks a flaming shade of crimson. "S-sorry," she croaked, realising Áine was the one who had come to her rescue. Placing the bowl aside wordlessly, Áine handed her a glass of water, but Neala flinched away from it, worried that she'd be sucked into it again.

A firm hand on her shoulder made her look up. Meeting Eilìs' gaze, Neala listened as the woman said sternly, "Drink it. You need to hydrate now more than anything else. It's safe - your power is shielded for the moment."

Still feeling hesitant, but unwilling to argue with Áine's imposing sister, Neala sipped the water carefully, trying not to think about becoming water herself. After she'd taken a drink, Neala wiped her mouth and looked sheepishly across at Torin.

"Sorry I'm such a mess," she muttered, her face still burning. Torin hung his head shamefully, and Eilìs scowled.

"It's hardly your fault. What were you *thinking*, Tor? Letting an untested Bard try something like elemental connection? Did you even stop to consider what her attributes may be?"

"I-I didn't think she would be so strong. Áine and I have done heaps of little experiments but nothing like this has ever happened to us."

"Oh, have you now?" Eilìs asked tersely, glaring at Áine, who stared down at her feet. "Seriously? You guys are lucky I hadn't left yet - what would you have done then? Neala could have been halfway to Scotland before you found someone to help. Next time, ask yourselves if attempting water bonding while a storm is building overhead would be a stupid idea, perhaps?"

Torin gulped and closed his eyes. "I thought I could shield us well enough."

Eilìs let out a long breath, massaging the bridge of her nose. "You're only a second-year, Tor - this was way beyond you. Frankly, given Neala's natural bond with storms, the only one who could have *possibly* shielded her sufficiently would be Ovate Clodagh, or Finley, of course. You never stood a chance." She clapped him on the shoulder and gave a squeeze.

"And as for you," Eilìs turned to Neala, who peered up at her wearily. "Your power has a wickedly-strong affinity with storms - with clouds and lightning. Until you've had proper training, do *not* try to connect with them."

She paused, chewing her lower lip. "In fact, with only a couple more weeks to go 'til you're at Birchtree, I'd suggest not trying to actively access your power at all. Once you're tested, you'll have a better idea of where your strengths lie, and how to safely use your magic. For now, I've put a temporary barrier around your power, so it won't leak out of you while you're sleeping or anything. It'll wear off by tomorrow afternoon, most likely."

Neala swallowed hard, a trickle of fear running down her spine. The thought of slipping off to join the storm in her sleep filled her with dread. Forcing her tone to stay level, she said, "Thank you, Eilìs. I'm sorry about all this."

Eilìs shrugged and patted her on the shoulder gently. "We've all been there, love. Now, if you lot can keep out of trouble for five minutes, I'll be off. Colleen should be up soon with dinner. Enjoy the rest of your night."

Giving them all a little salute, Eilìs turned and strolled over to the doorway, picking up her bag and disappearing, leaving Neala and her friends in awkward silence.

Áine, who had been quiet for some time now, shuffled restlessly. "I, uh, I'm just going to see if Colleen needs any help." Without looking back, she hurried out after Eilìs, rubbing her forehead with a frown.

Still feeling a little ill, Neala closed her eyes again and leaned back against the couch. She heard Torin clear his throat.

"Neals, I really am sorry —"

"Enough apologizing - it's all good. Truly," Neala muttered, placing her hands on her clammy cheeks. "You didn't know I was going to take off and become part of a storm. What is that - like some Bard version of running off to join the circus?"

She heard Torin snort and opened her eyes to grin at him. "Seriously, though, don't worry about it. It was actually pretty cool, until I couldn't figure out how to come back."

A pang squeezed Neala's heart, and she reached into her pocket for her phone. "Speaking of, I just want to ring my mum quickly, do you mind?"

With a nod, Torin reached out and placed a warm hand on her knee. "Not at all. I'll go give Áine a hand, we'll be back in a bit."

Neala smiled at him gratefully, then swiped her phone screen. There was a text from her mother there already:

Thank you, baby. Have fun with your friends. Am here if you need anything, always. I love you more than words xo

Tears sprang into Neala's eyes, and she took a shaky breath. Pressing the call button, she placed the phone to her ear and waited. Glancing at the large grandfather clock in the corner, she realised it was only seven o'clock, and she raised her eyebrows. *Is that all? Seriously?*

The sound of ringing stopped abruptly, and she turned her attention back to her phone, heart pounding a little.

"Neala? Hi, sweetheart, are you okay?"

"Hi Mum. I'm fine, I just..." A lump formed in her throat. "I just wanted to apologise for being so horrible after...after last night."

Dana let out a long breath. "Oh, honey, you haven't been horrible, don't even think that. You have every right to be angry and upset. This has been a huge shock for you - of course it would be difficult."

"Did you speak to Nanna?"

"Yes, I've told her everything that's happened. She would love to see you, obviously, but she understands if you need some space. Maybe...maybe you could pop by the shop tomorrow and see her? Just to let her know you're okay?"

"Yeah, of course. She wanted me to help show Tilly the new coffee machine anyway, so that's fine." She paused, then blurted out, "Mum, I used my magic."

Dana gasped. "Your magic? Baby, what happened?"

In a rush, Neala explained everything - about connecting to the water element, and the overwhelming pull of the storm. When she was done, she waited for her mother to speak, holding her breath.

There was a long pause, then Dana said gently, "Oh, sweetheart. I'm just glad you're okay. Elemental work is tricky; they have their own spirits and don't always co-operate how we'd hope. Are you all right now, though? Do you need anything?"

Neala sighed. "No, I'm okay. Áine and Tor are bringing pizza up, then we'll probably just watch a movie or something. Whatever normal teenagers do at a slumber party, I guess. No more magic."

Dana sounded relieved. "That sounds great, honey. I..."

Neala waited, pressing the phone to her ear. Out the corner of her eye, she spotted Áine leaning around the doorway, looking to see if she was finished with her call yet. Neala gave her a little nod, and she crept into the room, followed by Torin carrying a large tray of pizza.

Her mouth had started watering, but she turned her attention back to her mother when she heard her speaking again. "I'm glad you called me. Enjoy the rest of your night, darling, and I'll see you tomorrow. I love you."

"Love you, too, Mum," Neala said, eyes welling a little. "Good night."

"Sweet dreams, sweetheart."

As Neala signed off, she smiled at her friends. "That smells awesome, Áine. I feel bad I didn't get to thank Colleen, though."

Áine flicked her hand dismissively. "That's okay, you'll meet her in the morning, most likely. She's gone back to her cottage now, but she's nearby if we need her. Anyway, have some pizza. I'll set up the tv, then we can pick a movie."

Grabbing a large slice, Neala settled back against the couch and sighed happily.

*****

Just before midnight, Torin rubbed his eyes wearily and stretched his arms above his head. Glancing at the two girls either side of him, he rolled his eyes affectionately.

Áine, as elegant as ever, was draped over a large cushion, sighing softly in her sleep. Neala, however, was sprawled across the couch, head lolled to the side and hair falling into her face. Worried that she was about to slip and fall onto the floor, Torin stood carefully, reaching for the remote control.

After switching the T.V. off, he turned back to Neala and gripped her gently under the arm, rolling her onto the couch more securely. With a snort, she curled up against the cushion. Smiling softly, Torin reached out his hand and tucked a stray strand of hair behind her ear.

Making his way over to the chest where the Holloways kept their throw rugs, Torin opened it and pulled out two soft, warm blankets. As he spread them over the girls, he smiled fondly. Stifling a yawn, he turned and headed to the door, dimming the lights until they were almost dark.

Just before he went upstairs to the spare room, where he used to sleep, he paused, tapping his thigh and thinking. Eilìs had said she'd shielded Neala's power so it wouldn't leak out while she slept but, just to reassure himself, Torin leaned back into the loungeroom.

With a flick of his fingers, he sent some of his purplish magic out to wrap around Neala, coating her like fine cobwebs. Once he was satisfied that she was shielded properly, he nodded happily and went up to bed.

~ 12 ~

Her dreams had brought her to the crossroads once more. Looking around, though, Neala noticed that something was different. It took her a moment, but her brows lifted in surprise when realised the fog was completely gone, and she could see clearly.

Suspicious, she called out, "All right, I think I get it. This place represents me and my magic somehow, yes? The more I learn, the clearer these paths and things get, is that right?"

When she got no answer, she continued, filling the eerie silence with chatter. "Like, when I made the decision to go to Birchtree, that path over there," she pointed to her left, "got clearer. Now that I've actually used my power, the fog is gone completely. So, what now? Do I take one of the paths?"

The silence continued. Throwing her hands in the air, Neala growled. "Fine, what if I go this way, huh?"

Taking several steps to her right, Neala looked around, waiting for a reaction. When none came, she started walking more purposefully down that path. Glancing to the side, she saw endless forest, silvery tree trunks glowing in the moonlight. There were no noises other than the sound of her footsteps, and Neala was starting to regret leaving the clearing.

Just when she thought about turning back, she saw another crossroad up ahead. Curious, she pressed on, emerging into the open with a satisfied smile.

But her grin only lasted a few seconds; she realised almost immediately that she was back at the same clearing she'd started at. Exasperated, she clenched her fists and stomped the ground hard.

She let out a curse, then yelled, "What is the *point* of all this? Why do you bring me here just to make me stay in the same place? Am I supposed to be learning something, or what? This is stupid! If you don't have anything to say, send me back and let me get a decent sleep for a change!"

"That is no way for a young lady to speak."

Whipping around, Neala saw the black fox sitting in the middle of the left-leading path, bushy tail flicking slightly. Scrunching up her nose, Neala retorted, "I'm not a bloody lady."

The fox's whiskers twitched in what Neala could only describe as the fox-like equivalent of a smirk. Cocking its head to the side, the fox studied Neala with its unnaturally-bright blue eyes. *"Have you figured it out yet? Where you are?"*

Neala rolled her eyes. "Like I said before, this place represents my magic somehow. The more I understand it, the more is revealed. Tonight, or yesterday, or however time works here, I used my power for the first time, and now the fog is gone."

"And how did it feel, using your magic? What did you learn?"

"To avoid storms, that was the key lesson," Neala muttered, shuddering as she remembered the panic of not being able to get back to her body.

The fox yipped in annoyance. *"Then you have learned nothing."*

Neala placed her hands on her hips and glared at it angrily. "Excuse me? I connected with the water like I was supposed to, but then it raced off to join the storm and I got sucked along with it. I couldn't get back - I didn't know how. Eilìs had to come and rescue me. It was terrifying!"

"Was it, though? Truly?"

About to snap back with some more unladylike language, Neala hesitated. Recalling how it felt to be a cloud, racing alongside her brothers and sisters, jostling and playing to create lightning, that feeling of joy when the thunder rolled around them...

Neala scuffed her feet and hung her head. That was all the answer the fox required.

"You are needed, Neala Stormbringer. We have been waiting for you."

*****

With a gasp, Neala sat upright, almost falling off the couch. A cold sweat had broken out across her forehead, and she clutched the blanket tightly around herself. To her right, Áine stirred, then rolled over, tucking herself more firmly against the back of the couch.

Squinting at the clock in the corner, Neala was surprised to discover it was just before dawn. With a sigh, she threw her blanket aside and carefully padded out of the lounge and down the hall, trying to remember where the bathroom was. Once relieved of her urge, she headed for the kitchen.

After staring at the fancy coffee machine for several moments, Neala begrudgingly accepted that there was no way she was going to figure out how to use it. Turning her attention to the kettle in the corner, she filled it and set it boiling, wondering if a family as rich as the Holloways would even have any instant coffee anywhere.

To her delight, she stumbled across a plunger and some ground beans, and she breathed in the comforting smell gratefully. While she waited for it to brew, she thought to herself, *Three days ago, I was normal. I was going to a music school - that's all it was. How did everything get so crazy, so quickly?*

Tears pricked at her eyes as she bit her lip. *It's all too much.* Unable to contain it, Neala leaned her back against the cupboard and slid to the floor, tucking her knees up to her chest and hugging them tightly. She bowed her forehead and let the tears come.

As her sniffles faded, Neala wiped her face and leaned her head back against the cupboard, hiccupping lightly.

For the first time in a long time, she felt like a weight had lifted from her shoulders.

She gave a little half-smile and opened her puffy eyes. "Seems I just needed a good cry after all," she muttered, sniffing one last time.

Getting to her feet, Neala poured the coffee into her mug and topped it up with plenty of milk, just the way she liked it.

Feeling restless, she padded back out of the kitchen and toward the front door. Easing it open, she stepped out, sucking in a breath as the chilly air hit her face, and giving a little shiver. Despite the cold, Neala felt better being outdoors. Plonking herself on the steps, she sipped her steaming coffee and looked around.

A faint mist hung over the pristine gardens, the lawn shining with dew in the palest light of dawn. With a contended sigh, she tilted her head back and stared up at the sky, watching as the blue-grey clouds slowly began to glow with shades of pale pink and yellow.

Looks like we're in for more rain today, maybe, she thought, admiring the bright beams the sunlight made through the building clouds. Despite what had happened last night, she still enjoyed watching the clouds morph and shift, seeming to dance in the wind far above the earth.

Neala smiled softly to herself, pressing her mug against her lips. She had loved camping back in Australia. She had always been more of a morning person than a night one, preferring the peaceful calm that heralded the start of a new day, when it felt, just for a moment, like she was the only person in the world - just her, and the plants and animals.

Closing her eyes, Neala sat back and focused only on listening to the world coming to life around her. It was so peaceful, just allowing herself to enjoy the moment. It seemed this kind of quiet serenity was getting harder and harder to come by, nowadays...

After a while, she heard the door handle turning behind her. Glancing over her shoulder, she nodded a greeting when she spotted Áine peeking at her curiously. The girl gave a small smile in return, and joined her on the step, lowering herself down with a grace that made Neala feel like a dumpy sack of spuds.

Áine had brought a blanket out with her and she offered half of it to Neala wordlessly. Wrapping herself in the warm, fleecy blanket, she thanked Áine softly. In comfortable silence, the girls sat and watched the sun rise fully in the distance, just enjoying the moment.

It was Áine who finally spoke. "Neala," she croaked, coughing a little to clear her throat.

"Mm?" Neala replied, turning her now-empty coffee mug over in her hands.

"How are you holding up? I mean, for real? You've had such a big couple of days, it must have been a lot to take in. Is there...can I help with anything?"

Neala was opening her mouth to give a dismissive answer, but then she paused. Shifting her weight, trying to work the blood flow back into her legs, she tilted her head to the side.

"You know what? I think I'm honestly okay. I mean, it all still feels kind of surreal, like any minute someone is going to yell 'surprise!' and it'll all turn out to be a secret T.V. show or something," she snorted, closing her eyes.

"But, at the same time, it feels...right, if that makes sense? Like, you know the old cliché about things happening for a reason? It kind of feels like that. Since the day I arrived, things have been...strange. It's almost like - like I'm being led somewhere, guided almost. Everything's falling into place so neatly."

She shrugged. "I suppose that's what makes it even more unbelievable. Like I'm in some kind of fairytale or something."

Nodding slowly, Áine pulled the blanket closer around her shoulders. "I can kind of see that, I guess. For me, I knew what Bards were from the moment I was born, so I can't relate as well as perhaps Torin can. But it must be such a shock. I've been lucky to have Eilìs to help me, and Colleen."

"What about your mum and dad?" Neala asked curiously.

Áine sighed. "Oh, they're rarely home. They travel all the time for work - they run a charity for orphaned kids; that's why Finley brought Poppy and Torin to us. When my parents *are* here, it's usually only for a week or two, and they only come back every couple of months. Colleen has practically raised us. Then there are the other staff, like our tutors, the gardeners, a couple of maids. Otherwise, it's usually just Eilìs and me. When she isn't at Birchtree, of course."

Neala's heart gave a squeeze. "That must be hard," she said softly.

Áine rested her chin in her hand and sighed. "It gets pretty lonely, sometimes. It was better when the others lived here; it gave Eilìs and I someone to hang out with. But after what happened to Poppy, Torin didn't feel happy here anymore, so he moved out as soon as he could. Mum and Dad weren't thrilled, but they keep an eye on him, just in case."

She raised a delicate brow. "They offered to buy him a house, you know. But he turned it down. He said they'd already given him more than he needed, and he wanted to take responsibility for himself. The unit he has in the city is pretty small, and he boards with a couple of university students, but he likes it. Of course, he lied about his age so they'd let him rent. But he'll be eighteen next May, so it hardly matters."

"Does he work? How does he keep up with rent?" Neala asked, surprised.

"Oh, he does odd jobs for people. You know, helping elderly people with their shopping or gardening, fixing things, dog-walking, even baby-sitting. Whatever people may need help with, he does it - like a handyman of sorts.

"It's all cash-in-hand, obviously, but when he's at school he uses any money he's saved up to cover his rent while he's away. His housemates are pretty good, too; they reduce his share by half when he's boarding instead of leasing his room out, so that helps him a lot." Áine grinned proudly. "He's pretty amazing."

Neala nodded in agreement, giving a low whistle. "Yeah, you're not wrong. I used to think I worked hard back home, but that's nothing compared to what he does."

"At least you *did* something," Áine muttered. "Even if I could, my parents would throw a fit if I tried to get a job or anything. Eilìs and I, we're expected to take over the charity eventually, so they see no point in us doing anything else. After all, we hardly need the money." She gestured around her with a sour expression.

"We are to study, and to practice our Bardic magic - that's it. Did you know I could already speak fluently in three different languages by the time I turned twelve? But I don't even know how to iron a shirt. I can tell you *how* to do it in French, Spanish, or Japanese, though." She laughed bitterly.

Neala, not knowing what else to do, shuffled closer and put an arm around her shoulders.

Meeting her eye, Áine cringed. "I'm sorry, I must sound like a spoiled brat."

"No, not at all," Neala reassured her hurriedly. "You know, growing up, I sometimes wished Mum and Dad were rich, and we lived in a big mansion where I could play all day, and never needed to do chores, or shovel animal crap, or get covered in dust and flies and sweat. But I guess it isn't always what it's cracked up to be, hey?"

Áine chuckled. "I mean, I never dreamed of shovelling *poop*, I'll admit. But I did sometimes wonder what it would be like to eat a family dinner in front of the T.V., or to play catch, or make mud-pies; to just be a normal kid for a change."

The girls fell into silence again, lost in their own thoughts. Eventually, Neala sighed and gave Áine a gentle squeeze. "Well, shall we go see what the lad is up to?"

Áine nodded and met Neala's eyes warmly. "Thanks for listening, Neala. I'm glad you're here."

With a grin, Neala rose to her feet, and followed Áine back into the house.

The night before she was due to leave for Birchtree, Neala lay awake, staring at the ceiling. A few days ago, Finn had rung her to say that he would be picking her up and taking her there himself, which surprised her. Surely she could just take a bus, couldn't she? When she suggested as much, Finn had only laughed and told her he would see her at dawn on Saturday.

Though she hadn't had a chance to see Áine or Torin again, they had both reassured her they would be there on the first day. Neither could tell her how to get there, but they reminded her that Finley was the best person to show her.

Neala had spent several days helping in the shop and was pleased to see Tilly was a fast learner and a very bubbly girl; she would do just fine as her replacement. To her surprise, Nanna had hardly mentioned anything about Neala's powers when she saw her. In fact, she hadn't spoken about Bardic magic at all.

Before she'd left the shop, though, Nanna had given her a gift to take to the school; a silver music box with an intricate engraving of a stag. It had belonged, Nanna explained, to her great-grandmother. "This is precious to our family, Neala. I am honoured to be passing it down to you."

Neala had thanked her profusely for the gift, but before she could ask any questions, Nanna had hurried her out the door with a quick kiss and a promise that she would see her in the winter holidays.

Once Neala had arrived home she'd fiddled with the music box clasp, but it wouldn't budge – it appeared to be fused shut. Though it made her curious, she'd eventually placed the box down and subsequently forgotten about it, caught up in the flurry of last-minute packing.

Now, several days later, she stared at it through the darkness, wondering whether she should try again. A flash from her phone distracted her, and she picked it up, blinking as the bright screen illuminated her face.

Hey Neals. If you can't sleep either, text me back!

Yawning, Neala propped herself up on her elbow and typed a reply to Torin.

Of course I can't sleep. My brain feels like it's stuck on spin cycle!

His reply came within seconds.

Haha! That sucks. Do you want me to sing a lullaby for you? Fair warning, I'm a terrible singer ;P

Neala giggled and sent back:

I think I'll be all right, tempting as that is. Anyway, better try get some rest. Thanks Tor, I'll see you tomorrow. Eeeeeeeek!

Placing her phone back on the windowsill, Neala sighed. Breathing in the smell of her linen, her stomach gave a twinge; the butterflies just wouldn't settle down. Tucking her blanket over her head, she shut her eyes tightly, trying to will herself to sleep. But a soft squeak made her eyes shoot open again.

Lying still, hardly breathing, Neala heard another squeak. It was louder this time - almost a yip. Clutching her blanket to her chest, she slowly rolled over, heart pounding. The faintest beam of moonlight lit her floor, and she froze when she spotted a glowing pair of eyes under her desk. Biting her tongue to stop herself crying out, Neala peered into the shadows, trying to see better.

"Sox?" she called tentatively, already certain that it wasn't the cat. At the sound of her voice, the eyes blinked, and the owner let out another firm yip.

In disbelief, Neala watched as a tiny little fox pup stumbled out from under her desk, smoky-grey fur making it appear as little more than a shadowy blob with legs.

Pressing her hands to her face, Neala groaned. "One day. Could I just have *one* day without something odd happening to me? Please?"

Peering through her fingers, Neala watched the chubby pup toddle over to the side of the bed, where it sat and stared up at her, blue eyes glinting in the light. Neala turned and placed her feet carefully either side of the pup and reached down with a sigh. Petting the fox's head, she closed her eyes and slowly counted to ten.

"And just how did you get in here, hmm? Where is your mama?"

Upset at being left on the ground, the pup whined and pawed at Neala's leg, bouncing on its hind feet in an effort to jump.

Smiling despite herself, Neala sighed and picked the fox up, clucking her tongue softly. "Demanding little thing, aren't you?"

Shuffling until her back was resting against the wall, Neala placed the pup on her lap and stroked it absently, enjoying the softness of its fur. She closed her eyes and let out a long groan.

"Oh, why is this be happening now? Little one, I can't look after you, I'm leaving for school in less than eight hours. I'll talk to Mum in the morning; she might be able to take you to a vet or something on the way to work."

The fox whined again, curling up on Neala's lap and resting its nose on its paws sadly. Shaking her head, Neala closed her eyes. "Hush now. I need to get some rest, okay?

I'm going to be a wreck tomorrow as it is. So, here's what we'll do: I'll set you up on a comfy pile of clothes, you will go to sleep, and I will deal with this in the morning. Well, later in the morning, I guess - it's after midnight now. Point is, it's time to sleep, okay? C'mon, you can use this old jumper."

Easing herself off the bed, Neala tucked the fox in the crook of her elbow as she bundled up a used jumper from the washing basket, fluffing it into a nest-like shape on the floor beside her desk.

Placing the pup carefully onto the makeshift bed, she pointed her finger at it sternly. "If you have to pee, do it on this paper, okay?" Neala dropped a scrap sheet of paper on the ground and climbed back into bed, pulling the doona close around her ears. "And I don't want to hear a squeak out of you, understood?"

As she drifted off into a fitful sleep, Neala wondered, not for the last time, if she had finally gone mad.

*****

She was certain that only five minutes had passed before she heard her alarm blaring, and she slapped it off with a growl. Grabbing her pillow, she shoved it on top of her head, mind swirling with exhaustion. *This is great. Just awesome*, she thought to herself wearily.

A yipping sound made her jump, then she remembered her strange midnight visitor. Leaning over the side of her bed, Neala poked her head out from underneath her pillow and peered down at the floor.

The little fox was standing beside her bed, whining softly as it stared up at her. When it spotted her face, it gave an excited bark and tried to jump higher.

Letting her hand fall to the ground, Neala scratched the pup's furry tummy. "So, you weren't a dream, then. Well. Okay. Sure, that's cool." With a sigh, she lurched to her feet, picking up the little ball of fluff resignedly.

Easing her door open, Neala stuck her head out to see if her mother was up yet. Hearing the shower running, she let out a breath and padded to the front door, thinking the pup would probably need to relieve itself.

Once she had placed it on the ground outside, she sat on the porch step and rested her chin in her hands. "How did you even get inside, hmm?" she muttered, watching as the pup sniffed at the ground, looking for a good spot.

Neala wondered briefly if it would run off, now that they were outside, but the thought was swiftly quashed when it finished its business and came bounding back over to the porch, looking pleased with itself.

Placing a paw on Neala's foot, it demanded to be picked up once again. Sighing, she clucked her tongue at it. "Look, you - don't go getting too fond of me. I'm literally leaving here today. Like, in an hour. Mum will take you to the vet and figure out what to do with you. But no getting attached."

The fox listened to her voice attentively, watching her with its head cocked to the side as she spoke. As she opened the door to go inside, Neala could have sworn she heard it snicker. "That better have been a sneeze..." she muttered, unnerved.

Cuddling the pup against her chest, Neala wandered over to the kettle and set it boiling, reaching for her mug. Turning her thoughts to Birchtree, she wondered what the other students would be like. She already knew Áine was in the same year as her, but Torin was older, about to start his second year there.

Ruefully, she realised she hadn't asked her friends much about the actual *learning* part of going to Birchtree; she had been more interested in how the magic worked in general.

Curious, Neala closed her eyes and reached within her mind, looking for the pool of magic she had discovered during her ill-fated experiment with the storm. Before she could reach it, she heard her mother emerge from her bedroom, and she dragged herself back swiftly, reeling with dizziness. The little fox whined worriedly, and nuzzled Neala's sleeve.

Dana gave her a quick smile, then glanced back into her room, holding onto the door handle. "C'mon, lazy bones," she called to Sox, trying to get him to leave the warmth of her bed. "You need to give Neala a cuddle before she leaves."

The ginger cat padded into the kitchen, but stopped suddenly, nose raised. With a hiss, he fluffed his fur up and glared at Neala. Worried, she knelt down and held her hand out, wondering what was wrong.

"Soxy, what's the matter? It's me," she crooned, wiggling her fingers. A squirm against her chest reminded Neala that she was holding the fox pup, and she gasped, worried she was squashing it.

Before she could move, Sox gave a last yowl and scuttled back into the bedroom, tail stiff as a brush. Dana stared after him, mouth open in shock. Turning back to Neala, she raised her eyebrow.

"What was that all about? He's never done anything like that before."

Neala glanced down at the furry bundle in her arms. "I think he smelt this little critter - it was in my room last night. I have no idea how it got there, but I was hoping you could maybe take it to the vet this morning?"

She tucked her hand gently under the fox pup and held it out to her mother, who approached curiously. Taking it in her arms carefully, Dana gave a low whistle.

"Well, you are an unusual visitor, aren't you?"

While Dana looked over the pup, Neala poured herself a coffee and took a long drink. Wrapping her hands around the mug, she leaned back against the counter. "I heard it squeaking around midnight, it was hiding under my desk. I don't know when it came in - I didn't see it at all before then."

"Maybe it got in during the day and fell asleep under your desk?" Dana mused. "Though it's still a mystery how it got into the house in the first place. Sox's reaction was weird, too. We rescued a few foxes on the farm before, remember? Much to Dad's disgust, of course."

She gave Neala a sheepish smirk, before quickly replacing it with a frown. "But Sox has never had a problem with them before; I wonder what was so strange about this one?"

Neala nodded, thinking of the many orphaned animals they had nursed back to health on the farm. Foxes, kangaroos, even a possum – Sox had been friendly with all of them. Was there something wrong with this pup?

"This one has been acting a little different to the ones back home, smarter almost. Like it understands me somehow..." Neala's brow furrowed as she remembered the black fox she had seen in her dreams, the one with the fur as dark as shadow...

A shiver ran down her spine and she gulped another mouthful of coffee. "But, like I said, it was late when I found it, maybe I imagined it."

Dana watched Neala with an odd look on her face. Giving her head a shake, she smiled and cocked her head to the side. "Did you manage to get any sleep, honey?"

Neala ducked her head with a wince. "Maybe a couple of hours, not much."

Dana laughed, turning away from the bench, the pup still tucked in her arms. "I'm not surprised. Finn should be here any minute, do you have everything packed? I'm just going to get this little one all comfy in the cat-cage, it can ride with me in the van while I drop off this lot of deliveries, then I'll take it to the vets. Make sure you eat something, okay?"

While Dana rummaged in the laundry cupboard for the carry-cage, Neala weighed up what she could stomach before choosing a pear from the fruit basket. Taking a bite, she walked into her room, giving her suitcase a pat as she passed it.

As she changed, Neala felt the butterflies in her stomach churn wildly once again. Sitting on her bed, she tucked her knees up and rested her forehead on them, trying to breathe.

Once she felt less light-headed, she pulled on her jeans and an oversized jumper, then yanked a brush through her hair before tying it in a ponytail to keep it off her face. Looking at herself in the mirror, Neala screwed up her nose. *Too casual? But what if I dress up and everyone else is in normal clothes - I'll feel like an idiot.*

She sighed and turned away from her reflection. "At least Torin and Áine will be there."

*****

Several moments later, Neala glared at the text message, her teeth clenched.

So sorry Neala, something has come up. Not sure if we will be there in time, will try not to be too late. Will explain soon. Sorry again xx

Dana glanced sidelong at her daughter. "What's up, honey?" Neala tossed her phone onto the bench and stared out the window.

"That was Áine, she might not be there this morning. Something's come up." Neala's fingers began to tap on her thigh, thrumming out a nervous rhythm. "Hopefully Torin is still coming, I might just check."

Grabbing her phone once more, Neala quickly typed out a message, muttering to herself, "I honestly thought I would have heard from him by now."

Hey Tor. Just checking you're still going to be there this morning? Áine is busy and may be late. Let me know!

Letting out a long breath, Neala flicked her gaze over to the fox pup, who was curled up in the carry cage, little nose poking out the bars. With a grin, Neala turned back to her mother. "I wish I could keep it. It'd be nice to have a pet at school."

Dana chuckled. "Nice try, kiddo." Stifling a yawn, Dana jumped when she heard a knock. Neala's heart gave a leap as she stared at the wooden door, knowing Finn was waiting for her on the other side.

"Well, this is it, sweetheart. We'd better get you sorted. Go let him in," Dana muttered, flapping her hands as she reached for Neala's suitcase.

Jumping off the stool, Neala tripped and almost fell. "Coming!" she called, getting herself under control. Once she was composed, she reached for the door handle, ignoring her sweaty palms.

Finn was standing on the other side, looking relaxed, with his hands shoved in his pockets. He grinned when he saw Neala and raised his eyebrows. "G'morning. So, are you ready to go?"

"Ah, yep, pretty much. Mum is getting my suitcase and I have a pack to carry with me, like you said."

With a nod, Finn asked, "Do you mind if I come in for a moment? We need to deal with your suitcase. I may as well do it now, saves lugging it all the way into the city. Lucky thing, you are."

Neala was confused, but stepped aside so he could get in. Striding over to the case, Finn dragged it back out the door, finding a spot on the lawn beside the garden path. Neala watched, enthralled, as he crouched down, tapping the earth lightly with his knuckles, almost like he was testing it.

A grin crossed his face and he straightened with a groan. "Stand back, Neala." He wheeled the suitcase a little closer, lining it up on the spot he'd chosen. He placed his hands on the earth once more, then...

The suitcase was gone, vanished into thin air. All that remained was a large hole in the ground, as if the suitcase had just burrowed into the earth like some kind of mole. Neala stared, open mouthed.

Meeting her eye, Finn chuckled. "It's okay, I've just sent it straight to Birchtree. The earth will make sure it gets there safely. There are baggage drop areas all over the place for our Bard students. Secret tunnels with a direct line to the school grounds. A valuable time-saver, don't you think?"

Neala must have looked clueless, because Finn pursed his lips and shook his head, berating himself. "Sorry, I'll explain more on the way. I didn't mean to overwhelm you this early."

Turning, Finn extended his hand to Dana, who was still waiting on the doorstep. "I'll watch over her, I promise."

Wordlessly, she shuffled down the path toward him and gave it a squeeze. Neala knew that her mother was fighting back tears, and her own eyes welled up. Finn gave her a tiny nod, and muttered, "I'll meet you over by the road when you're done, Neala."

He patted her shoulder gently as he passed, clicking the garden gate closed softly behind him. Neala faced her mother awkwardly, not sure what to do now.

Dana moved towards her, holding her arms out. As Neala embraced her, she felt as though she were suddenly a small child again.

"Oh, honey, I am so proud of you. Be good, stay out of trouble, and always remember that I...that I love you," Dana broke off, voice cracking with emotion.

Knowing that if she stayed any longer, she would never leave, Neala gave her mother a tight squeeze, then let go.

"I know, Mum. I love you, too. I'll be home in a few months any way - you'll hardly even get a chance to enjoy the peace before I'll be back. Enjoy it while you can!"

Dana sniffled and wiped her tears away, chuckling. "Oh, don't you worry, I have a nice champagne on ice ready to celebrate with tonight."

Neala giggled, then hoisted her pack onto her back.

"Wait, I need to..." Neala didn't finish her sentence, too focused on striding up the garden path and back into the cottage.

Finding Sox curled up on the couch, she gave him a quick cuddle, scooping the ginger cat up and pressing his soft fur to her face. Moving over to the little fox pup, she poked her fingers through the cage gate and stroked it gently.

Obviously exhausted by its adventures, the pup continued snoring, fluffy stomach rising and falling with steady breaths.

"Bye, little one. Thank you for the visit." Ignoring the nagging feeling that this fox hadn't arrived by accident, Neala rubbed her cheeks, telling herself firmly, *It's nothing. Coincidences happen, right?*

Nodding firmly, Neala opened the door and hurried back down the path toward the road. Dana was now standing beside the gate, arms wrapped loosely around her middle.

Hitching her pack more securely, Neala stepped closer to Finn, who had been standing beside the road with his eyes closed, breathing the morning air deeply.

Neala huffed out a shallow breath. "All right, I think that's just about it."

Finn nodded, smiling warmly. "Excellent, then we'll be off. Nice to see you again, Dana, and we'll keep in touch."

Dana untucked her arms and lifted a hand, waving vigorously.

"Have fun, honey! I love you!"

Neala waved back, then turned around, looking for Finn's car. She was puzzled to see no kind of transport anywhere. Before she could ask, Finn explained, "We have a little walking to do, I hope you don't mind?"

With a shrug, Neala replied. "Not at all." Frowning, she continued, "I never really asked where the academy is, did I? Is it far from here?"

Finn chuckled. "Let's walk and talk - I can't be late." Turning, they waved to Dana one last time, then started walking down the track Neala used when she would go on runs to the beach.

Feeling a little nervous - she hadn't been that way since the púca attack - Neala gripped the straps of her pack and strode forward in what she hoped was a confident manner.

The pair walked in silence for a while, enjoying the calm and quiet stillness of sunrise. In the distance, Neala heard a starling singing and she took a deep breath, filling her lungs with the fresh air.

It was Finn who spoke first. "You asked about how far away Birchtree is. It's a little complicated to explain, honestly. To break it down as simply as I can, all the Bards in each county have a meeting place, a sacred landmark, where we gather before entering the school grounds. Each county also has a *maor*, like a warden, who is responsible for making sure all their students get there safely."

Placing a weathered hand on his chest, Finley grinned. "For our area, that would be yours truly. Now, the students are responsible for getting themselves to their particular meeting place by midday on the appropriate date. If they are late, then they will have a very hard time getting through."

Neala wasn't sure if the explanation had answered her question, or just made it more confusing. Thinking about earlier, she asked, "What about my suitcase? Where did that go?"

Finn paused, crouching down to tie his shoelace. "Ah, yes. So, to make travelling a little lighter for the students, luggage is handled separately. There are designated collection points all around the county, where students can take their cases. These spots are hidden tunnels, disguised so that humans wouldn't notice them. For example, your closest tunnel is a sewer grate on the corner of West and Silverborough, marked with a special symbol. In the future, you will just need to take your suitcase there and literally drop it in. The earth will automatically transfer it to Birchtree." He chuckled loudly. "And I promise it won't smell anything like a sewer when it arrives."

Stumbling a little, Neala didn't realise her mouth was hanging open. Magic tunnels? The earth transporting suitcases at the Bards' requests? Torin had explained that a part of a Bard's power was the ability to manipulate the elements, but hearing actual evidence of this happening was entirely different.

Swallowing hard, she let out a shaky breath. Noticing, Finn stopped her, placing a gentle hand on her arm. With concern, he asked, "Are you sure you're okay? It can all be very overwhelming at first, especially for one so new to our world. And it only gets stranger from here, I'm afraid."

Neala mentally berated herself. *Great, now he thinks you're a delicate snowflake. Seriously, Neala, harden up. This is your life now - you need to get used to it.* Forcing a smile on her face, Neala turned and started walking again. After a moment's hesitation, Finn followed, falling into step with her once more.

"Okay, so that's the luggage dealt with. But what about us? How do we get there?" Neala asked brightly, trying to convince Finn she was fine.

Finn hesitated, then answered cautiously, "It's much the same, in essence. The difference is the level of protection. Of secrecy. Luggage is one thing - allowing people in is another issue entirely. We'll have to pass through a very ancient, very wise security system. But if you aren't considered to be a threat to the academy, or your fellow Bards, then it should be straightforward. I—" Finn cut off, startled by a ball of light which raced down from the sky, stopping in front of his face.

Frowning, he turned to Neala. "Please excuse me, there seems to be a problem. I'll be back in a moment." Dropping his pack, Finn strode back down the way they had come, the light ball following behind.

Once he was far enough away that Neala was out of earshot, he reached a hand towards the ball.

Feeling a little abandoned, Neala put down her own pack and looked around. They had diverted a little from her usual track, heading towards the dense woodland rather than following the curved path which led to the beach.

Neala breathed a secret sigh of relief. Fishing her sand spiral out from under her shirt, she stroked it absently. True to her promise, she had turned it into a necklace, securing the fragile shard in a wrought-silver cage pendant, and had worn it ever since. She hardly noticed its constant humming now, vibrating ever so lightly against her skin.

Wondering how much longer they would be walking, Neala turned back to Finn, watching as he spoke to the light ball. She frowned when she saw his face; usually he was so calm, but now she could see deep furrows of worry etched across his forehead, and he had his arms crossed tightly over his chest.

Within moments, the light ball disappeared, and Finn was walking back towards her, still looking concerned. Pursing his lips, he muttered, "I'm sorry to do this, Neala. There's a problem with one of the students - I have to go and track him down."

Pointing towards the woods, Finn said, "The meeting place is in there, it will take around two hours to reach it if you walk at a steady pace. Your mother says you're quite fit, so I figured this wouldn't be an issue?"

Neala shook her head, feeling nervous.

Fishing in his pocket, Finn pulled out a smooth, flat stone, black as pitch, a fraction smaller than his palm. It had been polished so brightly that it was almost as reflective as a mirror. He waved his hand over it, and Neala gasped when she spotted a glowing white spot appear inside it.

Handing it to Neala, he explained, "This is a mapstone - I've just programmed it to lead you to the meeting place. The dot will move around the circle, showing the way. Like a compass, but pointing to the specific place that you need to go. Give it a try."

Neala obeyed, turning and walking a few steps to her left. The glowing dot moved across the stone until it stopped near the top right. Walking back to where she started, she watched as the dot followed, coming to a stop at the top of the stone.

Satisfied, Finn hoisted his pack up with a grunt. "Good, it's working okay then. Now, when you reach the correct location, the dot will glow brighter and begin to pulse, all

right? I have to be there at midday to open the portal anyway, so don't panic."

Meeting her eyes steadily, he asked, "Now, are you sure
you will be okay?"

Neala's stomach was churning, but she didn't want to
cause him to worry any more than he already was. Shut-
ting down her fear, she forced a smile on her face and said
jovially, "I'm sure. It's the perfect day for a stroll in the
woods, anyway."

Wrapping her hand around the strap of her pack, she
adjusted it on her shoulders and gave him a small wave.
"Good luck with the student, I hope everything's okay."

Though he still looked unconvinced, Finn nodded and
replied, "I'll see you soon, okay?"

"Bye Finn!" Neala chirped, taking a few steps toward
the forest. Finn seemed to take the hint.

With a sigh, he let his muscles relax, and Neala watched
transfixed as his body began to fold in on itself, turning to
sand before her eyes. A strong breeze swirled around her,
whipping her hair against her cheeks, then the sand was
whisked away, spiralling into the distance.

Ignoring the trembling in her knees, Neala took a deep
breath and continued walking, trying to shake the image of
her friend crumbling to dust from her mind. "Definitely not
like the movies...not like the movies at all," she muttered,
fighting back the urge to drop her pack and run home.

Realising she was still clutching the mapstone, she held
it out and looked at it, checking to see where the dot

was pointing. Adjusting her direction slightly, she grit her teeth and said out loud, "All right, stone, let's do this. I'm trusting you, okay? Don't you dare get me lost."

Convincing herself that the stone hadn't just gotten warmer in her palm, Neala set off toward the tree line and whatever lay beyond.

~ 14 ~

Neala stared blankly at the ring of trees. *Is this some sort of joke?*

Inside the circle of trees, emerald grass swayed slightly in the breeze and a single butterfly zipped clumsily about, fragile wings fighting against the puffs of wind. Glancing around, she adjusted her pack and stared at the mapstone once more.

Sure enough, the ball had settled in the middle and was glowing with a pulsing light, just as Finn had promised her it would.

Just to be sure, she turned back the way she'd come and started walking away. In moments, the light dulled and stopped blinking. Returning to the tree circle, Neala watched as the light brightened and resumed its pulsing.

Scowling at it, she grumbled, "You know, it's almost like you're laughing at me, stone. Control the attitude."

She blew out a long breath and shoved the stone in her jeans pocket. She had been walking for close to three hours now, after briefly getting lost not long after entering the woods. It hadn't taken her long to get the hang of the mapstone, though, and she was now rather fond of it.

Looking around, she breathed in the unique wood-y scent of trees, water, and the sweet smell of soil. About to take a step into the ring of tall, silvery-barked trees, Neala heard a shout.

"Hey! Wait for the rest of us!"

Startled, she spun with a gasp, the weight of her pack throwing her off-balance. With a thump, she hit the ground hard.

Laughter echoed around the clearing as a group of young men and women approached from the path, led by a curvy, dark-skinned girl with the strangest eyes Neala had ever seen; they seemed almost purple in colour, like amethysts. Her teeth shone white against her skin as she guffawed, stopping to rest her hands on her knees.

Once she had caught her breath, the girl reached a hand towards Neala. "Sorry to scare you there. Are you okay?"

Neala's cheeks were burning with embarrassment, but she took the offered hand and let the girl pull her to her feet.

Brushing off her rump, she mumbled, "All good, I suppose. I wasn't expecting anyone else to be out here."

The girl cocked her head to the side and grinned wickedly. "What, you're the only Bard heading to Birchtree today, are you?"

Neala scowled, not liking the girl's tone. "Well, no, of course not. But that doesn't mean you can sneak up on people and not expect them to get a little surprised."

"Go easy, Jaz - she's obviously a newbie," a boy called out as he leaned against a tree.

Neala raised her brows; she'd not paid much attention to the others who'd come with the girl called Jaz, but now she looked around properly.

There were three girls and five boys, all older than her, and they had spread themselves around the clearing, sitting on the moss-covered logs or leaning against their packs.

With a start, she realised all of them were giving the silver trees a wide berth, as though they were worried about getting too close. Unnerved, Neala took a cautious step away from the trees, following the lead of the others.

Turning away from Jaz, Neala pulled out her water bottle then dropped her pack on the ground and sat on it, shifting her weight until it was comfortable. With a soft groan, she rubbed her legs, not realising how sore they were until she had stopped.

The boy who had told Jaz to back off met her eye and grinned. "So, you're an initiate? A first-year?"

Neala quickly swallowed her mouthful of water and nodded shyly. "Yeah, I moved here from Australia with my mother a few months ago. I'd never even heard of Bards or anything until Finn - Finley Talbot - found me."

The boy laughed. "Yeah, he does that. What's your name?"

"Um, Neala Moran."

"Nice to meet you, Neala. I'm Eamon." Gesturing to his friends, Eamon continued, "You've met the clearly-shy and quiet Jadzia, or Jaz. Sweet as pie, she is."

Overhearing him, Jaz rolled her eyes and gave him a rude sign with her fingers, drawing a laugh from him.

Unruffled, Eamon went on, "This here's Helena, then there's Seamus, Jasper, Christie, Cameron and Angus. You probably won't remember the names, but at least now the social custom has been completed."

Neala giggled, feeling more at ease. The others gave her a scattered variety of greetings, some waving, some merely nodding in acknowledgment.

Pushing away from the tree, Eamon moved over to where Neala was sitting and flopped onto the ground with a sigh, lying back and folding his arms behind his head.

Now that she had a closer view, Neala saw that Eamon was a very handsome man. His dark hair flopped charmingly into his blue eyes and his smile made her tummy flutter. But there was something else that she couldn't put her finger on; being this close to him was making her feel jittery, almost like a magnetic pull.

Before she could wonder about it, Eamon closed his eyes and started to chat.

"So, Australia, hey? What brought you all the way to the other side of the world?"

"Um, well, my-my family used to own a large farm, but my dad passed away last year, and it got too difficult to manage. Mum was born here, so it made sense that she wanted to come back, and my grandmother still lives here.

"So, Nanna gave us some work in her gift shop and helped Mum set up her floristry business here, and, well...that's it, really. I was working in the shop for a while, too, until I found out about Birchtree and all that."

"I'm sorry about your father, that must have been hard."

Neala shuffled and turned her water bottle around in her hands shyly. "Yeah, I try not to think about it much." She swallowed hard, the knot of grief in her chest threatening to unravel.

Hurriedly moving on, she continued, "But, enough about me, I'm not very interesting." Indicating the circle of trees with her head, she asked, "What's with the trees? I don't really understand what we're meant to do here."

Rolling onto his side so he was facing her, head propped in his hand, Eamon opened his mouth to answer just as Jaz bounded over, folding herself down beside him in one fluid motion.

Grinning at Neala, she held out her hand. "We didn't quite get off to the best start did we, Newbie? Sorry about that. I'm not actually that rude normally."

Eamon pretended to choke back a cough and Jaz shoved him jokingly, sending him sprawling onto his back. "Yeah, okay, so I can be a bit...blunt. Anyway, I'm sorry. We're all good, yeah?"

Neala took the offered hand and shook it cautiously. "Yeah, it's all good, no worries," she murmured, and Jaz laughed with delight.

"Oh, you sound so Aussie, I love it. So, what were you kiddies talking about?"

Eamon rolled his eyes affectionately and leaned toward Neala, whispering loudly, "Be careful with this one - she's the biggest gossip at Birchtree."

Jaz stuck out her tongue and Neala gasped as several twigs lifted off the ground and flew at Eamon's face. Swatting them away, he waved his hand lazily and Jaz's fuzzy black locks suddenly turned a vibrant shade of purple.

Jaz gasped, slapping Eamon's arm hard enough to send a loud whack echoing around the clearing. "Oh, you've done it now." She tugged one of her curls in front of her face, going cross-eyed as she focused on it. "You just wait – I'll get you back for this, you cheeky devil!"

As the others laughed, Neala heard more voices approaching. Shouts of greeting rang out as they welcomed the new arrivals - a group of five students ranging in age from sixteen to early twenties.

Feeling a little overwhelmed, Neala stood and moved her pack further into the shadows of the woods, placing her water bottle back inside before propping her back against it. With an understanding grin, Jaz followed her, still patting her vibrant hair ruefully.

Plopping down beside Neala, Jaz gave her a gentle nudge with her shoulder. "Wow, you look like a deer who's just run into some headlights. What's up?"

Neala opened and closed her mouth several times, trying to un-jumble the flood of questions pouring into her brain. Finally, she blurted out, "Your poor hair!"

Jaz stared at her for a moment then roared with laughter. Clutching her side, Jaz sucked in breath after breath, trying to compose herself. Once she was calm, she wiped the tears from her cheeks and gave Neala a warm pat on the arm.

"Oh, I like you, you're a good one. Don't worry too much; it's just a glamour – an illusion. A permanent one, most likely – Eamon's magic tends to stick. It probably won't come off until I cut it or something."

She raised her eyebrows and blew a wisp of fluorescent purple hair off her face. "He's on a completely different level, the things he can do. I'll never get rid of this myself, I should've known better than to tease him. Oh well, I suppose it could be worse."

Leaning back on her hands, Jaz turned her face up and closed her eyes, breathing deeply. "So, was that really all that was bothering you?"

Neala hadn't been paying attention. The moment Jaz had mentioned illusions, she was reminded of the night on the beach, when the púca had attacked. The man who had come to her rescue had used illusions, too.

The Fitzpatrick twins - Eamon and Lorcan...could this Eamon be the same one? Which means the one who saved me must have been Lorcan, then? Absently, she fingered the glass pendant.

It was several moments before she realised Jaz was still talking to her. Shaking her head, she flushed and said, "Sorry, I zoned out there."

Jaz waved a hand dismissively. "It's okay, most people do that when I talk. I was just saying, it won't be long now and we'll be ready to go, do you have all your things?"

Neala's eyes widened. "That's what I was asking Eamon. Where exactly are we going? The mapstone Finn gave me led me here, but there's nothing but trees. Where's the academy?"

Jaz grinned wolfishly. "You're going to love this. C'mon, grab your pack - the last of our lot are about to get here."

Neala was about to ask how she knew that, but then she, too, heard the voices on the wind. If the clearing had felt crowded before, it was nothing compared to now. Looking around, Neala saw people everywhere, milling about in groups, exchanging hugs and chatting with one another. Frowning, she could have sworn the space amongst the trees had grown; it had felt a lot smaller when it was just her standing there.

Shrugging it off, Neala grabbed her pack and made to follow Jaz when she heard a familiar voice call out her name.

Heart soaring, she turned to see Áine making her way over, followed by Eilìs. Her smile drooped when she saw

Áine's expression, though; she seemed to be on the verge of tears.

Meeting her eyes, Neala asked worriedly, "What's the matter?"

Glancing around, Áine leaned close and whispered, "It's Torin - no one can find him."

Neala frowned, casting her gaze around the clearing. "Surely he's just running late or something?"

Áine shook her head vehemently. "No, Eilìs and I were supposed to pick him up and bring him with us - that's why we're so late. But he wasn't home. The unit was unlocked, and his bags were still there. His roommate wasn't home, either."

"But he texted me at midnight, making sure I was going to sleep," Neala said confusedly. "What could have happened?"

"I don't know. But apparently sometime between then and this morning, he disappeared. Eilìs scried the winds for him, but there's no trace anywhere. That's why we called Finley."

Neala raised her brows. "It was you who sent that light ball? Finn was about to lead me here when he got called away. Why didn't he tell me it was Torin who was missing?"

Áine shrugged, brows furrowing. "Maybe he didn't want to worry you? Anyway, we haven't heard anything yet, and we can't open the portal until Finn gets here—"

Neala opened her mouth, but before she could speak, a streak of white-hot light slammed into the ground nearby with a thunderous crack. People were shrieking as they ducked for cover.

A few of the older students were already scrambling to their feet and summoning various-coloured magics to their palms, ready to attack whatever had appeared; Neala could see Eilìs shielding Áine as she drew a whirlwind around them.

A huge pressure had begun building in Neala's ears. Deep inside, she felt her own magic surge, awakened by whatever force had just crashed into the clearing. She clutched the sides of her head, dropping to her knees with a shout. Her blood pounded deafeningly in her ears, roaring with power. As though a storm were beginning to roil within her veins...

Overwhelmed by the rush of magic swamping her body, Neala saw the world swim before her eyes, then she blacked out.

*****

"Hey, Newbie, wake-up. C'mon now, everyone's staring."

Feeling a gentle pat on her cheek, Neala's eyes fluttered. As she regained consciousness, she realised Jaz was leaning over her, tapping her lightly.

Áine's face swam into view, tear-streaked but still lovely. Propping herself up on her elbows, Neala blushed furiously as she realised she'd fainted. Once Jaz knew she was awake, she rocked back on her heels and chortled. "Ah, you are good value, Neala. Are you going to be okay?"

Neala carefully flexed her muscles, but whatever power had overtaken her before, it seemed to have calmed now; all she felt was a mild ache in her temples. Squinting her eyes tightly, she rubbed the back of her head and scowled.

"I don't think my pride will ever recover after today. And it's not even midday yet!"

Jaz laughed heartily and rose to her feet, offering Neala her hand. "Is it just me, or does this feel a bit like déjà vu, huh?"

Allowing Jaz to pull her to her feet, Neala let out a snort. A small tug on her jumper made her turn, and guilt bit at her as she realised she was completely ignoring Áine. Holding out her arms, she gave her friend a hug for reassurance.

Over the rumble of mutters and murmurs around her, Neala could make out the sounds of an argument, and she let go of Áine. Looking for the source of the commotion, she noticed a circle of students had formed around a large, burned-out crater in the ground.

Hurriedly muttering to Áine that she would be back, Neala pushed through the crowd, wanting to see what had happened – what had triggered her magic so strongly? Something about it seemed vaguely familiar, but she was too distracted to place it.

Reaching the front, Neala gasped as she saw the extent of the damage; it was like someone had blown up a heap of dynamite. In the centre of the crater, Eamon was standing toe-to-toe with another man, gesturing angrily at the chaos around them.

"-endangering people, you idiot! Seriously, Lorcan, what is wrong with you? Are you trying to get yourself killed? Or just everyone around you?"

Lorcan was standing casually, arms folded across his chest, unfazed by Eamon's anger. Neala's eyes widened in recognition – this was definitely the man who'd rescued her that night on the beach. Her breath caught in her throat. *What was he thinking? Sending a lightning bolt this close to people?*

A girl next to Neala was whispering to her friend, and she overheard her say, "No wonder they call him 'the Eastwind'. He shouldn't be allowed back to Birchtree - why don't they just kick him out and be done with it? He's too dangerous."

Eastwind? Neala thought to herself. *Why 'Eastwind'?* Absently, she rubbed her glass pendant.

In the crater, Lorcan suddenly perked up, as though someone had called his name. Turning away from Eamon, who was still lecturing him, he stared straight at Neala, head cocked to the side.

Startled, she froze, captivated. Those green eyes...she remembered them from the beach. But there was something else, something she couldn't name. Like an echo, a calling that sent her skin prickling. Her magic stirred once more, a faint tingling in her veins.

Lorcan hesitated, jerking back as though he, too, had felt something pass between them. Brows creased with curiosity, he took a step toward her.

But before he could come any closer, Eamon reached out and grabbed him by the shoulder, snapping, "Don't you dare walk away from me!"

Quick as a snake, Lorcan whirled, thrusting a hand at Eamon, who was propelled backwards, landing on his back with a thud. The crowd of students gasped and exchanged startled glances. Lorcan gave a low growl, snarling so softly that it was barely audible, "You don't control me, Eamon. Not anymore."

His lip curling into a sneer, Eamon let out a sharp curse, rolling to the side and slamming his fists into the ground. A crack opened in the earth, racing toward Lorcan, who leapt a little too late, his foot catching in the rift and throwing him off balance.

As he fell, he summoned a breeze to surround him, and it lifted him into the air. Eamon, who had now scrambled back to his feet, shouted angrily, and the wind around Lorcan turned to ice, crashing back to the ground.

Eyes wide with shock, Neala glimpsed a light flicker inside the chunk of ice, and it melted away as Lorcan emerged, body cloaked in flames. The other students were no longer cowering – in fact, many were cheering and shouting, egging the duellers on.

Just as Lorcan was gathering the flames into a fireball, a dust storm rose from the crater, engulfing the brothers and stinging the eyes of those gathered around them. Neala threw her hands up to her face, coughing as the dust whirled around her, eyes watering.

Almost as soon as it had appeared, the wind settled and Neala lowered her hands, still blinking out the grit.

Gazing back at Lorcan and Eamon, she was shocked to see that both were encased in stone up to their shoulders, unable to move. Between them stood Finley, an expression on his face that Neala had never seen before. His eyes crackled with anger, and she could feel power rippling off him in hot waves.

An eerie silence filled the clearing, all the students now silent and still, watching Finn cautiously. A tap on Neala's elbow made her glance to the side, spotting Áine, who was staring wide-eyed at the scene before them. Neala felt a chill run down her spine; how powerful was Finn, truly? How powerful were *all* of these Bards?

In a voice barely more than a whisper, Finn hissed, "I will deal with you two later. Eamon, you know better than this. Lorcan, you have been warned, several times over; do not test my patience."

Closing his eyes, Finn let out a long, whistling breath. As the sound echoed around them, Neala knew that whatever pressure had been filling the air was melting away. It was like a calming wave washing over everyone, with the other students visibly relaxing around her.

Eamon and Lorcan, too, were being freed, the stone caging them crumbling to dust around their feet. By the time

Finn opened his eyes again, it was as though nothing had even happened, apart from the giant crater marking the earth. Meeting Áine's gaze, Neala raised her eyebrows.

With a cough, Finn cleared his throat and called out, "All right, we're nearly out of time. Hurry everyone - please form a circle around the ring of birches. Newcomers, observe what the older ones do. Once in place, please take the hands of those beside you."

Neala felt Áine clasp her hand, palm sticky with sweat. "We can't go yet - where's Torin?" she whispered anxiously. Neala shrugged helplessly, feeling a little panicked. Finn wouldn't leave Torin behind, would he? Surely that meant he was safe?

Whipping her head around, Neala tried to understand what they were all doing, hesitantly pulling Áine toward the silver-trunked trees. A firm, broad hand took hold of Neala's free one and she jumped.

Lifting her gaze, she found herself staring into Lorcan's face, his green eyes locking with hers. Unsmiling, he turned away, tugging her toward the nearest tree. Áine was still gripping Neala's other hand, and she squeezed it tightly.

Parting her lips, Neala licked them nervously, about to ask Lorcan if he remembered her from the night at the beach.

Before she could speak, Lorcan leaned close, his breath tickling her ear and making the hairs on her neck stand up. "Just be still. Close your eyes if you get motion sickness."

Frowning, Neala opened her mouth, then closed it again. Her skin had started to prickle uncomfortably, like pins and needles. *Maybe it's coming from the trees?* she wondered, face screwed up in discomfort.

Glancing back at Áine, who was now also clutching the hand of an older student beside her, Neala whispered, "Don't you know what this is? Hasn't Eilìs ever told you?"

Áine gave a small shake with her head. "There's a secrecy bond - she can't tell me anything about how to get there. No one can talk about it; the magic is binding."

Neala gulped, trying to slow her racing heart. So lightly that she wondered if she'd imagined it, she felt Lorcan give her hand the tiniest of squeezes.

Finn's voice rang out from somewhere on the opposite side of the ring of trees. "For those of you attending Birchtree for the first time, allow me to explain. Before you can enter the school grounds, you must ask permission from the Waykeepers - these ancient birches.

"You will need to clear your thoughts and focus your mind only on the trees before you, and request that they allow you access. They will assess you and determine if you may pass through. Don't be worried; in all my many years, only a handful have been refused access through this portal. So, take a deep breath, and let's begin."

A hush fell over the clearing, and Neala held her breath, wondering what was about to happen. Remembering what Finn had said, she closed her eyes and tried to push her doubts and fears about being rejected aside.

Bringing into her mind an image of the trees which formed the ring, Neala focused on the one at the forefront, the one she was standing before. Its silvery bark swam into her vision, the leaves rustling softly in the breeze. Breathing deeply, Neala reached for the pale teal light inside that was her magic.

As she touched it with her mind, the image of the tree swayed slightly. Feeling a little silly, she called silently, *"Great and ancient one, protector of the Bards. I am Neala Moran, and I wish to enter Birchtree Hall, so I may learn to harness my power and use it for...for the greater...good?"* She cringed, feeling silly. Was she even saying the right things?

There was a slight pause, then an ancient voice sighed, *"You are expected, Neala Stormbringer. We know of you, and of your purpose. Tread cautiously; your path is a dangerous one."*

This time, Neala did gasp. She had the strangest sensation that she was being sucked into a whirlpool, though there was no water to be found. Her body was spiralling, and she felt her hands being pulled from Áine and Lorcan's grasp with a sharp tug.

Keeping her eyes tightly closed, Neala waited for the rushing to stop, understanding now why Lorcan had warned her about the motion sickness.

The whirling stopped abruptly, and she landed with a thud, falling onto her backside for the third time that morning.

Once her mind had stopped spinning, Neala opened her eyes, blinking as she adjusted to the bright sunshine after spending so long in the dim light of the woods.

Taking in her surroundings, she realised she was sitting on an expansive lawn, with the sound of a river rushing nearby. All around her, other students were materialising, their bodies spinning like tops as they emerged from glowing balls of light. It was nauseating to watch, and Neala shut her eyes tightly again, resisting the urge to be sick.

A rush of wind next to her made her squint one eye open cautiously, and she sighed with relief as Áine appeared beside her, landing roughly on her knees with a squeal. Her joy at seeing her friend was short-lived, though, as Áine immediately leaned forward and vomited.

Horrified, Neala shuffled over to give her some space. In moments, Eilìs swooped in from nowhere, rubbing Áine's back and chuckling softly as she murmured words of comfort.

Feeling more composed, Neala climbed to her feet, wondering if the trees had allowed everyone through. Curious, she glanced to her left, where Lorcan had been standing. She felt concerned that she hadn't seen him arrive yet.

Distracted from her thoughts by a thump on her shoulder, Neala gasped as Jaz's smiling face popped up in front of her. "Congrats, you survived. Now the craic can really get started, aye? I'll see you around."

Neala started to stammer out a reply, but Jaz was already bouncing away, greeting people as she went. Shaking her head with a smile, Neala watched as a new lot of glowing balls began to appear. *Finn said there were meeting points all over the place, in all the counties; this must be another lot coming in. I wonder how many Bards there actually are?*

A sudden sense of overwhelm gripped her chest, leaving her slightly breathless. She scanned the lawn, looking for Finn and wondering if he was too busy to speak to her. Spotting him some distance away, she started making her way toward him, but stopped when she noticed Eamon.

He was talking in hushed tones with a girl Neala didn't remember seeing in the clearing. She had waist-long black hair, creamy golden skin, and large, almond-shaped eyes. Unable to take her eyes off her, Neala thought she reminded her of a wild cat, like a panther or jaguar.

Sensing she was being watched, the girl glanced up and narrowed her eyes at Neala. Awkwardly, Neala gave a little wave, but the girl just sniffed and turned back to Eamon, leading him further away where they wouldn't be overheard. His expression seemed neutral, but Neala noticed the tension in his jaw and the way his fists clenched and unclenched at his side.

Feeling a little put-out, Neala looked once more for Finn, but he had disappeared. Tucking a lock of stray hair behind her ear, Neala adjusted her pack and made her way back to where Eilìs and Áine were standing.

Thankfully, Áine had regained some of her colour and was sipping on a bottle of water, looking mortified. Eilìs gave Neala a nod and said warmly, "Welcome to Birchtree Hall, Neala. How was your commute?"

Neala sniggered. "I can't fault the speed, but the comfort levels leave a lot to be desired." The girls laughed, and Neala gestured around them. "So, what happens now? Do we have to wait for everyone to get here? And where is the actual academy? Is there a proper building, or is it just more trees?"

Eilìs flicked her head at the hill in the distance. "It's on the other side of that - it takes about twenty minutes to walk there from here. I can take you there now, but you'll have to wait out the front, being initiates and all. There are a few orientation things to go over and what-not. If you're up to it, sis, we can make a start?"

Áine nodded, gulping down a last mouthful of water. "Yes, I'm okay." Pausing, she frowned. "But I want to ask Finn where Torin is. Why didn't he come with us?"

Eilìs shrugged casually, but Neala could see the worry in her eyes. "Maybe he was in another county and is coming through their portal? You know Finn wouldn't have just abandoned him. If he isn't here by dinner, we can find out more, okay?"

Neala and Áine nodded, but a heavy weight was still lodged uncomfortably in Neala's chest. Trying to ignore it, she followed Eilìs as she led them towards the hill. Around them, Neala could see other students were beginning their treks, too, branching off into little groups as they made their way from what she had dubbed 'the landing zone'.

Turning back, she saw yet another group of students beginning to appear, and she shook her head in wonder.

"Hey, Eilìs?" Neala asked curiously, jogging to catch up with her.

"Yeah?"

"I was just wondering – what's the deal with Eamon and Lorcan? Why were they trying to pummel each other?"

Eilìs sighed dramatically. "Oh, that. I've known the twins for ages – they were here when I started, and they've always been...how do I put it?" She chewed her lip. "Exceptional. They are *crazy* powerful, and they know it. Eamon is a little less arrogant about it than the Eastwind, but still – they're kind of the unofficial kings of Birchtree."

Her mouth twisted sourly. "They've always been really close, but then there was this whole big thing last year, apparently, involving Eamon's girlfriend, Darci Shae."

An image of the gold-skinned girl flashed in Neala's mind, and she raised a brow but didn't interrupt. "Anyway, she and Eamon were together for ages, a few years, at least. Then, just before last Yule break, she suddenly left him for Lorcan, out of the blue. It was the talk of the school. Since then, the twins have been at each other."

Eilìs shrugged. "Rumour is he's dumped her already, though."

"Hmm. Well, that explains the, ah...fighting," Neala muttered, eyes wide.

Eilìs grinned at her. "There's never a dull moment here at Birchtree."

As they topped the rise, Neala's face broke into a grin of delight. Birchtree Hall was everything she had hoped for; the central building was as grand as anything Neala had ever seen, framed by two large turrets with arched walkways stretching around from the massive staircase leading up to the entrance.

Two more buildings fanned out from it like wings, lined with windows to allow the sunshine to stream in. Neala suspected these were the dorm rooms, but she was too awed to ask. A wide path wound its way from the bottom of the hill to the front of the school, passing a lake to the left and a bunch of greenhouses to the right.

Trees ringed the entire area, and Neala felt as though they were watching the students eagerly, waving their branches in greeting. Excitedly, she glanced at Áine and beamed. Her friend smiled back, but her eyes were still shadowed. Neala's smile dimmed, wishing they had answers about Torin.

Feeling guilty, Neala shuffled her pack on her shoulders and looked around, hoping Torin had somehow appeared while they were busy. Eilís spotted some friends in the distance and bid the other girls a hasty farewell.

"Okay, you two. If you head to the main building, someone will be there to help you and the other initiates to settle in. I have to go, but I'll see you later at dinner, all right?"

Giving Áine a quick squeeze around the shoulders, Eilís whispered, "Finn's never lost something he couldn't find again, sis. Torin will be here soon enough. I bet he'll be stuffing his face at the table with us tonight, just wait and see. Love you, monkey."

Áine gave her sister a shaky smile and let out a breath. "Thanks, Eilìs, we'll be fine from here. See you tonight!"

With that, Eilìs strode off, waving to her friends as she went. Turning back to Neala, Áine gave a trembly smile. "I suppose I shouldn't worry, but it's just hard not knowing." With a sigh, she steeled her shoulders and started walking down the hill, Neala following close behind.

Looking around, Neala realised she still hadn't seen Lorcan arrive yet, either. About to say something to Áine, she closed her mouth again; there would be plenty of time to talk over dinner.

The pair walked toward the mansion in silence. Neala could see Áine was worrying about Torin, but she didn't have anything to say that would cheer her up. Instead, she took in her surroundings, admiring the endless lush green of the grounds and the stretch of shadowy hills in the distance.

Once they had made their way around the lake, she came to a halt. Áine took a few more steps before noticing her friend wasn't beside her, and she looked back curiously.

Neala took a deep breath, suddenly overcome with some strange emotion. Standing in front of Birchtree, she felt a mix of homesickness and exhilaration. The grand building, with its detailed carvings and fretwork, looked even more imposing close-up, and she tried not to stare. Spotting a little table out the front, she nudged Áine.

"Look, it says something about initiates over there. C'mon, let's go see what we need to do."

The girls approached shyly, smiling at the older woman sitting behind the table. She peered over her glasses, pursing her lips as she studied Áine and Neala.

"Excuse me, we're new here, can you direct us to where we need to go next, please?" Neala asked politely.

The older woman's face softened slightly, and she raised an eyebrow. "Yes, of course. I'm Druid Keyes, the librarian here at Birchtree. Before the introductions tonight, you will need to be assessed by Druid Orwyn in order to determine your attributes. Assessments take place by the greenhouses; take a number from here before you go." She indicated the stack of numbered cards in front of her.

"You will be called in numerical order. Once your assessment is complete, please make your way to the conservatory in the West Wing, where you will undergo a brief orientation. If you get lost, please just ask one of the older students to direct you."

Neala and Áine exchanged wide-eyed glances. With a mumbled word of thanks, the girls took a number from the stack in front of Druid Keyes, Neala pulling number seven while Áine drew eight. A line was forming behind them now, and the librarian shooed the girls on hurriedly before repeating the instructions for a boy behind them who looked as though he were going to be sick.

Moving a small distance away, Neala halted Áine and rifled in her pack for her water bottle. After a few sips, she said nervously, "I didn't know we'd be tested on our very first day here. What kind of assessment is it? And what are our 'attributes'?" Áine frowned, looking as confused as Neala.

"I honestly don't know, Eilìs has never mentioned them. Which means they're either secrecy-charmed, like the location of the portals, or they're really unimportant, so she didn't bother talking about them." Given Áine's tone, Neala could tell she hoped it was the latter.

Placing her water back in her bag, she hoisted her pack back up and sighed. "Well, whatever they are, we'd better head down there so we don't miss our turn. Here's hoping these assessments are incredibly boring and not at all stressful or terrifying."

~ 15 ~

Neala watched in terror as the wall of fire raced toward the boy, who covered his face with his hands. Panicking that maybe he had spontaneously combusted, she let out a relieved squeak as the flames disappeared, leaving him white-faced and gasping for air.

The elderly Druid who was conducting the tests made a note on his parchment and mumbled something to himself.

Neala still didn't entirely understand what was going on; since she and Áine had arrived, she had seen the Druid douse the current student in water until she was sure he would drown, lift him ten feet in the air with a mini tornado, and now he had set him on fire.

Dreading what was going to come next, she whispered to Áine, "He still hasn't done an earth test, has he?"

Áine had just opened her mouth to reply when the Druid clicked his fingers, and the ground opened up beneath the petrified boy. He barely had time to cry out before he was dropping away and the earth closed above him, trapping him underground.

Neala couldn't stop herself crying out this time, and Áine shrieked and covered her eyes. Unfazed, the Druid tilted his head to the side and clucked his tongue. A few moments later, the boy's hand burst from the ground like a scene from a horror film, and the Druid beamed.

"Ah, excellent - as expected. Well then, up you pop." He gave the ground a sharp stomp and the boy shot out of the earth like a cork out of a champagne bottle, landing back on the lawn with a thump.

Neala stifled a giggle, reminded of how much time she had spent falling on her butt so far that day.

Trembling, the boy got to his feet and asked nervously, "I-is that it? Am I done now?"

The Druid scribbled another note on his pad, then looked up at the boy, smiling. "Yes, yes, Master Doyle, you're free to go. Your learning schedule will be made available to you tomorrow at breakfast. Enjoy the festivities."

On shaky legs, the boy turned and tottered back towards the academy, shaking his head and hugging himself tightly. Neala's mouth felt dry, and she dreaded the words she knew were coming.

"Number seven? Is number seven here?"

Stepping forward tentatively, Neala squeaked, "He-here. I'm here." The Druid turned to face her, and she froze. She hadn't noticed before, having been too absorbed in the various trials the boy called 'Doyle' had endured. But now she realised that the Druid's eyes were milked over, the white veil all but erasing the bright blue irises beneath. He was blind.

"Do you have a name, lass? Or is it just 'Seven'?"

"Oh, sorry, yes, my name is Neala. Neala Moran." She blushed furiously.

Druid Orwyn frowned thoughtfully. "Moran, hmm? Not from old Liam Moran's line?"

Neala shook her head. "I doubt it; my father's family has lived in Australia for several generations now. But my mother was a Kennedy, before she married. She's where I get my, ah, my magic from."

The old man stared at Neala, pale eyes seeming to grow brighter. "Hmm, yes, I can See that trace in you. But don't discount the Moran line of power either, child; it is more subtle, but it's there. Aye, an ancient family, that one is. You'll need to be careful, lass. Misfortune follows that House, to be sure."

Turning back to his clipboard, the Druid clucked his tongue. "Anyway, there will be plenty of time for lineage discussions later. For now, let's determine your attributes, shall we?"

As though sensing her curiosity, the Druid tapped his clipboard with a small smile. "Don't you worry about how I'm taking these notes, little cat. Eyes are not all that are needed to see, after all."

Neala wasn't entirely sure what he meant, but she pushed her confusion aside to concentrate on his explanation.

"Now, attributes. There are three categories we tend to use to define the nature of each Bard's powers: regenerative, cohesive, and destructive." He bobbed his head lightly. "I can already sense that you're quite attuned to water, so to use that element as an example, let's look at water in each aspect.

"Water in a regenerative capacity is healing and soothing – think of soft rain encouraging new growth from tiny seedlings. In its destructive form, however, the water element can crumble cities to ruin, as typhoons and tsunamis. Cohesive—"

Druid Orwyn paused to clear his throat. "My apologies. As I was saying, the cohesive category simply means that the force of the element is balanced, a blend of passive and wild." He tapped his parchment once more.

"None of these tests will cause you harm, but they *will* help me to assess how your magic responds to each element; it will either try to expand the power being used, absorb it, or try to convert it to a gentler form. If you are ready, I will begin."

Neala knew she resembled a fish gasping for air. A strangled, garbled noise made its way out of her mouth, and the Druid chuckled. "I'll take that as a yes. Well then - here comes your fire test."

With a flick of his wrist, he sparked the flint in his hands and called the flames to rise until they were racing toward Neala, who shrieked and covered her head with her arms.

Before she could run, Neala felt the flames prickle over her skin, the heat pressing against her. To her surprise, she realised she was not actually burning, but was encased in a tornado of flame, which caressed her, inviting her to play.

Her fear was quickly replaced with awe, and she reached for the flames, wanting them to grow and burn brighter, sensing their desire to break free and unleash their full power. The intensity left her breathless, and she had to bite her lip hard to stop herself from pouring all of her magic into the fire – if she did, the resulting inferno could be disastrous.

Before she could send her magic to join them and start a wildfire, the flames disappeared. Neala was sorry to see them go – she'd enjoyed the thrill of their potential. But a small part of her also heaved a sigh of relief. *Was that the kind of destructive power he meant?* she pondered fleetingly, a tiny sliver of fear lodging in her heart. *I don't think I like that...*

With a wave of his hand, Druid Orwyn summoned a funnel of water from a large barrel nearby and sent it racing toward Neala, who was caught unawares. Despite her surprise, a grin stretched across her face as the water enveloped her.

As though greeting an old friend, the funnel swirled around her, tugging cheekily at her hair, and brushing against her like an affectionate cat. She didn't feel the intense rush of power that she had with the flame. Instead, she felt a total calm, at peace with this element. With a wistful sigh, she watched the water flow back to the tub, sloshing reluctantly back into stillness.

Air was the next element to greet Neala, the tornado rising from her feet until it stretched far above her head. She let out a giggle as the tornado tugged at her, willing her to ride with it into the atmosphere. Not wanting to resist, Neala let the winds scoop her feet from beneath her, and she poured her magic into it, watching as the tornado's height increased. Before she could go much higher, the Druid called the winds away, and she dropped gently back to the earth.

Leaving her no time to react, the ground below her feet divided, and she fell with a gasp, panicking slightly as the earth closed above her head. Curiously, she wasn't buried in the ground, as she had believed she would be, but was pocketed in a burrow of sorts.

She reached for the magic inside of her and sent it out cautiously, unsure how it would react with this element. Her power spread out lazily, calmly. She was of the earth, no different to the plants that sprouted delicately through the soil. With deliberate slowness, she eased her hands above her head, and the earth around her seemed to sigh happily as it helped her to rise gently back to the surface.

Opening her eyes, Neala swayed a little, her body humming with the power of the elements she had just met. As she stared at her hands, she watched as the faint teal glow faded from her skin, her magic settling once more into that still place deep within her.

Druid Orwyn gave her a curious look, his blind eyes seeming to look beyond her physical form, studying her soul. With a quiet chuckle, the Druid made one last note on his paper and nodded his head slowly.

"Interesting. Very interesting. Well, Miss Moran, you are done here for now. Please make your way up to the conservatory for afternoon tea - the rest of your classmates will join you there shortly."

Glancing back at Áine, Neala gave a little wave, hoping to send reassuring vibes her way. Áine looked a little pale, but she straightened her back and nodded, summoning her courage.

With a final nod to her friend, Neala slung her pack over her shoulders and started trudging back to the main building, ruminating over her tests. What were the categories again? "Destructive, regenerative and...oh, cohesive. I wonder which I was for each?" she muttered out loud. "Pretty sure fire was destructive. Better watch out for that one..."

As she wandered around the bend, lips pursed at the memory of the flames' wild power, she glanced up and froze. Not far ahead, leaning against the wall of the closest dorm building, was Lorcan. Her breath caught in her throat; she'd been wondering if he'd made it through the birch tree barrier or not. To her surprise, a small knot in her stomach eased.

Neala was debating whether to speak to him, and what she'd possibly say if she did, when she heard another voice call out his name. Hesitating, she watched as the golden-skinned girl she'd seen with Eamon earlier sauntered across the lawns, making a beeline for Lorcan.

Raising his head, Lorcan spotted the other girl, and a strange look crossed his face. Without pausing to say hello, she pressed herself against him and raised her lips to his, greeting him as only a lover would.

Feeling completely awkward, Neala tried to look anywhere but at the couple, a slow burn crawling over her cheeks. Ducking her head, she shuffled past them swiftly, willing herself to turn invisible. *If that's the 'Darci' Eilis was talking about, I have a funny feeling Lorcan didn't dump her after all...*

*****

Pulling away from Darci's embrace with an exasperated sigh, Lorcan was about to ask her what the hell she was doing when he spotted Neala, her head tucked to her chest as she hurried away.

He raised an eyebrow curiously; had she recognised him earlier? He'd known who she was immediately. Even if he hadn't, that piece of his lightning she was carrying around would have told him—

"I'm sorry, am I boring you?" Darci was sneering up at him, her dark eyes flashing with annoyance as she glanced around, smoothing her hair back from her face. Jabbing him sharply in the chest, she growled, "You've been ignoring me all summer, despite your promises. Now you won't even look at me?"

Lorcan pushed aside his musings about Neala, folding his arms across his head as he stared down at Darci. He chuckled dryly and shook his head. "Look, I've already told you – whatever this was, it's over."

Dark eyes flashing with hurt, Darci hissed, "But you promised – you *promised* you'd help me get rid of this curse, remember? I trusted you with my secret – I've never told anyone, not even Eamon, about the...the incident." She closed her eyes tightly, as if blocking out the memory.

Somewhere deep inside, a twinge of guilt jabbed Lorcan's stomach. But he swiftly shoved it away; he'd learned long ago not to indulge himself with petty things like emotions. They only brought pain.

"You told me you had answers, that you knew why it was happening. But you haven't helped me at all. I thought, maybe if I could cure it, then perhaps things would...be better. That I could finally go home." Darci's tone had turned pleading now, her eyes drifting to the side as her shoulders drooped.

There it was again – guilt. Pity. He wouldn't allow it to consume him. Not again. Taking a step back, Lorcan sighed. "I'm still looking for answers, okay? That hasn't changed. I will keep my word. But I never promised you anything more than that; it was your decision to leave him. Perhaps breaking my brother's heart to chase after me wasn't the wisest choice after all?"

Not again. Never again. His eyes hardened. "I'll never love you, Darci. Whatever fantasy you dreamed up about us, it's never going to happen. Do you understand that? I don't care about you. I never have. I needed answers from you, and I got them."

Lorcan steeled himself to deliver the final blow. "If you want someone who actually gives a damn about you, go back to Eamon; he's the one who truly wants you." He lifted his mouth in a cruel sneer. "Until he learns the truth about you, anyway."

Darci's mouth opened in shock, her eyes blazing with a mix of hurt and fury. Raising her hand instinctively, she moved to slap Lorcan across the face. But with a snap of his fingers, Lorcan froze her hand in place and tutted, gently lowering it back down to rest by her hip.

"Now, now - no need for that. Haven't you hurt enough people already?" Releasing his magical hold on her, Lorcan planted a cocky grin on his face and gave her a sly wink. "I'll see you around, Darci."

He didn't wait around to watch the hot tears fall from her eyes. Turning, he shoved his hands in his pockets and strode toward the main building, looking every inch like the heartless monster they believed him to be.

Those students nearby who had heard the exchange were throwing him glares and sneers, whispering to one another about how cruel he was. How arrogant and selfish. The Eastwind. The cold, bitter master of destruction and pain.

Good, he snarled in his mind. *All is as it should be.* He would never allow himself to care for anyone again. Better to be hated and feared. Love just made you weak. Vulnerable. He clenched his fists, sparks shooting from between his knuckles as he clenched his teeth. *The Eastwind cares for no one.*

The conservatory was a beautiful, airy room, walled in glass and filled with sunlight. Plants covered every inch of the space, trailing from baskets, from the roof, even from the windows themselves. Giggling, Neala watched as a particularly friendly ivy specimen draped itself over a girl's shoulder, making her shriek.

Marvelling at how quickly she had adjusted to the plants in this room moving of their own accord, she sipped her orange juice and absentmindedly stroked the fern that had pressed up against her arm. Áine returned with her own drink and Neala raised her glass in a toast. Áine smiled as the girls tapped their cups.

"Here's to our new lives," Neala said, grinning. Looking around, she counted the other initiates. Aside from Áine and herself, there were just over a dozen other sixteen- and seventeen-year-olds milling around. Neala asked Áine if that was a good number.

"I think so. Eilìs had around twenty in her initiate year, Torin had eighteen last year. There are less than three hundred students here most years, apparently."

Neala raised her brows. "Only three hundred? Really? I would have thought there'd be way more."

Áine shook her head sadly. "No, the numbers seem to be dwindling each year. Eilìs said the Druids are worried. With so many people now moving to other countries or places where Bards are unknown, there may be hundreds out there who don't know how to access their powers. A bit like you. Imagine, if your mother hadn't already known she was a Bard, how would you have ever found out?"

Neala frowned, lost in thought.

"There has been talk of establishing schools in other countries, but the logistics seem to be problema—"

"Hi, sorry to interrupt, I'm just making my way around the room and wanted to introduce myself."

Startled, Neala glanced up into a pair of bright blue eyes surrounded by a cloud of golden-brown curls.

"Oh, hello. Hi. I'm Neala."

The new girl beamed, showing off the kind of dimples that made Neala think she must have had her cheeks pinched by old ladies regularly when she was a child.

"Neala, that's pretty. I'm Gracie. It's lovely to meet you. And you?"

Áine flushed, her shyness taking over. Neala swept in to rescue her before she could get too embarrassed. "This is Áine Holloway, she's my best friend. Well, one of them. Our other friend, Torin, is a second-year here." *Assuming he actually arrives*, she thought worriedly.

Gracie looked from Neala to Áine happily. "A pleasure." She paused, tapping her lip. "Holloway, was it? Why do I know that name?"

Finding her voice at last, Áine murmured, "My mother and father run a charity - 'Havenhand'. They help all orphaned children, but specialise in assisting homeless Bard kids, mainly."

Gracie's eyes widened. "Oh, yes, now I remember. They're foster parents to that poor Poppy girl, aren't they? The one who went mad a few years ago? I heard she passed away yesterday, my brother said. He was in her group here. Such a sad thing. Anyway, if you'll excuse me, I was on my way to grab another drink. I'll see you at dinner later, ladies."

Seemingly oblivious that Neala and Áine had frozen in shock, Gracie skipped away, waving at a boy as she passed.

Neala's skin was rippled with goosebumps, as though someone had dumped a bucket of ice-water over her head. Staring at Áine, she saw that her friend's cheeks had turned the colour of milk.

"Poppy...as in, Torin's sister?" Neala's voice trembled. Remembering her shock when her mother had told her about her dad's accident, how it seemed like her whole world had imploded, she started shaking. *Oh, Torin...no, no...*

Áine could only nod. Swallowing sharply, tears welling in her eyes, she stammered, "And she's Eilìs' best friend. Oh, Neala, do you think it's true? Why didn't anyone tell Eilìs and me? Do you think Mother and Father know?"

Áine had started to shiver, so Neala wrapped an arm around her shoulders.

"I don't know if it's true. It would explain Torin's absence, though. But news also gets stretched and warped away from the truth when it spreads, so maybe she isn't actually *dead*; she may have just taken a turn or something and Torin went to be with her?"

"Then why couldn't Eilìs find him when she scried? She checked everywhere and couldn't find him, so how could he have been in the city? She's never failed to find us before."

Neala felt helpless, and it made her irritable. Without meaning to, her tone turned harsh. "Look, I don't know, okay? I don't have all the answers. I'm still getting my head around all of this as it is, how am I supposed to know why someone else's magic isn't working, or if people are dead or not?"

Mortified at her words, Neala yanked her arm from around Áine, her mouth gaping open in shock. "Oh, Áine, I'm so sorry, I didn't mean —"

But Áine was already stepping away from, her eyes overflowing. "No, you're right. You don't know everything. How would you know how much Poppy means to us, to Torin?" She swiped at her eyes angrily. "I'm going to find Eilìs, she needs to be told."

Turning on her heel, she strode away, leaving Neala sinking into a pool of remorse at her selfishness and lack of empathy. But Áine hadn't gone very far before the large glass doors at the end of the conservatory opened and a dark-haired, imperious looking woman greeted them.

"Initiates, welcome. I am Imelda, head Druid of Birchtree Hall. By now you should have all had your attributes tested by Druid Orwyn. Is there anyone who has not done this? Please raise your hand."

Neala and the other students exchanged glances, but no one seemed to be moving. Druid Imelda nodded. "Good. There's usually at least one who forgets, so this is encouraging. In a short while, we will be moving into the dining hall where dinner will be served, then you will be escorted to your new dorm rooms by your Dorm Masters. Druid Brian is in charge of the boys, and Ovate Clodagh cares for the girls.

"The boys' dorms are in the West Wing, girls' dorms are in the East Wing. You will each share a dorm room with one other student. We try to accommodate you with a friend or someone you know, but this is not always possible, depending on student numbers. If you have a particular dorm-mate in mind, please make this clear to your Master as soon as possible. Keep in mind, not everyone will necessarily have the room-mate they request."

Neala tried to catch Áine's eye, wondering if she still wanted to share with her. But Áine was staring straight ahead, not making any eye contact with her whatsoever. Fighting against the lump forming in her throat, Neala stared down at her folded hands.

With one last scan around the room, Druid Imelda checked her pocket watch. "All right, the rest of the students should be settled by now. Come, follow me."

Lining up behind a tall boy with a long, dark ponytail, Neala chewed her lip and thought about Torin. Was it true, what Gracie had said about his sister? *'She's the one who went mad'...Tor never said why Poppy was in hospital, did he? Only that it was an accident...*

"What did Gracie even mean? 'Went mad'...that's a bit vague," she mumbled, causing ponytail boy to glance over his shoulder at her. Dropping her gaze down at her feet, Neala shuffled along with the others, mind racing.

Lifting her gaze once more, she caught sight of the coal-coloured ponytail and was reminded quite unexpectedly of the fox pup who'd been in her room last night. She hadn't even told Áine about that yet.

Peering behind her, Neala spotted Áine a few places back. Her heart sank when she realised her friend had been weeping steadily, eyes puffy with tears.

Druid Imelda clapped her hands once, the noise startling the initiates into silence. "Now, make your way to the side of the dais and wait silently, please. You'll be introduced to everyone before taking your seats. You are free to sit wherever you choose, but please do so quietly. Keeping in line, follow me."

Pushing open the large double doors, Druid Imelda strode down the centre of the room. Neala felt like a small child, following the line of students as they trudged forward. All around them, the older students sat in groups at large round tables, studying the newcomers curiously. A strange, prickly sensation, similar to what she'd felt in the birch grove, crawled over Neala's skin as she entered the room.

When she was only halfway down the aisle, she heard a strange noise, like a raspy squeal. A few other students must have heard it, too, because she noticed several people getting to their feet, pointing curiously at something back in the doorway.

While attempting to look over her shoulder, she tripped and nearly overbalanced, stumbling headlong into the person sitting at the table to her right.

A strong pair of hands gripped her arms and helped her straighten, and Neala found herself staring into Eamon's deep blue eyes through her lashes, blushing furiously.

Eamon simply shook his head with a crooked grin and released her. Indicating with a thrust of his chin, he gestured to the hall doors. "I think she's here for you."

Confused, Neala stared behind her, where students were standing and pointing at a fuzzy little blob of fur scampering its way clumsily up the aisle, making a beeline for her and yipping angrily.

Neala's jaw dropped open in shock. "No way...there is no freaking way it could be..."

She was still staring in disbelief as the little black fox pup toddled over to her on its chubby legs, huffing with exhaustion. With a sigh, it flopped on her sneakers and whined, begging her to pick it up.

Ignoring the whispers and smattering of laughter, Neala scooped up the ball of fluff and cuddled it to her chest. Her hands were trembling, and a cold sweat had broken out on her face. Not knowing what else to do, she turned back to Eamon desperately, but he could only shrug.

Druid Imelda, however, was striding toward her, her expression stern. In Neala's arms, the pup was already snoring, its muffled breaths squeaking as its furry belly expanded and deflated.

Neala swallowed hard; she knew without a doubt that this was the same pup she had left with her mother that morning, the one that had snuck into her room overnight. It was not possible for it to be here.

Druid Imelda came to a halt in front of her, dark eyes narrowing as she took in the furball in Neala's arms. Pursing her lips, she turned away, clapping her hands sharply, and the hall fell silent.

Tightly, she said to Neala, "It's Miss Moran, isn't it? Pets are not allowed here at Birchtree. How did you bring it through the portal?"

Neala gulped, mouth dry as sandpaper. "I-I swear, I have no idea how it got here. It's not a pet, it just kind of *appeared* in my room last night, but I left it with my mum to take to the vet before I came here, honest." Her eyes had begun to prickle, and she bit the inside of her cheek hard.

Imelda's gaze softened, and she clucked her tongue. "What kind of creature is it, anyway? Show me."

Carefully, Neala shifted her arms so she wouldn't drop the little fox, and held it out to the Druid, keeping her eyes fixed on the ground. "A fox pup, ma'am. I have no idea where it came from, or how it got here."

There was a lengthy pause. Unsure what was happening, Neala lifted her gaze to peer up at the Druid's face. She was startled to see that Imelda seemed to have paled ever so slightly. But within moments, her face became stern once more, and she cleared her throat sharply.

"I will give this creature to Ovate Clodagh for now; she will place it in your dorm, along with some food and water for it. We will discuss it further in the morning. Please, hand her to me."

Reluctantly, Neala handed the sleeping fox pup over to the Druid, who tucked it carefully in the crook of her arm. Giving Neala a nod of dismissal, Druid Imelda addressed the rest of the room.

"There is nothing more to see here. Initiates, please proceed to the dais as instructed. The rest of you, resume your seats and we will continue with proceedings. Clodagh, may I speak with you a moment?"

Lining up with the other students, Neala knew her cheeks were glowing scarlet. Try as she might to block it out, she could feel the stares boring into her, could hear every whisper and mutter about what had just happened.

Closing her eyes, she folded her hands before her and bowed her head, wishing she could disappear.

Off to the side, Druid Imelda had a short, muffled conversation with a plump, grey-haired woman, before handing over the fox pup and returning to the dais. Taking her place on the stand, she raised a hand for silence. Once the room was settled, she began her address.

"Welcome, everyone, to another year at Birchtree Hall. For those of you who are new here, let me give a brief history of this academy, and what we do. First and foremost, Birchtree Hall was established as a safe haven for Bards to practice their magic away from the prying eyes of humans, following the separation of the worlds almost three hundred years ago. Humans distrusted those who were touched by the Fae, believing them to be cursed or unnatural. Many Bards were executed, accused of being witches and practicing dark magic.

"In order to protect our kind, Birchtree Hall was established by an unnamed Bard, about whom little is known. It was designed initially to be a home of sorts, for those of our blood. But it soon expanded into a place of learning, where young Bards were instructed by their elders, the Druids, in the ways of our power. Over time, it evolved into an academy, and thus remains.

"As the years passed, humans began to forget about the existence of the Fae, the Otherworld, and those ancient powers who ruled over the land - the Elementals and the Deities of the trees and rivers - believing them to be no more than myths and folktales. It became safer for us to come out of hiding and to live amongst them once more, keeping our powers concealed. But the education of young Bards is still required, and thus, Birchtree Hall continues to exist as a safe place for Bards to call home, once they come into their power, to learn and to understand their magic.

"All of you here today carry with you the blood of the Fae, the Elders, and the keepers of the secrets of the Otherworld. You are attuned to the natural flow of life, the great Song that binds us all and keeps the natural world in harmony. As Bards, it is our responsibility to keep the Song playing and to add our own unique melody to the fabric of the universe. Here, you will learn what it means to be part of the Song, and how we all have a role to play."

Neala's head was spinning, and her heart was pounding wildly in her chest. The power in Druid Imelda's words was undeniable; every sentence seemed to be etched in Neala's soul, and she could almost hear her magic humming deep within her, awakened and alive.

She was acutely aware of every brush of air on her face, could feel the solidity of the earth beneath her feet. The flames burning in the candles surrounding her seemed to dance, and out beyond the walls of the Hall, Neala swore she could hear the lake lapping gently under the light of the setting sun. It was at once overwhelming and glorious, the feeling of connection that had opened to her.

Deep in the shadows of her mind, a wild power stirred. It had a primal energy to it, unlike anything she had felt before. This wasn't her Bard power – this was far more ancient, far stronger. It seemed to be calling to her from the darkness, a sweet, mournful melody echoing through her soul.

Somewhere outside of her awareness, Neala knew she was dropping to her knees, her hands gripping the side of her head as she howled, her heart shattering with the despair in the song consuming her. The mark on her shoulder had begun to burn and pulse; she could feel it even here, in the depths of her soul.

"You must right the wrongs, Neala Stormbringer. You must restore the balance..."

The voice whispered through her mind, filling her vision with the image of a great tree, a tree whose branches and roots echoed one another in perfect harmony, in perfect balance. Flares of light danced around her, swirling faster and faster, until everything came to a sudden halt, and Neala knew nothing more.

~ 17 ~

When Neala's eyes finally opened again, she blinked groggily against the bright light shining on her face. Confused, she tried to pull herself into a sitting position, but a sharp pain in her head forced her to lie down once more, groaning softly.

A gentle hand touched her forehead, the coolness a relief against her skin. "Neala, are you okay? It's Áine. Oh, we've been so worried. Neala, Torin's here. Are you awake?"

The word 'Torin' broke through her haziness, and she forced her eyes to stay open, searching desperately to see his face. "Tor? Are you okay?"

Scrambling to rise, she flailed her hands uselessly, trying to find something to help pull herself up. A strong hand gripped her arm, and she blinked her eyes several times, trying to focus.

The room slowly came into view. She was in a small, cosy bedroom lined with cream and blue wallpaper. Sunlight streamed through a window to her right, a slight breeze fluttering the lace curtains.

In a chair to her left, Áine was eyeing her with relief, looking as flawless as ever, though the dark circles under her eyes betrayed how tired she was. On her right, Neala found the face she had been looking for.

Torin's bright blue eyes were gazing down at her worriedly, almost glowing against the bruises surrounding them. Neala stared at his face in alarm, noting the split lip and cut on his eyebrow. Struggling further upright, she gestured to Torin's battered face.

"Oh my god, what happened? Where were you?"

A tentative grin played at the corners of Torin's mouth before he winced in pain and his expression clouded over once more.

"I'm doing okay now, Neals. But let's forget about me for a moment, aye? Are you all right? I heard you had a bit of a dramatic start to life at Birchtree, huh?"

Neala squinted, trying to remember how she'd ended up here. The last thing she could recall was Druid Imelda making her welcome speech, then there was a rush of power...the song, the tree, the strange voice...and then she'd fainted.

Pressing her hands to her face, she groaned. "Oh no. No, no, no...what did I do? Áine, please tell me - was it really that embarrassing?"

Áine took one of Neala's hands and tugged it away from her face. Stroking it gently, she stammered, "I wouldn't say it was embarrassing so much as...it was all quite scary, really. Druid Imelda was just starting to introduce us when you...you kind of...well, you had a fit or something. Your eyes rolled into your head, and you collapsed on the floor.

She licked her lips, unable to meet Neala's gaze. "You were making an awful screeching noise, like you were in some kind of terrible pain, and you were jerking all over the place. It was terrifying - I thought you were dying."

A faint memory stirred in Neala's mind. Her birthmark had been burning again, and her heart had been consumed with a deep, inconsolable grief. Holding her breath, she listened dimly as Áine continued.

"That boy, Eamon, he got to you first and managed to calm you down before Druid Imelda came over and called for the Healer. She got Eamon to carry you out of the hall. Everyone was freaking out, no one knew what had happened. But the Druids made everyone settle down and we kept going with the introductions and had dinner." Áine gulped and met Neala's eyes cautiously.

Neala was sure her face was as red as a stop sign. She closed her eyes and groaned. "I can't believe it. That's so much worse than I thought. I'll never be able to face anyone here ever again."

Torin snorted. "Oh, don't be so bloody dramatic."

Taken aback by his unusually harsh tone, Neala opened her eyes and gaped at him. Running her gaze over his cuts and bruises, she immediately felt ashamed.

Giving her head a light shake, she murmured softly, "I'm so sorry, Tor. You're right, I'm being ridiculous. Forget about me - what happened to you? Is Poppy—" Neala broke off, gulping.

Torin bowed his head and sat on a chair next to Neala's bed with a thump.

"She's gone."

Neala heart sank. "Oh no, I'm so sorry..."

Torin glanced at her, then ran his hand through his hair. "No, I didn't mean - it's not like that." He let out a deep sigh. "See, it all started when I got into a fight with my housemate. He'd been out drinking with his mate, this absolute tool whose always hated me. Anyway, the gobshite must've gotten into his head, 'cause when he got home in the wee hours of the morning, he just barged into my room and dragged me out of bed, telling me to get the f—"

He paused, glancing at the door with a raised brow and a sheepish twist to his mouth. Deciding to proceed with some less colourful language, he went on, "Well, he quite rudely told me to get out. Seems he's had enough of me not paying as much rent when I'm here at school. Said he's going to get the tool mate to move in with him instead."

Torin leaned back in his chair, folding his hands over his stomach. "We got into a bit of a barney, then I just left. Not knowing where else to go, I went to see Poppy. I knew it was late, but I was hoping the hospital folk would take pity on me. I looked a right mess, anyway. Figured at least I could beg them to clean me up a bit."

"After the doc had checked me over, I asked if I could pop in and see Poppy for a bit. It was getting close to dawn, I just wanted to say goodbye before I left. The nurses must've taken pity on me because they took me up to her room, despite grumbling a bit about how early it was.

"But...she was gone. Like, disappeared. Her bed was empty, and all her clothes were gone. The nurse set off an alarm, and the place went into lockdown while doctors searched the whole building, but there was no trace of her anywhere."

Torin took a deep breath and folded his arms across his chest, a shadow drifting across his features. "I spent the rest of the morning talking to the police, answering questions about where she might have gone, if we had any relatives or anything she may have called. But I had nothing – no clue what may have happened to her.

"Eventually Finn came and got me, telling the cops he was my guardian and stuff so they'd let me go. Before we left, though, he snuck up to Poppy's room to get a read, to see if he could Track her. Nothing. Not even *Finn* could sense what could have happened, or where she'd gone."

Huffing out a sigh, he shrugged at Neala. "I got here just in time for dinner, but you'd already been taken away, Neals. I saw Áine and Eilìs, though, so explained everything to them. Eilìs still doesn't know why she couldn't see me when she scried, she said they'd looked."

His shoulders dropped dejectedly. "There's still no word on Poppy, though. Finn's been scrying on and off for the past couple of days but can't find any trace of her."

Neala's ears pricked up. "Wait, what do you mean 'the past couple of days'?" Her heart jolted. "How long have I been sleeping?"

Torin and Áine exchanged glances. It was Áine who finally answered, "Neala, we arrived here three days ago."

The words echoed around Neala's head. When she was able, she stammered, "Th-three days? I've been here for three days?"

"Mercy said you'd had a huge shock to your system. She thinks something had taken over you, some kind of power that she'd never encountered before. It wasn't Bard magic, but something else. She wouldn't tell us anything else, saying the Druids would get to the bottom of it and not to worry."

Neala lay back and stared at the ceiling. "Of course it'd be a mystery. Weird is my thing now, apparently."

A sudden realisation hit, and she sat bolt upright again. "The fox pup, what happened to it? Where did it go?"

Torin frowned, confused. "What fox pup?"

Áine shook her head. "Sorry, I completely forgot to tell you about that, what with everything else that's gone on. Ovate Clodagh has been looking after it, Neala. She brought it to you the day after you got...sick. The little thing didn't want to leave your side, but, eventually, Clodagh managed to get it to go with her. No doubt she'll bring it back to you soon."

Without warning, Áine lurched out of her chair, knocking it backwards. "Oh, crumbs, I was supposed to let Mercy know the moment you woke up. Sorry, I'll be right back."

As Áine hurried from the room, Neala felt a laugh bubble up in her chest quite unexpectedly. Unable to hold it in, she let it burst from her mouth, startling Torin.

Once she was composed, Neala gulped down several breaths and explained, "Sorry, Tor, I just-just didn't realise people actually said things like 'oh, crumbs' in real life."

Neala was taken by a fit of giggles once more, and this time Torin joined, his deep rumble warming Neala's heart.

It wasn't long before Áine returned with the Healer, Mercy. Neala glanced at her curiously. Mercy was a slender, dark-skinned woman with a serious face. Her black hair was close-cropped and there were several tattoos winding their way up her neck, like vines.

Her sharp eyes assessed Neala in an instant, and she clucked her tongue. "Well, you are an unusual one, that's for sure."

Neala was fascinated by the woman's accent; it was not one she could place.

"Whatever took hold of you had you tight. But I am pleased to see you have come back relatively unharmed."

"Wait, something took *hold* of me? Like, possessed me?" Neala asked incredulously.

Mercy gave her a long look, her amber eyes revealing nothing. She gave a short nod. "Oh, yes, something had its mind locked on you, girl. It was draining your essence, that

I know. Though how, and for what purpose..." She shook her head. "I cannot say. You are lucky to be here."

Turning to Áine and Torin, she flapped her hands, shooing them out the door. "Now, I must ask you two to leave. This one will be free to join you once I have made sure she is completely healed. Tell Druid Imelda that she will come to her office after midday. And you, boy - keep using that ointment on those cuts, twice a day. I'll know if you don't."

Neala's friends didn't argue. They gave her a quick wave, then hurried out the room, leaving her alone with Mercy. Licking her dry lips, Neala opened her mouth to ask more questions, but Mercy, quick as a cat, turned and held out her hand.

"No. I cannot tell you what was after you, or where it came from. The only advice I can give you is..." She cocked her head as though she was listening to someone. "Heed your dreams. She is coming, and you are needed."

Mercy's face softened for the briefest moment, and Neala saw deep sorrow flash in her eyes. But, as quickly as it had come, it was gone just as swiftly, replaced by the serious expression once more.

Mercy cleared her throat and gave her head a quick shake. Moving closer to Neala, she checked her over promptly and efficiently, examining her eyes and turning her face side-to-side.

Holding out her hands at the Healer's request, Neala felt coolness like water flow over her, and she sighed, every muscle relaxing as the magic seeped into it. When the sensation faded, she opened her eyes and watched as Mercy nodded in satisfaction.

"Yes, you are free to leave. I will escort you to the dining hall so you may have something to eat. I suggest eating lightly, perhaps fruit and some yoghurt or some fresh greens. The others will be coming in for the midday meal shortly."

Neala's stomach gave a flutter at the thought of facing the other students. What would they think of her? That she was some kind of freak? Gulping down her fear, she swung her legs to the side of the bed.

Mercy placed a hand on her shoulder, stopping her from standing. "Go slowly - your muscles will be weak."

Neala nodded, and rose carefully, her thighs trembling slightly with the effort. Realising she was dressed in nothing but a nightgown, she frowned and asked Mercy nervously, "Um, is there any chance I could get changed before we go to the hall?"

The faintest hint of a smile tugged at Mercy's lips. "Of course. I had Miss Holloway bring some of your things up here, including clothing and toiletries. Come, I'll assist you."

Feeling like a child, Neala allowed Mercy to help her change into a clean pair of track pants and a soft, grey jumper. Tugging her hair back into a ponytail, she ran her tongue over her teeth, grimacing at the layer of fuzz covering them.

Trying not to think about how bad her breath must be, she pulled the backpack Áine had packed her things in onto her shoulder and followed Mercy out of the room.

As they walked in silence, Neala concluded that she had been in Birchtree's equivalent to an infirmary; several doors branched off from a central room full of cabinets stocked with potions, tinctures and herbs. She noted that none of the medicines were like the ones she knew from the hospitals at home, and she said as much to Mercy.

The Healer snorted. "Of course not. We use natural medicines here - herbs and plants infused with magic to make them more potent. You will learn to make them as part of your studies, if you have the right attributes."

The word 'attributes' grabbed Neala's attention. "I almost forgot about the attribute test. What was it all about? What do attributes do?"

Mercy chuckled softly. "Your attributes determine your strengths – where and how your power is best used. To be a Healer requires an affinity for water and earth, ideally with regenerative attributes. I ask you - would you care for a Bard with destructive earth powers to offer you healing treatment? Or one who is more likely to drown you with water than to soothe you? I would imagine not." Neala frowned, puzzling it over.

The corridor from the infirmary to the dining hall was short, and Neala's heart started to pound as they drew closer. Voices were already filling the room with chatter and laughter; the other students must be arriving for lunch. Feeling slightly ill, she lowered her head as she followed Mercy's vibrant skirt through the doorway.

A hush fell over the room, and Neala wished she could sink into the floor. Mercy's voice rang out, clear and commanding, "Do not let me distract you from your meals, young ones. Please, go about your business."

As the babble of voices and scraping chairs started up again, Neala felt a rush of gratitude for the steely Healer. Wanting to thank her, she lifted her gaze, but Mercy was already striding away, heading for a door on the opposite side of the hall.

Feeling alone and exposed, Neala hunched her shoulders and scuttled over to the corner where the servery was. Joining the line of students, she grabbed a tray and clutched it to her chest like a shield.

A sharp slap on her back forced Neala's breath from her and she gasped. A familiar voice rang in her ear. "Newbie! Long time, no see. Bit early to be faking sick and skipping out on classes, don't you think? How's that poor buttocks of yours? I'll be surprised if it isn't red as a baboon's, the number of times you've fallen on it."

Neala giggled despite herself, a wave of relief washing over her as she recognised Jaz's teasing.

"Don't remind me," she groaned. Gathering a bread roll, some dried peaches, and a small bowl of yoghurt and honey from the buffet spread, she looked around to see if Áine and Torin were there yet. When she couldn't spot them, she shifted awkwardly from one foot to the other, hoping

Jaz might take pity on her. Noticing her movements, Jaz smirked.

"Yes, you can sit with me, wee lost lamb. I'll protect you from the prying eyes of society." Patting her fuzzy hair ruefully, Jaz chuckled. "Besides, with my hair still this alarming shade of magenta, no one will look at you twice."

Neala blinked, remembering the moment Eamon had transformed Jaz's locks from midnight black to garish purple.

"It suits you so well, I'd almost forgotten it wasn't intentional. You haven't figured out how to turn it back yet?"

Jaz shook her head, grabbing her own food tray and leading Neala to a table off to the side of the hall. "Nope. Eamon could turn it back if I begged, but, honestly, I've grown pretty fond of it. Still, I think I'm probably going to just cut it back short, anyway. I need a change."

As she settled herself on the chair opposite Jaz, Neala took the opportunity to properly take in her surroundings. The dining hall was immense, its walls panelled with various hues of wood, except for the eastern side, which consisted entirely of windows. The mid-morning sunshine was streaming into the room, casting a green glow over the trails of ivy that wound around the frames.

The rest of the walls were decorated with tapestries and paintings of all sizes, depicting trees, oceans, and a variety of creatures. Some were the animals Neala was used to, but others showed strange, unworldly-looking beasts and inhumanly beautiful people who could only have been Fae.

Students sat around small, round tables scattered haphazardly about the room, with no particular order. It reminded Neala more of a dining room you'd find in someone's home, rather than anything that would exist in a normal, everyday school. She mentioned as much to Jaz.

"Well, Birchtree isn't really a *school* as such, not like the humans have. Remember, it started out as a refuge home for Bards who were locked out of the Otherworld when the portals were sealed. We call it an academy, and we do come here to learn, but I think you'll find that it's pretty different to what you're used to back home."

Neala glanced down, the corners of her mouth lifting in amusement. "Probably not. I was home-schooled by my mother; I never went to a mainstream school."

Jaz swallowed her bite of sandwich and raised her eyebrows. "Oh, well, then I take it back. You're probably going to find it is way more your style, then. See, there's no real curriculum or lesson plans, exams, all that sort of thing here. We're grouped with those who have similar powers to ours, based on our attributes, and allocated to one of the Druids, who teaches us how to use our powers to the best of our ability."

She cocked her head to the side. "See, rather than trying to squash us all into the way they *think* we should learn, they adapt to what we *need* to learn. As an initiate, you'll complete your first year with the other newbies, but after that they divide us based on our skills and talents, rather than by what year we're in."

Neala frowned, chewing one of her peach slices thoughtfully. "So, how do you know when it's time to graduate? Like, when do you know you've completed your final year of study?"

Jaz grinned. "You don't."

Seeing the blank look on Neala's face, Jaz giggled. "Coming here is entirely optional, Newbie. After your initiate year is complete, you are free to choose if you continue to come back and keep learning. I mean, it's not like we need to graduate in order to get jobs, is it? What we learn here won't get you a career in journalism, or into medical school or whatever, right?

"It all comes down to how much you want to know about your power. Some people are fine just knowing that they can control it, and they go back to an ordinary, non-magical life. Others want to learn more about healing so they can go out and be doctors with that little bit of an edge over the human ones. See, we have to be subtle about using our powers out there in the 'real' world."

Jaz tossed her head. "After all, they used to burn our kind at the stake way back in the day, didn't they? Anything unusual or magical, the humans can't handle it. So, they fear or destroy it. That's why this world, the one we're stuck in, is called the Cursed World, did you know that? The Otherworld, where the Fae come from, that's where magic is welcomed and can be used freely. Lucky us, being stuck this side of the Veil, hey?"

It was the first time Neala had seen Jaz look so serious. Pursing her lips, she glanced down at her half-eaten food and poked at her bread roll. "It sounds like you'd rather be there than here."

Jaz met Neala's gaze sadly. "I'm just sick of being hated because I'm different. My skin is usually enough to get me in trouble; if not that, then it's my size." She gestured to her curves. "Add in a strange magic that sometimes causes me to do things people can't explain, so they call me a freak?"

With a sigh, she leaned back in her chair. "I used to go to a normal human school, up until my powers emerged. It was the best thing that could've happened to me – I could finally get out of the hell-hole I'd been enduring all those years." Her lips curled into a crooked smile.

"I choose to come to Birchtree every year because it means I can escape the human world and finally be myself. Most of us do. This is my third year coming back here, but some of the others have been here way longer than that. Eamon and Lorcan have been here the longest; no one knows for sure how many years they've been coming here. They got their powers real early, people say, like, around ten or something.

"So, you see, Newbie – we all belong here; it doesn't matter if we're different. But out there..." Jaz shrugged dejectedly. "There's always something wrong with you. Too dark, too fat, too skinny, too ugly, too weird...We're always too much of one thing, or too little of something else."

Jaz reached for her apple and took a big bite. Replacing her sombre expression with her usual carefree one, she drew her arm back and hurled the apple over Neala's head.

Gasping, Neala turned around just in time to see Torin catch it with one hand, balancing his lunch tray precariously with the other. Jaz let out a barking laugh, her melancholy forgotten.

"Nice catch, Rambo." Jaz winked as Torin sat down beside Neala. He rolled his eyes good-naturedly and polished the apple on his shirt before taking a bite out of it.

"Hope you didn't want this back," he muttered, juice spraying from his lips as he spoke. Neala grimaced but couldn't help grinning. Jaz stuck her tongue out at him and stretched her arms over her head.

"Anyway, that's my cue. You kids enjoy the rest of your lunch. Tor, I'll see you later this afternoon. It's sure to be good craic." Grabbing her tray, she beamed at Neala. "Laters!"

Watching as she sauntered away, Neala chewed her lip thoughtfully, Jaz's words echoing in her mind. Her ponderings were interrupted by Torin nudging her gently with his shoulder.

"Penny for your thoughts."

Smiling at her friend, Neala shrugged dismissively. "Nah, they aren't worth it - keep your penny." She leaned back in her chair, tapping her fingers on the table. "Where did Áine get to, anyway?"

Torin gave her a sidelong look but didn't question her further. "She wanted to see Eilìs - they haven't really spent any time together over the past couple of days. But she said to tell you that you'll be are sharing a dorm, as long as you don't mind? She was a bit worried you'd still be mad about the little tiff you had the other day."

Neala frowned. She had forgotten all about that. Shaking her head, she smiled. "Of course I'm not mad - she has more right to be upset about it than me, I'm the one who was rude. I'll apologise properly when I see her. Speaking of, I should probably go; I haven't unpacked any of my stuff." Her eyes widened. "And I need to find out about that fox pup, too."

She gave Torin a sheepish look. "I'm sorry, it feels like I'm abandoning you when you just sat down."

He shrugged. "It's fine, Neals. You have a lot to catch up on today; we can talk more tonight after you're settled in, aye? I think you still need to see Druid Imelda first though, don't you?"

Neala closed her eyes and let out a sigh. "Yeah, I'd forgotten about that, too. I'd better go, I'm so sorry."

Torin winked at her. "I'll see you tonight."

Neala hurriedly gathered her things and made her way to the servery, dropping her tray off with the other dirty ones. It was at that moment she realised that she had no idea where Druid Imelda's office was.

About to go back and ask Torin, she felt a gentle hand touch her elbow. Turning, she found herself face-to-face with Eamon. She felt her stomach flutter and her cheeks flushed. With a charming smile, he asked, "You look a little lost there, can I help?"

Stumbling over her words, Neala replied, "Um, yes, I need to go to Druid Imelda's office, do you know where it is?"

Stupid question, of course he knows that, dum-dum, Neala winced. *He's been here since forever.*

Eamon nodded happily. "Sure, I do. Why don't I escort you? Just to make sure you don't miss it." Neala smiled gratefully. Placing a warm hand on her back, Eamon gestured for her to lead the way out of the dining hall.

Once they were out in the main entrance area, he fell into step beside her. "Here, we need to go up those stairs over there." He pointed to a staircase leading to the second-floor landing. As they climbed, Eamon glanced down at Neala curiously.

"So, how are you feeling now? You gave everyone a bit of a scare the other day."

Neala sighed, screwing up her nose. "Embarrassed, mainly. No joke, I'd never fainted, not once in my life, before coming to Ireland. Now it seems to be the norm for me."

"Really?"

She nodded. "Yeah, I fainted on the beach a while back. Then again in the woods, when Lorcan arrived in that lightning bolt, just before you started fight—" Neala broke off, placing a hand over her mouth. Eamon's mouth twitched but he forced a rueful smirk.

"Ah, yes. My brother has that effect on people - he isn't the best at making a subtle entrance. I'm sorry it affected you so badly, though."

Wanting to change the subject, Neala glanced around her. They had reached the landing now and Eamon was turning down a smaller corridor to the left. The walls were covered in more tapestries, and Neala paused in front of one that caught her eye.

It was a woodland scene, with an image of a young woman standing beneath a large ash tree, one hand resting on the trunk, and her other hand seeming to beckon to Neala. At her feet, a shadowy creature, like nothing Neala had seen before, wound its way around her legs, a tail-like shape coming to rest at the woman's knees.

Neala couldn't take her eyes off the woman's face. It was ethereal and inhuman, almost catlike. But it was the antlers that fascinated her the most; they resembled those of a deer, strewn with vines and flowers, proudly sprouting from the woman's auburn hair. Realising she'd stopped, Eamon came to stand beside her.

"Ah. This is Elen of the Ways, an ancient woodland goddess. It's said that she was known as the way-shower, and she would help people who were lost to find their way again. Physically and metaphorically."

"What's this thing - this creature?" Neala asked, reaching her hand toward the shadowy form.

Eamon tapped his lips thoughtfully. "No one's entirely sure. It's not from our world - it belongs in the Otherworld. Finley has suggested it may be a shape-shifter, like a púca, but it's hard to confirm; they have never been seen in their natural form. As in, they always appear as something corporeal, like a horse or a dog. Others have said it's a phantom, or even Elen's familiar. But no one can seem to agree on what it is."

With a last glance at the tapestry, Eamon shoved his hands in his pockets and cleared his throat. "Anyway, we best not keep Imelda waiting. Come, her office is just down here."

Tearing herself away from the goddess' haunting eyes, Neala turned and followed Eamon's broad back down to the doorway at the end of the corridor.

Coming to a halt in front of the ornate knocker shaped like a ring of flames, Neala turned to Eamon, wanting to thank him, but he had already lifted the knocker and rapped it hard three times.

"Come in," the Druid's voice called, and Eamon smiled warmly at Neala.

"I'll leave you to it. I'm sure I'll see you again, Neala." With a nod, he strode back down the corridor, his long legs making short work of the distance. Realising too late that she never did thank him, Neala shook her head and pushed the door open nervously. Peering around the side, she gasped in surprise.

Expecting to see the head Druid sitting behind a desk, she was shocked to see the room was filled from floor to ceiling with plants, vines, and flowers. Trails of ivy wound their way down beams, and flowering honeysuckle arched overheard, drinking in the light streaming through the roof, which was composed entirely of glass panels.

In the middle of the room was a rug emblazoned with runes and symbols that Neala had never seen before, gold thread glowing against the deep navy wool. Seated on the rug was Druid Imelda, delicately shaping a bonsai tree to follow the wires she'd laid out for it. Glancing up at Neala, she cocked an eyebrow.

"Well, close the door behind you."

Startled from her staring, Neala hurriedly closed the door and took a few steps into the room. Carefully, making sure she wasn't treading on any plant tendrils, she came to a halt at the edge of the rug, unsure if she was expected to sit on it or not.

Without taking her eyes off her bonsai, Druid Imelda asked, "How are you feeling now, Neala Moran?"

"I'm fine, thank you, ma'am."

"It's Druid Imelda, Neala."

Neala flushed. "Sorry, Druid Imelda."

With a final pinch, Druid Imelda removed a single yellow leaf from her miniature tree and sighed happily. "There, that is a much better shape for you, my old friend."

Letting out a tired groan, she got to her feet and carefully lifted the pot, placing it on a shelf behind her where dappled light played over its dark green leaves. Turning back to Neala, she fixed her with a sharp gaze.

"Mercy would never have let you out of her care if she believed you were not fully healed. Regardless, I ask that you continue to rest for today. You may join your fellow initiates for lessons tomorrow morning. I have your attribute papers here. Since you missed orientation the other day, I will quickly run through what they mean."

Rolling her shoulders to stretch out the muscles, Druid Imelda walked over to a desk hidden beneath a canopy of ferns. Reaching into a drawer, she pulled out a scroll and unfurled it, brows creasing as she read.

Neala waited impatiently, shifting her weight from one leg to the other. A tickle on her ankle made her look down, and she spotted a Devil's Ivy tendril shyly winding its way over her foot. Trying not to giggle, Neala looked up and realised the Druid was watching her, a tiny smile tugging at the corners of her mouth.

Clearing her throat, Druid Imelda explained, "Based on Orwyn's trials, these are your elemental attributes: fire, destructive; water, cohesive; air, destructive; earth, regenerative. What this indicates is the way elements are likely to respond under your influence, and where your strengths and talents lie."

She tilted her chin at the Devil's Ivy. "For example, that plant currently cuddling up to you like an affectionate cat is drawn to you because your earth power is regenerative. It is instinctive for you to grow things and coax nature to do your bidding, rather than to send tremors to crumble buildings or force the earth to open up beneath your feet."

"However," she added with a note of caution, "your fire and air attributes are destructive, which means those elements are more likely to behave wildly under your influence. For you, sending fire to light a candle, for example, is fraught with potential disaster; you would more likely cause the candle to explode rather than to produce a small, gentle flame."

Druid Imelda was pacing now, hands locked behind her back as she spoke. Neala was listening intently, not wanting to miss a thing. The Devil's Ivy was not helping her focus, though; it had now wound its way up to her knee and its yellow-striped leaves were waving joyfully at being near her. Holding back a smile, Neala tried to concentrate on the Druid.

"Of course, your attributes only reveal what comes more *naturally* for you, not the limits of what you can or cannot do. Bards with destructive attributes can also learn to tame their power and complete gentler tasks. Conversely, regenerative attributes can certainly be used for destructive purposes if the Bard has the intent behind it.

"Ultimately, the main purpose of identifying your attributes is that they help us to determine what training you will benefit most from while you are here. You and your fellow initiates will be grouped together to begin with, but if you choose to return after this first year, you will be placed in classes more tailored to your personal learning needs. I have a lesson schedule for you here."

Druid Imelda halted her pacing and turned to Neala, handing her the attribute scroll and another, smaller one tied with a silver ribbon. "Your initiate year will be very broad in its learning, covering the basics of all the elements, as well as history, lore, and modern Barding practices. Music is an essential - all Bards are required to learn it. Additionally, there are optional dance and visual art teachings available outside of our typical learning hours. Animal husbandry is also an optional class."

She turned and stared out her window, which overlooked the lake below. "Ultimately, Neala, Birchtree Hall is a place to learn who you are and what you are capable of. The Bards who found themselves on this side of the Veil when the portals were sealed have endeavoured to continue our traditions and practices in a safe way, away from the fearful eye of humans. I hope you will find the answers you seek while you are here."

Turning back to her plants, Druid Imelda waved her hand at Neala in dismissal. "Your fox is with Ovate Clodagh in the girls' dormitory. You will be responsible for it at all times, understood? I will not have it causing distractions to the learning here."

Neala nodded, then realised the Druid couldn't see her. "Yes, Druid Imelda."

Glancing back over her shoulder, Imelda stifled a grin. "Oh, and please take that fellow with you. I couldn't bear his misery once you were gone. Consider it a gift."

Neala glanced down at the ivy, which was squeezing her affectionately. Tracking it back to its pot, Neala gently coaxed it to let her go. "All right, little one. You can come with me, just – yep, just let go. Easy now, that's it. Back to your nice little trellis, okay?"

Once the tendrils had wrapped themselves around their original climbing frame, she hefted the pot and balanced it on her hip. Aware that Druid Imelda was no longer paying her any attention, Neala awkwardly reached for the door, clutching her scrolls in one hand while she supported the pot in another.

Once she was out of the office, Neala let out a long breath. She wasn't entirely sure what to make of the aloof Druid leader. Glancing down at her new plant, she raised an eyebrow. "Well, at least I got a gift, I suppose."

"Talking to plants now?"

Neala jumped, almost dropping her ivy, which wrapped a tendril around her arm tightly. Ahead of her, leaning against the wall, was Lorcan. Annoyed at being startled, she snapped, "Do you do anything besides lean against walls looking mysterious?"

Lorcan let out a scoff, eyes lighting up. "Oh, she bites. And here I was thinking you were just a poor, quivering creature inclined to scream and faint at the slightest surprise. Like a frightened goat."

Flushing despite herself, Neala squared her feet, trying to look like his words hadn't affected her. "Is there any particular reason you're lurking in corridors? Or are you just a common stalker?"

His mouth twitched in amusement. "If you must know, I was looking for my brother. Someone said they saw him heading towards Druid Imelda's office. I heard her speaking to someone, so thought I'd wait it out and see if it was him." He shrugged and pushed away from the wall. "Now I know it was only you, I see I've been wasting my time."

Neala bristled. "Wow, how dare I waste your precious time. I'm so sorry, your highness. I didn't realise you were so important."

Lorcan smirked, all humour vanishing from his eyes. "You are a curious little thing. Tell me – do you have the faintest idea who I am? Or what I'm capable of?" He raised an eyebrow at her, then took one slow, deliberate step forward. "I'd wager you don't, or you'd have scarpered away down the hall by now. So, I'll tell you this once, and once only..."

He had moved so close to her that she could count the tiny freckles on his nose. Swallowing hard, Neala forced herself not to flinch, even as he leaned close to whisper in her ear, "For your own sake, stay the hell away from me."

Neala screwed up her nose and glowered at him, unable to stop herself rolling her eyes. "Seriously? *You're* the one who's been following *me!*" She wasn't sure if it was her irritation, or something else, but her skin had started prickling like it was crawling with ants, and it made her temper flare.

"Do you really have such an arrogant opinion of yourself? 'Don't you know who I am?' Give me a break."

So fast she wasn't sure if it had even happened, a spark seemed to leap from her, zipping across the space between her and Lorcan, straight into his chest.

He jerked back from her, his fingers rubbing the spot vigorously, green eyes widening in surprise. About to ask him what had just happened, Neala held her tongue. A strange tension had filled the air. Like static, almost.

Gripping her plant for comfort, Neala stood her ground despite the trembling in her legs - he towered head and shoulders over her. Meeting his scrutinising gaze, she did her best to make him believe she had even half a hope of beating him to a pulp if it came to it. Her skin was on fire now, as though electricity was racing through her veins.

As though drawn like a magnet, Lorcan's eyes zeroed in on the lightning-struck sand she had turned into a pendant. In an instant, his face relaxed and his mouth turned up in a knowing smile that made Neala shiver. Taking a step back, he let out a dry laugh.

"Nice trinket you have there. It was made by lightning, I believe? I seem to recall the moment vividly."

Reaching out, he flicked the pendant lightly and winked. "Listen to what I said, Neala Stormbringer. It's for your own good."

The colour drained from Neala's face. No one knew about her dreams, about the mysterious voice that referred to her as 'Stormbringer' - the same name the birch tree had called her by. She hadn't told a single soul about that. So, how did Lorcan know? Mouth gaping, she watched as he winked and walked away down the hall, whistling to himself.

It was several moments before Neala realised she was holding her breath. Letting it out in a huff, she drew in a gulp of air and tried to settle her nerves. Her plant caressed her face gently with its tendrils, bringing a shaky smile to her lips.

Once she was calm, Neala raised her eyebrows; the prickling sensation had gone. She ran a hand lightly over her hair, to see if it was sticking up, but it was still smoothly pulled back in its ponytail. *Curious. So, it wasn't static electricity or anything, then*, she mused.

Steeling herself, Neala made her way down the corridor, trying to remember which side of the building the girls' dorms were. "Who cares about that jerk anyway?" she muttered to her plant. If she tried hard, she could almost convince herself that she certainly didn't.

~ 18 ~

Neala was huffing by the time she reached the Dorm Mistress' door. Even after getting directions from several students, she had still gotten confused about where she was going. In the end, an older girl had taken pity on her and walked her to the dormitory entrance and pointed out which room belonged to Clodagh, the head of the girls' dorms.

Feeling hot and flustered and over it all by this point, she pounded her fist on the door much harder than she meant to. Her plant trembled and Neala cringed with remorse. Stroking its leaves gently as an apology, she waited for the door to open.

When no one came, she knocked again. "Maybe she's out?" she wondered aloud. "That'd be my luck today."

It was a surprise when the door suddenly opened, and Neala came face-to-face with Clodagh. "Oh, I'm sorry, Druid. I didn't mean to knock so loud."

Clodagh was a short, weathered old woman with wispy grey hair covered by a soft veil. As her brown eyes met Neala's, a wave of calm washed over her. Smiling more genuinely, she continued, "I'm Neala Moran - sorry that we haven't met yet. I've been told you have my – I mean, the little fox that followed me into the hall the other night at dinner?"

Tilting her head to the side, Clodagh nodded and gestured for Neala to come in. Curious, she entered the room. Unlike Druid Imelda's room, Clodagh's was simple and uncluttered. There was a little wooden table with two comfy couch chairs either side. A bed was set up against the far wall by the window, partly obscured by a screen decorated with a border of Celtic knots. Plants adorned the mantlepiece, but there was little other decoration.

The most striking feature of the room was the bookshelf, which took up the entirety of the right-side wall. Every inch of the shelves had been crammed with books, scrolls and papers. Neala itched to read them.

Turning away from the temptation, she heard a tiny yip, and her face broke into a grin. Hidden in a pile of blankets by the fireplace, she spotted a fuzzy black head popping out of the bundle and she giggled.

Placing her plant on the ground beside her, she crouched and held out a hand. "Hello, little one. I have a lot of questions for you." The fox scrambled out from the blankets and bounced over to Neala, tiny legs almost disappearing in the fluff of its body.

When it reached her, it whined with joy, trying desperately to climb up her knee. Hoisting it into her arms, Neala stood, beaming as the fox nuzzled her chest and licked her chin. She looked for Clodagh and found the woman stand-ing off to the side, hands folded as she smiled warmly, revealing several missing teeth. "Thank you so much for looking after her, Druid Clodagh—"

Clodagh raised a hand and shook her head. Gesturing to herself, she shaped a word with her hands. Neala stared at her, puzzled. Seeing Neala's frown, Clodagh tottered over to the table and picked up a well-worn notebook.

Opening it to a new page, she wrote a word on it and held it up for Neala to see. "'Ovate'?" she read aloud. "Oh, Ovate Clodagh, is that correct?"

Clodagh beamed at her, and Neala smiled. "Sorry, Ovate Clodagh. I remember now, the others have called you that. I'm still learning the different titles. Is an Ovate different to a Druid, then?"

Clodagh nodded but waved her hand dismissively. Scrib-bling on her paper, she held it up for Neala to read. "'No time to explain now. For lessons.'" Neala nodded sheep-ishly. "Of course, sorry. I can be a little curious sometimes."

Looking for a distraction, she turned her gaze to the fox, which was watching Clodagh with its ears pricked up. Changing tack, she asked, "I don't suppose you can explain how this little one got here? The last I remember seeing it, it was getting dropped to the vets with my mother back home."

The Ovate chuckled, a breathy sort of hooting. She shook her head and her brows furrowed. Writing in her book once more, Clodagh held up the page.

"No. She is a female, that is clear. But she is no true fox."

Neala read the words several times and felt a chill run down her spine. "Not a fox? But...what else could she be?"

"No one here can tell."

Neala bit back the flood of questions and swallowed hard. Taking a deep breath, she stared at the fox-creature, which stared straight back at her with eyes the colour of sapphires. Reminded again of the fox that had appeared to her in her dreams, Neala shuddered.

Hurriedly, she stammered out, "Well, thank you again, Ovate Clodagh. If you could show me to my dorm, I'm feeling pretty tired again. Mercy said I may feel a little sluggish over the next day or so, since I'm still healing and all..." Aware that she was babbling, Neala stopped herself.

Nonplussed, Clodagh nodded and pointed to the door. Stooping to pick up her plant, Neala realised there was no way she could carry her scrolls, the fox, and the plant at the same time. A gnarled pair of hands came into view, wrapping around the pot, and she gave Clodagh a grateful grin.

Following the Ovate's curved back down the hall, Neala noticed that none of the dorm room doors had numbers on them. Rather, each had a picture of a flower on it. When they reached the end of the hallway, Clodagh indicated the stairs leading to the upper floor.

Neala nodded, and ascended into another hallway, these doors marked by images of different species of leaf. Clodagh led her a short way down the hall and stopped before a door marked with a shamrock. Neala chuckled to herself. *The luckiest room in the building*, she thought amusedly.

Handing her a small key wrought of copper and tied with a shamrock charm, Clodagh gestured for Neala to unlock the door. Carefully placing the fox pup down on the ground, she turned the key and pushed the door open with her shoulder, eyebrows raising in surprise. She wasn't sure exactly what she had been expecting when she thought of the dorms, but it was not what greeted her.

Looking more like a motel room than a school dorm, there was a bathroom on the right-hand side, and two beds were lined side-by-side against the wall to her left. Across the room, a window offered a view of the lake in the distance, lace curtains waving softly in the breeze. There were two desks positioned either side of the window, and Neala could see Áine had already decorated hers with photos and books.

Against the wall next to the bathroom door was a double wardrobe, presumably for her and Áine to share. The wallpaper was mint green, printed with dark grey triquetra, and there was an ornate brass candelabra overhead, as well as smaller wall lamps with candles above each of the desks. It was cosy and welcoming, and Neala felt tears welling in her eyes. For a brief moment, she felt desperately homesick.

Before the tears could fall, Neala turned and thanked Ovate Clodagh for showing her to her room. With an understanding pat on the arm, she carefully placed Neala's plant on the bed and backed out of the room, closing the door softly.

Alone at last, Neala lay down on the bed and folded her arms over her face, the fox pup curling in beside her. More exhausted than she thought, she drifted off to sleep.

*****

This time, in Neala's dream, the landscape had dramatically changed. No longer surrounded by woodland, she found herself standing in the very centre of the clearing, where the four roads met, and could see no further through the darkness. Just as she spotted a shape moving toward her from the gloom, Neala heard Áine's voice. "Neala? Wake up."

She sat upright with a jolt. For a moment, the room appeared as dark as the woodlands in her dream, and she gasped. A wet nose pressed against her palm, and she was instantly calmed.

As the dorm came into focus, Neala realised the fox was eyeing her carefully, one paw on her hand. Mind still groggy, she muttered, "I really need to give you a name, fox."

Áine was eyeing Neala apologetically. "Sorry to wake you, it's just - it's tea-time and you haven't had much to eat lately, so I thought you wouldn't want to miss it."

Neala stretched her arms over her head, wincing as her shoulder clicked. "Thanks, Áine, I appreciate it." Meeting her eyes, she added swiftly, "I also want to apologise for the other day, about not being a very caring or considerate friend. You know I wouldn't choose anyone else to bunk with here, right?"

Áine beamed. "I know. I'm sorry, too. I was just so stressed about Poppy, and Torin missing, and everything that was going on, it made me snappy. It was silly. Let's just forget about it and move forward, okay?" Her eyes widened with excitement. "I can't wait for you to start lessons with us, it's so much fun. Did you get your attributes?"

Neala nodded, amused by her enthusiasm. "Yep, they're right here." Unfurling the scroll, she held it out to Áine while she opened her lesson schedule, the neatly-tied bit of parchment that she hadn't looked at yet.

As Áine read through the attribute sheet, Neala scanned her lesson plan. "Awesome, music with Finley is the first class tomorrow. Ooh, history and lore, too. Then we have water and air lessons...free time...earth...fire...modern Barding...then optional animal husbandry, dance or visual arts."

She frowned. There was only the one list of classes. It said nothing about which days of the week the classes were on. Puzzled, she asked, "Is it the same schedule for every day?"

Áine nodded absently. "Yes, the lessons are at the same time every day. Once we get through our initiate year, we are allocated to one Druid who will educate us for the rest of our time here, so they keep the schedule this way so the Druids can work it in with their groups.

"For example, Finn's personal group has free time for their first lesson every day, then they spend the rest of the day learning with him. Orwyn, who teaches the initiates history and lore, gives his students free time for the second lesson so he can teach us, and so on. It makes it far easier for them."

"So, once we complete our first year, we only get one teacher for every year after that?" Neala checked, remembering that someone had mentioned that earlier. *I hope I get put in Finn's group.*

Áine nodded, rolling the scroll back up and tying it neatly with the emerald ribbon. "Yes. Eilìs is one of Druid Imelda's students. After her initiate year, they determined that Druid Imelda was the best fit for what Eilìs needed to learn, and so she is educated solely by her. It is the way the Druids have always taught, taking small groups of students and teaching them the ways of Bards in the style that suits them best. The masters and their apprentices."

Neala nodded, mulling it over. "I suppose that makes sense. Kind of." Shaking her head, she got to her feet and scooped the fox pup into her arms. "Now, back to you, little miss. You need a name. What about...Shadow?" She screwed up her nose. "No, too obvious. Um, Dusky? Nope, that's worse."

She blew a hair off her cheek. "This is harder than I thought. You're something mystical, curious - you deserve a name that's special."

"*Keia.*"

"Sorry, what was that?" Neala asked Áine distractedly.

Áine gave her a strange look. "I didn't say anything."

Neala squinted. "Oops, sorry. I thought I heard something."

"*Keia.*"

Certain she had heard someone whisper that time, Neala flicked her head around the room. Áine watched her worriedly. "Neala, what's wrong?"

Neala growled, "I keep hearing something, like a whisper, but I don't know where it's coming from."

A soft nip on her finger made her gasp, and she glared down at the fox. "What was that for?"

"*Keia. Name.*"

Neala froze. The fox was staring at her pointedly. In her mind, she heard the voice speak once more. "*My name. Keia.*"

Startled, Neala almost dropped the fox as she stepped backwards. "Y-you? It's *you* who's speaking to me? What the heck is going on?"

"*Keia sent here. Help you. Help Stormbringer.*"

It was the same way the fox in her dreams had spoken to her; the same voice in her mind, but younger. Neala recognised it now. Goosebumps crept over her as realisation dawned. "It can't be...no way..."

Feeling dizzy, Neala thrust the fox pup at Áine and stammered, "I need to go. I'll see you at dinner. Please just, just put her down somewhere, I'll-I'll be back later. I just – I need to get out for a minute."

"Neala, wait, what—"

But Neala had already bolted out of the room, leaving Áine and the talking fox behind. In a few short leaps, she was down the stairs and racing down the corridor toward the hall, dodging the other students on their way to dinner.

Almost slipping on the slate floor, Neala turned and raced to the entrance doors, slamming them open and jumping down the steps in one motion. A light rain had begun to fall, and the drops trickled down her face as she ran, heading to the lake.

Finally coming to a halt beside a large willow tree on the bank, she sat and rested her forehead on her knees.

"What is *wrong* with me? I should be used to crazy things like this by now. Haven't I seen enough of magic over the past few weeks to just expect the supernatural at this point?" She leaned her head back against the tree trunk, feeling the raindrops filter through the leaves and splatter on her skin.

"Maybe I am just a poor, quivering creature, like Lorcan said. No one else has been this sensitive - I'm the only one falling apart at every strange little thing that happens."

"When you're finished feeling sorry for yourself, let's talk."

Neala gasped, then let out a sigh of relief. Standing off to the side with his hands shoved in his pockets was Finley Talbot. "Finn, hi. Sorry, I didn't think anyone was out here."

Finley shrugged, then folded his lanky body until he was sitting cross-legged opposite Neala. He didn't appear fazed that he was getting slowly drenched by the rain. "So, what brings you out here to mope?"

Unable to keep it all inside anymore, Neala told him all about the dreams she'd been having since she arrived in Ireland, about the crossroads, about the black fox that spoke to her in her mind, and how she kept being called 'Stormbringer'.

Then there was her curiosity about the tree she'd touched in the yard, her mother believing she was some kind of Lorekeeper, her grandmother giving her an unopenable music box, and the secrets they'd kept from her.

She explained about finding the fox pup in her room, then having it appear here at Birchtree, and how it may not be a fox at all, but some other creature...

"...And just now, I heard it speak to me, in my mind." She tapped her head. "Just like the one from my dreams. Though, that one was full-grown, not a pup. She told me her name is Keia and that she is here to help me, to help the Stormbringer."

Finley had listened patiently the whole time, not interrupting or making any comment. Now, he stared down at his hands and nodded his head slowly.

Unsure what he was thinking, Neala sat awkwardly, shifting her weight to try and coax feeling back into her numb backside.

After several moments, Finn raised his head and met her eyes. His expression was unreadable as he murmured softly, "I can see why you're feeling overwhelmed."

With a sigh, he ran his hands along the ground and plucked a blade of grass, twirling it between his long fingers. "That is certainly a lot to take in over such a short amount of time."

Cupping the grass, he raised it to his lips and blew. Neala was surprised to hear a thin, high-pitched whistle come from his closed hands. As she listened, he played a short, squeaky tune.

Glancing at her with a smile, Finn asked, "Have you ever made a grass whistle before?" Neala shook her head, bemused.

Picking another bit of grass, he handed it to her. "Here. Hold it tightly between your thumbs, squeezing it with your tips and your palm." Neala fumbled, trying to make it stay in position.

Once she had it secured as best she could, she looked at Finn again. He nodded. "Good, okay, now blow through that gap, where the grass is being held. It takes some practice, but it will eventually make a whistling noise. Watch."

Neala concentrated as he opened his hands, leaving only his thumbs touching one another. Placing his lips on his hands, he blew gently, making the grass vibrate and give off a whistle. Wanting to try, Neala copied him, but all she produced was a fart-like raspberry.

Despite herself, Neala giggled. Finley chuckled and blew his grass whistle again, opening and closing his hands to change the tone of the notes.

Determined to get at least one whistle out of hers, Neala kept trying until, finally, a brief squeak emerged. Buoyed by her success, she sat back and let the grass blade fall from her fingers.

Letting his own drop, Finn's expression turned soft as he looked at her. "Everything is important in the Song of Life, Neala. Everyone tends to focus on the loud noises; the thunder of a storm, the crash of waves, the howling of winds, and the everyday sounds, like birdsong, animal calls, music made with instruments. It all has its place, of course."

His eyes were distant as his voice lowered until it was barely audible. "But the little things contribute, too. Oftentimes, they are what make the experience all the richer. Even the smallest blade of grass can make music if we stop to observe."

Finn reached out his hand and patted Neala's knee gently. "You are part of a bigger picture that's unfolding. There is much we still don't understand, and many mysteries still to solve."

He sighed wearily. "I can't give you many answers now, as much as I wish I could, and for that I am truly sorry. But please know that you are not alone, you are not weak, and there is definitely nothing wrong with you."

Rising to his feet, Finn held out his hand to help her up. "Thank you for telling me all of this. In future, please come to me if there is anything bothering you, okay? Or go to Clodagh, or Imelda. If I may, I would also advise you to confide in your friends - I am sure they care for you and want to help, if you will just let them in."

Indicating with his head, Finley gave her a wry smile. "Now, shall we go in? Those same friends are probably worrying about you right now. A belly full of warm food will also help, I am certain."

Neala nodded, a shiver running down her spine. She had almost forgotten about the rain while she had been speaking to Finn, but now she was aware of just how chilled she was.

By the time they reached the stairs, Neala's teeth were chattering so loudly that even Finn could hear it. With a chuckle, he said, "Hold still a moment." Placing his hands above her head, he closed his eyes.

Within seconds, Neala could feel the water evaporating off her like steam, warming her from her toes to her scalp. Gasping with delight, she realised she was completely dry. Beaming at Finn, she thanked him with a laugh.

Swiftly running his hands over his own clothes, he joked, "Nothing like a good steam clean to make you feel refreshed, is there?" Thanking him once more, Neala turned and walked into the dining hall.

Spotting Áine and Torin at one of the tables, Neala quickly loaded a tray with some hot stew, some crusty bread, and a cup of pumpkin soup. Her stomach growled hungrily, desperate for food. Adding a bowl of chocolate pudding to her tray, she hurried over to join her friends.

Áine's brow was creased with concern and she asked, "Neala, thank goodness. Are you okay? What happened earlier?"

Neala ducked her head apologetically. "I'm sorry, Áine. I'll explain everything, I promise. If I can just have some soup first, before my stomach bursts out of me, I swear, I'll tell you all about what's been going on."

To their credit, Áine and Torin listened intently to Neala's story, the same one she had told Finley. Between mouthfuls, she told them all about her dreams, about Lorcan and the púca on the beach, about feeling like her world was being turned upside down.

Once she had finished, Torin let out a low whistle. "No wonder you've been so jumpy." Leaning forward on his elbows, he frowned. "'Stormbringer', you said? I wonder...remember when we did that experiment at Áine's house? The one with the water? You were sucked up into a thunderstorm and nearly carried away, until Eilìs brought you back. Do you think that's linked somehow?"

Neala sat back, eyebrows raised. "Maybe. Eilìs said something then about me being sensitive to storms, didn't she?"

Áine had been quiet, but now she perked up. "She did say something like that, Neala - maybe we should talk to

Eilìs about this, too?" She gasped, her eyes lighting with interest.

"You said that Lorcan called you 'Stormbringer', too, right? He has power with lightning, something no one else has ever been able to master. Surely he has experience working with storms? Or, at the very least, he may have some knowledge about how you can connect with them so easily." She squinted at Neala thoughtfully. "Maybe you should speak to him?"

"Ah, yeah, I'd rather not." Neala screwed up her nose, remembering their last interaction. "But maybe I can talk to his brother? Eamon is a lot less...prickly."

Changing the subject, Neala asked Áine, "How was the fox – I mean, Keia, after I left? I feel bad for abandoning her. After all, she hadn't seen me for several days, then I slept the whole time I was with her."

Áine smiled gently. "Honestly, she did seem a little sad, but then she kind of just sighed and curled up on your pillow, like she was resigned to waiting. I'm sure she'll be fine. It's curious that she can speak to you, though. I honestly didn't hear anything. Do you think she really is the fox from your dreams? Well, except, not a real fox, obviously."

Torin had been lost in thought, but now he raised his head, eyes worried. "You don't think she's some kind of shape-shifter, do you? Like the púca?"

Neala frowned. "I don't think she's dangerous. But, after my run-in with the one on the beach, Finn explained to me that púca can be malevolent *or* helpful, so what if she is one of the helpful kind?"

"Either way, she's obviously an Otherworld creature; she has to be - nothing like that exists here. But the portals were sealed several centuries ago. How are they getting through?"

Neala exchanged glances with Áine. "I don't know, Tor. Finn didn't have any answers about that, either. He did say that there is a lot we don't know, and that there are mysterious things happening that they're trying to understand. I'm assuming 'they' are the Druids here."

Torin tapped absently on the wooden table, face cloudy. "I just wonder if it all has something to do with what's happened to Poppy. What if some Otherworld creature is the thing that took her?"

Neala's eyes widened and Áine placed her hand over her mouth. "But...surely Finn would have picked up on a magical Trace, though? If something like that had happened to her?" Áine whispered. Torin shrugged dejectedly.

"These kinds of creatures haven't been seen here in centuries, perhaps he can't sense their kind of magic? Or maybe whatever it is can shield itself from Trackers? We really don't know anything about what exists over there, only what the myths and legends have told us. If the Veil is lifting..."

The three fell silent, expressions ranging from fearful to unsure.

It was Neala who finally broke the silence, trying to lighten the mood. "Well, on that pleasant note, shall we head off? We're pretty much the only ones left down here." Gesturing to the almost-deserted hall, she spotted Eamon chatting with some friends at one of the far tables, including the girl she'd seen kissing Lorcan.

Her stomach twisted, and she decided there was no rush to talk to Eamon about his brother. That could wait for another day. Realising Torin was still distracted, Neala sighed and raised her eyebrows at Áine, looking for help.

Áine caught on and let out an exaggerated yawn. "Oh, yes, I am so tired. Come on, Tor, let's head to bed. We can think about this all again tomorrow. I'll talk to Eilìs at some stage, too."

Finally, Torin seemed to hear them. His eyes were still shadowed, but he smiled his familiar crooked grin at the girls. "All right, I can take a hint. Let's get out of here. 'Early to bed and early to rise, keeps a man healthy, wealthy and wise', right?"

The trio headed out of the dining hall together, before splitting off in the entrance hall, Áine and Neala heading to the left corridor. Torin bid them goodnight before loping down the right-side corridor to the boys' dorms.

Padding along silently beside Áine, Neala chewed her lip, lost in thought. It wasn't until they were inside the shamrock dorm that Áine spoke.

"Neala, do you really think some kind of awful creature took Poppy?" she whispered. Neala shrugged sadly, not having any answers. At the sound of Áine's voice, Keia pricked up her ears and stared at Neala, blue eyes almost glowing in the light of the moon shining through the window.

Striking a match from the box on her desk, Áine carefully sent little balls of flame to the candelabra, filling the room with soft light. Neala watched her with awe.

"When did you learn to do that?"

Áine blushed shyly. "My fire element is regenerative - we practiced lighting candles on the first day." The corner of Neala's mouth twitched wryly.

"Hmm, with destructive fire as my attribute, I may leave the candles to you, if that's all right?" Áine giggled, and Neala's whole body relaxed. For the first time since arriving, she felt light and happy.

It feels good to have gotten that all off my chest, she mused as Áine gathered her things for a shower. *Hopefully things will be easier now.*

As Áine washed, Neala sat on her bed and reached out a hand to stroke Keia's soft fur. The fox was still wary, but she shuffled a little closer so Neala could touch her. "I'm sorry, little one," she murmured. "I'm still not used to all this magic stuff. I hope I didn't hurt your feelings. I'm glad you're here with me." Keia's tail twitched and she shuffled closer, leaning her chin on Neala's thigh.

"Happy with Stormbringer."

Prepared this time, Neala didn't flinch when she heard Keia's words in her mind. Deciding she would leave her shower until the morning, Neala went to the wardrobe to find some pyjamas. Someone had packed away her belongings and placed her empty suitcase on top of the wardrobe.

She sighed gratefully, making a mental note to thank Áine later, and pulled her clothes from the drawer. Wondering how she could still be so tired, Neala could barely keep her eyes open as she climbed into bed, Keia moving up to cuddle on the pillow next to her. She was asleep before Áine had even finished her shower.

~ 19 ~

Neala had been staring at the ceiling for hours, watching the sunlight slowly creep into the room, dissolving the shadows. Next to her ear, Keia was snoring softly, occasionally twitching her tail or her ears, lost in some dream. *I hope it's not as confusing as mine*, she thought to herself as Keia's fluffy tail tickled her cheek once more.

Apparently there had been some unfinished business from Neala's dream the previous afternoon, because as soon as she was asleep, she found herself back at the pitch-black clearing. The scene was exactly as it had been when Áine had woken her from her nap.

With a weary sigh, Neala had called out, "Is anyone there?" Like usual, no answer had come.

Deciding to wait it out, she'd tucked her legs beneath her and lay down on the damp grass, splaying her arms and legs like a starfish. "I wonder what would happen if I fell asleep in these dreams? Or would that break the space-time continuum or something?" she'd wondered aloud, trying to fill the silence.

Even the mournful owl had vanished in this alternate dreamscape. The fox, too, was gone. *Presumably she's now sleeping beside my body in the 'real' world*, Neala had thought with amusement. Humming to herself, she'd crossed her feet and closed her eyes, knowing from experience that someone or something would soon come to speak with her.

"Well, aren't we a sassy one."

Neala had jumped. "Finally..." she'd muttered, pulling herself up on her elbows.

Standing at her feet was an old crone, her face obscured by the hood of a tartan cloak. In her gnarled hand, she held a wooden staff topped with a silver handle. Without warning, she'd rapped Neala smartly on the ankle with it.

Yelping with pain, she'd scrambled to her feet. "Excuse me? What was that for?"

The crone had laughed, a harsh sound like a crow cawing. "Because I can. Respect your elders, dearie, or there will be more where that came from."

About to snap back, Neala's words had caught in her throat. The old woman was pushing back her hood, revealing the ugliest face Neala had ever seen.

One eye had been lost somehow, leaving her with only a puckered eye socket on one side, while her other eye was unnaturally blue and bulbous. Her skin was covered in warts and when she'd cackled, Neala could see that her maw was mainly blackened gum with hardly any teeth to speak of.

What remained of the crone's hair was straw-like and white, almost like whiskers poking from her scalp rather than soft, fluffy clouds. Trying not to stare in horror, Neala focused on the crone's shoulder instead.

"What is it, child? You would rather a beautiful maid - someone more like my sister?"

Neala could not bring herself to meet that unnatural eye when she'd answered, "I can't judge, I don't know your sister. Or who you are, for that matter."

The crone had clucked her tongue angrily, making Neala cringe at the sucking sound her toothless gums made. "Of course you don't. No one cares for the Old Ones anymore in this Cursed World."

Her voice had grown soft, and Neala had shivered as a chill swept over her, goosebumps springing up all over her body. "I am winter, child. I am the storm and the ice and the cold of the mountains. I am as old as time and wiser than the most ancient of beings. They call me 'An Cailleach Bhéara'."

Neala had begun to tremble then, a mix of the cold and a growing sense of trepidation. As the crone had spoken, her voice had changed, echoing with the howl of wolves and the screech of wind through rock.

It had chilled Neala to her bones, and it took everything she had to remain standing. Closing her eyes, she'd spoken through chattering teeth. "I-I am sorry if I have offended you, C-Cailleach. I didn't mean to."

At once, the oppressing weight that had been filling the clearing abated, and Neala had hugged herself tightly, still shuddering. She felt like her entire body had been frozen; like she would never feel warm again. Forcing herself to meet the Cailleach's stare, she inclined her head politely.

Cawing with laughter again, the crone jabbed Neala with her cane. "You are young. Young people are prone to rudeness. I will forgive you this time. But learn from your mistakes."

Wincing as she rubbed her freshly-bruised shoulder, Neala had chewed her lip before asking tentatively, "Are you the one who has been sending me these dreams, the ones with the crossroads? Is Keia yours?"

The crone shook her head, lips pursed. "No, she belongs to another. Though both had come here at my command. I believed sweet little Keia would be less...distressing for you, at first. Unlike scary old me."

Neala opened her mouth again, but the Cailleach silenced her with an icy glare. "No more questions – I have already meddled enough. You are nearing the point of no return, my Stormbringer – things are falling into place swiftly now. A storm is coming, like none we have ever seen – which way the winds shall blow will depend on you."

Waving her hand, the Cailleach had tottered away from Neala, hobbling toward one of the roads leading out of the clearing. Neala had taken a step closer, listening intently. Was she going to get some answers at last?

Gesturing with her cane, the crone had explained, "As you can see, the ways forward from here are unknown. In all mortal destinies, there comes a time when we Divinities must step back and allow you to exercise free will, as is your mortal right. The path you choose next will change the course of the future, child – for all of us. The fate of both worlds rests with you."

The crone paused, her face darkening. "I cannot visit you in this place again – She is already growing suspicious. The risk is too great." She'd cupped Neala's chin tightly in claw-like fingers. "I will be waiting, Neala Stormbringer. Do not disappoint me."

As soon as the Cailleach had finished speaking, Neala had woken, drenched in a cold sweat. Dazed and confused, she had lain still, waiting for her heartbeat to slow and her muscles to stop trembling.

Now, with the sun almost completely risen over the horizon, she decided it was light enough to get up and have a shower without feeling guilty if she woke Áine.

Moving carefully so she wouldn't disturb Keia, she pulled an outfit from her wardrobe and crept into the bathroom. Letting out a long breath, she stripped and turned on the hot water, watching as the shower filled with steam.

Once she was clean and dressed, Neala stared at her reflection in the mirror. *'The fate of both worlds rests with you'...What does that even mean? Why me? I'm nothing special...am I?*

Poking her tongue out at herself, Neala swiped her hand over the mirror, smudging the steam. "No. Today, I am just a girl going to her lessons. I am nothing more. No more talk of crones or storms or destinies."

Resolute, Neala pulled the door open and stepped out, checking to see if Áine had stirred, but she was still fast asleep, face barely visible under her plush doona.

Keia, however, was awake and shifting restlessly on the bed. Neala raised her eyebrows and whispered, "I suppose you need a toilet break, huh?"

Keia whined pitifully, and guilt jabbed Neala's stomach. "Sorry, Keia, I'll organise some sort of litterbox or something in here, okay? Then you won't have to wait for me every time."

Patting her ivy as she walked past, Neala carefully scooped Keia up and carried her gently out of the dorm and through the building until she got to the doors. Easing them open, she placed her on the ground as soon as she was able, and Keia wasted no time in finding a patch of grass to relieve herself on.

Standing on the entrance steps, arms folded against the morning chill, Neala stared out over the grounds. Ahead of her lay the hills they had landed in when they were teleported by the birch trees. It was hard to believe this would be her first proper day of lessons since arriving.

"Better late than never, right?" she mumbled to herself as Keia scrambled back up the steps toward her. With a final glance at the peaceful landscape stretching away before her, Neala breathed deeply, allowing the serenity to fill her from head to toe, then made her way back inside.

*****

Joining her friends for breakfast, Neala wondered if she should tell them about this latest dream. But a tightening in her chest stopped her. *They've gone along with it all so far, even accepting the mind-talking dream fox. But a storm deity? Fates of worlds resting on a choice I have to make? Yeah, I might leave that story for another day.* Reaching for her cup of juice, she brightened. *At least the lessons will distract me today.*

Flicking her gaze from Áine to Torin, Neala suddenly realised something obvious. "Oh, Tor, you won't be at lessons with us, will you? I forgot you had your initiate year last year. Who is your Druid?"

Torin had just taken a huge bite of his bacon and egg sandwich, and he rolled his eyes at Neala in mock exasperation. Once he'd swallowed, he answered, "I'm part of Druid Brian's group. He finds unusual ways to teach us, usually through doing something hands-on or physical rather than with books and things. It works better for me because I can't read that well."

Neala's eyebrows raised in surprise. "Really? I didn't know that."

Torin shrugged, picking up the last half of his sandwich. "It's no big deal, I just struggle with letters and things sometimes. They get all jumbled together and I can't make sense of them. Finn thinks that's why dance is easier for me than playing an instrument. Reading music does the same thing - it mixes up in my head. I play by ear, when I have to, but dance comes easier." He grinned. "Are you going to take the dance elective, Neals?"

She shook her head vehemently. "No way. I'm hardly coordinated enough when I'm walking, let alone dancing. I was thinking animal husbandry might be fun. I did work with animals a lot on the farm, so it's something familiar. What about you, what elective have you chosen?"

Neala turned her attention to Áine, but found her staring into the distance, a thoughtful look on her face. Spotting her plate, Neala noticed that she'd hardly touched her banana or porridge. "Áine? Is everything okay?"

Áine blinked and turned back to Neala, still frowning slightly. "Oh, yes, sorry. I was just...thinking. What was the question?"

"Neala was asking about your elective," Torin replied, before Neala could answer.

"I signed up for visual arts. Eilìs does it and she loves it, so I thought I'd try it, too. Animals aren't really my thing, and I'm not passionate about dance like you, Tor, so it seemed like the logical choice. Well, apart from not choosing one at all."

Áine pushed her porridge around with her spoon, then dropped it into the bowl. "Sorry, I'm not feeling very well this morning, I'll meet you in music soon, Neala." Abruptly, she stood and hurried out of the dining hall, the other two staring after her worriedly.

"Did she mention anything to you this morning? About feeling unwell?" Torin asked Neala.

She shook her head with a frown. "No, I hardly saw her. I got up early to let Keia out, but Áine was still asleep. By the time I got back, she was already gone. I hope she's okay."

Torin folded his hands behind his head and leaned back in his chair, tilting it dangerously far. Casting his gaze around the room, his eyes settled on Lorcan, seated alone at the table closest to the door. Hiding his sneer, he jerked his head at Neala, muttering, "There's your mate."

Turning to see who he was talking about, she sighed. "I don't know why I got so mad talking with him yesterday. I couldn't stop myself, I was feeling so irritated; my skin was really itchy, like it was burning."

Shaking her head, she turned the conversation back on Torin. Imitating his head-flick, she gestured to Jaz, who was holding court at a nearby table, her companions giggling and laughing as she relayed some amusing story to them. "What about your mate, then, *Rambo*?" she teased.

That made Torin snort. "I dare you to name one person here who isn't Jaz's mate," he chuckled. "She's in Druid Brian's group with me."

He pinched the bridge of his nose, sighing in amusement. "Jaz is a league unto herself. Giving people ridiculous nicknames seems to be her favourite hobby, too. The moment she found out my sport is boxing I was stuck with

Rambo. Which doesn't even make sense - Rocky was the boxer. But that's Jaz." Shrugging, he asked, "What has she dubbed you?"

Neala grimaced. "Newbie."

Torin screwed up his nose. "Wow, she's slipping. That's not overly original. Perhaps she'll find something better for you later on." He leaned forward, eyes glinting wickedly as he grinned at Neala. "Is there anyone else you want me to tell you about? Since we're indulging our inner gossips, of course?"

She giggled, shaking her head. "No, I think that will do me for today. Thanks, though."

Expression changing to one of concern, Neala started gathering up her things. "Anyway, I better get going. I want to check on Áine before we go to our music lesson, she seemed really off this morning. What are you up to next?"

Torin gave a big stretch, then pushed his chair out from the table. "This morning we're heading down to the lake, we're going to look at manipulating water like a physical object. You know, holding balls of it in our hands and stuff. It's pretty cool. If you see me walking around with soaked trousers later, that's totally the reason, okay?"

Neala laughed and stood, grabbing her tray. "Of course. I'd never assume anything else." With a wink, she carried her tray over to the servery.

As she was leaving the hall, she spotted a tiny figure hiding in the shadows by the doorway. Raising an eyebrow, she watched as Keia toddled forward, looking as sheepish as a fox can. "Excuse me, missy? And how did you get down here, huh? I left you napping on my bed."

Wearily, she reminded herself that this was the same creature who had magically found her way out of Dana's carry cage, through the birch tree circle, and into the entrance hall without breaking a sweat.

"Hmm. So you're able to do all that, yet, somehow, you still need me to take you outside for toilet breaks, do you?" Keia huffed out a breath, turning her nose up snootily. Neala giggled. "You definitely aren't a real fox, are you?"

Kneeling down, she gestured for Keia to come. "C'mon, then. If you insist on being with me, I'll have to find something to carry you around in." Scooping her furry companion up, Neala made to walk off when she felt her skin prickle.

Running her tongue over her teeth, Neala turned slowly, already knowing who she would find. Lorcan had come to a stop in the doorway, but his expression was not what Neala was expecting.

Gone was the usual self-assured smirk. Instead, his face was stony and pale, and a light sweat had broken out on his upper lip. Staring at Keia tucked in Neala's arms, he whispered hoarsely, "I knew it. You *are* the one. The one who..."

Before she could say anything, Lorcan's face turned thunderous, and he balled his hands into fists. Clutching Keia to her chest, Neala could sense the air around them heating, pressure building in intensity.

Just when she was about to cry out in pain, he suddenly stopped and a strange expression crossed his face. If she didn't know any better, Neala would have said he looked distraught. Just like that, the pressure dropped and the air cooled.

Without another word, Lorcan strode towards the entrance doors, thrusting his hands forward. A rush of wind blew before him, slamming the doors open with a bang. Within seconds, he was gone.

Neala stood, stunned, as several Bards nearby started muttering angrily, pointing to the doors. "Bad luck follows when the east wind blows," a deep voice murmured behind her.

Turning, she spotted a man she hadn't seen before. He was tall, taller than anyone Neala had ever met, with skin as dark as ebony. Black eyes stared down at her from a broad face, his expression unreadable.

As suddenly as he had appeared, the giant Bard left, his strides eating up the ground as he beelined toward the boys' dorm corridor.

Shaking her head, Neala stroked Keia absently. *Bad luck follows when the east wind blows'? Is that why they call him that?*

As she let out a long breath, Neala felt the sudden urge to call her mother. The time had passed so quickly, she'd hardly given a thought to the fact that she had never been apart from Dana so long. Guilt gnawed at her stomach. There had been no point bringing her phone with her; she figured there was unlikely to be any service here. But she wondered if perhaps Druid Imelda had a phone she could use.

Vowing to ring her mother during free time that afternoon, Neala muttered to herself, "All the weirdness can wait until later. I have a music lesson to get to. Preferably without any more drama, am I right?"

Keia had been staring at the entrance doors, ears pricked, ever since Lorcan had burst them open. Now, she tore her gaze away and looked up at Neala.

"*Music.*"

Neala smiled. "Yes, music. Exactly." Wondering whether she had enough time to return to the dorm and check on Áine, she wandered into the entrance hall, looking for a clock. Instead, she found Finn, who was descending the stairs, looking thoughtful. Spotting Neala, he grinned.

"Ah, you're the first one here. Excellent. The others shouldn't be far away, then we'll head out."

Neala was puzzled. "Out? As in, outside?"

Finn beamed. "Of course. Where better to practice music than surrounded by nature? We'll pop by the music room first, though, so you can choose an instrument. The classroom is upstairs on the second floor, but I rarely use it for anything other than storage."

He leaned against the stair railing and tapped his fingers lightly. "What made that bang before, do you know?"

Neala felt sheepish, despite knowing she hadn't done anything wrong. "It was Lorcan. He came out of the dining hall, then went all weird and pale when he saw Keia and me. He muttered something about –"

She hesitated. "Um, well, I didn't really hear it properly. Then he made some wind blow the doors open and stormed out."

Finn's eyes narrowed for a moment, before returning to a neutral expression. "Hmm, interesting. That's fine, I'll speak to him later and work out what happened. In the meantime, here come the others."

Turning, Neala saw that several Bards had begun filtering in. She recognised one or two but felt a little awkward when she remembered that her fellow initiates had already spent several days together while she was in the healer's rooms.

Keia seemed to sense her nerves and gave her hand a gentle lick. Smiling gratefully Neala tried to ignore the curious stares and looked for Áine.

By the time she raced in, face flushed, Finn was just clapping his hands together. "All right, attention you lot. Today we have Neala joining us at last, so make her feel welcome. Let's head on up and grab your instruments, then we'll make our way out to the greenhouse to start with. It's a lovely clear morning for a change, so we may even go into the woodland a ways. Understood? Good - let's go. Neala, over here with me, please."

Giving Áine an apologetic shrug, Neala shuffled closer to Finn while the other students brushed past her, chatting amongst one another as they climbed the stairs. Falling into step beside him, she listened as he explained more about his lessons.

"As you already know, music is the core of our power. Without the ability to understand the natural rhythm and flow of nature, our magic can't be fully utilised. The elements have their own songs and tend not to bother with someone who can't tap into that. By studying music in this form - through instruments - we learn to centre ourselves, to listen for the slightest change in tone or pitch, and to work in harmony with one another.

"Many Bards struggle to see how important music is; they are more excited to make fire dance in their palms or summon a whirlpool with their mind. But, without the fundamentals, we cannot realise our full potential. Music is the language of the universe, Neala. Everything is part of the Song of Life, and it is important to understand that."

Clapping her lightly on the shoulder, Finn moved further ahead, squeezing past students until he was at the front of the group.

Neala hardly noticed Áine move in beside her as they walked down the hallway, heading the opposite way to where Eamon had taken her to see Druid Imelda. Her mind was playing Finn's words over and over. The way he'd spoken about music, his passion for it...

It wasn't until they came to a halt that she quickly whispered, "Sorry, I was completely lost in thought then. Finn's words were so powerful."

Áine smiled softly, mumbling back, "I know, he gave us the same speech on our first day. I got goosebumps."

About to ask what instruments she had chosen so far, Neala was cut off by Finn raising his hand. "Now, as always, remember to cleanse your instrument before you use it, okay? Neala, I'll show you what I mean in a moment. Everyone else, no pushing or shoving this time. Once you have made your choice, head back down to the entrance hall, please."

Swinging the door open, Finn stepped aside as the eager students pushed past to find their instruments. Once Neala reached him, he said, "You can choose any instrument you like, but before you take it, bring it to me and I'll explain how to cleanse it. Every time someone uses an instrument, they pass their essence, their magical trace, to it. Those who are sensitive to it can sometimes feel it and it throws them off; they can't play purely through their own power, because they can sense the other magic on it. Not everyone is that sensitive, but it's a good habit to get into regardless."

Neala nodded, already itching to explore her options. Keia wriggled in her arms until she was forced to put her down or risk dropping her. With a snort, Keia sat beside Finn's boots. *"Stormbringer choose. I wait."*

Grinning, Neala nodded and walked into the music room.

Her mouth opened in awe as she looked around. Every wall was hung with instruments, from guitars to harmonicas. Lyres, harps, violins, cellos – there were so many stringed instruments to choose from.

The woodwinds were just as numerous, with flutes, clarinets, saxophones, piccolos, even traditional Irish tin whistles. An assortment of brass instruments, including trumpets and various horns, were stacked on shelves in the corners, along with several giant tubas. Percussion was not forgotten, with drums of all sizes scattered around the room, from traditional hide drums to a full modern kit.

Unsure where to start, Neala closed her eyes. Listening to her instincts, she opened her eyes and headed straight for the woodwinds, reaching for the flutes. It was the instrument she felt the most comfortable with, having been the first she had learned, taught by her mother.

Feeling a tug in her chest, Neala ran her hands along the numerous flute cases until she felt her palm itch. Drawing the case from the shelf, she clicked the clasps open.

With a gasp, Neala realised this was not the kind of flute she was used to. Unlike her silver one at home, this flute was made of redwood, with only its keys and connector sections wrought with silver. It was beautiful to behold, and she loved it immediately.

Spotting Áine, who was holding up two lyres to compare them, Neala noticed that, despite being the last to enter the room, she was one of the first to choose her instrument. Feeling pleased, she carefully closed the case and took her flute over to Finn, who smiled broadly.

"I knew you wouldn't take long. Who did you choose today?"

"This one, she called to me straight away," she answered, flushing slightly. Keia yipped at her, and Neala shushed her with a finger, though a smile tugged at her mouth. As Finn drew the different parts from the case and assembled the flute, Neala watched the others for a little while.

She vaguely recognised one of the girls, the one with the bouncy curls who had told them Poppy had died, and she remembered the boy with the long, jet-black ponytail, but the others weren't familiar.

As she glanced around, she heard one of the girls, who was rolling her eyes and looking bored, lean over to pony-tail-boy next to her and whisper, "This has to be the most useless class here. It's not even magic - it's just music. Even humans can do this, this sucks."

The boy nodded in agreement, carelessly dropping the saxophone he'd been looking at onto the floor.

Neala felt heat rise in her cheeks, fists clenching at her sides. She wanted to speak up for Finley and scold these Bards for being so disrespectful. But a gentle hand on her shoulder made her pause, and she turned to see Finn giving her a sad smile.

"Let it go, Neala."

"But, Finn, they can't—"

"Like I said before, some people just want to do the 'big' magic - the dramatic and showy things. Others, like you, can appreciate the smaller, fundamental magics. Like music. Or the humble blade of grass." With a wink, he handed her the wooden flute.

She sighed and nodded, ignoring the other Bards and giving her full attention to Finn. "Now, to cleanse something, you are washing any trace of other magics off of it. In cases like this, that magical trace will be minimal, like a tiny layer of dust. The more magic an object has had worked into it, the trickier it gets to clean. And some objects can't be cleansed at all, no matter how hard you try. Something that has had blood on it, for instance, will forever have that trace of magic on it, because it has been imbibed with the literal lifeblood of the Bard, or Druid, or whatever creature."

"Is that how you Track people? Like how you're Tracking Poppy?"

Finn jerked his head back and gave her a stern look. In a low whisper, he muttered, "This is not the place for such talk, Neala." His mouth twitched slightly. "But, if you must know, yes. That's how it works for most Trackers. Not all, though."

Tapping his nose secretively, Finn stood straight again, a smile tugging at his lips. "Now, back to cleansing. What you need to do is send your magic to the object and, basically, wipe it over. Like you would with a cloth or rag. Envision your magic flowing over the object, lifting the traces of foreign essence and forcing them to separate from the item. Once they are loose, you call on whichever element you feel most drawn to, to dispose of them.

"For example, I tend to bury them, giving them back to the earth. Others may burn them, or wash or blow them away. Whatever you choose, you need to make sure it is gone completely from you. The natural world can handle absorbing most magics, but we cannot. Our magic is far weaker and more easily corrupted by the powers of others. So always make sure you give it to one of the elements."

Neala was listening intently. Apart from her attribute tests, she hadn't deliberately used her power since her ill-fated experiment with the water at Áine's house, and part of her was nervous to access it now.

Sensing her reluctance, Finn folded his arms over his chest. "I'll help you for the first one, okay? It will soon become straightforward, but, for now, I'll walk you through it once we're outside. As for the rest of you," he raised his voice to address the whole room now. "Make your choices and move out - we're wasting the morning."

As the other students clamoured to select their instruments, Neala picked up Keia and cuddled her against her chest, realising Finn was still carrying her flute.

Without hesitation, Finn strode over to the rack of guitars and drew one off its hooks. Using it to gently nudge his students from the room, he marched them down the stairs and out into the crisp morning air.

20

The summer heat was making way for autumn chill now, and the air frosted Neala's breath slightly as she followed the others to the greenhouses. Áine, carrying her lyre carefully in her arms, moved up beside her.

Neala gave her a sidelong look and asked worriedly, "How are you feeling, Áine? You didn't seem like yourself at breakfast."

Áine gave her an over-bright smile and flicked her hair over her shoulders. "Oh, yes, it must have just been a headache. Maybe I slept funny? I'm fine now, truly."

Neala didn't believe her for a moment; Áine was a terrible liar. But she decided against pushing further.

Playing along, she mirrored Áine's smile and said, "Oh, that's good. I'm glad it was nothing serious."

Gesturing to Neala's empty hands, Áine asked, "Didn't you choose an instrument?"

Neala tilted her head at Finley, who was chatting with some other students as they walked. "Finn has my flute; he's going to show me how to cleanse it when we get to the greenhouse." Something she had been wondering played

309

on her mind now. "By the way, aren't we supposed to be calling him Druid Finley or something? Isn't that, like, the term for the teachers here?"

"No, Finn isn't a Druid. There's a whole process to earning the Druid rank - years and years of study and work. The Ovates, like Clodagh and Mercy, are those who are gifted in the arts of Seeing, or have more psychic-type powers." Her voice hitched, but she quickly covered it with a cough.

"They're basically at Druid level, but with extra abilities. Finn is one of the strongest Bards in the world, and is certainly capable of being a Druid, but he's never undertaken the initiations. He prefers to just be...Finley."

"Ohh," Neala nodded, making connections in her mind. "That's why Ovate Clodagh is different - she's a Seer? I have a million more questions about that, but I suppose I'll have to be patient."

She shook her head, confiding in Áine softly, "I feel so...lost here. I don't know if it's because I knew so little about all this before I came here, but it feels almost like I'm playing catch-up on even the most basic things that everyone else just does automatically."

Áine nudged her gently, giving her a proper smile this time. "You can't expect to just know everything, otherwise what is the point in learning?"

Her eyes lit up. "What if I show you the library during free time this afternoon? It's loaded with books and things, and Druid Keyes is happy to help with any questions." Cheeks flushed slightly, she added, "I spent a fair bit of time there while you were in the infirmary. I'd be happy to go with you?"

Neala beamed excitedly, then remembered the promise she'd made to herself earlier. Rubbing her forehead, she muttered apologetically, "I would love to, really, but I was hoping to find a way to call my mother this afternoon. I haven't been apart from her this long since forever, and I want to check in and see how she's going. But what about after dinner tonight? We can squeeze in a little time before curfew, right?"

Áine nodded, her face drooping slightly. "Yes, of course."

Neala didn't miss the flash of sadness that crossed her gaze, and she hurriedly apologised, "Oh, Áine, I'm sorry. Have I upset you?"

"Oh, it's nothing. I just – I wish my mother worried enough to check on Eilìs and me. Every year, Eilìs would come to Birchtree, but Mother never really made an effort to see how she was going. I mean, Eilìs and I would exchange letters through the year, but Mother and Father were always too busy with their projects, so I usually kept her up-to-date and I'd throw in the odd 'Mother misses you', or 'Father says hello', but that was about it. Now that I'm here, too, I wonder if they will even bother sending a card or anything?"

Now it was Neala's turn to nudge Áine's shoulder reassuringly. "How about, instead of worrying about them sending you letters, you focus on the fact that, this year, you don't have to write to Eilìs? You get to experience everything with her here and now. I heard someone saying there are lounges and things all over the school, what if you find one you and Eilìs like and make a regular catch-up date? Say, every Wednesday night you meet up with her and have a cuppa or something before bed? You couldn't do that before, could you?"

Coming to a halt, Áine met her eyes gratefully. "Yeah, you're right. I do love that I'm here with Eilìs now; I always missed her so much when she was away." She sighed. "All told, she's always been more like a mother to me than my real one ever has."

With a giggle, she continued, "And I'll still send letters home, but I'll write to the staff instead. I miss Charles and Colleen more than them, anyway. Maybe Colleen will even send some of her famous shortbread, if I ask nicely?"

Pleased that her friend had been cheered up, Neala glanced around. The rest of the class were now settling in around them, some leaning against the glass walls of the greenhouse while others sat cross-legged on the grass.

Gesturing for Áine to join her, Neala eased onto the grass and folded her legs, trying carefully not to jostle Keia too much. Wincing, she straightened her legs out, placed Keia on her lap, and leaned back on her hands instead. *Flexibility is not my thing*, she thought wryly as she rubbed her knees.

Her thoughts were interrupted by Finley clapping his hands loudly. "All right, everyone - today the focus will be on harmonising, okay? Getting everyone to work in-tune with one another. By now, you should all be familiar with the basics of what the notes are and how they are used in sheet music. But a lot of what we learn will be instinctual. We aren't a Secondary School band, after all." The students chuckled, glancing at one another.

"As Bards, music is in our nature, our very DNA. The Fae are master musicians, and they make the sweetest music anyone ever heard." His eyes were distant, as though his mind was elsewhere. "Not by reading it out of a book, but by playing from their very souls. That's where the magic happens."

Shaking his head, he refocused on the students in front of him. "Today, we are going to split into small groups and practice playing in harmony with one another, without pre-written music to follow. But first we cleanse the instruments."

Nodding firmly, he walked over to Neala. "I'll help you with this part, then we'll get to it. The rest of you, you know what to do."

Watching as her fellow students all sat up and placed their instruments in their laps, Neala saw various flashes of light beginning to surround them.

The boy with the long ponytail was placing his hands on the deer-hide drum resting on his knees and a scarlet light was flowing around his hands as he began running them over the instrument.

Neala was fascinated, watching the different colours coming from each person. Áine's magic flowed from her hands like butter, the pale-gold illuminating her face with its warmth.

Curious, Neala looked at her own palms. She remembered the blue-green of her magic, the pool she had seen within her when she tapped into her source. The cool teal of a mountain lake.

She had almost forgotten Finn was beside her until he gave a short cough. Guiltily, she met his gaze and mumbled, "Sorry, I was just wondering about the, uh..." She fumbled to find the words. The light? The glowing?

Finn chuckled. "About what colour your essence is? Admittedly, not everything we do with our power gets covered in pretty sparkles like this." He gestured to the circle of rainbow magics. "That's because, more often than not, our power is moving *through* something else. Like this."

He gestured to a stray leaf on the ground, which suddenly lifted into the air, spiralling in the mini-tornado he'd conjured up.

With a wave, he released the leaf, and it fluttered back to the ground. "All I did then was coax the wind to do my bidding; it wasn't *my* power that did that, do you see? It was the wind, acting on my request. That is essential to understand; believing that they are controlling the elements has led many Bards to disaster."

A shadow flashed across his features, and Neala was reminded inextricably of Torin. His face had made an almost-identical expression when he'd explained the same thing to her, about Bards trying to control elements. Had they witnessed it? The consequences of trying? It piqued her curiosity no end, but she pushed her musings aside, not wanting to miss what Finn was saying.

"The elements cooperate with us if we ask them, and if they want to. But things like this, like cleansing - that is coming directly from you. You are sending your *own* magical essence out to do a job, not the elements. Some Bards can use this power, known as the fifth element, or the element of Spirit, to work magic like they would any other element, but it is much harder to control, and much more dangerous."

Finn's face grew stern. "Using the spirit element means exactly that - pouring part of your own soul into performing magic. If you aren't careful, you can drain your entire life-force without even noticing until it's too late."

Neala nodded, eyes wide. She remembered the feeling of her essence being bonded with the water, back at Áine's house, and how she had become one with the storm, slowly being dragged further and further from her body. The memory still made her shudder.

Soft paws pressed against her chest, and she stared down into Keia's worried eyes. *"Stormbringer cold. Why afraid?"* Taking a deep breath, Neala stroked her gently and gave her a soft smile.

"I'm okay, little one. I just—" She screwed her nose up. "I just understand what Finley means, about being careful with our personal magic."

Finn gave her a tight-lipped smile. "Ah, yes, the storm bonding. That is a great, and awful, example of the kinds of things that can go wrong. When," he handed her the wooden flute, "you aren't under the careful watch of an instructor, at least." Neala grinned at him.

"For now, you will only be using a tiny amount of your personal power, just to give this girl a good dusting, really. And I'll be here to bring you back if something goes a bit ends-up."

He eyed her with raised brows. "Now, as I explained before, all you're doing here is running your power over the flute, gathering up any traces of other magic, and sending it away. My suggestion would be to just hand it over to the earth - that would be far simpler than any other method, since we're outside and sitting on the bare ground.

"Start by closing your eyes and breathing deeply, centring yourself, then take a strand of your power and send it through your hands as you wipe over the flute, okay? I'll observe for now, just in case."

Neala sat straighter, reluctantly folding her legs under her until she was sitting cross-legged. As if knowing she would be in the way, Keia scrambled out of Neala's lap and sat beside her instead, head cocked curiously as she watched.

Holding the flute in her hands, Neala took several deep breaths, focusing as hard as she could on letting her mind drift. Realising the irony in what she was doing, she smiled, and relaxed, releasing her grip on her thoughts.

As her muscles slackened, her breath slowed and she found herself facing inwards, staring at the pool of magic that was hers. Glinting in the darkness, her power stirred, rippling softly as it sensed her presence.

Stretching a hand toward it, Neala's mind-self touched the surface gently, drawing a sparkling thread away with her. Allowing the magic to spread over her hands until they glowed, she turned her mind-self away from her source and drifted back to her awareness.

She could feel the weight of the flute in her lap, could hear her quiet breaths drawing in and out of her lungs, and the steady pounding of her heart. Not wanting to lose concentration, Neala raised her hands, seeing them with her mind, still glowing with her power.

As she ran them from the head of the flute to the base, she noticed a strange tingle, like an itch in her magic. If she had to describe it as a physical sensation, she would have said she had a thorn in her palm.

Another little stab, and she now had two thorns attached to her. That seemed to be all, but she stroked the flute once more, to make sure she hadn't missed anything. Now it felt smooth under her magic - there was nothing more there.

Placing the flute back down, Neala plucked the magical 'thorns' from her palms and sent a trickle of her power down into the earth beneath her. A sigh escaped her lips; the earth was so solid, so comforting. A rumble made her magic tingle, and she realised the earth was humming.

"Yes, little one. You called?"

"I, um, please, Earth Mother, would you take these thorns - these traces of magic - from me? They are itching me."

"Of course, my Daughter. Place them down, I will gladly remove them for you."

Neala lay her palms flat on the ground, feeling the coolness of the grass and soil on her skin. Before she could even ask what she needed to do next, the itchy feeling in her magic was gone, and she felt clean again. Gratefully, she sent her magic deeper into the earth. *"Thank you, Mother."*

"Daughter, when you are overburdened, come to me with your troubles. I will always be here."

With her heart full of gratitude, Neala drew her magic back into her palms, then sent it to her source, letting it settle back into the teal pool at her core. Slowly, she drew her mind back into focus, feeling her muscles tensing as she blinked.

Becoming aware of how uncomfortable her legs were, she winced as she slowly unfurled them, rubbing her thigh as pins and needles raced down to her feet.

Clutching her flute, she looked at the other students, wondering if she looked as dazed as they did. Finn was beside her, running his hands swiftly over his guitar and flicking them to the side, as though he was swiping mud off it. Neala blinked in awe; Finn's power was copper-coloured and shone so brightly that she could hardly look at it.

In moments, he had brushed the last of the traces off the guitar and opened his eyes, beaming. Nodding as he glanced around, he met Neala's eyes.

"How did you go? You seemed to have it under control well enough."

Neala nodded, still feeling relaxed from her grounding with the earth. "Yeah, that went much better than last time."

Finn snorted and addressed the rest of the class. "Now that's all done, let's have a play." He started strumming absently on his guitar as he spoke, tuning it occasionally. "What we're going to do first is break off into small groups of three or four. There's, what, fifteen of us? So, let's do three groups of four, and one of three. Your job will be to work out how to play together in harmony, without sheet music to follow."

He gestured to the landscape around him. "You can split off into the woods or wherever if you don't want to be disturbed, but don't go too far. Neala, Áine, you two can come with me, the rest of you split into groups of four."

Neala and Áine exchanged glances but gathered their instruments obediently as the other students chatted loudly around them, calling for friends and picking partners. Once they had all been sorted, Finn called, "I'll bring you all back in around twenty minutes. Use the time wisely!"

As the students wandered off to secluded areas to practice their harmonising, Neala and Áine hung back, fiddling with their instruments absently. Finn left them briefly, answering a call from one of the groups. A string on one of the boys' guitars had snapped and he was looking panicked.

Unsure what else to do while she waited, Neala placed the flute up to her lips, feeling the familiar keys under her fingers. Blowing as softly as she dared, she ran through a quick C-major scale, the sound barely audible.

She placed it by her side again once she saw Finn start striding back over to them, his face expressionless. Áine sucked in a soft breath, hissing, "Neala, something's happened with Poppy – he's heard something."

Neala stared at Áine incredulously. "What? How could you possibly know that?"

But Áine only shook her head, not meeting her eyes. As soon as Finn was in earshot, she whispered, "Is there news about Poppy?"

Finn seemed taken aback. "How did...Well, yes. But I only found out early this morning. How do you...?" He narrowed his eyes, studying Áine thoughtfully, but she just looked away, rubbing the side of her head and avoiding his gaze.

Letting out a sigh, he continued reluctantly, "One of my scouts has heard some rumours - other Bards had been reported missing up north. There was a pattern, moving down the west coast. No one had really noticed as the Bards who were disappearing had all returned."

He scratched his chin absently. "And *that* was the pattern - they would disappear for a few days, sometimes up to a week, then show up again, completely unfazed. But the odd part is, none of them seemed to have any idea that they'd been gone at all. Like they'd been there the whole time."

Áine gasped. "Has Poppy returned, then? Like the others?"

Holding up a hand, Finn frowned. "Not exactly. My friends, Trackers like me, are searching, but there's no trace to follow, only rumours and whispers. What I am certain about, however, is that whatever is causing these disappearances, it's an Otherworld creature. They are difficult to track as they never leave a trace that we can follow, unlike humans or other Bards."

Finley turned away, rubbing his forehead in frustration. "I feel like I should *know* what we're dealing with, but it's been so many years, I can't remember..." He let out a frustrated growl. "I've been over here far too long. There's too much I've missed. For all I know, it's something new, something I haven't encountered before..."

Áine stared at him oddly. "But...what do you mean, you don't remember? No one has seen any Otherworldly creatures here for centuries, there's nothing *to* remember."

Finley jerked, apparently unaware that he'd been muttering aloud. Hurriedly back-tracking, he shook his head and said, "I just mean in my reading, that's all. I can't remember everything I've ever read about them."

Hoisting his guitar up, he glared sternly from Áine to Neala. "Now, girls, I promise I'll keep you updated if I hear any more about Poppy – Torin, too, of course. But, for now, we have a lesson to focus on. C'mon, let's go."

Turning away, he walked over to a patch of lawn in the sunshine, head bowed. Neala narrowed her eyes and glared at his back as he walked away. Áine nudged her as she gathered her lyre.

"He's lying. Well, not lying exactly...more like, only telling half the story," she muttered as the girls followed their teacher slowly. "I don't doubt he *has* read about the creatures of the Otherworld, but it almost sounded like he meant - that he..."

"That he should remember because he's *seen* them," Neala added. She hadn't missed his choice of words and was hardly convinced they had been accidental.

Keia chose that moment to wake with a jerk and begin scrambling to get out of Neala's arms. Surprised, she leaned over and let Keia jump to the ground. The fox landed with a light thump and restlessly started shaking her fur out, blue eyes eyeing Neala sidelong and ears pressed flat against her head.

Noticing they had reached Finley now, Neala pushed her suspicions to the back of her mind and sat down beside him, placing the flute on her knees. Áine took a seat on the other side, so they formed a triangle.

Calmer now, Finley replaced his angry expression with his usual friendly one. "All right, now, working in harmony is the focus today, girls. One of the easiest ways to get started is to have someone begin playing, setting the tempo and the key, then the rest join, adding their part to the music, okay? Slowly building the harmony piece by piece."

He glanced from one to the other. "Neala, why don't you start us off this time? Then Áine, you join her, and I'll come in at the end. You can play anything you want, whatever you feel – it's our job to match your song, okay?"

Neala didn't realise how hard she was clutching the flute until she felt the keys digging into her palm. *What do I play, though? Do I play something I know, like, something by Beethoven? No, we aren't playing orchestra songs, he said that. I guess I'll just...make it up, then.*

Not knowing what else to do, Neala took a deep breath, closed her eyes, drew the flute to her lips, and blew. The notes were deep and rich, the wooden flute giving a much clearer sound than her silver one had. Turning away, Neala tuned out all thought of Finn and Áine. Instead, she played her story.

She played for her sorrow, the grief over the loss of her father, that still clung to her like a shroud, even when she thought it had faded. She played for her anger, for the betrayal that she had felt when she learned her mother had lied to her. She played for love, for the friends she had made, and for the magic she had found since coming to Ireland. On and on she played, releasing everything through the notes that sang from the flute.

*****

As Neala's confidence visibly grew, the magic she was sending into her music expanded, creating shimmering pictures in the air, glittering echoes of the images in her mind as she played. Finn and Áine were watching it unfold, their hearts humming with the emotions Neala was conjuring.

They felt her pain, her loneliness, and it brought Áine to tears. Finn, too, felt it sink under his skin, and he closed his eyes, the depth of Neala's power making him sigh.

After a while, the song became lighter, echoing the happiness which had replaced her grief. Watching curiously, Áine and Finn saw images of their own faces form through Neala's magic, along with Torin and Jaz, and even Eamon.

Feeling compelled to join now, Áine settled her lyre in her lap and strummed the strings, adding her own notes to the song.

*****

As the new notes sounded, Neala's ears pricked. She could feel Áine's presence in her mind, a glowing yellow shape forming at the edge of her awareness. Wondering what was happening, she opened her eyes and almost gasped. Not wanting to halt her playing, she kept her breath steady, blowing across the flute even as she marvelled at the scene before her.

There were images playing out in the air between them, glowing with the teal of her magic. Flickering her eyes at Áine as yellow images merged with the teal, Neala's heart gave a leap. A rush of gratitude for her friend filled her magic, and she watched as the images shifted, changing to reflect the shift in her emotions.

Flicking with golden and teal-blue light, the combined magics transformed into the girls faces smiling at one another, blurring then reforming as them sitting beside one another, talking sombrely. They were playing in harmony, their music forming the images of their friendship.

Áine took over the melody, then, and Neala stepped back to provide the harmony. As Áine led the song, the images changed to snippets of her life; of her and Eilìs as young girls, of nights spent listening to Colleen read her bedtime stories, of a tiny Áine clutching her mother's skirt while she tried to prise herself away, a suitcase gripped in her hand.

Stroking Keia softly, Finn watched thoughtfully for a moment, then reached for his guitar. Neala lifted a brow curiously as he strummed some chords, then added his own melody. Copper-orange fire surrounded the yellow and teal, then the song began to tell Finley's story.

In her mind, Neala felt Finn's presence, and it almost overwhelmed her. It was as though she were looking into the sun.

As Áine joined her in the background, providing the harmony, Finn's melody took over. Neala felt a new wave of sorrow, one far greater than her own, which was quickly replaced by an overwhelming sense of duty, of the acceptance of fate and placing all trust in destiny.

There was love and joy and loss, anger and hope, all merging into an endless stream, flowing like a river across the breadth of time. Compared to her story, Finn's stretched for a lifetime and beyond. It was enough to make her breath catch in her throat, but she played on, not wanting to disrupt the music.

Finn's melody slowed now, and Neala knew he was playing for the day he'd met her, when their paths converged. A key drifted into view in the air before her, a key in the shape of a leaf, just like her birthmark. A ring of six other keys, all with different leaf shapes, materialised behind the first one, which swirled once before slotting into place and completing the circle.

As the ring of keys disappeared, the song began to change, becoming softer, less certain. Realising it was drawing to a close, Neala took a deep breath and blew one last note, listening to it waver until it finally faded.

Somewhat sadly, she watched as the last traces of teal, yellow, and copper sparkles faded away. Swallowing hard, she was startled to discover her cheeks were soaked with tears. Turning, she saw Áine wiping her hand over her own cheeks, and Finn was sitting with his guitar in his lap, rubbing his face.

No one spoke straight away, each lost in their thoughts. Neala felt raw, like all her emotions has been brought to the surface. *Not just mine*, she realised. *I'm feeling theirs, too. Áine's and Finn's.*

With a sigh, Finley leaned back on his hands and stared up at the sky. "That was very well done, girls. Perhaps a wee bit more intense than I'd planned, if I'm being honest." He winced. "Be sure to connect with the earth now, to ground yourselves. Otherwise you'll be all out of sorts for the rest of the day."

Rising to his feet, Finn groaned, stretching his back. Once he was sure Áine and Neala were okay, he moved away and raised his hand to his mouth. With a loud whistle, louder than should have been possible, Finn summoned the rest of the students back. Once they were all assembled, he glanced around at them all.

"So, who successfully harmonised with their group?" A scattering of hands rose, while other students scowled. The girl who had been so dismissive of Finn's class earlier sneered, rolling her eyes. Neala noticed her hand stayed firmly by her side.

Finn noticed too, and he ran his fingers lightly over his guitar. "Well, that's a good start. For those who may be wondering about what this has to do with anything," he deliberately raised his eyebrows, "the lesson is this: unless you can learn to work in harmony with the energies around you, you will find it difficult to convince the natural elements that they should work with you. It goes both ways – they will respect and listen to you only if you respect and listen to them.

"So, if your ultimate goal is being able to do something like this—" he strummed a sharp chord, and the earth below the students' feet began to rumble. The snooty girl shrieked, losing her balance as she fell to her knees in the dirt. Neala managed to ride the wave out, grinning at Finn, who winked. "Then you'd best keep practicing. Until next time, you are free to go."

Neala and Áine hung about awkwardly while the other students gathered their things and began moving back toward the school building. Sensing their unspoken questions, Finn ducked his chin to his chest and sighed.

Quietly, so only they would hear, he murmured, "Girls, you need to get to your next lesson. Don't worry about Poppy - I'll find her and work out what's happening. I promise." He slung his guitar onto his back and reached out to pat Neala on the shoulder. "I know it's been a very overwhelming couple of months. If you need to talk to anyone, you know where to find me."

Turning to Áine, he continued, "And as tempted as you will be to speak to your sister about Poppy's disappearance and all of this, please keep it just between us for now. You already know more than you should – until I have more answers, stay quiet."

He raised a finger to shush Áine when she opened her mouth to protest. "No, I mean it. Now, if you would get along, I need to speak with Torin and Imelda, to give them the same update."

With that, he nodded at the girls and turned on his heel, striding away towards the lake, guitar bouncing against his back. Neala pursed her lips tightly but didn't call after him.

With her flute in one hand, she scooped Keia up with the other and cuddled her tightly against her chest. Áine had a glazed look in her eyes, one Neala recognised; she had no doubt Áine would be making a trip the library the first opportunity she got.

Sighing, she pressed her face into Keia's soft fur. "I've never liked mysteries, have I mentioned that?"

Keia rubbed against Neala's cheek, and the girl laughed. "Okay, except for you. You're by far my favourite mystery."

Giving Áine a gentle prod with her flute, she asked, "Shall we head back up? We need to drop these instruments off before the next class."

But Áine still looked dazed, and she muttered to Neala groggily, "Actually, I...I think I need to lie down for a while. I'm still not – not feeling well."

Neala glanced at her in concern. Áine's skin was always pale, but now it was almost green, and her eyes were still unfocused and bleary – they almost looked milky, reminding Neala alarmingly of Druid Orwyn.

Worried, she placed Keia on the ground and linked her arm through Áine's. "Yeah, you don't look good at all. Something's wrong with your eyes...Here, let's get you to Mercy, we'll find out what's wrong."

To Neala's surprise, Áine wrenched her arm out of her grip, and she stumbled away, lyre still clenched in her hand. "No, just leave me alone. I'll – I'll see you later. I have to go – now. I just – I just have to go."

"Áine!" Neala called, but she was already hurrying away, one hand pressed against her forehead as she followed the path back up to the manor.

Neala stared down at Keia, who tilted her head up to meet her gaze. "Well, I guess we'll just...leave her to it, then," she muttered worriedly. With a sigh, she started walking, mumbling to Keia, "I don't suppose you know where our next class is held, do you?"

21

The history and lore lessons, Neala soon discovered, were taught by Druid Orwyn in a room on the top floor of the school. Once she had returned her flute and caught up with her fellow initiates, Neala followed them up to what they called 'the Blue Room'.

It resembled a large study more than a classroom. There were no desks; the room was filled with mis-matching couch chairs and lounges, and there were shelves loaded with books along every wall, as well as tapestries and paintings. Blue flower-patterned wallpaper revealed to her how the room had earned its name. A fireplace took up centre-stage against the far wall, but it remained unlit for now. Neala imagined it would be well-used during the coming winter months.

Glancing around, she saw that Áine hadn't arrived yet. Concerned, she was about to head out and look for her when Orwyn shuffled through the doorway, a cane in hand, though he didn't appear to need it.

Neala tapped her hands on her thighs, wrestling with her guilt at not looking for her friend, then decided to take a seat. She hastily moved over to a free chair in the corner by the door, and sat down, placing Keia on her lap.

As the rest of the students found places to sit, Orwyn scanned the room with his blind eyes, nodding to himself. He paused when he reached Neala and grinned, chuckling softly. "Ah, yes, our strange visitor. Welcome, little Keia."

Neala blushed and sank back into the cushions as the eyes of the other students bored into her, some curious, others narrowed in envy. Keia, ignoring them, sat up and gave her fluffy tail a small wag.

With a stamp of his cane, Druid Orwyn called the class's attention back to him. Standing by the fireplace, he folded his hands over the top of his cane and began to speak.

"As you remember, over the past few lessons we have been discussing the history of the Tuatha Dé Danann and their journey to the Otherworld. Neala, you will need to catch up in your own time, I will give you some material to read."

Neala nodded, hoping she wouldn't be singled out in every lesson today.

"We will eventually delve deeper into their fascinating history, but, for today, I want to discuss more about how Bards came into existence."

He cleared his throat. "As you should all know, a Bard is the offspring of a Faerie and a human. A blend of both, we possess many powers of the Fae, but merged with human DNA. Some would argue that we have the best of both worlds; for all that the Fae have vast magical abilities, they can be aloof and lack the essence of what makes humanity so interesting. There is a certain coldness to the Fae; they don't experience feelings and emotions the same way humans do.

"Not to say that they do not have the ability to love, or to feel anger or sadness. But they do not appear to be able to regulate these as humans do; the emotions are much more raw and intense. Love can very easily become obsession for a Fae, and anger an uncontrollable wrath.

"There are many legends and myths about human encounters with the Fae, both here and in the Otherworld, before the Sealing of the Worlds. The Fae were indescribably beautiful, but they were unable to distinguish the subtle emotions of a human. When they fell in love, for example, they would stop at nothing to make that human theirs. Trickery, kidnapping, murder - all were commonplace.

"Equally dangerous was their fury. They would hound a human they took grievance with until the end of their days, and many people feared the Fae, whether rightly or wrongly. Often, they would refer to them as the 'Good Folk', or 'Fair Folk', afraid to even speak their name, lest it draw their attention."

Neala was transfixed. Like most children, she had grown up with fairytales, the stories of humans who encountered supernatural beings and learned a lesson of sorts. She even knew some of the darker, original stories. But hearing Druid Orwyn speak of it, in his whispery, ancient voice, and knowing now that these tales were not just made-up warnings to children, but possibly real events in history, it stirred her stomach and she felt oddly afraid. She huddled deeper into the couch and wrapped her arms around Keia, grateful for the fox's warmth.

"Nevertheless, many humans found themselves falling in love with a Fae man or woman. After all, it is hard to resist that kind of beauty, and the intensity of their devotion. As a result, many children were born, a combination of Fae and human blood.

"Over time, they became known as Bards, the lore-keepers - masters of music and song, with the ability to connect deeply with the natural world and influence the elements. Our Fae blood gifted us magic, but our humanity made it possible to understand the subtleties of life and creation, something the Fae lacked. For many years, Bards lived in harmony with both humans and Fae, able to transition from one world to the other freely and easily."

Orwyn sighed and shifted his weight from one foot to another. "But things never seem able to remain at peace for long. Soon, the Bards began to experience resentment from both worlds. The Fae grew jealous of the ease in which the Bards were able to integrate with the humans. They began to see them as rivals for human affection and refused to acknowledge them as peers any longer.

"The Fae distanced themselves further and further from the world of humans, and Bard children were often left with humans to be raised, the Fae no longer desiring to have them in their world.

"By now, a fairly large number of Bards and humans resided in the Otherworld, and they soon created their own kingdoms - a world within a world. The Fae shared this existence with them, but remained separate, each with their own laws and way of life.

"Meanwhile, here on our side of the portals, magic was becoming more and more feared. New religions were replacing the old, and many of the old magics were becoming outlawed, being viewed as dark and dangerous. Bards, unfortunately, were labelled witches and were hunted. A great number perished; in fact, almost the entire Bard population of America was destroyed."

Orwyn paused. "But that is the topic for another lesson. For now, we will centre our learning around the differences between the Bards, humans, and the Fae." Letting out a short groan, he shuffled over to one of the long shelves lining the walls, tapping his cane carefully as he navigated his way around the various armchairs.

Running his hand along the books, he drew out a thin, leather-bound one and smiled. Moving back to the fireplace, he held the book tightly against his chest and cleared his throat. In a voice as smooth as velvet, he began to recite a poem:

> "'Twas there beneath the moonlight gleaned,
> Her skin like ivory shone within
> I watched the maiden low and bow,
> And under hand did bloom so there

A single rose of red.
With keen and sorrow did lie the maid
Beside the bloom of fire bright
Weeping tears of gold and shimmer
That did tear my heart asunder
For the wails of despair.
Against all hope I came upon
Reaching with hand that trembled sore
To touch that face, ah, the wild made form
So nevermore would my life be mine
I was hers in thrall.
Those peerless eyes upon my face did gaze
Echoes of starlight in endless dance
In my hand she placed that blood-red bloom
And in voice at once both feared and b'loved did sigh,
'Until the end of days.'"

The silence in the room seemed to stretch for eternity. With a sad smile, he placed the book down on the mantle-piece and let out a long breath.

"That verse is from one of the many tragic ballads of Clìodhna, the Banshee Queen of the Tuatha Dé, and her mortal lover, Ciabhán. The full tale is contained within here," he gestured to the book, "if anyone wishes to read it in its entirety.

"What we can learn from accounts such as that of Ciabhán and his encounter with Clìodhna is that mortals were often consumed by their love for the Fae, and there are many accounts of them being held 'in thrall'. There are numerous tales of women becoming enthralled by Fae as well, particularly the males of the Tuatha Dé."

His tone shifted from wistful to a louder, more commanding one. "For our next lesson, I would like all of you to research and memorise a ballad, song, or poem, describing an encounter between a mortal and a Fae. It can be one of overwhelming desire, like the sample I have given today," he waggled the book in his hand, "or one with darker elements. I will expect you to recite several verses of it in tomorrow's class."

He chuckled. "After all, we Bards are the lore-keepers of old. It would not do to be unable to memorise even one tale, would it?"

With a wave of his hand, Orwyn dismissed them. Neala was surprised; the time had passed so quickly. As the others slowly started getting to their feet, chatting in hushed voices as they made their way out of the room, she remained seated, Keia cuddled against her.

Once they were alone, she tentatively got to her feet and shuffled over to Druid Orwyn shyly. Alert to her presence, Orwyn turned his head to the side and raised his tufty brows. "Miss Moran, is it not? What can I do for you?"

"Um, Druid Orwyn, I was just wondering if, well," Neala stuttered, "if you know of a prophecy – see, you mentioned Bards being 'lore-keepers', and it reminded me of something my mother said...about Lorekeepers and...and this weird birthmark I have."

Orwyn's expression changed to one of curiosity. "A prophecy? Hmm, I know many prophecies. Could you elaborate?"

A flush had crept over Neala's cheeks, and she squinted her eyes shut, regretting even mentioning it. "I...well, I have this birthmark on my shoulder in the shape of an ash leaf, and my mother seemed to think that was important – that it marked me as some 'Lorekeeper'. But, well, if *all* Bards are known as lore-keepers, then maybe it's...maybe it's nothing."

A silvery sheen flashed in Orwyn's cloudy eyes, and the corner of his mouth twitched ever so slightly. He pursed his lips and tilted his head to the side. "All Bards are keepers of lore, Miss Moran, but only a few are Lorekeepers. A very rare few, in fact."

Pausing, he gave a light shake of his head, disappointment creasing his wrinkled brow more than usual. "I'm afraid I cannot discuss this further with you today; my students are waiting for me. But this will not be the last we speak of it, aye?"

He tapped his lip thoughtfully. "I noticed Miss Holloway was not in attendance today. Please let her know what your task is for tomorrow's lesson, if you please? I hope she is not unwell. The headaches do pass, eventually – tell her she may come see me about it any time, if she requires."

Neala quickly thanked him and hurried from the room, unsure about how she was feeling. Orwyn had not given her a clear answer to her question, though he had implied they would discuss it again. This lifted her spirits slightly; perhaps there was hope of finding answers yet.

But her concern for Áine dimmed her optimism somewhat. During the lesson, she had been too captivated by what Druid Orwyn was saying to notice that Áine had not arrived. Chewing her lip, she knew she only had a short time to look before her next class.

It was morning tea-time, which gave the students a fifteen-minute break between classes. Walking faster, Neala decided she would try the dormitories first, thinking perhaps Áine had gone for a lie down.

With Keia tucked in her arms, she ground her teeth as she strode swiftly down the corridor. *I wonder if I could find Druid Orwyn again after dinner? Would he have time to speak with me then, maybe?*

She was so lost in thought that she wasn't paying attention to her surroundings. Without warning, she crashed into someone with a thud. Keia yipped in panic as she tried to avoid getting squished, and she leapt from Neala's arms.

Neala managed to stay on her feet, but she stumbled awkwardly for a moment. Giving her head a shake, she apologised profusely, trying to see who'd she'd bumped. Heart sinking, Neala watched as Darci Shae picked herself up off the ground, fuming as she brushed dust off her top.

"Darci, I'm so sorry, I wasn't concentrating, are you—"

"Shut up," Darci hissed, turning her gaze on Neala. Her dark eyes flashed dangerously, burning like hot coals. Neala took a step back, shocked at her reaction.

Sensing her fear, Keia scurried back toward Neala and crouched in front of her protectively, ears pressed flat against her head as her lip curled in a silent snarl.

"I just – it was an accident," Neala stammered, not understanding Darci's malice; she hadn't bumped her on purpose.

Darci took a step toward her, but Keia growled softly, and she hesitated. Placing one hand on her hip instead, she sneered, "Look, just stay away from me, all right? You think you're something special, with your little pet, and your whole 'I'm so new to this, it's so overwhelming' bit?"

Neala flinched. She had no idea why Darci was attacking her like this, but her words stung like daggers, each one laced with the venom of her deepest insecurities.

"It was a dramatic entrance you made - throwing that ridiculous fit, screeching like some feral animal and flinging yourself all over the place." She rolled her eyes. "*Please*, it's pathetic. Eamon may have fallen for it, but everyone else just thought you were insane, or maybe desperate for attention."

Neala's hands were balled into fists by her side, and her teeth were aching from being clenched so tightly. Barely controlling her fury at the undeserved lashing, she spat, "*Excuse* me? You don't even *know* me; you don't know anything about me. What the hell have I ever done to you?"

Darci's eyes narrowed, and her voice grew darker. "Lorcan promised to help me - he *promised*. But now it seems he's gotten distracted by the shiny new toy. Since you arrived, he hasn't spared a single second to help me find a cure."

Her face slackened for the briefest moment, before the angry mask was back. "I won't let anything, or *anyone*, get in the way of that. Consider this your official warning, mouse: you go near Lorcan again, you'll be sorry."

With that, Darci turned on her heel and stalked toward the doors, shoving them open and disappearing into the sunshine.

Neala felt like she'd been slapped. Her eyes prickled, but she swiped them quickly, pressing her tongue to the roof of her mouth so she wouldn't cry.

Now that the threat was gone, Keia relaxed, moving back to Neala's side and placing a paw against her leg. Reaching down, Neala rubbed her behind the ears, not trusting herself to speak yet.

Darci's words were coursing through her veins like poison. *'Everyone else just thought you were insane...you think you're something special? ...it's pathetic ...'*

Neala closed her eyes tightly, willing it to stop. Darci had confirmed her greatest fears; that everyone at Birchtree was laughing at her or thinking she was a freak.

"Not true. She lied."

Keia's voice was loud in Neala's mind, emphatic. Glancing down at her with tear-filled eyes, Neala whispered, "How do you know that? What if it's true, and they all think I'm stupid?"

The fox pup barked, her body jerking with the force of it. *"Stormbringer knows better – you are important."*

Unconvinced, Neala drew in a shaky breath and planted a smile on her face, reaching down to Keia. "Come on. I was going to try find Áine, but we'll be late for our next class if we waste any more time. Maybe she'll join us there?"

Keia eyed her warily but consented to being picked up. As Neala turned to head out the doors, Keia whined softly and nuzzled her chin. "Thanks, Keia," Neala murmured. "At least I have you, hey?"

*****

By the end of the day, Neala was sure her head was going to implode. Her elemental lessons had been intense, and it had taken her full concentration to keep her powers in check. Though water had been willing to cooperate with her, she had found the air and fire elements to be far more troublesome.

Understanding at last what her attributes meant, Neala had struggled to rein in the destructive nature of her relationship with these two. Fire, in particular, had rebelled against her requests; every time she had tried to coax it into a gentle flame, it would flare up and consume her firewood in seconds, mocking her.

Naïvely, she had believed that the earth element would be more cooperative, being her one regenerative element.

However, she'd found working with it to be just as draining, though for a different reason.

While it had readily agreed to aid in her request to speed along the growth of the hedge plants they were working with, it was hard work to keep them from getting excited and throwing out too many new shoots, which would stress them. Neala now knew what everyone had meant when they told her that she was at Birchtree to learn control.

Áine, thankfully, had returned to classes after midday, apologising to Neala for how she'd spoken to her. "I had the most horrible headache, closer to a migraine. I went to the dorms initially, but, in the end, I was feeling so rotten that I had to go see Mercy. She didn't seem too concerned, but she wants me to monitor how I feel over the next few days, and report to her if there are any more problems."

She'd looked miserable as she muttered, "I hope it's not the flu or anything, I've never been sick in my life."

Neala had offered her words of comfort and reassurance, but Áine had sensed her distraction. When questioned, though, Neala had convinced her that she was just feeling tired after a busy morning. While not a complete lie, she didn't elaborate on what was really bothering her – that she had taken Darci's words to heart.

Though she had intended her free time to be used to speak with Ovate Clodagh about contacting her mother, Neala realised belatedly that the Ovate would, obviously, be busy with her own students during that time. Instead, she had taken Keia for a walk in the woods, exploring the grounds around Birchtree. She hadn't wanted to be around others, not even Áine.

Once she returned for her Modern Barding lesson, Neala was feeling a little more like herself. The walk in the woods had helped to clear her mind, and she had even managed a laugh, watching Keia chase a butterfly across the lawns.

Although she was feeling more cheerful, Neala had quickly concluded that this class was her least favourite by a long way. Miranda, the Bard who taught the lessons, was young and enthusiastic, but Neala couldn't shake the sadness that settled over her as she learned about life on this side of the Veil; how Bards had to work to hide their magic and adapt to life in a world where they didn't belong.

Her final class for the day had been animal husbandry, the elective she'd chosen. Unsure what to expect initially, Neala had immediately loved it. Back in her element, she had relished the chance to be around animals again.

However, she had swiftly discovered that Keia was not a good companion to have with her for that class; the moment the animals in the menagerie had gotten a whiff of the Otherworld creature, they had panicked, leading the Druid in charge, Cathal, to ban Keia from coming within a hundred-metre radius of the area. Keia chose to sulk at the edge of the forest instead and complained to Neala that the other animals were just being rude.

By the time the lesson had ended, Neala was starving. Lining up to collect her food, her stomach growled. The smells of lamb and herbs and buttery vegetables invaded her nostrils, and she could focus on nothing else. Once she had her meal, she looked for Torin, spotting him at one of the tables near the doorway.

Carefully making her way over, trying not to bump into anyone, she set her tray down beside his and flopped into her seat. Turning his head to look at her, Torin asked her in a low voice, "Have you heard? About Lorcan?"

Neala was about to take a bite of her bread roll, but stopped abruptly, roll halfway to her mouth. Her stomach flip-flopped. "No, I haven't. What's wrong?"

Torin frowned. "He's disappeared. No one's seen him all day - Eamon's been asking around."

"I saw him this morning, just after breakfast. He-" Neala paused, remembering how upset Lorcan had been when he'd spotted Keia. Glancing at her fox, Neala wrinkled her nose. "He seemed angry about something, then he stormed off, out the front door. I don't know where he went after that."

Piercing a bit of meat with his fork, Torin ran it around his plate to gather the last dregs of gravy and popped it into his mouth with a shrug. "Well, he's a big boy, I'm sure he can take care of himself. He's been known to disappear for days at a time, this isn't a huge surprise. More a curiosity, don't you think?"

"Mmm, I suppose..." Neala poked at her vegetables with her fork, remembering. "Did Finn get a chance to speak to you? About Poppy?"

Torin's shoulders slumped and his tone turned sour. "Yeah, he told me. I'm glad he's getting some answers, but still...It's worrying. Not knowing what's going on out there – I wish there was some way to keep an eye on things, you know? I just want to know that she's safe."

Wondering how to answer him, Neala was distracted by Áine plopping her tray down beside her, grinning excitedly. "Neala, I just saw Ovate Clodagh. I know you were hoping to contact your mother somehow but hadn't gotten around to asking. So, while I had the chance, I asked her for you. She explained that she can't call her or anything, but she can scry for her, and you could see her, at least. If that's what you want? She'll be in her room tonight after dinner and she would be happy to help."

This news did perk Neala up. "Oh, Áine, thank you - that would be great." Taking advantage of the change of topic, she asked, "So, how were your lessons today, Tor?"

Settling into casual conversation, Neala kept all thoughts about Darci, Lorcan, and disappearing Bards from entering her mind.

*****

Lying in bed that night, Neala felt as though a great weight had been lifted from her shoulders. True to her promise, she had gone to Ovate Clodagh's room, to see if she could scry for Dana. Clodagh had magicked a bowl of water into a scrying glass, allowing Neala to watch her mother cooking dinner, humming to herself. Neala's heart had ached so painfully she felt it would split in two.

Her mother looked the same as always, though it seemed she'd had a haircut after Neala left – her long, brown hair was now styled into a sleek bob. The kitchen had been filled with flowers and Sox was curled up on the chair Neala usually sat in.

After a while, the Ovate had let the image fade away, and Neala thanked her profusely. Once she'd arrived back at her dorm, she had written a long letter, vowing to drop it to Clodagh the next morning so it could be sent to her mother.

"Who cares about what Darci Shae thinks?" she whispered, half to herself, half to a sleepy Keia, who was curled up beside her on the bed. "I'm going to be a great Bard and make Mum proud – and Dad. No matter what." With a yawn, Neala settled more comfortably on her pillow, then drifted off to sleep.

~ 22 ~

By mid-October, Neala had almost forgotten what her life was like before coming to Birchtree. It hadn't taken her long to get into routine, attending her classes and bonding with her friends.

It had quickly become apparent that Neala was a natural, and she was beginning to excel in her lessons. Despite what Darci had said, she had been increasingly welcomed by the other students, and was often greeted by name as she passed through the halls. No one batted an eye at Keia anymore, either; the girl with the shadow-coloured fox was just another part of life at the academy now.

As Neala and Áine made their way down to their usual music class, breath misting in the crisp air, Neala clutched her violin tightly, feeling oddly nervous. Finley hadn't seemed his usual self that morning; he'd been tense, tapping his hands on his legs restlessly as they'd chosen their instruments, and talking to them in short, brisk commands.

Turning to Áine, she whispered, "Do you think Finn's okay? He's been really odd this morning."

Áine was silent for a while, considering her answer. "It's been weeks since he heard any news about Poppy, or those other strange disappearances. Perhaps he's getting worried? It must be hard, if he has to be here teaching but also wants to help his friends with their investigations. Finn would be really torn."

Neala pondered this, then nodded slowly. "I suppose that could be it. I wonder what—"

"Girls," Finley called, gesturing for Neala and Áine to hurry up. Embarrassed, Neala realised they had been so engrossed in their conversation that they'd almost walked straight past the rest of their class. Shuffling over to the others, Neala and Áine exchanged guilty smiles.

Focusing their attention on Finn, he raised his brows at them, then addressed the group. "Today we're going to do something a little different. You've all come a long way in harmonising with one another, and I'm satisfied you all have a grasp on that particular skill. Moving forward, I want you to go off and find a quiet place where you can just play."

The students glanced at one another, not understanding.

A smile tugged at the corner of his mouth. "Listening to silence is just as important as working with others. Once you feel like you are tuned in to the sounds of the environment around you, your challenge will be to play your instruments in a way that enhances the natural vibration around you and doesn't clash with it.

"The Song of Life, the force that binds all living things, is everywhere, at all times. Your task is to listen for it and join it with your music." Waving his hands at them, Finley shooed them off. "Go on - you may go anywhere in the area, as long as you are close enough to make it to your next class on time. Not in pairs, Jasper and Scarlett; this is an individual task."

As the students separated and wandered off, Finley strode over to Áine and Neala, gesturing for them to wait. Neala's mouth went dry; something was wrong. Once they were alone, Áine blurted out, "It's Poppy, isn't it? Something's happened."

Finley hesitated, studying Áine curiously, then nodded. "Yes. One of my friends, Megan, contacted me late last night. It seems Poppy was found wandering the moors just outside Ballyconneely. It is unclear exactly how she got there, but it seems she has woken from her coma at last. But her mind is still, well..."

He trailed off, looking sad. "Apart from being dirty and cold, she seems relatively unharmed, which is unusual. She's been missing for over a month; we expected, at the very least, that, if she were even found alive, she would be malnourished and very ill. Whoever kidnapped her must have taken care of her, that much is clear."

He rubbed his face with his hands. "We're still no closer to finding out who took her, but, for now, she's back at your parents' house, Áine, being cared for by nurses around the clock. It was agreed that she couldn't return to the hospital, not until we find out more about what happened."

Neala let out a sigh, her muscles trembling. She hadn't realised how much she had tensed up as Finn spoke. "But she's alive and safe, right?" she reiterated, shifting her weight to her other foot.

Keia, who was sitting beside her, suddenly tucked her ears back and let out a low whine, a noise Neala had never heard her make before. The three Bards stared down at her, and Neala crouched worriedly. "Hey, what's up, little one? What's wrong?"

Keia was pressed low to the ground now, as though in pain. Her whines had risen higher, and her paws were scratching at the ground. *Bad is here. Not safe, danger.*

Neala reached a hand toward her, wanting to comfort her. But Keia flinched away, lips pulling back in a snarl, teeth snapping sharply. Shocked, Neala yanked her fingers back. She had never seen Keia behave like this.

Finn had been watching curiously, and now he knelt beside her. Without taking his eyes off Keia, he asked softly, "What is she saying, Neala?"

"She says something bad is here, that there's danger," Neala answered, brows furrowed in concern.

Finn asked in a low voice, "Keia, what is it? What is the bad thing?"

Keia whimpered piteously, pressing her tummy low to the ground. *Her creatures - the changers. They're here.*

Neala relayed the words to Finn, and his face paled. With a thump, he sat on the ground, eyes flicking from side to side as his mind raced, his features taut. "Of course. Stupid, *stupid*..."

He dropped his face into his hands with a growl. "Oh, I'm an idiot. It had to be them - why didn't I see it earlier? I'm so fecking *stupid*! This means, all this time..."

Jerking his head back up, he pressed his hands into the dirt, which rumbled warningly beneath him. "They're all in danger. I have to go." Abruptly, Finn got to his feet, mouth a hard line.

Something seemed to snap in Neala. Stepping in front of him so he couldn't leave, she hissed, "What the *hell* is going on? Why is my fox acting like she's being tortured? Who's in danger?"

Finn hesitated, meeting Neala's eyes at last. Her fists were clenched at her sides, and she felt ashamed of speaking so rudely. But she wanted answers.

In a softer voice, she pleaded, "Please, Finn. You asked me to tell you everything - about the dreams, all the strange things that have been happening. And I have - I've told you everything, all I know. Don't you trust us enough to tell us what's going on? Torin's our friend, my best friend - if Poppy's in danger, we need to be there for him."

Áine moved up beside her now. "I agree with Neala," she squeaked. "If she's in trouble, it's only fair that we know - that Torin knows."

Running a hand over his thinning brown hair, Finn grappled with his thoughts, his mouth tense. Resigned, he slumped his shoulders. "You're right, and I agree with you. Things are moving quicker than we thought - we need to start training you all immediately."

He looked into Neala's eyes gravely. "I give you my word, I will explain everything. There are things we have been keeping from you, I admit it." He nodded at Áine. "From both of you. But please trust me when I say it needs to wait. Just for a little while longer."

Finn reached down and scooped up Keia, who was now panting in exhaustion. "If what Keia has told you is true, I can't waste another moment. The creatures she warned us about - the 'changers'...If my suspicions are correct, then changelings have crossed from the Otherworld. And that could spell disaster. It could be what has happened to Poppy - it all fits. If so, she is in grave danger."

Neala shook her head, feeling like an outsider again. "What is a changeling? Why is it so dangerous?"

"Changelings are shape-shifters, like the púca, but much more efficient. They're born from the spirits of deceased Fae children, or sometimes created with enchanted wood imbued with the soul of the child. The Fae are astonishing in many ways, but they don't understand how to love like humans do. Faerie children are not doted on like their human counterparts - they are given the essentials they need to ensure they survive until adulthood, but little more.

"Longing for the love and affection that they were denied in their short lives, they change places with a human, impersonating them completely; they can even imitate a Bard's magic, to a degree. Once they acquire their target's essence, usually through touch, they retain every thought, feeling, and memory of the one they replace."

Rubbing his face, Finn scowled. "It can be near impossible to tell a changeling from the real person – the only sure way is to listen for a heartbeat; changelings don't have one."

His expression turned sombre. "If it's true, and changelings are responsible for the mysterious disappearances - and subsequent reappearances - that have been going on, then I need to help track them down. The Bards they've replaced..." His throat bobbed as he swallowed "The changelings have either hidden them somewhere, or they've..."

With a wince, Finn hung his head. Neala and Áine didn't need to think hard about what the alternative could be.

Gulping down her panic, Neala shuddered. "I'm sorry, Finn. I was rude before. These changelings sound..." She shivered. "Like something from a nightmare. Of course you have to go, we're sorry for pestering you."

Neala shot Áine a glance. "Just, well...would it be okay if – if we told Torin what's happening? It doesn't seem fair otherwise."

"And Eilìs," Áine added, eyes hard. "Poppy was - *is* her best friend. She deserves to know, too."

Finn raised his head and nodded gravely. "I'll talk to Torin. Áine, you may speak with Eilìs, but please, and I cannot stress this enough," he raised his finger and gave each of the girls a sharp look, "keep this to yourselves. Just for now. If word got out, there would be a panic, and we need to know the facts before things get out of hand and rumours start spreading. Is that clear?"

Áine and Neala nodded, faces drawn.

Satisfied, Finn continued, "I do need to speak to Druid Imelda, though. Things are...complicated. There is more going on than I realised, and more than I can tell you now. For that, I am truly sorry. But you'll know everything soon, I swear. I'm doing my best to understand what's happening, but even I can become overwhelmed at times." He smiled faintly at Neala.

"Imelda knows everything I do, and she will handle things here while I'm away. Until then, girls, please try not to worry. Keep at your lessons - keep learning all you can."

With a stretch, he glanced at the sky. "Class is almost over, anyway. I'm sorry to have kept you. You'd best get ready for your next lesson."

Placing a hand on each of their shoulders, he murmured, "Don't worry about Poppy, okay? I'll find her and work out what's happening. I've never lost something I couldn't find again, remember?"

With a final nod, Finley turned and strode off, head down and hands in his pockets. Watching him go, Neala felt a rush of sadness; she would miss Finley terribly. Biting down on her trembling lip, she turned shakily to Áine, who was also staring after Finn with tears in her eyes.

Unable to think of anything to say, Neala crouched and placed a hand on Keia's soft head, reassured by her warmth. Áine muttered something about going to class, then wandered off, rubbing her forehead absently. Neala stared after her, feeling empty.

The story about the changelings had sent a chill down her spine which wouldn't ease, and she cuddled Keia close. Pressing her face into her fur, she sighed. "Oh, Keia. What is going on out there?"

"Danger."

Despite her worries, Neala bit back a snort. "Well, you aren't wrong." Rising to her feet with a groan, she started walking after Áine. "Could you be more specific? How did you know that changelings were here? That they'd come?"

Trotting by Neala's side, Keia's little nose snuffled, and she flicked her ears. *"She told me. The wise one."* Neala paused.

"The Cailleach?"

"No, the other. The one who sent me here."

"Who sent you? From where?"

Keia whined softly. *"Can't remember."* Neala gave her a gentle squeeze.

"Hey, that's okay. You're only a baby, how can you have memories of where you're from? I'm just glad you could warn us. That was very helpful."

Keia's tongue lolled from her mouth, and she flicked her tail proudly. Neala grinned, then her smile faded. "Well, I guess we just keep carrying on as normal, then, huh? Because 'normal' is something we have in abundance these days. Easy, right?"

*****

Grabbing a muffin from the basket, Neala glanced around the dining hall, but it was practically deserted. The morning tea break was only short, so many of the students just grabbed a snack and went to one of the lounge rooms or outside to laze about before resuming their lessons. Neala, though, was on a mission; she had to find Áine.

After their music lesson, Áine had complained of a headache and had told her to go on to their next class without her. Neala had been concerned, but Áine had waved her off, telling her it was nothing. But she had been getting lots of headaches lately, Neala noted.

Over the past week, Áine had even been waking in the middle of the night, gasping and sweating after another nightmare. When Neala pressed her, Áine had refused to tell her anything about them, other than they were just bad dreams – nothing to worry about.

Knowing all too well how strange dreams could be in this place, Neala hadn't pushed her, but she remained suspicious. Now, though, she wanted answers.

As she wandered out into the entrance hall, she spotted Druid Imelda walking down the stairs from the second floor, face drawn and tired. Wondering if Finley had spoken to her yet, Neala took a hesitant step forward and opened her mouth, but the Druid caught sight of her and frowned, placing a finger on her lips.

Gesturing for Neala to follow her, she wandered toward a deserted hallway. Neala toddled behind her, Keia at her heels.

Once she was sure they were alone, Druid Imelda stared down her long nose, mouth tight. "Neala Moran. Before you fire a dozen questions at me - yes, I have spoken with Finley Talbot, and I am aware of what occurred this morning."

Glancing down at Keia, her face softened. "You are a mysterious creature indeed, young lady."

Turning back to Neala, Imelda's mouth tightened. "As it happens, I was just coming to find you. Your friend, Áine Holloway, has been admitted to the infirmary. She collapsed on her way to the dormitories after first lesson."

Imelda raised a hand to stop Neala from interrupting. "She is fine, she just needs rest. You may visit her during your free time this afternoon."

Pulling a watch out of her blouse pocket, she nodded. "Regarding what Finn spoke to you about, I will be in touch as soon as I have made arrangements. Miss Holloway should be recovered soon enough, and there is no time to waste. I will speak to both of you again soon. Until then, I must continue on; I have students waiting for me. And you need to get to your next lesson."

Neala's head was feeling overstuffed, but she managed to gather her wits long enough to thank Imelda and promise she would get straight to her next class. With a nod, Druid Imelda walked away, leaving Neala to collect her thoughts.

Chewing her lip, she turned her attention to Áine. Though Druid Imelda had told her not to worry, Neala was concerned for her friend and desperately wanted to go see for herself that she was okay.

"But I just said I was going to go to my lesson. If she finds out I've skipped class..." Neala glanced down at her fox for guidance, but Keia just stared at her, blue eyes giving nothing away.

Huffing out a breath, Neala nodded, resigned. "Of course I'm going to see her, who was I kidding? C'mon, Keia. There will be time for lessons later."

Wandering down the halls on her way to the infirmary, Neala was startled to see Torin up ahead, sitting against the wall with his head in his hands. Her chest gave a tug as she hurried over, wondering if Finn had spoken with him yet.

Placing Keia on the ground, Neala shuffled closer and knelt, resting a hand on Torin's arm. When he glanced up at her with bloodshot eyes, she knew immediately that he'd been told about Poppy – about the changelings. Not knowing what else to do, Neala opened her arms and wrapped them around Torin's broad shoulders.

Face scrunching with pain, Torin leaned his head against Neala's neck, taking several shaky breaths. "You heard, too," he whispered. It wasn't a question.

"I'm sorry, Tor, I truly am," Neala mumbled, cheek resting against Torin's curls. Keia moved closer until her furry body was huddled next to his legs, trying to offer him comfort as best she could.

After a little while, Torin leaned away from Neala and she lowered her arms, settling in to sit beside him instead. Drawing his knees up, Torin linked his arms around them and leaned his head back against the wall with a sigh.

"I don't know if it's better or worse than before, when I didn't know where she was." He rubbed a hand across his face. "Changelings. I've heard of them, but always thought they just took babies, you know? I asked Finn if perhaps they could've taken her back to the Otherworld somehow, through whatever crack in the Veil they'd snuck through, but he didn't know. The thing pretending to be her may have – she might be..." he trailed off, voice hitching.

Neala leaned her head on his shoulder, unable to find any words to comfort him. They sat like that for some time, before Torin let out a long breath.

"Finn said it was Keia who sensed the changelings, Neals. Is that true?"

Keia's ears pricked up, and she looked at Neala. *"No - I was told. By my Lady."*

Neala frowned. "She says she didn't sense them, not like that. She was told by –" Neala glanced at Keia, to make sure she got it right, "by 'her Lady'. Someone - or something - spoke to her and told her that changelings were here, then she got all scared."

Torin nodded, lips pursed. "Well, that raises more questions than it answers, but never mind. I just thought, perhaps she would be able to help Finley track them down quicker? If she could sense them, that is."

Keia whined softly, pressing her nose into her paws. Torin didn't need Neala to translate that time, and he reached a large hand out to scratch the little fox behind the ear.

"It's okay, wee lass. I know you'd help if you could. At least you helped solve one mystery, hey?" He met Neala's eyes. "Though, it seems we have a new one to figure out. You heard about Áine?"

Neala nodded. "Yeah, I ran into Druid Imelda, and she told me Áine had collapsed. I was actually looking for her - she'd skipped our class because of another headache - but I didn't know it was this bad. Druid Imelda said she was fine, and she'd be okay with a bit of rest," she shrugged sheepishly, "but I had to check and make sure she was okay anyway. Then I saw you, and, well..."

"You had to make sure I was okay, too," Torin finished for her with a crooked smile. Rising to his feet, he held out a hand to pull Neala up. "You're never going to learn how to be a Bard at this rate; you're too busy helping out everyone around you."

He gestured down the hall with a flick of his head. "C'mon, then. We may as well go together."

Falling into step beside him, Neala let her mind wander. What had Finley told Druid Imelda to arrange? What was the secret they were hiding? Clenching her jaw in frustration, she tried to push the thoughts aside.

Reaching the door to the infirmary, Torin raised his hand to knock just as Mercy opened it. Neala smiled at the Healer, but she just glanced from one to the other and rolled her eyes. "Of course it's you two. I suppose your classes will just carry on without you, hmm? Are you not here to learn?"

Resigned, she sighed and stepped aside. "Come - she is in here."

Leaving the door open, Mercy disappeared, bright-coloured sarong swirling behind her. Torin and Neala exchanged suppressed smiles and followed, Neala making sure Keia was trailing after her. She tapped her hand rhythmically on her leg as she walked, feeling strangely nervous.

Mercy was waiting for them beside a pale-yellow door, arms folded as she watched them move closer.

"She is in here, resting. Her latest vision has obviously overwhelmed her, but she will be fine after some rest. My guess is that she will be awake in a few hours, perhaps by dinner. She was exhausted, too, which did not help, so I have put her into a deep sleep. You may visit briefly now, if you wish, but do not expect much from her."

Torin's forehead was furrowed. "What visions?"

Neala stared at Mercy in shock. "Visions like...like a Seer?"

Mercy looked surprised. "Oh, yes, she has been Seeing things for several weeks now - both in her dreams and, more recently, waking visions. Did she not tell you?"

Torin and Neala exchanged a look, brows raised. Clearing her throat, Mercy tapped her foot impatiently. "Hmm. Well, if you are finished with your curiosity, I need to get back to work."

Neala thanked her and watched as she grabbed several jars of herbs and made her way into another room. Turning to Torin, she flicked her head at Áine's room. "Shall we go in?"

Turning the ornate handle, Torin edged into the room as quietly as he could, Neala close behind. Áine was tucked into the bed, lying on her back and breathing deeply, blonde hair spread about her like a halo. She reminded Neala of a princess in a fairytale, waiting for her prince to awaken her from her slumber.

Spotting a chair, she gestured for Torin to take it while she perched carefully on the end of the bed, making sure not to crush Áine's feet. Once Torin had sat, he leaned back and folded his arms behind his head, looking pensive. "So, a Seer, huh? I wonder why she didn't tell us?"

Neala nodded slowly. "Did she think we'd react badly or something?"

Torin rubbed his chin thoughtfully. "There's no history of Seers in her family. Well, none that she's mentioned. Perhaps she thought we'd pester her to See visions of the future if she told us? It's hard work, sometimes, being a Seer. At any moment, the future can change; it's totally subjective. One choice can change everything – it can alter a person's path completely.

"I've heard stories of Seers going blind because of it – some even go mad, trying to look into the future and seeing so many constantly-changing paths ahead that they lose their minds. Perhaps that's why she kept it secret? Waiting until she had a handle on it in case it turned or something?"

Neala digested this, stroking her forearms softly as she thought, *It's just like the Cailleach told me. The potential futures are always changing, based on our choices. Imagine trying to see what's coming when even the smallest decision could change everything? Poor Áine - no wonder she's been getting headaches, especially if she can't control the visions yet.*

Feeling like they had found more questions than answers, Neala let out an exasperated breath. "You know, I kind of miss my life on the farm. Sure, it was hard work, but it was simple. Get up, do my chores, do some schoolwork, do more chores, eat, and sleep. Since coming here, everything has gotten so complicated."

Snorting, Torin beamed, dimples forming in his cheeks. "Like you would trade it for anything else, Bus Girl."

Hearing his old nickname for her, Neala met his eyes and grinned. "You had no idea what you were getting into that day, did you O.B.G?"

Falling into comfortable silence, she turned and placed a hand on Áine's ankle. She didn't react, chest rising and falling in steady rhythm. "I know I should get back to class, but it just feels wrong to leave her here by herself."

Torin nodded. "I know what you mean. Here, what if we hang here until midday, then get back to it after lunch? Mercy said she'd likely be up by dinner, so that seems like a fair deal."

Neala relaxed, agreeing with Torin's suggestion. "Sounds like a plan."

With a thud, Neala plopped onto her seat, eyeing the bowl of stew wearily. The rest of her day had passed in a blur, her mind distracted by thoughts of Finley, and Poppy, and changelings, and Áine.

Unable to concentrate, she'd almost caused an accident in her fire lesson, allowing the wall of flame she was supposed to be keeping contained to slip past her defences and race away. Druid Imelda, sensing why she was slacking, had called the wildfire back and reprimanded Neala for her carelessness. Dinner time had not come quickly enough.

Torin had almost finished eating by the time Neala placed her tray down beside him. He mumbled a quick hello before running the last chunk of bread around his empty bowl. She had barely spooned the first bite of soup into her mouth when she was distracted by a blonde figure walking shyly into the dining hall, glancing from side to side as she looked for them.

Dropping her cutlery with a clatter, Neala waved excitedly, "Áine, over here!" Torin's head whipped up and he grinned broadly. Spotting them, Áine hurried over, Mercy following close behind.

Neala pulled a chair out and Áine slid into it gratefully. Torin gathered his tray and said warmly, "It's great to see you up and about. Do you want me to bring you something to eat, since I'm going up there?"

Mercy held up a hand, stopping him. "Only something small and light for now, until she has recovered fully. Perhaps some bread, cheese, and fruit?" Torin nodded and returned to the servery, placing his own dirty tray down along the way.

Turning back to Neala, Mercy looked at her sternly. "Do not let her over-exert herself. She is to eat, then to go to bed. Understood?" Neala agreed meekly, not daring to argue with the imposing Healer. With a final glance, Mercy patted Áine gently on the shoulder and left.

Neala was about to ask Áine how she was when they were interrupted by a light cough.

Surprised to see Druid Imelda standing in front of her, Neala froze. Her stomach, obviously annoyed at still being unfed, grumbled loudly, and she blushed. Druid Imelda raised an eyebrow. "I won't keep you from your meal for long."

Directing her words at Áine, she continued. "Mercy has kept me updated on your condition. I know it is a big ask, and that you need rest, but I must speak with you as a matter of urgency. And you, too." She turned her dark eyes on Neala's face briefly. "After dinner, when the eighth hour strikes, please meet me in the Blue Room. It is vitally important."

The girls glanced at each other, nodding slowly. Before the Druid could say more, Torin returned, awkwardly pausing to wait for Imelda to move so he could give Áine her dinner. With a pointed look at the girls, Druid Imelda reminded them, "Eighth hour, in the Blue Room."

As she walked away, Torin slid into his seat, looking puzzled. "What was that about?"

Neala replied slowly, "Apparently she wants to meet with Áine and I tonight in the Blue Room. She didn't say why."

Torin frowned but didn't press further. Instead, he waved his hand at the girls' untouched plates. "C'mon - eat up, then. Neala, your food must be getting cold by now."

Reminded of her growling tummy, Neala picked up her spoon and dove into her dinner. As she ate, Torin spoke to Áine.

"So, how are you feeling?"

Áine poked absently at her bread. "A little woozy. It was the strangest feeling. I was so upset after Finley spoke with us—" She gasped, eyes wide. "Oh, Tor, it's about Poppy. She—"

Torin raised a hand, expression sad. "He's already told me."

"Are you okay? I'm so sorry."

"It is what it is," Torin replied with a sigh. "I trust Finn - I know that he won't stop looking until he finds her. But I was asking about you, aye. Let's focus on that for now."

Áine still looked worried, but she pursed her lips and continued. "So, anyway, I was coming back up here and I just...it was as though I was walking through a dream world. Everything got blurry and I felt like I was walking in slow motion. My ears were ringing, like there was some kind of song playing in the distance, just out of range, and bright lights were dancing all around me. Then, this vision came into my mind, and I Saw..."

She tilted her head to the side and squinted her eyes closed, searching for the memory. "I was in a cave, a cave filled with fog. There were people there, but I couldn't make out their faces. There was this flash of light, through the fog, then it all went black."

Neala had been listening intently, poking at her dinner. The feeling Áine had described - the ringing, the song, the dancing lights...it reminded her of the day she'd arrived at Birchtree, when she'd fainted. She'd felt the same back then - as though she had been floating, like her soul was being drawn from her body. "And the voice..." she mumbled.

"What voice? Neala, are you okay?" Áine was looking at her curiously.

Realising she'd spoken aloud, Neala flushed and scooped up some more of her soup. "Yeah, sorry, I was just thinking out loud. But tell us more; why didn't you tell us you were getting visions? You're a Seer - that's pretty cool."

Áine shook her head, turning her bread roll over in her fingers. "It is cool, I guess. But it's also very confusing. The visions come when I'm least expecting them, especially when I'm tired. It started off just being random things, like seeing someone fall over. I mean, I'd be staring at a patch of lawn, then I'd See a vision of a girl tripping and grazing her knee on that same spot, but...different. Like a mirage or something. Then it'd disappear as quickly as it had come."

She blinked tiredly. "Trying to work out what was real and what was a vision took me a while. Then the dreams started - little snapshots of things that I couldn't make out, like someone showing me a movie but only giving me a two or three-second glimpse every time. I thought I was going mad, until Ovate Clodagh realised what was happening. I've been working with her and Mercy in the evenings, just getting a handle on how to control when I See things, and how to filter what's important and what isn't."

Áine shrugged, blushing. "Mercy says I'm a very strong Seer; that the number of visions I'm getting every day is pretty high. Which is kind of good, I guess, but it's also frustrating. I am sorry for not saying anything, I didn't know what was happening and I was, well...scared, to be honest."

Neala and Torin reassured Áine that they weren't angry - they were just glad she was okay. Once Áine was smiling happily, Torin placed his hand over his mouth, stifling a yawn. Tiredly, he asked, "So, what does Druid Imelda want to see you about, do you know?"

Neala swallowed the last bite of her vegetables and pushed her plate aside, leaning on her elbows. "I'm not sure. It mustn't be about Poppy, otherwise surely she would have asked you to come, too?" Torin wrinkled his nose, turning away and frowning thoughtfully.

"Perhaps it's about my visions?" Áine wondered aloud. "Maybe Mercy told her about the cave I Saw, and it means something to her?"

"Maybe." Neala wasn't convinced. "But then why would she need me there?" She cringed. "I stuffed up pretty badly in my class with her today, maybe she has a punishment for me? Do they do detention here?"

Torin cleared his throat, pushing his chair back. "Well, whatever it is, keep me in the loop, okay? I'm going to head to the lounge; if I don't see you again tonight, tell me all about it at breakfast. Here, I'll take your trays."

The girls thanked him and stood, Neala reaching down to pet Keia and feed her some scraps she'd saved from dinner. Keia snuffled the food quickly, then got to her feet, fluffing out her fur. With a final wave to Torin, Áine and Neala wandered out of the hall, turning toward the staircase.

"You don't think we're too early?" Áine asked nervously.

"Better that than late, I guess?" Neala answered, suddenly shy.

In silence, the girls climbed to the second floor and wandered down the hall until they found the Blue Room. Pushing the door open, they quickly realised they were not the only ones there. In a chair by the fireplace sat a large, dark-skinned man, a heavy book lying open on his lap. His eyes, black as coals, studied the girls curiously.

Neala barely had time to wonder why he looked familiar when she suddenly recognised him; he was the giant who had spoken about the east wind that day, when Lorcan had blasted the doors open and stalked off. 'Bad luck follows when the east wind blows', Neala remembered.

"Hello," the man said in his deep, gentle voice. "I am Orion Akinjide. Can I help you with something?"

Áine and Neala exchanged glances; they hadn't expected anyone else to be here, and it had caught them unawares.

Stuttering a little, Neala answered, "Oh, um, hi, it's nice to meet you. I'm Neala Moran, this is Áine Holloway. We're meant to be meeting Druid Imelda here at eight..." She trailed off, feeling self-conscious.

Orion looked thoughtful. "Holloway. You are the sister of Eilìs?"

Áine nodded, seemingly unable to speak. Neala edged further into the room, not knowing why she was feeling so nervous. "Yeah, she is. Anyway, is it - I mean, do you mind if we just hang out in here until Druid Imelda gets here? We don't want to be a bother."

The man chortled, the sound reverberating through Neala's entire body. "Of course, please sit. I, too, am waiting for the Druid. We are the early birds, it would seem?"

Neala raised her brows. "Oh, okay, that's good." She wondered how many others Druid Imelda had invited. "Did she happen to tell you what we're meeting about?"

Orion tilted his head to the side, reminding Neala of a wise old owl. "No, she did not say."

Feeling somewhat disappointed, Neala shrugged and walked further into the room. "Oh well, I suppose it will make sense s—"

"Hi guys, what's the craic?"

Neala was stunned to see Jaz flounce into the room behind Áine, who jumped in surprise. Spotting Neala, she beamed, eyes lighting up. "Newbie! Long time, no see. You've been summoned, too, huh?"

"Summoned?"

Jaz rolled her eyes. "What else do you call it when the boss calls you to a meeting? Hey there, Rye, how's it going?" Her attention had shifted to Orion now, and he smiled affectionately as Jaz bounced into a chair beside him.

"Hello, Jadzia. It is good to see you."

"So, anyone know what we're here for?" Jaz asked, flicking her eyes from Neala to Áine. The others shrugged and shook their heads. Jaz ran a hand over her hair, which had been cut very short, Neala observed; it was little more than fuzzy stubble.

"What's with the buzzcut?"

Jaz grinned, turning her head from side to side. "I told you a while back that I needed a change, right? Why play it small?"

Neala snorted and took a seat opposite Jaz and Orion, Áine quickly tucking herself into an armchair beside her. No sooner had they sat down than another figure slipped into the room.

Keia, who had been sitting quietly by Neala's side, twitched her ears and pressed herself further into the chair. Neala's heart sank. In the glow of the firelight, she recognised the scowling eyes of Darci Shae.

Even Jaz fell silent, her smile drooping. Nonplussed, Darci flicked her hair over her shoulder and walked purposefully over to a chair furthest from the others, draping herself into it with catlike grace.

Sensing the change in the room, Áine nudged Neala's arm, looking confused. Whispering as low as she could, she asked, "Who is that?"

Neala murmured back, "Remember that girl I told you about? The one who went all crazy when I knocked her over that day?"

Áine's eyes widened and she shot a quick glance back at Darci, who was staring at the wall, ignoring the others stubbornly. With a quiet huff, Áine turned back to Neala.

"That's her? That's Darci?"

"Yep, that's the one. She told me to stay away from Lorcan, remember?" Neala rolled her eyes. "Because I'm totally following him all the time, right? Like a crazy stalker or something." She frowned. "Even if I was, it's not like he's ever around; he seems to come and go as he pleases."

Áine nodded. "I've noticed that. His brother is always trying to find him, asking people if they've seen him—"

As if on cue, Eamon's head poked around the doorway, looking puzzled. He grinned when he saw Jaz and Neala, but his mouth twitched when he spotted Darci in the corner. Fixing a smile on his face, he walked into the room, greeting them with a wave. "Druid Imelda's called you all in, too, huh? Does anyone know why?"

Jaz seemed surprised. "If anyone knew, it'd be you, surely?"

Eamon folded his body into a chair by the doorway, barely able to squeeze his broad shoulders into the cushioned armrests. Rubbing his chin, he frowned. "Nope, she didn't mention what it was about, just that I needed to be here." His frown deepened into a scowl. "And that I needed to bring my brother."

Unable to help herself, Neala glanced at Darci, who sat taller in her seat, studying her fingernails. Eamon, too, had flicked his gaze her way, before clearing his throat and planting a neutral expression on his face. "But I couldn't find him in time. Hopefully Druid Imelda understands."

Orion spoke, his voice a low rumble. "It is almost eight, I'm sure she will be here soon."

The others nodded and fidgeted, a strange tension now filling the air as they all pondered the reason for the meeting. Neala's heart had begun to pound; when she'd thought Druid Imelda only wanted to see her and Áine, it hadn't seemed like a big deal. Looking around, she knew now that something more serious was going on.

*Perhaps...*Her eyes narrowed. *Finley said he was going to speak to Imelda before he left, something about starting some kind of 'training'...what if...*

Before she could expand on this thought, Neala heard Druid Imelda's voice coming down the corridor. She was speaking to someone, though Neala couldn't make out the words. Feeling a mix of excitement and dread, she sat straighter and took a deep breath.

Druid Imelda floated into the room, austere as always. Her companions were a surprise; behind her came Druid Orwyn, cane tapping lightly as he navigated the furniture, followed by Ovate Clodagh and Druid Brian.

Brian taught the initiates' air element class, and he was tall and lanky, with greying ginger hair pulled back in a ponytail. His beard trailed almost down to his navel, and was speckled with strands of silvery-white amongst the fiery red.

While Clodagh and Orwyn found seats toward the back of the room, where Darci was sitting, Brian opted to stand, moving to the corner and linking his hands in front of him, hidden within his oversized sleeves.

Unlike the other Druids, who tended to wear regular, everyday clothes, Brian dressed more like the Druids in old paintings; flowing robes with a drawstring waist, the sleeves long enough to always keep his hands tucked away, out of sight. Though his expression was sombre, Neala liked the glint in his eye; he was someone who enjoyed a bit of mischief.

As the students stirred, exchanging curious glances with one another, Druid Imelda strode to the front, coming to rest beside the fireplace. Casting an eye around the room, her mouth tightened; Lorcan was a notable absence.

Clucking her tongue, she pulled a pocket watch out and glanced at it. "I'll give him five more minutes."

Eamon raised his hand, looking sheepish. "Apologies, Druid Imelda. No one has seen my brother much this week. Or most weeks, truth be known. I'm not sure he'll be coming."

Imelda's eyes narrowed, and she scowled. "Oh, he will."

Unsure how to respond to the finality of that statement, Eamon opened his mouth then closed it again, squaring his shoulders as he leaned back in his chair. His foot jiggled slightly, and he tapped his fingers absently on his knee. Neala was fascinated; she had never seen Eamon flustered before.

The other students shifted and twitched, time seeming to drag on. Moving her hand to scratch Keia's ears, Neala was shocked to realise her fox had disappeared.

Frantic, she searched the room, before noticing that Keia was curled up on Ovate Clodagh's lap, fast asleep. The Ovate met Neala's eye and smiled softly, nodding. Neala smiled back, relaxed now that she knew Keia was safe.

Druid Imelda seemed not to notice or care that the others were fidgeting, maintaining her stoic expression.

Glancing down at her pocket watch once more, she let out a frustrated sigh. "Well, then, I suppose I'll have to—"

With a rush of wind, the door to the Blue Room swung open and Lorcan strode in, hands in his pockets. Spotting Eamon immediately, Lorcan's face split into a devilish grin and he winked. "Good evening, brother mine."

Flopping into a chair, he swung one leg over the arm-rest and glanced curiously at the rest of them. He smirked when he saw Darci scowling at him, but when his eyes landed on Neala, his expression changed.

For the briefest moment, she thought he looked almost contrite. But it was soon replaced with his usual crooked grin. "Sorry I'm late, everyone - I just got word of this little gathering." He nodded at Eamon. "Thanks for leaving the note, brother. Very considerate of you."

Druid Imelda was fuming, her eyes burning like hot coals. Fighting to maintain her calm demeanour, she hissed through clenched teeth, "Where have you been?"

Lorcan tucked a hand behind his head and leaned back. "I had some business to attend to. But it's all sorted, for now." Gesturing to the rest of the room, he added, "Any-way, don't let me hold you up. What are we all meeting here for?"

Eamon's knuckles were white against his skin, fists clenched so tightly Neala's hands hurt just looking at them. Jaz, she saw, was fighting back a smile, while Orion seemed to be taking it all in, expression unreadable.

Darci was glaring daggers at Lorcan, and Neala could almost see the rage hissing off her like steam. Áine seemed slightly terrified of his brazen arrogance. Swallowing hard, Neala was almost afraid to look at Druid Imelda. She could feel her fury building, like pressure sucking the air from the room.

The Druid closed her eyes, took a deep breath, and released it slowly, the atmosphere in the room easing. Once she was calm, she clasped her hands in front of her and opened her eyes, meeting the gaze of each of them in turn.

"I've called you all here tonight to discuss events that have, unfortunately, forced our hand." Imelda cleared her throat, searching for the words. "As you all know, the portals between our world and the Otherworld were sealed almost three hundred years ago. It was believed, at the time, that the reason for this was to prevent humans from entering the Otherworld, and vice versa. This was the story that was told, and what has been taught to every Bard on this side of the Veil for hundreds of years."

Imelda began to pace. "However, over this past century, there has been a rumour building - one regarding the supposed *true* events that led to the closing. This rumour claimed that there was a threat to the Otherworld; a demonic force capable of destroying the Fae and all who called the Otherworld home. It arrived unexpectedly, without warning, and had to be stopped immediately.

"Acting swiftly, seven Druids, the greatest of their age, called upon the power of the Chieftain Trees. These trees were the First Trees, the ancient guardians of the Other-world. With the magic bestowed on them by the Chieftains, the Druids were able to close the portals between the worlds forever, sealing them behind the Veil. The threat, it seemed, was contained in this world - forever after known as the 'Cursed World'."

She paused, rubbing her temple as she breathed deeply. "How much truth there is to this rumour has been discussed at great length. There are many who believe it to be untrue - a myth created to make the history of the Sealing more interesting. Others believe there may have been a threat, yes, but that it was humans who were to blame; that they were the 'demonic force' referenced and that the story was embellished as it was retold over generations."

She shook her head in frustration. "Without knowing what is happening in the Otherworld, it is impossible to say for sure what is true and what is myth. We cannot understand what life is like for those who remained over there, as there is no way to communicate with them anymore. For all we know, they may be thriving and prosperous. Equally, they could all be extinct. The lack of information is a constant source of irritation to those of us searching for the truth."

Druid Imelda swept her gaze around the room, mouth pursed tightly. "Druid Orwyn, in particular, has researched the accuracy of this myth for many, many years. Through his efforts, and with the help of Finley Talbot, possible evidence about what happened at the Sealing was discovered in the north. There, in a long-forgotten cave, a Seer had sealed himself, seemingly driven mad by the visions he had Seen."

Neala felt Áine tense and she reached a hand toward her, squeezing her fingers reassuringly. Engrossed in Imelda's story, she kept listening.

"In his madness, he repeated the same words over and over until the day he died, explaining what he'd Seen. What they discovered," Ismelda bowed her head in acknowledgment to Orwyn, "was that the Seer had surrounded himself with winds, breezes that would never cease to blow.

"These winds had been captured and locked inside his cave with him, forever replaying the words that had been spoken to them centuries ago. Over time, the winds weakened, and many of the words were lost. But, from what Finley and Orwyn managed to decipher, it appears the Gate was indeed sealed by seven Druids, who perished in the process. Their spirits, though, were preserved, though it is not clear how or where.

"The prophecy the Seer had made prior to his death hinted that the Chieftain Trees would choose seven new wielders of their power, the Bards destined to ensure that the Veil remains intact, should the safety of the worlds ever be threatened once more. They would be known as the Lorekeepers, and trusted with the most ancient of magics – the magic of the trees. It was not specified when, or even if, the Veil would be broken, but there is evidence mounting that this may be happening now, in our time.

"The emergence of Otherworld creatures in our world over the past few years is a sure sign that, somewhere, there are portals opening once more. These creatures were locked away, all traces of them erased from our world; there can be no other explanation for their resurgence.

"Trackers have been hunting them for several years now, attempting to keep them contained, but the numbers are increasing rapidly. What is most troubling is the variety of creatures that have come through. From púca to cú-sìth...and now changelings, it seems."

She finally paused, letting out a heavy sigh. Rubbing her eyes with her fingers, Imelda gestured with her chin. "Druid Brian, I will hand over to you. Your knowledge of the trees and their magic is unparalleled."

All eyes turned to the Druid in the corner. As Brian came to stand by the fireplace, he removed his hands from their long sleeves and tucked them behind his back. Druid Imelda took a seat off to the side, still rubbing her temples.

"Thank you, Imelda," Druid Brian mumbled. Turning to address the students, he met each of their gazes in turn. "I know that was a lot to absorb, and many of you may be wondering what all of this has to do with you."

There were scattered nods and the exchange of glances, and Druid Brian pursed his lips.

"Most of you know my history, but for those who are new," he nodded at Neala and Áine, "you may not be aware that my life before coming here was..." He stared at the ceiling and chuckled. "Unorthodox."

Bringing his arms around to the front, Brian rolled up his overly-long sleeves and Neala gasped. Now she understood why he always kept them hidden during their lessons; his arms were covered in vines. Not just tattoos, but actual, living vines – miniature tree branches. They even had small leaves on them, which fluttered after being disturbed.

Áine clutched Neala's hand, but she couldn't tear her gaze away.

"As a boy, my family lived in the woodlands. My father was a tanner, and we would spend many months camping and moving around in search of animal skins. Though my family were Bards, they had closed off their powers, refusing to access them. I never understood why, because it was forbidden to talk about it. I suspect it was residual fear of being tortured and burned if discovered. Those were fearful times, back then. As a result, I tried to hide my own magic once it emerged, when I was fifteen."

Brian smiled wryly. "But we all know how well that works. To keep a long story short, my magic rebelled. I had a particular tree, an aspen, that always tried to speak to me, to encourage me to use my gifts. I continually resisted, not wanting my family to know I was using my power.

"Then, one day as I sat in the branches of my aspen, I fell asleep. My magic, kept restrained for so long, burst forth like a river bursting through a dam, and it dragged my soul into the tree beneath me. I was consumed by the tree. I *became* the tree."

He rolled his head from side to side. "For almost a century, I was trapped inside the aspen, unable to free myself. It was an old Druid by the name of Aoife who eventually found me, my family having long moved on. After much study and many failed attempts, she was able to free me, though I would forever be part-man, part-tree. It was thanks to her training that I learned control and became a Druid myself."

Neala gulped. An image of the tree in her yard swam into her mind, and she placed a hand on her shoulder uncomfortably; her birthmark was beginning to throb.

Druid Brian continued, his eyes shadowed. "The point of this is, I have lived life as a tree and understand the magic they possess. It is wild and ancient, far different from that of a Bard. The Druids of the Chieftain Trees - the legend claims they were gifted magic from the ancient ones, and they used it to create the Veil. If what the prophecy says is true, then the new Lorekeepers will be gifted with these same powers in order to prevent the Veil from being destroyed."

Druid Brian linked his long, vine-covered fingers and pressed them to his mouth. "There is no doubt in my mind that the seven new Lorekeepers are each of you."

Neala's throat felt so tight she could hardly breathe. Her heart was pounding so loudly that she could feel it in her brain, and it made her light-headed. "The leaf-mark," she whispered hoarsely, more to herself than anyone else. Druid Brian stared at her curiously.

"Yes, each of you would have a mark, like a white birthmark, in the shape of a leaf. How did you know that?"

"My mother, she told me, ages ago..." Neala stammered, letting go of her shoulder and tucking her hands under her armpits. "She said it marked me as a Lorekeeper, but no one seemed to know what that meant."

Brian's mouth twitched. "Your mother is a clever woman. Do you know which leaf yours is, from which tree?"

Neala cocked her head. "I think it's an ash leaf? The mark is on my shoulder – there was a tree in the woods just behind my home, an ash tree. When I touched it, my birthmark burned..." she trailed off, staring shyly at her lap.

"I have a mark, too," Jaz said, unusually serious. "Here." Pulling up the leg of her jeans, she gestured to a patch of white pigment on her calf, bright against her dark skin. Brian moved closer to inspect it, then smiled.

"Ah, the apple. Yes, that makes sense. Thank you, Jadzia."

Neala glanced around at all the others, wondering if they really did have a mark like hers. Áine was trembling as she lifted her hair, exposing the back of her neck. "Mi-mine is here, though it's very faint."

One by one, the students revealed the locations of their strange birthmarks. Darci pulled up her sleeve, showing a leaf pattern on her upper arm. Orion's was on his ankle. Eamon and Lorcan exchanged glances, then said in unison, "Mine's on my chest."

Druid Brian nodded slowly, lips tight. "Well, that confirms what we suspected."

"Suspected? But then...what was it that made you believe we were the Lorekeepers in the first place?" Eamon asked, leaning forward with his hand over his chin.

Druid Imelda rose and answered, "It is largely thanks to Finley that we knew you were all a little different. When he sees your magic, it shimmers in a unique way, different to anyone else. Once he raised his suspicions with me, you all would have been viewed by each of us," she gestured to her fellow Druids, "to confirm what Finn had seen. Ovate Clodagh, too, had visions of this moment; of us meeting in this very room, prior to your arrival here. Though we didn't understand then quite what it all meant."

Neala stared down at her hands. The audition Finn had arranged for her – it had never been necessary; it was just a ruse to allow the Druids to view her and see if she had the tree-magic, like he suspected.

A flash of hurt stabbed in her chest, but it was quickly squashed down. Yes, it had been another lie, but Neala was past feeling surprised by those anymore. *What's one more, I suppose...* She thought bitterly.

For some reason, Neala found her eyes drawn to Lorcan. While the others all seemed to be wide-eyed and in varying degrees of shock following these revelations, he was still draped over the chair, perfectly relaxed. She frowned, wondering why he didn't seem surprised by this development.

Shaken from her thoughts by Druid Imelda speaking once more, Neala turned her attention back to the teachers. "Now, this is a lot to take in, we know. We had not planned to take this step until we were absolutely sure of how to proceed, or what is required of you - and us, as your mentors."

Imelda covered her eyes with her hands and took several breaths. "After brief discussions today, we have decided that the logical thing to do right now is to begin training you to manage these strange powers. Druid Brian will assist you all to access your tree-magic, while Ovate Clodagh and Druid Orwyn will gather as much information as we can on what we should be training you for. Knowledge of the Veil, and so forth. After all, what was considered a myth has now proven itself to contain a grain of truth." She smiled wryly.

"Well, perhaps we should say there are seven grains of truth. Finley is off seeking more information, as is his want." She sighed. "In the meantime, you will all meet here, every Sunday evening at the eighth hour, where we will find a way through this mystery. Together."

Druid Brian stepped forward. "It would help me greatly to know which tree each of you is connected to. The Chieftain Trees are Oak, Holly, Scots Pine, Yew, Ash, Apple, and Hazel. Jaz has already been marked as the bearer of the apple's powers, and Neala as the ash, but if I could see each of your marks, it would help identify you." He gestured to Orion's foot. "May I?"

Obligingly, Orion removed his boot and rolled down his sock, showing his own pale mark. Brian studied it for a mere second before smiling. "Ah, scots pine. Fitting, indeed."

Turning to Darci, the Druid claimed her as the yew tree's chosen. Áine followed, named as the hazel, before Druid Brian turned to the twins, his gaze curious. "That leaves you two as the oak and holly. How fascinating. But which is which?"

"What's so fascinating?" Jaz asked, folding her legs under her until she was sitting cross-legged on her armchair.

Brian turned to her, face unreadable. "The oak and holly have their own legends, quite apart from their roles as Chieftain Trees. After all, they are the representations of summer and winter, are they not? You know the seasonal wheel, don't you, Jadzia; the cycles of the Holly and the Oak King's reigns?"

It was Orion who answered. "In the summer, the Oak King is the ruler, the mightiest tree in the forest. He governs all who frolic in the warmer months, a time of prosperity and life. But, as the wheel turns and the earth begins to darken and turn cold, his power wanes.

"At Midsummer the Holly King is born. Holly is the master of winter, untouched by the darkness and the cold that forces so many others to weaken and be still; he endures it all. By the time the autumn equinox comes, the Holly King is mighty enough to overthrow the Oak King and takes his place as sovereign.

"But, in turn, the Oak King is reborn at Midwinter and begins to grow stronger, as the Holly King weakens. The Oak King eventually reclaims his throne at the spring equinox, sending his brother back into the darkness, to be reborn at summer's peak. The two kings, forever defeating one another then being reborn. Oak for the summer, Holly for the winter."

Silence filled the room as the richness of Orion's deep voice faded. Neala realised she hadn't breathed for a while and sucked in a breath as quietly as she could.

With a crooked smile, Lorcan clucked his tongue. "Well, it should come as no surprise to anyone that I have the mark of the holly tree, then?" Unbuttoning his shirt, Lorcan revealed a silvery-white holly leaf mark just below his left collarbone, over his heart. Wordlessly, Eamon lifted his shirt, showing an oak leaf in the same place on his own chest. No one spoke.

"That is that, then," Druid Brian muttered, breaking the tension in the room. "Now that I know which tree has chosen each of you, I will research what kinds of powers may have been gifted to you. If you agree, Druid Imelda, I think it may be time for these young ones to get some rest, yes?"

Imelda nodded, face thoughtful. "Yes, of course. All of you, off to bed. We will meet again on Sunday night. If you need to speak about any of this, please come to one of us." She indicated the four teachers in the room.

"I will ask, however, that you do not discuss this amongst your fellow Bards. Until we know more, it is vitally important to keep this secret. This is uncertain territory." She closed her eyes. "For all of us." With a clap, she startled them all back into awareness. "Now, bed."

Neala found it harder to stand than she anticipated; her foot had gone to sleep, and she stumbled, almost falling. A second later she felt the prickle on her skin that told her Lorcan was close.

Sure enough, his hand was supporting her elbow, holding her steady. Not daring to meet his eye, she mumbled a quick thank you, then reached her free arm towards Áine, linking it through hers.

Surprised, Áine turned to ask what she was doing, but Neala just shook her head and pressed closer. "At the dorm," she whispered, nudging Áine towards the doorway. With a flick of her head, she indicated for Keia to come, and the little fox leapt off Ovate Clodagh's lap, weaving her way through the chair legs.

Without another word, Neala and Áine hurried from the room, eager to get to their dorm and debrief about everything they had just learned.

As Áine clicked the clover-leaf door closed behind her, Neala flopped back on her bed, Keia jumping up beside her. Shaking her head, she looked over at Áine. "Well, I can't say I was expecting *that*."

Áine hurried over and sat on the edge of Neala's bed, wide-eyed. "Can you believe it, Neala? Truly? It all just seems so...so insane."

Neala chuckled at Áine's expression; her eyes were almost bugging out of her head.

"I just can't wrap my head around it. What kind of magic do these Chieftain Trees have? Why have they chosen us - what makes us so special? And why now? What is causing the Veil to weaken? How was the Veil even created? Does it have layers, or is it just a meshing of the seven magics, interwoven like...like thread on a loom? Do we need to fix it? What if—"

"Áine, stop. Please, you're going to make my head explode." Neala closed her eyes, placing her arms over her face. "There are so many questions, we could spend all night just asking more and more. I mean, I also want to know whether this has anything to do with the crossroad dreams I've been having, or if the Cailleach is involved, and what 'Stormbringer' means..."

Áine was frowning, lost in thought, when her ears pricked up. "Wait, Neala, what did you say? Something about the Cailleach?"

Neala froze. She hadn't told her friends about her last dream, about being visited by the ancient storm crone. Kicking herself mentally, she sighed.

"I had one more dream, the last for a while, in our first week here. I didn't tell you or Tor because I thought, if I ignored it, I could focus on just being a normal student, without all the other craziness getting in the way. In it, I was at the crossroads again, like always, but there were no paths this time. It was all dark, except for the clearing.

"Then this old woman appeared, a one-eyed crone. She told me she was the Cailleach, the winter deity. She called me Stormbringer, and told me I was her chosen one, or something along those lines.

"The reason all the crossroad paths were darkened, she explained, is because my future now depends on the choices I make at this time. Until I make some decision about something, there are no potential futures laid out for her to see or to guide me on. This decision will apparently, she said, affect the fates of both worlds. I haven't had another dream since."

Saying it out loud, Neala blushed. "I'm sorry, that all sounds so arrogant of me."

While she'd been speaking, Áine had been listening thoughtfully. Now, she tilted her head to the side. "I wonder what that choice could be? And why a storm goddess has taken an interest in someone this side of the Veil? I know that back before the portals were sealed, the Old Ones, the elemental deities, used to favour people and worked much more closely with mortals than they do now. It was believed that they all chose to reside in the Otherworld, too. Like they abandoned this one or something. But perhaps that whole concept is wrong? Can they perhaps be in different dimensions of time and space simultaneously?"

Áine was speaking faster and faster. "After all, it's common knowledge that the Otherworld exists on a different earthly plane to ours, so in order to interact with you *here*, the Cailleach would need to be able to transcend these barriers and speak with you. Is that perhaps why she has only appeared in a dream?

"Your dreams seem to exist in an alternate reality, being more psychic visions than true dreams, so that makes sense. But, if that's true, then what does that mean for the Veil? It can't be breaking in our world if it's being weakened from the Otherworld side, because we aren't aligned with their space and time continuum.

"So, does that mean it has already *been* broken and we are just becoming aware of it now? Or is it going to be broken in the Otherworld future, and we have to stop it before it begins? But then wouldn't that create a time paradox? If we stop it before it ever begins, then we would never be there to stop it in the first place because we would not have anything to stop—"

"Áine, enough. I'm going to slap you in a moment," Neala groaned, head fit to burst. Áine gasped, eyes still slightly glazed.

Propping herself up on her elbows, Neala studied her carefully. "Are you sure you're okay? That was a lot of philosophical pondering you were doing. Did you – did you See something?"

Shaking her head to clear it, Áine murmured, "No, they're different - it wasn't a vision. I don't know what came over me, then. It was like, once my brain started thinking, all these ideas just kept coming, like this need to *know* that wouldn't stop." She shrugged sheepishly. "I know I'm a curious person, but that was a wee bit extreme, even for me."

Neala chuckled. "I think our brains are all in meltdown mode at the moment." She let out a yawn. "C'mon, let's get some sleep. Maybe things will be clearer in the morning. Do you want the first shower?"

Áine shook her head. "No, you go. I'll wait."

With a nod, Neala pushed herself up from the bed and gathered her pyjamas, cocking a brow at Keia. "Do you have anything to add, by the way, mysterious fox-creature?"

But Keia just sniffed at her and curled up in a tight ball, furry tail covering her face. Smiling to herself, Neala headed into the shower, willing the water to wash away the headache that was forming.

~ 24 ~

By the time Sunday evening rolled around, Neala could hardly sit still. Her leg was bouncing so hard that she bumped the table, sending Torin's plate clattering. He gave her a withering look and sighed. "I've never seen anyone so nervous about tutoring. It's not a big deal, Neals. Áine is your friend, and a great teacher. Nothing to be worried about."

Neala's stomach squirmed and she pushed her mashed potato around her plate, not feeling hungry. It had been awful, keeping their secret from him. After the events of the secret meeting, Áine and Neala had agreed to follow Imelda's advice and not tell anyone what they were up to.

When they'd met Torin for breakfast the next day, they'd told him that the Druid had asked Áine to tutor Neala for a little while, claiming she needed some extra help with her lore and myth work. Seeing as how new she was to Barding, this seemed plausible.

Torin had accepted their story, even offering to help Neala himself. Guilt eating at her, she had declined, explaining that he was busy enough.

As they waited for Áine to join them now, Neala again felt the overwhelming desire to tell him the truth. Instead, she bit her tongue and let her mind wander.

The rest of the week had flown by. A Bard by the name of Eve had taken over Finley's music classes; "Only while he's away", she'd assured them. During her lessons with the Druids who had been in the Blue Room that night, Neala had half-expected them to give some sort of hint about what they'd learned, but none of them had mentioned anything more to her or Áine, not even giving the slightest acknowledgement that they had met outside of class.

Glancing around the dining hall as she made patterns with her food, Neala wondered what the others were feeling. She hadn't even spoken with Jaz since their meeting. Lorcan had been notably absent, and on the occasions when she had seen the others, they had either smiled politely or ignored her point-blank (in Darci's case).

Áine had been coping in her own way; by spending all available time in the library, researching. Neala had joined her once, but she found more joy in being outdoors, or helping Cathal with the animals.

Sipping her glass of juice absently, she thought about her mother. They had exchanged several letters since Ovate Clodagh had scried her for Neala, and Nanna had even sent some of her famous butterscotch fudge, which Neala had been rationing to make it last as long as possible.

As much as she had wanted to explain to Dana what had been revealed in the past week, she'd kept her last letter very short, deciding she would rather tell her everything in person when they reunited over the Yule break. Poking her soggy mushrooms absently, Neala wondered what it would be like, seeing them again after all she had learned. Would they treat her any differently?

As the bell chimed the seventh hour, Áine came hurrying into the dining room, looking flustered. Throwing some food on her tray, she joined Neala and Torin, muttering a hasty greeting.

Torin raised his brows, looking from one to the other. "Geez, you'd think you guys were about to sit an exam, not do some revision. What's the big deal?"

The girls exchanged pained glances. "Oh, no, it's not that. I'm just a bit researched out, that's all," Áine muttered.

Torin chuckled. "Words I never thought I'd hear from you." Turning to Neala, he stifled a grin and reached towards her, plucking a piece of straw from her hair. "I didn't even notice that before. You can take the girl out of the farm, but not the farm out of the girl, am I right? Hanging out at the stables again, I presume?"

Neala smiled, running a hand over her ponytail in case there were more hidden treasures. A quick glance down at her shirt and jeans revealed a few dust marks, but nothing worse. Relieved, Neala pushed her plate aside and rested her chin in her hand. "Sorry, Tor. You should know what a grub I am by now."

He chuckled, leaning back in his chair. "Not half. But we love you anyway." He suddenly looked very nervous, and he rubbed the back of his neck awkwardly. "Anyway, ladies, I, uh, I'm going to cut this a little short. I have to, um, go and do some stuff."

Neala had never seen Torin look so uncomfortable. A faint blush was creeping over his cheeks, and she gave him a sidelong smile. "Do you just? Anything more you'd like to share with the group, pal?"

Rolling his eyes affectionately, Torin stood, scraping his chair back. "Not really, no," he teased, giving Neala a gentle shove on the shoulder. "Have fun tonight, girls. I'll see you tomorrow." Shoving his hands in his pockets, he strode from the room, shoulders hunched.

Neala watched him go, then gave Áine a pointed look. "Any idea what that was about?"

Áine glanced up from her half-eaten pudding cup. "Sorry, I wasn't really listening. I was just thinking about tonight, you know?"

Neala's leg started jiggling again, the brief distraction over. Turning her thoughts to that evening's meeting, she swallowed hard. She had no idea what to expect. Feeling the sudden urge to go for a walk, she sighed loudly. "Áine, would you mind terribly if I left? I don't want to leave you here on your own, but I just need to clear my head a bit before the meeting."

Shaking her head, Áine pushed her own tray aside. "No, I was done. I'm going to find Eilìs - I haven't seen her in ages and just wanted to check how she's going."

Áine's eyes drifted down and her voice grew hushed. "Honestly, I'm really nervous about tonight and kind of just need to see my sister." Neala nodded in understanding, gathering her tray.

"That works perfectly, then. I'll see you at eight, okay?" Áine nodded and Neala left, disposing her tray before leaving the room with Keia. Not having a real destination in mind, she walked outside, breathing in the cool night air. It was dark out, and the smell of rain was strong. Her magic prickled, sensing a storm not far away.

Deciding against being outdoors after all, Neala chewed her lip. With a huff, she turned on her heel and went back inside. She still hadn't explored the whole manor yet and wondered if she should go wandering.

But, she countered, if she got lost, she might miss the meeting. Growing more frustrated, Neala growled to herself. "I may as well just go to the Blue Room now, then," she muttered. "Let's go, little one."

Keia had been very quiet since the day Finley had left to hunt the changelings. Though she could still mind-speak to Neala when she needed, the occasions were few and far-between. Neala wondered what had changed.

Turning to Keia now as they walked, she whispered, "You've been pretty silent, are you okay?" The little fox was trotting along beside her, her short legs working hard to keep up with Neala's steps.

"Yes. Stormbringer needs to learn things for herself now. I must not interfere."

Neala stopped abruptly; she hadn't expected that answer. "That sounds an awful lot like what the Cailleach said, about not being able to guide my decisions."

Keia stared at her, blue eyes not revealing anything. Pursing her lips, Neala crouched down. "Someone has sent you to me - we know that much. But if it wasn't the Cailleach, then who?"

"My Lady."

Neala blew out a breath. "Yes, but that doesn't help to narrow it down." Rubbing her eyes, she stood with a sigh. "But one mystery at a time, I suppose. Otherwise I'll go mad." She chuckled. "Well, mad-*er*."

Continuing to walk down the hall, she mumbled sadly, "I do miss speaking with you, though."

Keia whined softly, butting Neala's leg with her furry head. *"I am still here."*

Neala smiled. "I know. And I am grateful for that, really. I don't think I could ever be without you now."

Arriving at the Blue Room, she pushed the door open softly, wondering whether Orion or one of the others would be there again this time. But it was quiet inside, only the crackling of the fireplace breaking the silence. With an internal sigh of relief, Neala entered the room, closing the door behind her.

Still unwilling to use her magic to light the candles - her attempts at working with fire safely were still proving a challenge - she grabbed a taper from the box on the mantlepiece instead.

Once the room was filled with a warm, cosy glow, Neala threw the stick on the fire and sat on one of the armchairs, Keia jumping onto her lap. Rain was beginning to fall against the windows, and she watched the drops run down the glass panes, stroking Keia rhythmically. It was hypnotising.

Unconsciously, she sent her magic out, sensing the closeness of the storm above. Keia growled softly but didn't interfere. Settling herself more comfortably, she rested her nose on her paws and waited, twitching anxiously.

*****

"Storm-daughter, you are welcome."

Neala's water-self opened her eyes, seeing the forest stretching below her. In the distance, cloud-Neala could see the wavering lights of Birchtree Hall, glimmering through the mist of her brothers and sisters. Joy filled her, and she excitedly bumped her companions, finally at home in the storm.

As they rolled over the land, she could feel the prickling energy of lightning surrounding them, growing stronger by the second. A part of her remembered feeling this in her human body, whenever Lorcan was near.

Lightning. Of course that's what it is. It's part of him - that's what I can sense. Neala's cloud family rumbled uncomfortably, sensing the humanity taking over their storm-sister.

Not wanting them to worry, she gave in to her water-self once more, returning to the dance, jostling her friends and building up the energy for a lightning bolt. The white-hot light burst forth, zig-zagging its way through the air until it met the earth below.

The echo of thunder rumbled, and the clouds cheered happily. Rain began to fall more heavily, and Neala had the same rush of fear she'd felt before; if she allowed herself to rain, she may be lost forever.

They were moving closer to the school now, and Neala wondered if she could somehow return to her own body. Last time, she'd been rescued, but leaving the storm and becoming human again was something she would surely have to learn for herself.

Closing off her connections to the other clouds around her, she focused on how it felt to be human. She felt the warmth of Keia, curled up on her lap; of the air filling her lungs as she breathed. The heat from the fireplace was pressing against her skin, and the sounds of the crackling wood filled her ears...

Opening her eyes, Neala realised instantly that she was back in her body. Outside, another bolt of lightning was followed immediately by a crack of thunder, telling her the storm was now overhead.

She gasped excitedly, cuddling Keia to her chest. The fox licked her face as relief coursed through her. "I did it! I didn't get caught up in the storm this time, I figured out how to come back." Neala laughed, still feeling the rush of being one with the clouds. "That was amazing!"

As the rain pattered harder against the window, her excitement was replaced with concern. "Still, I wonder what would happen if I stayed and became rain?" Thoughtful, Neala pressed her face into Keia's inky fur.

The sound of the door creaking open made her jump, but she relaxed when she saw it was only Eamon. He was followed closely by Orion and Jaz, and Neala greeted them shyly.

The others took their seats and chatted amongst themselves, all avoiding the one topic they longed to discuss. Even Jaz was unusually subdued, sticking to talking about the weather and their classes.

By the time everyone else had arrived, the anticipation in the room was so thick you could cut it. Like last time, Lorcan was still missing by the time Druid Imelda and Brian arrived, though he slipped in just before the door closed.

Giving him a stern look, Imelda resumed her position by the fireplace. Áine, who was curled up on the couch beside Orion and clutching a cushion to her chest, leaned across to Neala. "No Clodagh or Orwyn?"

Neala raised her eyebrow and gave a small shrug. She was a little distracted - her skin had started to prickle the moment Lorcan entered. Though he was seated on the opposite side of the room, she could feel the echoes of lightning power, as though it were coursing through her veins.

Wondering whether her brief connection with the storm had made her more sensitive to Lorcan's power, Neala's ponderings were interrupted by Druid Imelda clearing her throat.

Hands behind her back, she spoke to the group. "I know it hasn't been long since we last spoke, but how is everyone feeling? Have you all had time to absorb everything we discussed?"

Looking around at the others, Neala nodded slowly; everyone seemed reluctant to admit if they hadn't. Mouth a hard line, Imelda narrowed her eyes, but continued, "Good. Now, I have made contact with Finley. He is rather consumed with his own investigations right now. However, he wanted to pass on that he is thinking of you all and will do all he can to learn more about what is happening to the portals and the Veil.

"Until then, we will focus on discovering what your powers may be, and how best to manage them safely. Druid Brian, you can elaborate on this, yes?"

Brian was leaning against the wall, a bag of scrolls slung over his shoulder. Nodding curtly, he moved to the centre of the group and placed the bag down. "I've researched the magic of the Chieftain Trees. As you are all aware, our innate Fae magic allows us to connect with the natural world more closely than humans and the like, but there is a host of greater power out there that we cannot understand or comprehend.

"Every living thing has its own essence, its own form of magic. Trees are no exception. While the Chieftain Trees are perhaps the most powerful, every tree has its own spirit and abilities that it can share with those who seek it. The greatest examples I can think of are the sacred groves which guard the portals that lead here, to Birchtree. That is not *Bardic* magic, but a more ancient power - the magic of the birch trees themselves."

He stroked his beard absently. "I believe this is what the original Lorekeepers were gifted - the very spirit of the seven trees. That must have been what enabled them to use magic beyond their Bardic abilities to create the Veil. A power as strong as that could not have been produced by mere Bards, or even pure Fae. The Veil has strength enough to hold back deities – ancient gods and goddesses. That kind of power must be..."

With a shake of his head, Druid Brian cleared his throat and refocused his attention on the students. "But I digress. Back to the Chieftain Trees. My logic was to look at what properties each of the seven trees possess. This should give us some idea what to expect from your magic." Waving his hand, he tilted his head to the side. "Enough talk - it is easier to show you."

Holding out his hands, Druid Brian rolled back his sleeves. Though she was expecting it, seeing the tiny aspen leaves fluttering on their miniature branches within his skin still made Neala shudder. As she stared, the leaves began to dance and wave, an invisible wind stoking their movement.

Unable to look away, Neala's eyes grew hazy, as though a silvery mist was coating them. The leaves were blurring now, though they still continued to move hypnotizingly. As her vision cleared, she found that she could avert her gaze at last.

Blinking, she looked up and gasped. Staring across the circle at Jaz, Neala could see a tree sparkling within her, its image wavering and distorting. Tiny crab apples hung from its branches.

Shifting her eyes to look at Eamon, she could see the towering oak inside his body, shimmering like a mirage. The others were all staring, too, heads turning as they looked at one another in awe. Wondering what she looked like, Neala glanced down at her own body, but saw nothing; no image, only Keia staring at her, head cocked to the side.

As the magic started to fade, Neala hurried to get a glimpse of Lorcan. There, disappearing into his chest, was the spiky, glossy green of the holly leaf. Realising the image was gone and she was now staring into his green eyes instead, Neala flushed and looked away.

Druid Brian was pulling his sleeves down once more, a sad smile on his face. "I do not possess much of the aspen's magic anymore - only the ability to show what is hidden from plain sight sometimes. But that is an example of an unusual power that I can use, which I was gifted from the tree; it is not a Bardic ability. What each of you will be able to do should be much more enhanced, and closer to the natural powers of the trees who have chosen you."

He reached over and pulled a scroll from his bag, tapping it against his hand thoughtfully. "Surprisingly, there is little record of the Chieftain Trees and their magic. Our ancestors seldom used written communication, passing down knowledge and wisdom through story and song. But I have recorded what I have learned from speaking with the trees and from my reading.

"Druid Orwyn has also contributed with his knowledge of the myths and legends of the Otherworld. Frustratingly, much of the lore is contained over on the other side, so we are a bit limited. Still, it is a start."

Handing out the scrolls, he explained, "In each of these, you will find an image of your tree, plus its Ogham symbol. That is the ancient language of the Druids - their alphabet. You will also find a summary of what magic your trees have been known to produce, though it is not extensive. Have a quick browse, then we shall have some more discussion."

Neala unfurled her scroll excitedly. Drawn in ink, the illustration of the ash tree was extremely detailed, every leaf included. The markings on the bark were exquisite, and she silently commended Druid Brian's artistic ability.

Below it, a symbol was drawn, alongside the word 'Nion'. The symbol was a vertical line with five staves coming off its right side, like ladder-rungs. Written in jagged handwriting was a short description of the ash's properties. Scanning eagerly, Neala read:

A tree that connects the worlds – referred to as The World Tree, or the Tree of Life. Branches above are reflected by the complex root system below, symbolising the bringing-together of different worlds by the ash tree. Connection to water, but also fire and air. Possible abilities include mind-reading and scrying, particularly with water sources. Healing comes naturally. Association with lakes, oceans, and storms. Charms made from its wood can be used against drowning. It was often used to make boats as it is very strong. Power to open portals between dimensions.

Eyes wide, Neala placed the scroll down on her lap. She could feel her heart in her throat, and she swallowed hard. *Association with storms...connected to other worlds...opening portals...* Neala's hands began to tremble. *Is this why the Cailleach is interested in me? Is this what 'Stormbringer' means?*

She glanced up to see how the others were reacting. Jaz was scanning her scroll eagerly, beaming. Áine, like Neala, looked a little pale and in a state of shock. The older students didn't seem as fazed, though Eamon was staring out the window, rubbing his chin and frowning. Lorcan was watching her, brow creased with curiosity. Neala met his gaze, then looked away, itching to read what powers he may have.

Once he was satisfied everyone had read their scrolls, Druid Brian clapped his hands together lightly. "I hope some of that is resonating with you all. Does anyone have any questions thus far?"

Darci crossed her legs and leaned back in her chair, hiding herself deeper in the shadows. Squinting, Neala was shocked to see that her face was screwed up like she was trying not to cry.

In a voice that shook slightly, Darci snapped, "How come no one has ever told us this before? In all the years I've been here, why has it been hidden until now? Are you telling me no one's ever noticed that we can do...other things? Dangerous things? If my family knew this –"

She hesitated, tone changing from one of irritation to anger. "It's just stupid. I mean, *his* says he may be able to turn his skin to stone." She pointed at Orion's scroll with a sneer.

Orion looked annoyed that she had been reading over his shoulder, but Darci ignored him. "Surely someone would have noticed these things before?"

Lorcan started to laugh. "Oh, Darce. I've been using illusions for years, one of my so-called holly-gifted talents. Jaz, you're one of the most popular Bards here - I'm going to take a stab that one of your apple-gifts has something to do with being liked, yes? Like a gift of love or attraction?"

Jaz narrowed her eyes, but mumbled, "Infatuation is on my list."

With a smug twitch of his eyebrows, Lorcan turned to Orion. "And our giant friend over here. You weren't always this big - you grew almost two feet taller in a matter of months, just under year ago. I'd bet anything that is one of the elements of the scots pine, hmm?"

Orion nodded. "Yes. Rapid growth."

Satisfied, Lorcan sat back and met Darci's eyes pointedly. "It isn't a *separate* magic – not for us. We were born with these skills as part of our power. Everything we do is tainted by the tree magic, whether we mean it to be or not. That's what made it so hard to work out – without an obvious distinction between our own Bard abilities and those gifted by the trees, how could anyone guess why we could do these things?"

Mumbling softly, he added, "It's not a curse, Darci – no matter what others may have thought."

Turning away, Darci folded her arms and refused to meet his eye. Eamon, however, was staring at him with a sour look on his face, knee jiggling restlessly.

Screwing up his nose, Lorcan turned back to Druid Brian. "With all due respect - you only gained your additional powers *after* merging with the aspen tree, is that correct? They weren't there before?"

Contrary to what Neala expected, the Druid did not interrupt Lorcan or scold him for talking out of turn. Instead, he stroked his beard thoughtfully. "Yes. Prior to that day, my powers were no different to an ordinary Bard. I could always sense the aspen's power as something different from my own, like a magic within my magic; oil and water, if you will. Never mixing, but with the ability to access both as needed."

A crease formed between his brows. "If you are correct, and many of you are already displaying some of the traits listed, then it may be as you believe; you were gifted the magics from birth, so have never known any different. It is certainly an interesting idea."

Jaz huffed. "Well, if I have been using apple-tree power, I haven't been aware of it."

Lorcan rolled his eyes. "That's what I'm trying to say. You wouldn't know if you were using it, because you've *always* used it – whether you intended to or not. It's always been part of you. What we need to learn now is how to isolate and use the tree gifts *deliberately*."

The familiar smirk crossed his face. "Well...I mean, at least the rest of *you* do."

"Oh, that's enough. We get it - you can stop lording it over everyone here, Lorcan," Eamon snapped. "We're supposed to be a team. Unless you're willing to actually *help* everyone instead of just bragging, then you may as well leave."

Lorcan didn't hesitate. "Sure." He stood and gave Eamon a mocking salute. "Your wish is my command."

Neala expected Imelda or Brian to stop him, but the Druids watched calmly as Lorcan disappeared out the door. Wordlessly, Druid Imelda closed it, expression neutral.

Not returning to her seat, she instead addressed the remaining students in a tone that showed how tightly controlled her emotions were. "He is right. Your Bard and tree magics are so intertwined that it is virtually impossible to distinguish one from the other. Many things you have always believed were part of your Bard powers may truly be tree-gifted, after all.

"Until we practice specific magic related to your Lore-keeper abilities, we will not know. If Lorcan has already found a way to do this, and it sounds like he has," Imelda sighed, "then we will need to take his lead on where to go from here."

The two Druids exchanged glances, and Brian nodded, encouraging her to continue. Imelda looked more vulnerable than Neala had ever seen her, and it was frightening.

"The truth is," she half-whispered, "We have no idea what we're doing. This is unchartered territory; there are threats returning to our world that have not been seen for centuries. Old magics are awakening - things we do not understand. Our forebears, the ones who could traverse the realms on a whim - they would have knowledge of how to handle it. But there is little available to those of us who were left over here."

The steely look of determination returned to her eyes. "But we are strong, and we have adapted. We will continue to grow and roll with the punches. The next time we meet, we will be outdoors, so we can practice some of these new magics. Meet us at the greenhouses next Sunday, instead of here.

"In the meantime, learn as much as you can about what these abilities may mean for you. I will speak with Lorcan and see if he will cooperate rather than continue to hold himself apart from you all. Eamon is correct - you must work together." With that, she dismissed them.

Clutching her scroll, Neala stood, about to head out, but Eamon held up a hand to stop her. Curious, she paused, wondering why he'd made her wait. Darci had already left, followed closely by Jaz and Orion, the girl chattering non-stop at the gentle giant.

Áine was making her way over to the two Druids, who were hovering by the fireplace, no doubt about to gather as much information as she could. Realising she had no reason not to, Neala turned to Eamon. "Did you want to talk?"

Eamon nodded, answering in a low voice, "If I may?"

Neala gestured to the door. "After you."

As the two walked out of the room, Eamon glanced down at Keia. He smiled warmly. "You do have a shadow, don't you?"

Neala grinned. "She's pretty special."

"Indeed." Eamon frowned briefly, but then his face softened once more. "I'm sorry if this all seems a wee bit odd, I just wanted to ask you something. Away from prying ears."

Neala's stomach fluttered with nerves. What could he possibly want to ask her? Realising they were heading to a part of the school she hadn't seen yet, Neala started to feel a little anxious. She was relieved when Eamon stopped, staring absently at the ceiling.

"Um, what do you want to know?" she stammered. Eamon sensed her nervousness and his eyes lit with mirth.

"Oh, Neala, I'm sorry if I've frightened you or made you uncomfortable. I can see how this may seem, well...somewhat creepy." He ran a hand over his hair, looking sheepish. "No, I just wanted to ask about your relationship with my brother, that's all."

Neala was stunned. "Well, for starters, I'd hardly say we have a *relationship*. We've hardly even spoken." She screwed up her nose. "Honestly, the only proper conversation we've ever had was more of an argument than anything. I barely know him." Subconsciously, she reached up to fiddle with the lighting pendant around her neck.

"That's good. I mean, not that being friends with him is a *bad* thing - I don't mean to imply that. It's just, well, hmm..." Eamon sighed, rubbing the back of his neck. "I guess what I'm trying to say is...Lorcan can be dangerous. He is reckless, and doesn't consider other people's safety all that often."

"But why warn me? Like I said, we aren't close."

Eamon pursed his lips. "My brother has taken an interest in you. Despite our troubles, he's still my twin; I can read him well enough. I am just worried that you may get hurt."

He flushed slightly, shifting his weight from one foot to the other. "And I don't want you to come to any harm, that's all."

A blush was creeping over Neala's own cheeks. Unsure how to react, she stuttered, "Oh, um, okay. That's - that's really kind of you. I'll, um, I'll be careful, then."

Clearing his throat, Eamon nodded curtly. "Good. That's good. Well, I suppose I'll see you next Sunday?"

"Yep, I'll be there."

"Great. Have a, uh, good night."

Neala wished she could sink into the ground. "You, too."

With another nod, Eamon turned on his heel and walked away swiftly, clicking his fingers as he swung his arms. Fighting a grin, Neala rolled her scroll in her hands, feeling giddy.

Surely I'm just overreacting? Maybe he's looking out for me as a friend. Friends do things like that, don't they? Flustered, she suddenly realised she had no idea where she was. About to ask Keia if she could help find the way back, she paused.

So faintly she almost missed it, she heard the sound of a piano playing. Fighting the urge to yawn, Neala felt torn; she was desperately tired and longing for her bed, but her curiosity was itching to investigate. Resigned, she looked down at Keia. "Screw it – bed can wait."

She giggled as her fox gave her the most withering look she'd ever seen. Poking her tongue out at her, Neala began tiptoeing down the hallway, listening intently.

After a while, the music began to grow louder. Neala recognised the tune now; it was *'Für Elise'*, by Beethoven. Wandering down to the doorway at the end of the hall, Neala paused.

Listening to the melody rising and falling, she eased the door handle down, praying it wouldn't squeak. Peering around the door, her eyes widened.

The room was huge, with a large window providing a view of the lake and the woodlands stretching far into the horizon. In the centre stood the most beautiful grand piano she had even seen; pure white with gold inlays, it seemed almost too exquisite to touch.

The space had been specially designed to amplify the acoustics perfectly, so the notes were rich and full, filling the room with their music. Seated at the piano, his back to her, was Lorcan, head down as he played, lost in the moment.

Neala could hardly breathe; the power emanating from him was magnetic, drawing her in. Silently, she entered the room and padded closer to the piano. Keia did not follow this time; instead, she curled up just inside the doorway and settled down for a nap.

As he played the final chord, Lorcan turned his head to the side, a smile tugging at the corners of his mouth. "I don't usually have an audience."

Startled, Neala jumped, dropping her scroll on the floor. Hurriedly, she picked it up, face burning. "Sorry, I'm sorry. I just, I heard someone playing, I didn't mean—"

Lorcan laughed and played a quick flurry of notes before turning fully to look at her. "I never said it was a bad thing." He cocked his head at her. "What were you doing this close to my room, anyway? The Blue Room isn't near here, nor are the girls' dorms."

"Your room?"

"Yes, my room. That wasn't an answer."

Neala bristled. "If you must know, I was talking with your brother." Another flush crept over her cheeks at the memory. "Or, rather, I was being warned by your brother. About you."

Lorcan's eyes danced. "Really? And you being here shows how much you listened, obviously."

About to retort, Neala stopped. *My brother has taken an interest in you.* Though she didn't believe Eamon's suspicions, she was curious to see how Lorcan would react if she didn't fight him for a change.

Smiling warmly, she moved closer to the piano, ignoring the prickling of her skin. "So, *'Für Elise'*, hmm? What other songs do you know?"

Lorcan titled his head back curiously, not expecting this reaction. Without a word, he turned back to the piano and started to play another song Neala knew well: *'Rêverie'.*

Taking care not to interrupt, she slid onto the piano seat beside him. Shuffling sideways to make room for her, Lorcan didn't pause his playing.

Oddly enough, though she was the closest to him she had been in a long time, Neala noticed that the prickling sensation was gone. Shaking her head slightly, she watched as his hands danced nimbly over the keys, the familiar tune coming to life under his touch. Try as she might, she couldn't keep the tears from welling in her eyes.

Without looking at her, Lorcan asked softly, "What's wrong?"

Neala sniffed, rubbing her eye with a finger. "It's nothing."

His mouth lifted in a half-smile, but he didn't take his eyes off the keys. "If it causes tears, then it's never nothing. You can tell me."

"It – it reminds me of my dad. This song." Neala laughed, the sound coming out as more of a sob. "We used to tease him all the time, my mum and me. You see, he was obsessed with classical and jazz music; he never listened to anything else. Whenever he'd get home from work after a long day, he'd always do the same thing: make a cup of tea - black, no sugar - then settle down in his favourite chair by the record player and put on one of his usuals. Beethoven, Mozart, jazz legends like Miles Davis..."

Neala gestured to the piano. "Debussy, obviously. For exactly one hour, he would just sit, eyes closed, sipping his tea and listening. Then he'd turn it off and carry on with the evening. No one could talk to him when he was in his chair; it was 'his' time."

As Lorcan wound up the song, Neala wiped her cheeks and took several shaky breaths through her mouth, nose completely blocked now. Once the last note had faded, Lorcan lowered his hands and faced her. To her surprise, his eyes were full of kindness. "You really miss him."

Neala nodded. "He died last year in a car accident. That's partly why Mum and I moved here. I now know this—" she waved her hand around to indicate the school, "was the main reason."

Lorcan was silent, thoughtful. He played a few gentle chords, then asked Neala softly, "What was his favourite song?"

Without hesitating, Neala laughed and answered, "'Concerto de Aranjuez'. He used to laugh at me every time I'd try to pronounce it. I was almost thirteen by the time I realised it wasn't called 'Cornettos and Orange Juice'. Dad thought it was the cutest thing, apparently, and he always smiled when he listened to it."

She hurriedly moved on, wanting her own turn to ask the questions. "But enough about me. What about you? What are your parents like?"

A chill tinged the air as Lorcan tensed beside her, and his hands flexed slightly. Mouth twitching, he looked away. "They aren't very interesting."

Sensing the frosty wall being built up between them, Neala backtracked. "Oh, okay, that's fine. So, how long have you known about your tree magic?"

Lorcan glanced at her, eyebrows arched. "No. I'm not going to play this game – enough questions." Eyes softening, he frowned thoughtfully, then smiled. "I have a better idea."

He flexed his fingers, then gave Neala a sidelong look. In a gentler tone than before, he murmured, "Close your eyes."

Hesitantly, she obliged. As the first chords of the song played, Neala's breath caught in her throat; it was 'Cornettos and Orange Juice'.

In her mind, she could see her father, sitting in his favourite chair with his teacup, exactly how she remembered. Listening to Lorcan play, she began to tremble; the memory felt so real.

Next to her ear, she heard Lorcan mutter gruffly, "Open."

Blinking the tears from her lashes, she gasped and clutched his arm without thinking. There, reflected in the window, was her memory.

As though watching on a television screen, Neala could see her father, the chair, the cup. He was listening to his record player, eyes closed as he leaned his head back against the cushion, tea nestled in his large, calloused hands.

Rising shakily to her feet, she stumbled over to the glass and pressed her hand against the image of her father's face. The illusion of Gary smiled at her touch.

As soon as she touched the glass, the scene enveloped her, surrounding her. It was as though she had been transported back in time and was standing in her old living room. The details were everywhere; the ticking of the cuckoo clock on the wall, the painting of the tractor her grandfather had made, framed and hung on the wall above the record player. And her father, right there in front of her.

Neala breathed deeply; she could almost smell him - the faint whiff of dust and animals and sweat, tinged with the woody scent of his aftershave. Her heart ached, a combination of grief and love and joy.

Overcome with emotion, Neala dropped to her knees and rested her head on the arm of her father's chair. Light as a whisper, she felt his hand stroking her hair. It was all so real...

*****

All the while, Lorcan played, embellishing the song with magic. He had poured a lot of his power into this illusion, wanting to make it as special as possible for Neala. Frowning, he wondered what it was about her that made him lose focus like this.

What am I doing? This isn't part of the plan - I can't falter now, it's so close, he thought angrily, gritting his teeth.

In spite of his frustration, Lorcan glanced up and his stomach stirred; it felt good to do something nice for her, and he was honestly enjoying it. It had been so long since he'd cared about anyone but himself - he was surprised to feel as strongly as he did.

Almost regretfully, he reached the end of the song, allowing the notes to fade away, taking the illusion with it. The silence echoed as Neala pressed her face against the cool glass of the window, crying soundlessly. Unsure what to do, Lorcan made to stand, then stopped. Instead, he waited.

*****

Once her tears had dried, Neala pulled away, looking out at the view of the lake below once more. Turning back to Lorcan, she opened and closed her mouth several times, unable to find the words.

Shifting his weight awkwardly, Lorcan mumbled, "I, um, I'm sorry. I didn't mean to upset you - I thought it might make you...happy?"

A laugh burst from Neala's throat, and she hurried over. To the surprise of them both, she threw her arms around his neck, pressing her chin into his shoulder. "Thank you. Thank you, Lorcan."

Completely out of his depth, he patted her back, unsure what else to do. "Uh, you're welcome, I guess?"

Coming to her senses, Neala let go of him and sat back on the piano seat, face hot. Composing herself, she explained, "That was a really sweet thing to do. Thank you so much. It was like I was really with him."

She hesitated. "I didn't get the chance to say goodbye, you know? He just left to pick up some things in town, but never came back. It was nice to, well...to have that final moment with him, even if it wasn't real. If that makes sense?"

The silence was palpable, hanging between them like a thick blanket. Feeling vulnerable after sharing so much, Neala tried to lighten the mood. "I didn't think you'd know that song - that was impressive."

More at ease now that she wasn't hugging him, Lorcan adopted his familiar crooked smile. "I know everything. Haven't I made that perfectly clear already?"

Neala was beginning to recognise this bravado attitude, and she grinned. "Oh, only a hundred times. But who's counting, right?"

The pair chuckled, then fell silent, neither knowing where to go from here. Glancing over her shoulder, Neala spotted Keia snoozing by the door, and she realised it must be getting very late.

Sliding off the seat, she rubbed her hands on her jeans and stammered, "Well, anyway, this was lovely. I really should be getting to bed, though. Late nights and all that. But thank you again; that was – that was a very nice thing you did. I appreciate it."

Lorcan was giving her an odd look, something glimmering deep in his eyes. Before she could make sense of what it may be, he lifted a hand and cocked his head to the side. "Let's just leave it at: 'you're welcome, have a good sleep, and I'll see you tomorrow.'"

Mouth snapping closed, Neala nodded in relief. "Yes, that. Exactly." Turning her back on him, she walked swiftly to the door, murmuring for Keia to wake up. The fox stirred, shaking her fur out and stretching.

Holding the door open, she poked her head back into the room one last time. "Good night, Lorcan."

He smiled softly. "Good night."

As she closed the door, Neala heard the piano playing once more. This time, though, she did not recognise the tune.

~ 25 ~

Neala woke on Friday morning feeling very ill. Lying in bed, she placed her hands over her face and groaned softly. Her head was pounding, and she felt trembly all over. A cold sweat covered her body, leaving her skin sticky and gross.

Rolling to her side, she wondered briefly if she was going to vomit. Waiting for her stomach to settle, she sucked in some deep breaths. *Shower. I need a shower*, she thought to herself.

Once she could stand, she grabbed a clean sweatshirt and a pair of khaki cargo pants and hurried into the bathroom, being careful not to wake Áine. The water from the shower rolled over her skin, and she sent some of her power into it - just enough to make sure that whatever illness was trying to take hold of her body would be flushed away.

Rubbing her face with her hands, Neala tried to gather her thoughts. For the first time in a long time, her week had been uneventful - well, as uneventful as it could be, given the circumstances.

She had attended her classes, enjoyed relaxed lunches with her friends, and otherwise been a perfectly average Birchtree Hall student. Jaz and Eamon were constant companions at lunch times now, and she smiled at Orion in the halls. Darci was still being...Darci. Lorcan, however...

Neala chewed the inside of her cheek. She hadn't seen him again since Sunday night. Eamon had dismissed her concerns when she'd asked, explaining that it wasn't anything unusual. Still, it made Neala feel a little edgy. But, apart from Lorcan's absence, things were cruising along smoothly.

So why do I feel like something is about to burst, then? Neala wondered. Now that the water had healed her physical symptoms, she had isolated the origin to an overwhelming sense of dread. Every one of her senses was on-edge, though she had no idea why.

Once she had dressed and pulled her hair back in a braid, Neala returned to the main room to see if Áine was awake. But she was still fast asleep, and Neala soon understood why; the sky outside the window was dark, with only the faintest hint of pale blue light on the horizon. With a sigh, Neala sat on her bed, reaching out to stroke Keia. Instantly, she knew what was wrong.

Keia was gone.

Biting back her panic, Neala patted all over her blanket, whispering for her fox. She checked under her desk, and even leaned over Áine to make sure Keia hadn't curled up in her bed instead.

Unfortunately, just as Neala's shadowy form was looming over her, Áine's eyelids fluttered open and she screamed, slapping Neala's face hard, causing her to gasp and pulled back, cheek stinging.

Áine started apologising profusely. "Neala? I'm so sorry, I didn't realise - I just saw this shape leaning over me." Rubbing her eyes, Áine sat up and shook her head, golden locks falling over her face. "What are you doing?"

"Keia's missing," Neala muttered anxiously, hand still pressed to her smarting cheek. This made Áine wake up properly.

"Keia? But she never leaves you. Ever."

"I know," Neala hissed. "That's why I'm worried." Áine threw her covers back and got to her feet, reaching for her fluffy dressing gown.

Hesitantly, unsure how Neala would react, she muttered, "Um, well, the thing is...I've been thinking. You know how you said Keia arrived here strangely - that you *definitely* left her with your mother when you came here, but then she appeared in the dining hall?" Neala paused, meeting Áine's gaze.

She continued, voice stronger now, "Well, I've been wondering about that a lot. No one can say for sure what Keia even *is*, other than she's obviously some supernatural being, right? But..." she licked her lips, "What if she can teleport? No, hear me out." She held up a hand to stop Neala's protests.

"I'm not saying it's necessarily an easy thing - maybe that's why she doesn't do it often. But how else do you explain how she got here in the first place? Then there's your theory that she is the fox from your dreams, incarnated in physical form. What if she can travel through dimensions? That would explain how she got through the birch grove to be here, too. I've been researching what kind of creature she could be, and there's a few different possibilities, though none seem to match perfectly."

Neala had been listening to Áine's reasoning, slowing her mind so she could focus on what her friend was saying. Calmer now, she sat on the edge of her bed and folded her hands.

"Let's say you're right, and Keia can teleport around the place. That doesn't explain why she would just leave without letting me know. Like you said - she never leaves my side. Even if we have to be apart briefly, like when I'm working with the animals, she is always within earshot. This is just so out-of-character."

She explained to Áine how she'd felt when she woke up, the sense of foreboding that had made her so ill. Áine tilted her head to the side thoughtfully.

"You didn't have another dream, did you?"

Neala shook her head, trying to remember. "No, I don't think so. My special dreams are usually really vivid, like they aren't even dreams at all. It's almost like they're real, like I'm actually there but it's..."

They finished the sentence together, wide-eyed. "In some other world."

Áine sat beside Neala and gripped her arm tightly, eyes shining with excitement. "Neala, if that's true, then that could help explain how Keia came to you – moving from one world to another rather than materialising from a dream – and it answers a lot of questions about how the Cailleach could speak to you.

"Isn't one of your tree-magics something to do with connecting worlds, about opening portals? What if that's what these 'dreams' are? It could be you're actually transporting yourself, or astral-projecting into a different dimension, a between-world zone. Like some sort of limbo, where the Otherworld and our world meet.

"Think of them as concentric circles. After all, time isn't linear, and space is absolute, so there is a real possibility that you are able to transcend these boundaries." Áine's eyes looked as though they were about to pop out of her head, and she was breathing shallowly.

Neala felt woozy again, and she rested her head in her hands. Sensing her friend's distress, Áine placed a hand on her back. "Oh, I'm sorry. I did it again. Look, we'll find Keia, I promise. Why don't we ask around at breakfast, see if any of our friends have seen her or know anything that may help? You know she wouldn't have left you unless there was a very good reason."

Áine cocked her head to the side. "She has mentioned 'her Lady' quite a bit lately - perhaps she was called away for something? It's fair to assume this 'Lady' is a goddess or deity of some sorts. Maybe she needs Keia, or has a message for her?"

That twigged Neala's memory. Sitting straighter, she frowned. "She mentioned a little while ago that she hadn't been speaking to me much because I needed to learn things by myself, and that she couldn't assist me. I remember thinking then that it sounded eerily like what the Cailleach said to me. Whatever is happening, it seems like I'm on my own until I make some decision that will affect the potential futures ahead of me."

Neala sighed sadly. "I suppose you may be right. Perhaps she has left for now, until I make my choice." Punching her fist hard on the bed beside her thigh, Neala growled. "I just wish I knew what it was about. And why me?"

Áine wrapped her arm around Neala's shoulder and gave her a squeeze. "I wish I had the answers."

Neala leaned her head against her friend's neck and closed her eyes. "I know. I do, too."

*****

By the time breakfast was served, Neala felt much more refreshed. After their chat, Áine had decided to go back to bed, yawning, "You're the morning person – not me."

Neala, though, had decided to go for a run, swapping her khakis for leggings and throwing on her sneakers.

As she had jogged around the lake, she'd felt her mind clear. It had been too long since she'd really pushed herself, and now she felt the need to really pick up the pace. Focusing on nothing but her breath, on the thud of her feet pounding the solid ground beneath her as she ran, Neala had poured her energy into the earth, allowing it to anchor her.

Opening her power even more, she'd invited the wind to run with her, whipping and plucking at her clothes and her hair as it danced alongside her. Panting with exertion, she'd beamed, calling the water to join the wind and come with her. As the elements had merged around her, she'd sprinted as fast as she could, the combination of water and air surrounding her in a vortex; it was as though she were running through a tunnel.

It was so easy now, connecting with the natural world. Hands outstretched, she'd run her fingers through the water, whooping with joy. As her legs gave out, she'd sprawled on the grass, letting the water fall over her, washing away all her worries.

She had lay on the lawn by the lake for an hour, watching the sun rise in the distance. Legs trembling, she had eventually dragged herself to her feet and begun the slow jog back to the manor. Neala was pleased that the overwhelming feeling of dread had faded, and she was looking forward to the rest of the day.

Keia's absence was still a thorn in her side, though. Try as she might, Neala couldn't help but worry about her.

Whatever you're up to, please come back soon, she'd thought, wondering if Keia would hear her, wherever she was. *I feel lost without you.* But no response had come.

With barely enough time to change before breakfast, Neala had hurried back to the dorms, hoping no one would question why she was covered in grass and dripping wet.

As she popped a bite of pancake into her mouth, Neala looked around at her friends. Along with Torin, she was joined once more by Jaz and Eamon, and Áine had invited Eilìs to sit with them that morning, too. Mouth full, she listened as Áine explained to them about Keia's strange disappearance.

"...so, if any of you see or hear anything, please let Neala know."

Eamon was frowning. "There's something familiar about all this, I just can't put my finger on it. I've wondered for some time what Keia might be, what kind of creature she is. It's frustrating; I know it's in here somewhere." He tapped his head sharply, sighing in annoyance.

Eilìs nodded, twirling her spoon in her fingers. "I agree, there's something about her that rings a bell."

Áine sipped her juice and placed her cup down. "Perhaps we can meet in the library tonight? Try putting our heads together and finding some answers?"

The other two nodded, but Jaz interrupted with a yelp. "Count me out. I don't go near books unless I have to. You nerds can take care of the study - I'll put in the leg work." She grinned wolfishly, teeth white against her skin. "Rambo, you're with me, right?"

Torin raised his brows but didn't answer. He had been quiet all morning, Neala realised. *Come to think of it, he's been a little strange all week.* Deflecting Jaz's attention away from him, Neala teased, "By leg work, you mean kicking back in a chair on the lawn, right?"

Jaz winked at her. "Naturally." As the others laughed and conversation turned to other topics, Neala leaned over and poked Torin gently. He jumped, then relaxed when he realised it was her.

"What's up? Is everything okay?"

Torin looked down and jabbed his untouched eggs with a fork. "Yeah, I'm all good, Neals. I'm just worried; we haven't heard anything from Finn lately. I don't know how things are going with Poppy, whether they've found any more clues, or anything. I hate feeling this helpless, you know?"

A wave of guilt flooded Neala. With everything else that had been going on, she'd nearly forgotten about his missing sister.

"Is there anything I can do to help? I mean, I know I can't fix it, but perhaps we can do something later, while the others study? We haven't hung out in ages. What do you think?"

A slight flush crept over Torin's cheeks, and he huffed softly. "Actually, now that you mention it, I've been, um, planning something. For a little while now. See, there's this girl, one of the ones in my group. I've been wanting to ask her on a date, but I..."

His blush deepened. "I've never been out with a girl before. I mean, not for, you know, anything romantic. Would it be too much, if —" He shook his head. "Nah, it's stupid."

Neala's insides gave a funny twist, but she pushed the feeling aside. Nudging his arm, she leaned down until he was forced to look at her. "Tor, did you want to go on a practice date with me?"

He coughed, face positively glowing by now. Gruffly, he muttered, "Is that a stupid idea? I just thought, maybe if it was with someone I know - a good friend - I would be a bit more, like, confident or something."

With a grin, Neala leaned her shoulder against his and gave him a friendly shove. "I'm flattered. Of course I'll go on a not-a-date date with you. What did you have in mind?"

With a grateful look, Torin let out a long breath. "Is it too cheesy to invite you to a picnic by the lake? I was thinking the patch near those large rocks, you know the ones? Right on the edge of the woods. It gives a great view of the sunset over the hills. Or is that lame?"

Neala pretended to consider it seriously, tapping her chin and making the odd 'hmm' sound. Rolling his eyes at her, Torin laughed. "Give me a chance here, there aren't that many options to choose from."

Giggling, she shook her head. "No, it sounds lovely, for real. I was just teasing. What time did you want me to meet you there?"

"How about half-five, right on dusk? Don't worry about coming here for dinner, I'll make some arrangements." Torin sighed, rubbing his eyes. "Man, this conversation has been nerve-wracking enough. How am I ever going to ask Lexi out at this rate?"

"Her name's Lexi, huh? Interesting..." Neala said wickedly, standing to scan the room. "What does she look like? I bet she's a redhead. Is she tall? Short? Ooh, is that her over there, wiping her mouth with her sleeve?"

Torin pulled her back down, snorting with laughter. "Here, we're supposed to be friends. But you're a wee devil, that's what you are."

Neala leaned against his shoulder. "You'd be so bored without me."

Planting a quick kiss on the top of her head, Torin didn't argue. "Desperately. Now, if you'll excuse me, I have a not-a-date date to plan. And lessons to attend, I suppose."

As he said his farewells to the others and gathered his things, Neala watched him thoughtfully. He had been her friend from the very beginning - her first friend here. Things were so easy with him, comfortable. Would going on this date, even if it was just pretend, make things weird between them? She hoped not.

Kicking herself for already overthinking it, she placed her empty bowl on her tray and cleared her throat, getting the attention of her friends.

"I'm going, too. Áine, did you want to come? Eve said to meet her at the lake with our instruments today, we should go choose them."

Áine nodded, turning to Eilìs to finalise their plans for that evening. Wondering if she should tell Áine about her own plans for that night, Neala decided immediately that she shouldn't; Torin would probably be really embarrassed. Promising to keep it a secret, she started walking to the servery, knowing Áine would catch up.

Neala wasn't sure if it was her increasing nervousness about the date with Torin or the strangeness of not having Keia at her side that made the day seem to drag on. She had been unable to focus all morning, even earning a severe reprimand from Druid Brian during her lesson with the air element after losing control of her miniature whirlwind and accidentally destroying an old boat shed on the lake edge.

To her surprise, Druid Imelda led their water lesson that day. Clodagh, she explained, was in the infirmary. She and Mercy had both fallen ill, so they were being cared for by Miranda.

As a result, Imelda allowed the initiates to pair up with her own students and practice some of the things Clodagh had already taught them. Neala had been grateful for this, as it meant she didn't have to concentrate as hard. Still, she struggled to stay present.

By the time midday came around, Neala was feeling the full effects of her early start to the day. About to head to the dorms for a quick lie-down, she was stopped by Áine, who hurried up to her with a panicked look on her face. "Oh, Neala, there you are – listen, I need to talk to you. I-I'm worried about Torin."

Neala frowned, fighting a yawn. "What? Why?"

Áine seemed to be struggling to find the words. "It's – hard to explain. Up until now, I haven't Seen him in any of my visions. Which, you know, didn't seem overly odd at the time, but now they're getting stronger and I'm Seeing a lot clearer. He..."

Her eyes were darting from side-to-side. "It's like he's – like a ghost or something. I can sense him there when I See things, but it's...weird. Like I'm looking at him through fog or something. I don't understand it."

Cocking her head to the side, Neala asked softly, "Have you spoken to Mercy or Ovate Clodagh? Do they know what's causing it?"

"I can't – they're sick." Sighing, Áine pursed her lips. "Maybe it's nothing. I'm still figuring out how it all works; perhaps it's just because I'm so new?" She waved her hand. "Sorry, I shouldn't be bothering you with all this, not when Keia's missing – you're busy enough. Are you coming in for lunch?"

At the mention of Keia, Neala's heart sank. Shaking her head slowly, she mumbled, "Actually, I think I'm going to head to the dorm for a bit. I'm pretty tired and I have a – a busy afternoon ahead. But I'll see you later, okay?"

Áine studied her carefully but didn't press further. "Of course, that's fine. Go get some rest. You aren't sick, too, are you?"

"Nah, just exhausted. Thanks, though." With a little wave, the girls parted ways, Áine still watching Neala worriedly. By the time she reached the dorm, Neala's head felt like it was full of lead. Her eyes were closed the moment she hit the pillow.

~ 26 ~

Although she felt a little guilty about avoiding Áine for the rest of the afternoon, Neala really didn't want to have the awkward conversation about why she was skipping dinner that night. Instead, once her classes were over, Neala hurried straight back to the dorm to shower and scribbled a note for her friend.

Áine,
Didn't come to tea because I wasn't hungry. I've headed out for a walk to get some fresh air - I'll see you before bed. Hope the study goes well tonight!
Neala x

She felt bad for lying, but she told herself it was more of a white lie; after all, she *was* going for a walk that night. *And I'm too nervous to eat dinner anyway, so that's not really a lie, either.*

Hoping that Áine wouldn't decide to come to the dorm before going to eat, Neala opened her side of the shared closet and studied her options. It was rather disappointing.

Even though she kept telling herself it wasn't a real date, she still wanted to look nice and get dressed up a little. But she soon realised her clothing choices tended to lean more toward practical than pretty. After all, she hadn't planned on going on dates when she was packing for Birchtree.

Deciding her best bet was a nice top with some jeans, Neala pulled out her fanciest shirts. Laying them on the bed, she stared at them, weighing them up. After 'um-ing' and 'ah-ing' a few times, she threw several of them on the ground, leaving only her white blouse with the red polka dots, or a navy cross-over top studded with diamantes around the bottom.

Deciding the white was impractical if she was going to be sitting on the ground by the lake, Neala tossed it aside and pulled on the navy top, adjusting it until it sat comfortably.

Turning her attention to make-up, she hesitated. She didn't want to give Torin the wrong impression; if she dressed up too much, would he think she actually *wanted* this to be a real date? But, if she didn't try at all, would his feelings be hurt? With a groan, she covered her face in her hands.

Out of nowhere, she started to giggle. "Oh my gosh, it shouldn't be this hard. Imagine if it was for real - I'd be a wreck." Habitually, she turned to grin at Keia...

Her smile faded and she sat on the edge of the bed sadly. "Oh, Keia, where are you? I hope you're okay. Please...please come back soon. I miss you."

A short while later Neala was tottering down to the lake, rueing her decision to wear the only pair of boots she owned that were more fashionable than practical – the heel wasn't big, but she still felt like a baby giraffe taking its first steps.

She had ultimately decided against make-up, opting only for a swipe of lip-gloss. But she had made an effort with her hair; it hadn't been this long in a while, so she had decided to wear it down, pinning it so the rich brown waves cascaded over her left shoulder. It made her feel a little more special.

After all, this is my first date, too. Kind of. My first not-a-date date. Does that even count? she pondered as she walked, wincing as she rolled her ankle slightly on a rock.

In the distance, she could hear an owl hooting, heralding the arrival of night. Neala slowed, a tiny shiver running down her spine; it sounded eerily like the mournful cries she had heard in her crossroad dreams.

Wrapping her arms around herself, Neala continued on, following the trail around the lake which led to the spot Torin had mentioned. She'd seen it a few times on her morning runs; there was a flat clearing on the edge of the woods, raised above the lake. She hadn't been there on dusk, but she could imagine how stunning the sunset would look from there; a glowing orb sinking into the silvery water below. Heart beating faster, she peered ahead, wondering if Torin was there yet.

Spotting his broad shoulders in the distance, Neala grinned. Despite her nerves, she was glad to be spending some time alone with him. It seemed like an eternity since they had talked – like, *really* talked. Wrapping her hands around her mouth, she called, "Hey stranger!"

Torin's head whipped around, and his face lit with a broad smile. Moving down the path toward her, he gestured for her to stop. "Hang on - I had this whole bit planned, don't ruin it." Giggling, Neala halted, hands clasped in front of her.

When he reached her, Torin moved behind her and told her to close her eyes. "All right, you trust me, right? That I'm not going to push you into the lake or anything?" Neala smiled, closing her eyes and shaking her head. Her stomach was fluttering, and it made her feel giddy.

Gently, Torin gripped her upper arms. A tickle by her right ear told her he was leaning close, and he said warmly, "You look beautiful, by the way."

Despite reminding herself that this was not a real date, Neala couldn't stop the flush spreading over her cheeks. She allowed him to guide her forward, grateful for his hands to stabilise her as she shuffled cautiously in her boots. Vowing to take them off the moment she had a chance, Neala smiled, keeping her eyes tightly closed.

"Here we are. Just let me do something...one second," Torin mumbled, releasing Neala and moving away from her. She heard a rustle of paper and then he was instructing her to open her eyes. Peering through her lashes, Neala beamed.

Torin was standing in front of her holding a pretty bouquet of yellow and white lilies, their delicate scent permeating the air with their spicy sweetness. Meeting his eyes, Neala was surprised to see just how nervous he was. She reached out for the flowers, taking them from him gently.

"These are gorgeous. Thank you, Tor."

Torin ducked his head shyly and shrugged. "You're welcome. I, uh, I know they're your favourites."

The air between them had grown a little awkward, and Neala licked her dry lips and shuffled her feet. "Well, um, do you want me to - to sit down or something?"

Jolted out of his thoughts, Torin gestured to the blanket he'd set out on the grass, "Yeah, um, please - make yourself comfortable. I have drinks and a few things to eat - I'll grab you something. Do you feel like water, or I have juice? I was going to bring wine but wasn't sure if you drink or not? I guessed not, as you're a bit young yet, but Lexi's nineteen so I kind of felt, like, to practice properly, I should think about bringing some..."

Torin was clearly flustered as he knelt down by the basket he'd packed for the picnic, and Neala felt sorry for him. Crouching, she placed a hand on his shoulder.

"Hey - don't stress so much. It's just me, remember? You can relax a little; I'm not going to run off if you don't have the right colour serviettes or whatever."

Laughing, Torin sat back, dropping his chin to his chest. "You know what, you're right. The whole point of this was to practice, wasn't it? And I can't think of anyone I'd rather be on a not-a-date date with than you, Neals."

Patting the space next to him on the blanket, he beamed at her, looking much more like his usual self. "I'll just pull everything out then you can choose what you want, okay? That sounds way easier."

Neala giggled as she sat down, shifting until she was comfortable. "I hope Lexi is also this low-maintenance. What will you do if she's the type of person who *does* care about having the right colour serviettes?"

"Run for the hills," Torin muttered, rifling through the basket and pulling out two glasses. Neala took the opportunity to slip her boots off, sighing with relief as she wiggled her toes in the breeze. Noticing, Torin sniggered, shaking his head.

She stuck her tongue out at him. "What? I don't care what they say - these boots are definitely *not* made for walking."

Handing her a glass, Torin said, "Now, I have apple juice and some sparkling water I swiped from the kitchen - I mean, asked for politely and managed to acquire using my voracious charm, of course."

Neala cocked her brow at him. "Of course. Now, purely with the intent to be difficult - in order to prepare you for any potential high-maintenance dates in the future - I'd like my glass filled with one-third juice, two-thirds sparkling water. Garnished with a lemon wedge. And a little umbrella."

Torin stared at her, face deadpan. "Madame, I'm going to have to ask you to leave. You are obviously not my type."

Neala gave an exaggerated sigh. "Fine, fine...forget the little umbrella."

Opening the bottle of apple juice, Torin's face brightened, and he said jovially, "Now, that is far more reasonable. You may stay."

Once she had her sparkling apple juice mix, Neala leaned back on her hand and took a sip, staring out over the lake. The sun was almost completely set now, and the lake seemed to shimmer with gold and silver. All around them, birds were singing their farewells to the sun, and the leaves of the trees whispered in the breeze. It had been a perfect autumn day, with little rain.

Tilting her head back, she breathed deeply, enjoying the quiet. Before long, though, her thoughts drifted back to Keia, and her heart sank with misery.

Torin had just placed down a platter with various fruits, cheeses, and biscuits, when he heard Neala sigh. Glancing at her, he asked gently, "You okay?"

"Yeah, I'm just thinking about Keia. I can't shake the feeling that something bad has happened. Then I feel guilty that I'm not out looking for her, then helpless because I don't even know where to begin. It's all a mixture of emotions. I just wish I had a clue - some sort of sign that she was okay."

Torin ran his tongue over his teeth, eyes darting from Neala to the food. "Here, have something to eat. I know you're worried about her, but it's like Áine and the others said - she's an Otherworld creature with unknown abilities, she could be anywhere. I mean, heck, she materialised out of your dreams and managed to sneak through the birch portal while only a baby, so she must have some kind of power. It takes a lot to get through an ancient magic like that - not many creatures could do it."

Neala nodded, grabbing a handful of dried apricots from the platter. "I know, I'm sorry. Let's talk about you for a bit, I feel like I've made it all about me today. I want to know more about Lexi, what's she like?"

Raising an eyebrow, Torin asked in mock seriousness, "If I answer, are you going to stalk her?"

"Yes."

Throwing his head back, he chortled with amusement. "All right, fair enough. Well, where do I start?..."

*****

The moon was glowing in the sky by the time they fell silent. Torin yawned loudly, lying down on his side and propping his head up with his hand. "I don't think I've talked that much in my life. My throat feels all crackly."

Neala shivered slightly, arms wrapped around her knees. The breeze had turned chilly now, and she had forgotten to bring a jacket. Noticing, Torin shuffled closer, wrapping his arm around her back.

Neala leaned back against him, propping her head on his chest so she was tucked under his chin. Pressed close, she breathed in Torin's scent - a mix of cinnamon, earth, and his own unique smell.

Narrowing her eyes, she froze; something didn't seem right, though she couldn't put her finger on it. Torin started speaking again, his voice rumbling against Neala's ear.

"Thanks for coming tonight, Neala. It means a lot to spend this time with you."

She mumbled something back, too distracted by the goosebumps spreading over her arms to pay much attention to what she was saying. In the distance, she heard the owl again, its haunting cries echoing in her ears, louder now. A warning, almost...

A thrill of terror ran down Neala's spine; she knew what was wrong. And it turned her blood cold.

Pressed this close to Torin's chest, she could feel his warmth, could smell him, could hear the air moving in and out of his lungs as he breathed...but she couldn't hear his heartbeat. There was no thudding, no pulse that she could sense.

As subtly as she could, Neala shifted until her ear was pressed right over the place where his heart should be.

Nothing. Not a single, solitary beat.

Swallowing nervously, she leaned back, peering up at Torin's face. He was staring out over the lake, expression unreadable. Neala watched as a muscle in his jaw twitched, and his fingers pressed tightly into her shoulder to the point of painfulness.

"Ow, Tor, you're – you're hurting me," she whispered, voice shaking. Above her, Torin sneered, his face contorting with rage.

"You're all so fragile, aren't you?"

Neala struggled to sit up, eyes wide with fear. "Torin, what's wrong with you? What's going on?"

He let out a growl, rolling until he had pinned Neala's shoulders to the ground. She tried to scream, but he covered her mouth with a broad hand. "*Mortals*," he spat. "You're all the same; Bards or humans, it makes no difference. You can all die - can all bleed!"

He scratched the side of her face with a fingernail, drawing blood and making her cry out in pain, tears streaming from her eyes.

She kicked and thrashed, but Torin was much larger than her, and he held her down easily. With a gentler hand this time, he stroked her hair, pressing his face close to hers. Neala could feel his breath on her neck, and she turned away, sobbing helplessly.

"You are a pretty thing. He loves you, you know? Torin. Has since the moment he met you. It's pathetic, really, how much he longs to be with you. To hold you...to kiss you..." His lips brushed her throat and Neala screamed, finally getting her mouth free from under his hand.

With as much force as she could muster, she bit down, teeth tearing into his skin. Torin yelped and pulled back. It was all the opportunity she needed; twisting to the side, she slithered out from beneath him and scrambled to her knees, trying to get her feet under her. She could outrun him; she knew she could—

Before she could take a step, Torin was tackling her, knocking her to the ground. The force winded her and she gasped for breath. Rolling her onto her back, he straddled her and wrapped his large hands around her throat, cutting off her air supply.

Spots danced before Neala's eyes as she gasped and choked, kicking desperately. The edges of her vision grew fuzzy, and her body grew limp, unable to fight anymore.

Help...someone, please...help... Neala tried to cry out, but she had no voice, no energy. In the distance, the owl hooted once more, then everything was gone.

~ 27 ~

Neala was sure her throat must be lined with razor blades; they cut into her when she tried to swallow, stabbing her sharply. As she blinked, head pounding, she tried to speak, her words coming out as little more than breathy hisses. Her eyes began to focus, and she realised she was propped against the base of a large tree, her arms bound tightly to her side. She could feel the earth beneath her; she was seated on a damp, mossy patch of dirt.

Instinctively, she tried to send her magic down, but she was still too woozy to focus. Closing her eyes, she sucked in several breaths, wincing as her throat burned with every movement. The sound of footsteps nearby made her flinch and she whimpered.

Torin was standing before her, arms folded as he looked her over. Watching his familiar face sneer at her with loathing, a burning rage gathered in her chest, melting away her fear, and she spat at his feet. Swallowing hard, she forced out the words, "Who...where...Tor..."

"Your boyfriend won't be coming. I'd be surprised if he's still alive at this point, honestly." He moved toward her, and Neala turned her face aside, eyes burning with fury.

Shaking his head, Torin muttered sadly, "I wonder how he'd feel to know his love - his darling Neala - couldn't even tell the difference between him and a changeling? Wouldn't that just break his poor, wounded heart?"

Neala's face paled. "Ch...change..."

The changeling impersonating Torin rolled its eyes. "Changeling. Of course. Haven't you connected the dots yet? Think, idiot girl! Prove to me you aren't as stupid as the others, come on."

Eyes wide, Neala wracked her woozy brain, trying to work out when this...this *thing* could have taken Torin's place...

"Poppy. A changeling...took Poppy. You...went for Tor, too." Every word lanced her throat with pain, but she forced them out.

"Good girl, well done. Yes, I did, but not without a few hiccups." He rubbed his lip with a frown. "He was a fighter, your boyfriend; I didn't think he'd rough me up as much as he did. Still, using an argument with his roommate as a nice cover story for the bruises he gave me was believable, no?"

"I bet he kicked your ass," Neala choked out, a grim sneer curling her lip. "He would've pounded you into the dirt."

The changeling growled. "Then why I am I still here, idiot? And here I was thinking you were a clever one."

Neala felt sick to her stomach. Where was the real Torin? "

"But I suppose we can't all be as smart as me, can we? I forgive you – after all, you *are* just a poor, pathetic Bard child." Sneering cruelly, the changeling patted her cheek. She spat at him in disgust, but that only made him laugh harder.

"So, then – I defeated your 'oh so tough' Torin, then what? What was the whole point of it, do you think?"

Neala rolled her eyes. "Don't you know that villains should never get too chatty? That always gets them into trouble in the end. It gives the hero time to come up with a plan to defeat them, every single time." As she spoke, Neala attempted to send her magic out, now that she was more focused. But it seemed to die in her veins – she couldn't even draw it up from her core.

The changeling scoffed. "And who do you think is coming to save you, hmm? Your little friends? Or maybe the great Finley Talbot?" He bared his teeth. "Even he didn't figure it out, though, did he? That we had come. He's been given quite the run-around by my siblings – he's chasing shadows. I must say, he doesn't really live up to his legendary status. It's been quite disappointing."

Neala could feel the anger bubbling under her skin, and she reached out for the earth once more, hoping to open it up underneath the changeling and squash it flat. But there was nothing; her magic met an invisible barrier, as though it was surrounded by glass. Neala tried again, willing it with all her might.

Peering at her with Torin's eyes, the changeling noticed her struggling and let out a harsh, barking laugh.

"How many times have you tried to use your magic now, hmm? Are you having any luck? Maybe I should have mentioned it before - those ropes are enchanted." He smirked.

"You Bards may be the most powerful creatures this side of the Veil, but that's like boasting that you're a caterpillar amongst the worms; able to do things they cannot, but still a useless grub. Over there, where I'm from, you Bards are nothing. Nothing but worthless specks of dust. Even you, supposed Lorekeepers that you are. You wouldn't be fit to lick the dirt off Her shoes."

Slumping against the tree, Neala gasped. "How did...we haven't told you anything about the Lorekeepers. None of us has said anything about it to anyone else."

With an angry snarl, the changeling slammed his fist against the tree, just above Neala's head. She squealed and ducked, whimpering softly. "*I* know. I know everything about you, about this academy, about your precious little tree-hugger gang."

He started to pace in front of her, eyes bulging wildly. "None of the others have achieved what I have. I was the last one they expected to be chosen as a scout - no one thought I was good enough. But they'll see; when I present you to Her, I'll be rewarded beyond imagination. I dare the fleshies to call me 'Twig' then."

Neala wondered if she could loosen the ropes, whether that would allow her to use her magic. The changeling seemed to like the sound of its own voice. All she had to do was keep it talking. "Achieved? What kind of achievement do you call this? Kidnapping a teenage girl? That doesn't," she coughed, trying to clear her throat, "seem that - impressive."

The changeling's skin rippled, and Neala could see his features wavering for a moment. Turning away, he hissed, "'Kidnapping a teenage girl'? Oh, no. No, no - this is so much more than that. I couldn't believe my luck when I stumbled across you. You're the *one* - the one who can open the portals. When I bring you back to Her..." The changeling shivered. "I'll be rewarded beyond my wildest dreams."

"Why Torin, though? You could have become anyone. Finn, one of the Druids...Why him?"

Leering at her, the changeling walked closer. "I needed to gain your trust. From the moment I saw you, I knew you were one of them - one of the seven. You were with Torin and the girl, Áine. I could sense the ancient power in her, too, but the boy was nothing. A mere chess piece. It was an easy task to learn more about him, find out where he lived. I took on the skin of his roommate."

The changeling shrugged. "She usually prefers us to send the ones we select back through the portals to Her, so She can use them in her games, but, well...he was just a useless human. I disposed of him and took his place."

Neala felt sick to her stomach. Breathing deeply, she tried to focus on the ropes. Her wrists were stinging, but she could feel it beginning to slacken. Gritting her teeth, she strained as hard as she could, trying to loosen them until she could free her hands.

The changeling was lost in his story now, seeming to enjoy having an audience for his brilliance.

"But I suppose it's unfair to call him completely useless. After all, he did know about Torin's sister. It was all up in here." He rapped the side of his head lightly with his knuckles. "I mean, he didn't know she was a Bard, obviously, but he knew where to find her. My sister went to check it out while I was busy fighting our lad Torin – a Bard's a Bard, aye? Always worth investigating."

His eyes lit up. "And what did she find? Only a Bard who had enough power to stop a *hurricane.* That's impressive, I'll give her that. Such a pity that controlling it sent her mad, though. Tsk – 'you can't control the elements', how many times have these Druids said it?"

The changeling shrugged. "Too bad she didn't listen. Now my sister has her body, so it's much of a muchness. A quick fist fight later, and I have Torin's. Ta-da - he's off to the Otherworld and I'm off to Birchtree."

Neala was finding it difficult to swallow past the lump in her throat. Torin had never told her what was wrong with Poppy, why she was in the hospital. *Controlling a hurricane...a storm is hard enough. That must have been horrendous...*

Rolling his eyes, the changeling spat, "Enter Finley Talbot. Of course he'd come to investigate; he's never been able to keep his big nose out of things. He came to the hospital to get me. How he knew I was there..." He shook his head. "Not that it mattered in the end. Knowing he was distracted by Poppy's disappearance, I gave him some excuse about dropping my luggage off then slipped away."

He let out a frustrated sigh. "He really was so disappointing; nothing like the legends claim. Being over here so long has made him soft."

"The birch trees - they should have stopped you," Neala rasped. "You weren't there with the rest of us, though. I would've seen you – would've...would've noticed..."

Neala's chest was aching. Torin had never been at Birchtree with her at all; it had been the changeling this whole time. It had all been a lie. She felt tears well in her eyes. *I should have known. I should have known it wasn't really him.*

Pacing now, the changeling didn't even seem to remember Neala was there. His eyes were shining with madness, and he was speaking rapidly.

"That was my biggest hurdle. I was never going to fool those Ancient Ones - they're way too wise. But the Bards have one weakness in their system; the luggage tunnels. They don't consider them a threat, because they're designed to only allow inanimate objects to pass through.

That's what makes it impossible for humans to find their way here by accident – the earth would just reject them. But they never considered that the *unliving* could use them."

He cackled, thumping his chest. "No heartbeat, remember? I threw Torin's suitcase in then jumped right after it. The earth didn't hesitate, just sent me along my merry way. A good servant of the Bards, just doing its job. Not even Finley bothered to check how I – how *Torin* – got here in the end. Idiot."

Giving her right hand the slightest of tugs, Neala realised she could now slip it out of the ropes. Eyes wide, a rush of adrenaline coursing through her, she considered her next move. If she could just get the knot untied now... "That was – very clever of you. You fooled everyone."

The changeling nodded vigorously, clasping his hands in front of himself. "Oh, it was. It was. I got past them all - all the clever Bards and their clever tree-groves. From there, it was as easy as breathing. You and your friends...you're all so chatty and open with each other. When you started telling me about your dreams, it confirmed what I already knew; you were the portal-opener, the one I needed.

"If I could deliver you to Her, she wouldn't need to worry about the songs anymore, the ones keeping the Veil in place; She could use you to open a portal straight through the cursed thing – blast a hole through it and be free. Then once She creates her new world, I'll be favoured above all - King of the Changelings."

"But - why? Why do you need to do this?" Neala asked. "Who is this woman, and why is she so important?"

"She is no mere woman! She is our Dark Queen, our Goddess. I need to - I *have* to serve Her. She loves me - She gives all of us Her love. We are Her children. She cares for us, when no one else would..." For the first time, the changeling seemed hesitant, his eyes unsure.

Sensing his uncertainty, Neala kept pushing. "What if - what if you didn't, though? No one needs to get hurt - we'll help you." She coughed, mind whirling. "Let me go and we can tell the Druids. I-I'm your friend - I'll help, I promise. You could—"

"NO!" The changeling pressed his hands to his ears, eyes wild. "No one can help me but Her. She *loves* me - no one else ever could. Not you, not anyone. No one—"

A streak of white-hot light slammed into the ground so hard that the tree above Neala shattered. Screaming, she tucked her chin against her chest as branches and leaves rained around her, a sharp stick scraping her eyebrow as it fell. Blood poured into her eye, and she tried desperately to blink it away.

There was a burning smell in the air, and Neala knew her hair was singed. Despite it all, she felt sobs of relief burst from her aching throat.

Lorcan had come.

Through the blood and tears, she could make out a shadowy form in front of her and she cringed in fear.

"Neala, are you okay? Can you move?" Lorcan's voice was calm but firm.

She strained to move her arms towards him, but the ropes were still binding her too tightly. "Help, Lorcan, please—"

"Keia, help Neala with the ropes. I need to find the creature."

"*Keia?*" Neala whispered, hardly believing what she had heard. Then she felt the familiar brush of fur against her fingers, and she cried out in joy.

A gentle nip on her hand was accompanied by Keia's voice echoing softly in her head, "*Hush. It is still here.*"

"Keia, it was Torin. He - he—" Neala couldn't spit the words out. Shock was taking over her system, and she was fighting the urge to vomit. It was all she could do to keep herself from breaking into a wild panic.

"*Yes. Your friends are coming.*"

In an instant, the ropes loosened their hold on Neala, and she slumped to the ground, rolling herself into a ball. Everything ached, and she was trembling all over.

"*Neala! Run!*"

Keia's cry rang through her mind, even as a painful yelp sounded right beside her ear. Before she could move, a booted foot slammed into her side, and she screamed in pain. Another kick. Neala knew her ribs had cracked, and she gasped for air, trying to crawl away.

"You ruined everything!" the changeling screeched, reaching down to shake her shoulders hard. Neala's brain rattled in her skull, the dizziness almost enough to send her unconscious.

"You can't help me – you're a liar! No one could ever care for me, no one—" The changeling's cries of rage morphed into roars of pain as Keia came flying out of the shadows beneath the bushes, latching onto his forearm with her needle-sharp teeth.

Through the haze of blood and swirling nausea, Neala realised the changeling wasn't bleeding; instead, greenish-grey smoke was pouring from the wound Keia had inflicted. With a jerk, the changeling flung Keia to the side once more, and she yelped loudly.

Calling out to her, Neala tried to pull herself along on her elbows. A weight pressed down on her back, pinning her to the ground. Gasping for air as she tried desperately to free herself, she squealed in pain as the boot dug into the bones of her spine.

"Open the portal to the Otherworld and get me home. Now. Or you will die." The changeling's voice was distorted and laced with poison.

"No. You will."

Neala craned over her shoulder, watching in horror as Lorcan strode up behind the changeling and rammed his fist into its back. The changeling let out a terrible, high-pitched screech that would haunt Neala's dreams forever.

As Lorcan drew his hand away, she saw that his arm was coated in fire, his hand barely visible through the white-hot flames. The changeling dropped to the ground beside her, convulsing wildly as it burned from the inside out.

Even though she knew it wasn't really Torin, Neala couldn't stop herself from stretching her hand out toward him, hating to see her friend's face contorted with so much pain. "I'm sorry. I'm so sorry," she wailed, taking the changeling's hand in her own.

For the briefest moment, the creature's eyes locked with hers. No longer Torin's eyes, they were amber-coloured with speckles of green and brown, and full of fear. As Neala sobbed, the light faded from his eyes, and he lay still.

Within seconds, foul-smelling smoke surrounded the changeling's body. Once it cleared, only a bundle of charred sticks remained, tied into the shape of a poppet.

Breathing shallowly, Neala pressed her face into the ground and screamed. Over and over, she screeched and sobbed, no longer in control of her body. Keia limped over and brushed up against her cheek, resting her head on her shoulder.

Lorcan knelt beside her, placing a gentle hand on her hair. Murmuring that help was coming, he turned to face the woods, senses alert. In moments, he heard the sound he'd been waiting for.

"Neala! Where are you?" Áine's voice echoed through the trees, high-pitched in terror. "What's happening?"

Neala could hear Áine, but the tiny part of her mind that longed to respond was drowned out by the overwhelming shock currently taking hold of her body. The most she could manage was to bring her hysterical shrieking to a halt, panting wildly as she fought to regain her senses.

Hardly aware of what she was doing, she reached weakly for the charred remains of the changeling. With a shaking hand, she pulled one of the sticks from the bundle and tucked it against her chest, cuddling it close. *I'm sorry. I'm so sorry...*

*****

With relief, Lorcan called out, "Here, she's here. We need help - she's badly hurt." He watched as Áine stumbled into view, followed by Eamon, then Jaz, Orion and Darci. Spotting Neala, who had stopped screaming and was now shuddering violently as she hugged herself, Áine came to a halt, mouth open in shock.

Eamon stepped forward, hands fisted at his side. "What the hell is going on? What happened to her?"

Ignoring his brother, Lorcan focused on Darci. "I need your help. The usual magic won't be enough." Darci scowled, but after he glared at her fiercely, she sighed and crouched beside Neala, checking her over with her magic.

Neala's cries had died down now, and she was wavering in and out of consciousness. Lifting her head slightly, she tried to speak, but only a gurgling sound came out. In moments, Áine was kneeling beside her, hand stroking her hair.

"It's okay, shh - I'm here. It's all going to be okay." Leaning her cheek against Áine's knee, Neala closed her eyes.

As the others crowded around Neala's battered body, watching Darci curiously, Áine asked in a voice tight with tension, "How are we supposed to get her back to the school, to Mercy? Orion, are you able to carry her?"

Wearing an expression of someone who had just sipped sour milk, Darci shook her head and interrupted, not taking her hand off Neala's back.

"He doesn't have to. I can—" She sighed. "I can heal her."

Everyone but Lorcan stared at Darci in shock. Exasperated, she raised her other hand. "I don't like doing it. It's apparently one of my tree gifts, one I actually *do* know how to use."

She shot Lorcan a bitter look. "I can regenerate things - heal things. But it's not...it's not the same as what other healers do. I have to –" She swallowed hard. "I have to trade life to do it – as in, draw the life force from one thing and give it to something else."

A flash of sorrow crossed her eyes. "I've done it to heal someone before. Once. But it can be...difficult." Her expression was replaced with her usual mask of haughtiness. "Generally, I only use it for minor corrections."

"Like healing a pimple, hmm?" Lorcan interjected.

Darci sent him a look of pure loathing but continued, "Healing Neala's injuries will take more than just a drop of life essence from a pot-plant, though. The only one of us strong enough to endure it would be..."

She gazed up at Orion, brow raised. One by one, the others looked to see what he would say.

He shifted uncomfortably, not liking being the centre of attention. "Will it save her?"

"Yes," Darci replied. "But we must do it soon." She glanced down at Neala, who was breathing shallowly.

Without another word, Orion nodded. "What do you need me to do?"

Taking his large hand in her delicate one, Darci kept her other hand on Neala's back. Closing her eyes, she murmured, "Stay alive."

Neala woke with a start, sitting bolt upright. Her hands scrambled in the dirt beside her, and she whipped her head around, trying to see Torin. Something touched her shoulder and she screamed, lashing out at whatever was trying to hurt her.

Her fist connected with something solid, and a familiar voice groaned, "You have to stop doing that, you know." As her vision came into focus, she found herself staring into Lorcan's eyes.

"What the hell, Lorcan? What's going on? What time is it?" Her face paled and she stared at him in horror. "The changeling – you killed it. It is dead, isn't it?"

"See for yourself." Lorcan pointed at the charred stick Neala had been clutching, and she stared down at it blankly. She vaguely remembered picking it up, sort of. Curious, she turned it around in her fingers; the wood was scorched and blackened and smelled lightly of smoke.

"It was a lesser changeling." Lorcan's voice was a soft rumble in Neala's ear. "The kind made of sticks and imbued with a soul and glamour, rather than a flesh-and-bone Fae

465

child who has passed on. They are much more fragile. Fire is their greatest weakness."

The memory of the changeling burning before her eyes flashed in her mind and she winced. Oddly, though it repulsed her, she couldn't bear to throw the stick away. Shoving it securely into her top, she gasped. Lying not far from her, snoring softly, was Orion.

Glancing around, Neala became aware that she was sitting in a damp cave, surrounded by the other Lorekeepers. Keia was curled up by her side, sleeping soundly. Spotting Áine, tears sprang into her eyes, and she held her arms out. Her friend had been hanging back, but now she rushed forward, throwing her arms around Neala's neck tearfully.

"Oh, I'm so glad you're all right. How do you feel? Does anything hurt?" Áine sat back, holding Neala's shoulders gently. Neala shook her head, glancing over her body.

"No, I – I feel fine..." she trailed off as more memories surged in her mind; how was she healed? Her body had been bruised and broken. She stared at Áine in confusion. "How am I okay?"

Áine opened her mouth, then closed it again. With a sidelong glance at Darci, she mumbled, "You kind of have her to thank for that. And Orion," she added hastily. "Darci transferred some of his life essence to you, so your body could speed up your healing. You aren't one hundred percent healed, because that would have been too much for him to handle, but the worst injuries have been taken care of."

Neala's head was swimming. An image of Torin's face filled her mind and a vice-like grip seized her chest. She gripped Áine's hand tightly. "Oh, Áine, it's Torin. He's in the Otherworld - the changeling sent him there. I don't know how, or if he's even—" She couldn't bring herself to say 'alive'. "We have to help him. I can't bear the thought of him being in danger."

Eamon cleared his throat. He was sitting by the cave entrance, staring out over the woods. In the distance, the first rays of dawn were beginning to light the sky, reflecting off the clouds which heralded another rainy day ahead.

Turning to meet Neala's gaze, he said tersely, "Before anyone does *anything*, I think we need to make sure everyone is on the same page." He glared at Lorcan furiously. "*Everyone.*"

Rolling his head around on his shoulders, Lorcan shrugged. "I see no reason why not." Gesturing to Orion's sleeping form, he asked innocently, "But can someone else wake yon big lad? A punch from Neala I can handle, but he's likely to take my whole head off."

Jaz, who had not spoken throughout the whole turn of events, reached out and pressed a hand against Orion's shoulder. Giving him a gentle shake, she muttered, "C'mon, you old bear. Hibernation's over."

With a yawn, Orion sat up, blinking slowly as he turned his head from side to side, orientating himself. Sighing, he rubbed his face with his hands. Spotting Neala, his eyes softened in relief. "Ah, you're awake. I'm glad you are feeling better."

Neala smiled at him gratefully. "Thanks to you I am." She flushed, then sheepishly turned to Darci. "And you, of course, Darci."

The other girl just sniffed and muttered, "You're welcome."

With a wave, Eamon summoned a breeze to boost the small fire he'd lit to keep the cave warm, stoking it into an energetic blaze. One by one, everyone moved forward until they were all seated in a circle around it.

Neala reached out a hand to pet Keia, and the fox opened one bright blue eye to look at her. Her fluffy tail thumped happily. *"Stormbringer is safe."*

She was about to ask Keia what had happened to her - where had she been all day? - but the fox closed her eye once more, and Neala decided to let her sleep. There would be time for answers later.

"You need to tell us everything you know," Eamon demanded, glaring at Lorcan.

Crossing his legs, Lorcan leaned forward and ran his tongue over the front of his teeth. "All right. I'll tell you what you need to know."

Neala's eyes narrowed suspiciously. Eamon, too, looked a little wary, but he clenched his jaw and stayed silent.

Lorcan cleared his throat, then began to speak. "I've been aware for several months now that creatures have been coming through the portals to our world."

Raising a hand as Eamon started to question how, he stared at him icily. "You want me to explain things? Then don't interrupt."

Eamon's face was stormy, but he closed his mouth, placing one finger over his lips and resting his chin in his hand. Lorcan gave him one last glare, then continued. "Anyway, the first creatures people started noticing were the púca. Neala, the one you encountered on the beach? That was the fifth that I'd defeated. Some contacts I have, they've been hunting these things – keeping them under control.

"We were trying to work out why only weaker magical beings had managed to get through the Veil, compared to some of the others over there. Surely if anything was going to break through, you'd expect it would be something stronger, like a banshee or Black Dog?"

Taking a deep breath, he pinched the bridge of his nose. "Just before coming back to Birchtree, I heard a rumour that changelings may be crossing over. My contacts were pursuing the leads, but that was the last I heard. Until, of course, I met your mate Torin there."

Lorcan nodded toward Neala, who cuddled closer to Áine. Her body had started trembling again, residual shock settling in now. But her mind focused on what he'd said in sharp detail.

"You *knew*? This whole time, you knew he wasn't the real one?" Her heart thudded painfully.

"I suspected. Illusions are my talent, remember? And what is a shape-shifter other than a master of illusion?"

Deep inside, Neala could sense her rage building, but it was tempered by a deeper, more intense emotion - betrayal. In a choked voice, she spat, "So, you let this creature – this *monster* - who'd taken my best friend God-knows-where, possibly even *murdered* him, buddy up to me for weeks? Knowing the whole time what it was? You used me like - like *bait*?"

Lorcan's face was stonelike as he stared into her eyes. "Yes. I needed answers. How was it here? What did it want? It was fixated on you, that much was clear. I figured it would eventually reveal itself. Now we know that it was trying to get *you*, in particular. It makes sense – you're the ash tree, the portal-opener. If anyone is trying to break through from the Otherworld, you're the one they'd be after."

This was the last straw for Eamon. He slammed his fists into the ground and stood, towering over his brother. "You never learn, do you, Lorcan? You can't keep endangering people for your little experiments. Neala could have been killed - she nearly was. And for what? We're no closer to understanding what's happening with the Veil than we were before."

"I wouldn't say that, exactly," Lorcan argued, raising his hands in front of him. "When the Veil was created, it wasn't a physical barrier, but a collection of magical enchantments, one for each of the Chieftain Trees, right? I mean, obviously the 'Veil' isn't singular - it refers to the magic that closed all the portals simultaneously. But, somehow, holes are forming; enough that weaker creatures are slipping through unnoticed. Perhaps..." He cocked his head to the side.

"Think of it like a wall with some bricks missing – a lion would still be trapped behind it as long as the rest of the structure held, but rats would squeeze through the holes easily. If someone is commanding creatures like the changelings to cross, perhaps it means they're incapable of doing it themselves, which seems unlikely."

He shrugged. "Or they're extremely powerful and the Veil is still resisting them. Regardless, the changeling gave us some valuable clues – we're being targeted. Someone, or *something,* on the Otherworld side knows we exist, and where to find us."

Neala felt Áine shudder beside her. Eamon had gone still, eyes wide as he stared at the fire, weighing up Lorcan's words.

It was Orion who broke the silence. "But what does this mean for us? What do we do now?"

Eyes narrowed in concentration, Jaz tilted her head and frowned. "What if others come? We're targets, all of us. The Druids here, they admitted that even they aren't sure what's happening, or why the Veil is weakening. If Lorcan has these contacts - the ones who are going after the Otherworld creatures - then perhaps we should, like, team up with them or something? They seem to have more information than anyone else."

She stared at her hands sadly. "We're putting everyone in danger if we stay here – if one changeling managed to weasel its way into Birchtree, how long before more come? I think – I think we need to leave."

"What? Leave Birchtree?" Áine gasped. "But we haven't learnt anything about our tree powers; we haven't even tried using them yet, not properly. And Neala and I - we're only initiates. We've hardly even studied the basics of our Bard powers, let alone anything that could help us fight monsters or help defend portals or anything like that."

Lorcan whistled loudly, the sound amplified by the cave. Everyone covered their ears, wincing in pain. Neala's head was spinning, and she closed her eyes tightly. When she opened them, she came face-to-face with Eamon, his expression full of remorse.

"Neala, I'm sorry. You've just been through a terrible trauma; you should be resting." He sat beside her and wrapped an arm around her shoulders. "Come on - let's get you back to the academy. Mercy should be feeling well enough by now, she can take a look at you, all right?"

Mercy... Neala placed a hand on Eamon's leg, stopping him. Her eyes widened, and she turned her head slowly to look at Lorcan. Seeing the expression on her face, he shifted uncomfortably.

"Mercy and Clodagh: they're both Seers, right - able to see visons of things about to happen? Isn't it a little odd that they both fall ill on the same day? The very same day that I end up being attacked? Which leads me to wonder why Áine isn't ill? If the changeling was behind it, why didn't he try to get Áine out the way, too – he knew she's a Seer, we'd spoken about it."

She sucked in a breath. "Keia was missing, too. She's never left my side, ever. Do you happen to know about that, too? Is that something else you decided to just keep to yourself, Lorcan?"

Lorcan sighed. "The changeling had been planning this since your first day here, Neala. It had to have been - its plan was too well-executed. It couldn't be Seen by the Seers; the changelings' magic protects them from things like scrying and Tracking, but it wouldn't have been taking any chances. I suspect it poisoned them, to get them out of the way. Both are on the mend now, I swear."

Staring into the fire, he continued, "I honestly don't understand why it didn't poison Áine, too. Perhaps - and this is a stretch - it didn't believe her power would be strong enough? She is only a new Seer; perhaps it didn't consider her a threat? It's arrogance was its downfall." Lorcan chuckled to himself. "Because you did See it, didn't you?"

Áine jerked, not expecting him to call on her. Stammering, she muttered, "Um, yes. In the hall, before dinner." She turned to Neala. "I Saw you, Neala, walking to the lake. Then Torin was there, but...but it wasn't him - it was like he was covered in cobwebs or something, some kind of haze. It was the first time I'd Seen him properly - like I told you, he'd only been a ghostly presence before that. I had this horrible feeling when I looked at him - I felt really sick.

"Keia showed up next. I Saw her in the darkness, trying to free herself from some rope. The vision panned out and I saw an old well - it was where she had been this whole time. Then I Saw you, lying under the tree. You were...were..." Áine's voice trembled, and Neala leaned against her reassuringly.

"By the time it ended, I could hardly walk. Lorcan—" she glanced at him. "He was just coming in when I fell, and I knew I had to tell him what I'd seen. He told me to get the others – the other Lorekeepers - and go to the lake, to the place where I'd seen you lying in my vision. Then he left."

"Once Áine told me what she'd Seen, I knew the changeling was making its move," Lorcan took over, his voice gruff. "Tracking Keia was difficult; she'd been drugged the night before, probably at dinner, and stolen from your room. I'm surprised she hadn't sensed the changeling already."

He shrugged. "But then, she is still very young; perhaps her abilities are still developing? Anyway, it had stashed her at the bottom of an old well, deep in the woods. She was bound with the same ropes used to hold you, spelled to nullify any magic they contained.

"Once I'd freed her, we came looking for you. Áine's vision was, obviously, correct. I'm not surprised she could See the changeling when other Seers can't; part of the hazel tree's power is truth-seeing, so it would have revealed the true nature of the changeling, even underneath its illusion. But there was another part to your vision, wasn't there?

The part you told me...but haven't told them." He turned to Áine now, brow raised.

Stuttering, Áine flicked her gaze around at the others, focusing on their feet and avoiding eye contact. She clasped her fingers together, then released them, fidgeting uncomfortably. "I-I...there was...it was this moment. This." She indicated the cave they were in.

"After the vision of Neala faded, it changed to this scene; to all of us sitting here talking, just like we are now. Then there was a wave of fog, a flash of light, then it ended. I've had it before, always the same. But I've never understood what it meant."

Her voice had begun to shake. "That was all, I swear. I was too worried about Neala to even think on it again. I just wanted to make sure she was safe."

It was Eamon who looked pale now. He stared at Lorcan, and Neala felt him tense beside her. "Visions of the future, even Seer visions, are subjective, Lorcan. You know that. It doesn't mean anything."

But Lorcan was standing now, staring into the flickering coals of the fire. "Remember when we first came here, brother? We found this cave, and we sensed it then. I know you can feel it, same as me – the pull is much stronger now. It's finally time."

The others were watching the two brothers in confusion. Wordlessly, Darci stood and stalked to the entrance of the cave. Jaz called after her, "Where are you going?"

"Until everyone stops talking in cryptic little messages, I'm out of here." She folded her arms across her chest, face livid. "It's ridiculous. What are we even still doing here? Neala's fine. People will be noticing us missing soon and I don't particularly feel like playing twenty-questions all morning. I'm tired, I'm hungry, and I'm leaving."

"Darci, wait," Eamon called. She paused, glancing at him warily. Shoulders slumped, Eamon waved toward the back of the cave. "There's a portal here. In this cave. We found it years ago, Lorcan and I, but Finley forbid us from ever returning to it. As soon as we walked outside, it disappeared from our memories. It must be a protective mechanism, a way to keep people away from it, like the birch grove in the woods protects the school.

"But, for the past couple of weeks, I've been dreaming of this cave, exactly like Áine described – the fog, the flash of light... I know you have, too - it's what we've been talking about, right?" He glanced up at Lorcan, who nodded curtly.

"Lorcan suspects, and I am starting to agree, that we are being led here." Squaring his jaw, he made eye contact with every person in the cave. "We have to go through this portal. To the Otherworld."

There was a deathly silence. Then everyone tried to speak at once.

"Are you insane?"

"Go through what?"

"Why? What the—"

"How do you know?"

"I agree."

It was Orion's deep, soothing voice that overruled all the others, and they fell silent. Jaz, who was sitting next to him, craned her head around until she was staring into his face.

"How could you possibly think this is a good idea?"

Orion turned his solemn eyes on Neala. "I have dreamed it, too. This cave, this moment. And I never dream."

Neala's throat was tight, and it made her wince. "Well, if anyone else has been having dreams or visions about caves and portals, now's the time to mention it, I guess," she tried to joke, but it came out as more of a squeak.

Jaz shook her head, looking miffed. Darci, too, was rolling her eyes. "Dreams and visions. Is this what we've become? A group of hippies?"

Áine was giving Neala a pointed look. "Yes. Has anyone *else* had any dreams or visions they'd like to share? That maybe have to do with this *decision* we have to make right now?"

Neala's eyes widened and she opened her mouth in shock. Reaching for Keia, she touched her fur softly, remembering.

"The decision..." she mumbled. *'The path you choose next will change the course of the future, child - for all of us. The fate of both worlds rests with you.'*

Áine poked her in the arm, encouraging her to say it louder. Speaking only to Eamon, who still had his arm around her shoulders, she whispered, "I was told, in a dream a little while ago, that I have to make a decision; that my future paths will not become clear until I do. I think – I think this may be that choice."

In the back of her mind, she heard the mournful owl crying, and she knew. "The decision is whether to leave for the Otherworld or remain here." Saying it out loud, Neala felt a wave of clarity wash over her, and she sat straighter.

Lorcan noticed the change in her, and a smile tugged at the corners of his mouth. "Neala, you are the one with the ability to open portals between worlds. If we are to go through, it comes down to you."

Her heart was pounding. To cross over would mean leaving everything behind; Birchtree Hall, the Druids, Finley, her mother...Neala's chest ached, and she hugged herself tightly. *I was going to see her again soon. In the holidays...*

Eyes narrowing as she looked around the group, Darci spat tersely, "Um, hello? I'm still failing to see any logical reason to go through a portal to a *literal* Otherworld. Apart from all these dreams and things, is there an actual, compelling need to throw ourselves into uncertainty?"

She shook her head vehemently. "Why should we have to sacrifice everything? Put ourselves in danger to *possibly* fix something that may or may not even be happening? We don't even know what's over there – no one does. So why do we need to risk our lives on some whim? We never asked for this."

The others mulled over her words, lost in their own thoughts of what this decision could cost them.

It was Lorcan who answered first. "I look at it this way; we can either stay on this side and try to defeat whatever creatures come through for as long as we can - because they *will* keep coming, I'm sure of it - or we can go over to the other side and try to stop whatever is damaging the Veil in the first place.

"What we're doing now is putting bandages on bullet holes; we can try to stem the bleeding, but it won't stop them from shooting at us. We need to learn more - we need to know exactly who, or what, is trying to break the Veil and come through. More importantly, why? What could they possibly want from this side?"

"You must right the wrongs, Neala Stormbringer. You must restore the balance..." Memories of a voice, an ancient, powerful, and terribly sad voice, reverberated through Neala's skull. Clutching her ears, she clenched her teeth until the deep wave of sorrow had ebbed.

Breathing deeply, she raised her head and glanced from Lorcan to Eamon. What he'd said made sense, and it was something she had wondered herself in the quiet moments before she fell asleep at night. Why was the Veil breaking? Who could possibly want the portals opened once more?

Something pressed against her collar bone sharply, and she glanced down. The charred stick - the one she'd taken from the changeling - had shifted in her shirt and was poking her painfully.

With a grimace, she reached toward Áine, taking her hand. Her friend looked at her, eyes shining with unshed tears. Neala could feel her trembling, and she squeezed her hand tightly.

"Torin's over there," she whispered, her voice thick with emotion. "The changeling said that when he took over Torin's image, he sent the real one to the Otherworld. If we have a chance to save him, I..."

Áine's mouth quivered, but her eyes hardened, and she nodded vigorously.

"No. This is stupid - I'm not going. You imbeciles can go ahead and risk your lives, but don't drag me to Hell with you." Darci was still standing in the mouth of the cave, hands balled at her sides and glaring at them all. "You're all insane. We don't have a clue what we're getting into. You think the changeling was bad? There'll be worse over there."

She threw her hands in the air scornfully. "You want to walk into certain death, go ahead. Some of us have too much to lose."

It was Eamon who walked over to Darci and wrapped his arms around her, stroking her back and murmuring softly. In his embrace, Darci slowly relaxed, her body trembling as she rested her head against his shoulder, tears streaming down her cheeks.

"It'll be okay, love, I promise. You know I'd never let anything happen to you. Please, we need you - *I* need you."

Neala looked away, pretending she hadn't heard - his words were not meant for her. Whatever had happened between them, she could see that Eamon still loved Darci unequivocally.

Unable to resist, she stole a peek at Lorcan, wondering how he was reacting. But he wasn't even looking at them, having turned his attention to Jaz and Orion.

"What about you two? Jaz, you were the one who suggested leaving here to team up with my contacts and get some answers; this would provide far greater insight for us."

Jaz nodded slowly, rubbing her stubbly hair thoughtfully. Orion stood, towering over Lorcan. Neala was shocked; she knew he was tall, but Lorcan wasn't exactly short, either. Had he grown?

"I have no reason to stay here. I will go with you."

One by one, the others got to their feet, Orion's words seeming to confirm what they all knew, deep down – if they were going to fulfill their destiny as Lorekeepers, the ones chosen to protect the Veil, then they had to leave.

Neala leaned on Áine for support, her legs wobbly. Silently, eyes shut tightly as she willed the words to reach her, she sent a prayer to her mother. *Mum, I need to do this. You brought me here, knowing what my destiny was, even though it hurt you to do it. You made a choice, one that you hated having to make – now I need to do the same. I have to go; I hope you understand. Please, know that I love you with all my heart. I will come back to you, I promise.*

Gulping back her tears, Neala gripped Áine's hand tightly, making her friend wince. Eamon, with one arm still wrapped tightly around Darci's waist, locked eyes with Lorcan. "It looks like we're all in."

Nodding, Lorcan cast his eye over each of them, lingering on Neala before he turned away. "The portal will be shrouded in mist. Come on - we have to go deeper in."

The others fell in behind him as he led them further into the cave, a ball of flame cradled in his hand for light. Neala glanced around curiously; how far in did the tunnel go? She had seen the large hills surrounding the far side of the lake, but she never imagined there would be a cave system in them.

The walls were formed with dirt and moss, and the smell of the earth was all around her. Frowning, she doubted that any sort of mist was going to be able to form in here.

After several moments, she realised she was wrong. The faintest trails of silvery fog had begun to swirl around their feet, flowing and dancing as the air shifted with the movement of their legs. There was something familiar about it, something Neala couldn't place.

As they turned around a sharp bend, she gasped; there was a wall of fog ahead of them, misty tendrils streaming from it.

Áine huddled close to her, breathing shallowly. "Neala, what if this is a mistake?" She wanted to offer her friend some words of comfort, but she had none.

A shiver ran down her spine as she realised what was disturbing her; the fog was the same as she'd seen in her dreams - the one that had shrouded the paths and stopped her from following them.

Watching the fog intently, Lorcan came to a halt, turning to face the rest of them. "I'm guessing this is it."

It must have been the nerves affecting her, or perhaps delayed shock from her ordeal, because Neala began to giggle uncontrollably. One by one, the others started to laugh, too, the sound echoing eerily.

Even Lorcan smiled, shrugging his shoulders. "Yeah, okay. I guess that's not the most enlightening thing I've ever said."

Moving closer, he reached a hand toward the fog, wiggling his fingers lightly. With a grimace, he pulled back. "It's impossibly cold - colder than anything I've ever felt before. If we're going to get through, we're going to have to clear it aside. Neala, I think this is where you come in."

Stepping forward anxiously, Neala came to stand beside Lorcan, feeling weak and dizzy. "What do I do, though? I have no idea how to open portals." A wave of exhaustion washed over her, and her legs buckled.

Wrapping an arm around her waist, Lorcan supported her gently. Though her skin was still prickling a little in his presence, she hardly noticed it anymore. Keia slunk up, pressing her warm body against Neala's legs. She smiled down at her companion, feeling the strength returning to her.

"I am here, Stormbringer. It is time."

"Thank you, Keia. Let's do this."

Lorcan had been studying her carefully, and concern tinted his voice as he asked, "Are you sure you're up to this?"

Neala steeled herself. She was tired of feeling weak, of feeling like she was so far behind everyone else – like she would never belong with them. Closing her eyes, she thrust her hands toward the wall of fog.

Lorcan, sensing what was about to happen, took a step back, letting go of her reluctantly.

"Neala Stormbringer. What is your desire?"

Neala heard the whisper of the fog, felt it wrapping around her with its icy breath. For a fleeting moment, she was reminded of the Cailleach's voice, at once ancient and powerful, but as fragile as glass.

Keeping her eyes firmly closed, Neala replied, "We are the Lorekeepers, the ones chosen by the Chieftains Trees to wield their magic and protect the worlds. To fulfil that duty, we must pass through."

"You cannot pass. The Veil must hold."

"Please, we must. We want the same thing – to protect the Veil. But in order to do that, we have to go through to the Otherworld. Please move aside."

"No."

A rumble like thunder filled the cave, making the others jump. Gritting her teeth, Neala bore down with her will, sending her teal-blue magic deep into the fog, straining against the icy mist. "I am the Lorekeeper of the ash tree, the opener of portals and the connector of worlds. I *command* you to open!"

The fog swirled, writhing and twisting like a living thing. It hissed wildly, the sound sending goosebumps racing over Neala's skin. She tried to hold back her scream, but she couldn't stop the whining groan from tearing from her throat. It was like her entire body was being torn to shreds, molecule by molecule.

There was another crash of thunder, louder than before, which shook the cave walls and forced everyone to cover their ears, gasping with pain. Keia dropped to the ground, lips curled back and ears flat against her skull as she snapped at the air, not liking this feeling.

The fog flowed forward, enveloping Neala's friends. Their screams and cries surrounded her, all of them struggling with the sensation of dissolving into the mist. The last thing Neala remembered was a blinding flash of white light...

*****

Back in the silent Shamrock dorm, the light of dawn beamed through the window, warming the leaves of the ivy which wound its way up the curtain. As it slowly illuminated the room, caressing the two empty beds with sunshine, it flowed over the dusty wooden desk, covering it with a soft glow.

There, the silver engraving of the stag glinting brightly in the rays of sunlight, Neala's music box suddenly popped open and started to play a gentle, tinkling song.

Amanda Maynard-Schubert was born and raised in the Riverland of South Australia and grew up with a love of reading and writing, particularly fantasy stories. An international award-winning author, Amanda has also worked as an illustrator on several children's books. Following her attendance at a writer's retreat in Crom Castle, Northern Ireland, Amanda was inspired to write '*In the Whispers of the Trees*', which has been published internationally and has won numerous awards.
It is the first book in '*The Lorekeepers Trilogy*'.

When not writing, Amanda enjoys spending time with her family, gardening, playing field hockey, and practicing her craft as a green witch.

Instagram: @amandamaynardschubertauthor